WIDOW'S
MIGHT

A LIV BERGEN MYSTERY

SANDRA BRANNAN

GREENLEAF
BOOK GROUP PRESS

Published by Greenleaf Book Group Press
Austin, Texas
www.gbgpress.com

Distributed by Greenleaf Book Group LLC

For ordering information or special discounts for bulk purchases, please contact Greenleaf Book Group LLC at PO Box 91869, Austin, TX 78709, 512.891.6100.

Design and composition by Greenleaf Book Group LLC
Cover design by Greenleaf Book Group LLC

Publisher's Cataloging-In-Publication Data
(Prepared by The Donohue Group, Inc.)
Brannan, Sandra.
Widow's might / Sandra Brannan. -- 1st ed.
p. ; cm. -- (A Liv Bergen mystery ; [3])

Issued also as an ebook.
ISBN: 978-1-60832-372-2
1. Murder--Investigation--Black Hills (S.D. and Wyo.)--Fiction. 2. Man-woman relationships--Fiction. 3. Black Hills (S.D. and Wyo.)--Fiction. 4. Suspense fiction. I. Title. II. Series: Brannan, Sandra. Liv Bergen mystery ; [3]
PS3602.R36485 W53 2012
813/.6   2012937395

Part of the Tree Neutral® program, which offsets the number of trees consumed in the production and printing of this book by taking proactive steps, such as planting trees in direct proportion to the number of trees used: www.treeneutral.com

TreeNeutral®

Printed in the United States of America on acid-free paper

12 13 14 15 16   10 9 8 7 6 5 4 3 2 1

First Edition

*To Lisa
and the two mites,
Hunter and Jonathon*

SINCE
1854

MECHANICS' INSTITUTE

LIBRARY & CHESS ROOM

57 Post Street, San Francisco, CA 94104
(415) 393-0101

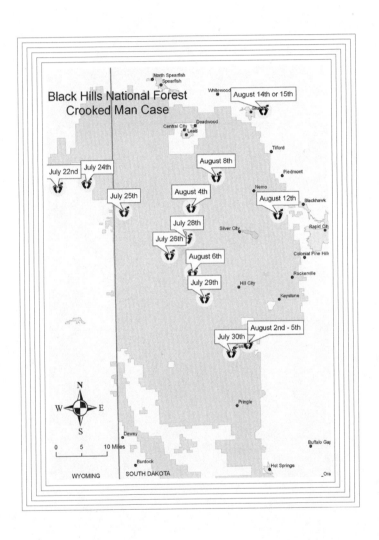

CHAPTER 1

HER BONES WERE AS delicate as Belleek china, her skin like ancient parchment stretched thin over aged, sinewy muscles formed during a life working the ranch.

The shape of her body under the blanket was like that of a grade-school girl whose height had outraced her weight. So thin. In the dark, he felt the faintly familiar warmth of arousal as he stared at her, imagining the ease with which he could wrap just one hand around her throat. How effortless it would be to squeeze the balance of her short life out of her insignificant body. But he wouldn't do that. Of course not. That would leave a mark, make her eyes bulge from her emaciated skull. Not a symptom of a woman who would die from the cancer that had eroded her from the inside out.

Instead, he would quietly slip a pillow over her face, covering those eyes that had always judged him. Her husband had warned her to be nicer to him, to mind her manners and be more hospitable. Ernif Hanson may have been known as a mountain of a man, but he knew differently. When Ernif so willingly flopped onto his belly on that rock, he proved he was nothing more than a mouse. Ernif laid down his life for his wife, a woman he couldn't control. A woman who refused to see his vision, to support the cause. His cause.

And now the all-powerful Helma Hanson lay here in the dark. Alone. Unable even to muster enough strength to roll her tiny frame over in her hospital bed. Struggling for every breath. Clinging to life instead of the pride that had caused her world to crumble only days ago.

Glancing at the glow of the numbers on her bedside clock that read 2:57 AM, he wondered if she was even aware that her husband's funeral was scheduled to take place in a short thirty-two hours. On Thursday. He wondered if she would even notice that her husband wouldn't be with her during her weekly oncologist's appointment later today. A doctor's appointment that Ernif had been so adamant about attending.

No matter—now, after thirteen long years of careful planning, the date had come. He would finally be vindicated, knowing that the Hansons, the final obstacle, would be extinguished as of today. August 7. The day he had originally intended for Ernif's glorious demise.

The bed next to Helma's was empty. Lucky him.

He poked his head around the door and glanced down the dimly lit hall to make sure the night nurse was nowhere to be seen. He strained to hear her heavy footfalls nearby in case she had varied from her scheduled rounds. But he saw nothing, heard nothing. And he knew the night nurse was probably leaning back in that soft easy chair at her desk, the volume on the television turned low, her head lolling forward with her chins resting on her massive chest as she snoozed.

He stepped quietly over to the edge of Helma's bed. Anchoring his resolve to the stillness, he reached over toward the empty bed and hooked his fingers around a pillow. Afraid the sound of his awkward movements would wake her, he stood motionless above her for a moment before slowly positioning the pillow over her face.

He hesitated briefly, wondering if he'd waited long enough, if Helma was indeed too weak to fight back. A sadness washed over him as he wondered if he'd waited too long, if Helma was so far gone she wouldn't even be aware of what was about to happen. He longed for her to be aware. He *needed* for her to be aware. He had something to tell her.

There was only one way to find out.

Just as he placed the pillow down on her thin nose and small mouth, he cooed, "Helma."

Her eyes snapped open, too late to let out a scream.

"You know what I told him, Helma? The last words Ernif ever heard?"

He pressed the pillow down hard on her face, feeling her struggle against him.

"There was a crooked man who walked a crooked mile. He found a crooked sixpence against a crooked stile."

With images from Sunday of Ernif's final moments of life on this earth flashing in his mind, the strength in him surged, as did the pure joy from feeling Helma's fight intensify beneath him.

It was not too late after all.

"He bought a crooked cat, which caught a crooked mouse," he said, pressing his hands against the pillow.

He was yet again experiencing the thrill. And the nursery rhyme seemed to further infuriate Helma Hanson.

She kicked and flailed, her deathbed creaking and groaning. Afraid the noise might attract the nurse's attention, he threw himself against her, a bony knee connecting with his ribs, his grip loosening on the pillow. A muffled croak sounded in the stillness, and he pushed harder on the pillow, feeling her tiny frame buck against him, her brittle fingers clawing at his hands.

"And they all lived together . . ."

He could no longer see her eyes, but he imagined they were widening with the realization that her life was nearly over. Those eyes. The piercing accusation they had made the instant before he covered them with the pillow. It was anger he saw in those wide eyes, not fright as he expected. Her eyes bore through him, her will strong and resilient.

Surprised by her resistance, he leaned into her ear. "In a crooked. Little. House."

He almost missed the warning. The hurried steps down the hall were not heavy, not those of the night nurse, Hester Moore. Instead, they sounded like army boots, quick and stealthy. He glanced over his shoulder at the fish-eye mirror hung over the door and saw a form racing down the hall toward the room. Toward him. It was most certainly not Nurse Hester, whose six-foot, 250-pound frame would have been unmistakable, even in the dim glow of orange. This person was not much more than five feet, weighing a fraction of Hester. And from her silhouette she appeared to be carrying a weapon and wearing a hedgehog as a helmet. He blinked, thinking it was he who had been deprived of oxygen, who was now delusional and conjuring up impish apparitions. But the figure kept coming, quickly and surely toward him.

Although Helma's bucking had slowed, her fingernails retracting from his wrists, he found himself out of time. He released his grip and pushed himself off the bed. He tossed the pillow aside and darted quickly for the door, ducking behind it just as the waif reached Helma's room.

"Helma?" a woman's voice whispered in the dark.

At first Helma lay still, giving no answer. He smiled in the shadows, thrilled to mark August 7th indelibly as his fondest memory to date.

That is, until Helma gasped. She choked to catch the breath he had stolen from her. The tiny figure rushed to the old woman's bedside and cradled her like a child against her chest, cooing and comforting the very-much-alive Helma Hanson.

"Are you okay? Helma?"

As Helma hacked and coughed, he studied the small woman, trying to make out details in the stingy light that touched her face. She was beautiful in an unreal way, like a fairy, her eyes disproportionately large, set within a heart-shaped face. But something about the way she carried herself reminded him more of a leprechaun, quicker and stronger than her beauty and size would otherwise suggest. She handled and manipulated Helma Hanson effortlessly, as if the imp were an ant able to carry ten or even fifty times her weight. Freakishly strong, and with hair that was every color of the rainbow. Spikes of bright blue, lemon yellow, cherry red, and the greenest green he had ever seen. Leprechaun green.

Who *was* this woman?

She rocked Helma in her arms until the sputtering and spewing turned to wheezing and whispering, harsh and hurried. He couldn't make out what Helma was saying to her through the shushing noise the fairy creature was making. He stood graveyard still, fixated as if under the woman's spell, wondering why he had never heard of this nurse before now. And he worried that Hester wouldn't be far behind, eager to snap on all the lights, his discovery inevitable. He began to work a plan out in his head, one that involved force, if necessary, and one that required calmness, patience, and careful consideration of timing that would allow him to disappear like a shadow in the night should Hester pad into the room.

Just as he was cursing himself for not considering that Hester may be training a new nurse, the woman added, "I came as soon as I got the call about Ernif. I am so, so sorry, Helma. I'm here now. Shh. I'm here."

He stiffened, confused by the proclamation, watching as she stroked the old woman's twiggy back and shoulder blades. Ernif and Helma were childless; he had made sure of that. Checked the records thoroughly and accumulated information from several sources. They had no nieces, no nephews. No one. So who the hell was this?

He found the simple act of swallowing difficult, an unfamiliar feeling creeping up his spine. He stood watching, still as the night, and studied her, introspection clouding his thoughts. It didn't take him long to finger the cause for his symptoms. It was doubt. And the mischief-maker who came out of nowhere to take up a bedside vigil by Helma Hanson was the deliveryman. Or woman. Women were always trouble, his father used to say. Father was always right.

His ruminations abruptly scattered as the imp shouted, "Nurse!"

His mind froze as he went rigid behind the door. Hester Moore was waddling down the hall, her footsteps so heavy and hurried he could feel the vibrations through the soles of his sensitive feet. He braced for action. Three women. Should he take out Hester first, then the waif, or vice versa? Either would be formidable, and both would be nearly impossible to take down easily. Just as he landed on a plan, Hester snapped on the light and bustled toward the bed, both she and the imp with their backs to the door.

Again his plans changed. He opted for stealth and slipped from behind the door, unseen, and down the hall.

Not, however, before he heard Helma cry out the imp's name, "Elizabeth!"

CHAPTER 2

I CANNOT STOP TREMBLING.

Three o'clock in the morning, and I'm riding through the spectacular Black Hills of South Dakota, a dog curled up on the floorboard at my feet, a hunk of man at the wheel next to me.

It's a warm night. I'm in good hands. I'm safe.

Yet a tremor erupted deep in my bones sometime during the past hour, and it has worked its way out from my core into my limbs to the tips of my fingers and toes. I am reminded of the time when I was six and broke through the ice at Wilson Park pond. We were playing "crack the whip" on a school outing, and, as the last link of the human chain, I was determined not to let go. I don't remember much after the deafening crack beneath the blades of my skates, which sank up to my shoulders in slushy ice through a soft patch, but I do remember Monsignor O'Connell's worried eyes locked on mine as I lay on my back, wet and shivering. I felt Sister Gabriella tugging the soaked leather skates off my frozen feet and heard her scolding me for allowing those older kids to talk me into such a dangerous game. I hadn't forgotten that I was cold, but I had forgotten the intensity until now: unable to warm my core; quivering for days; Mom regularly shoving a thermometer under my tongue and insisting I must have a fever. But I didn't.

"Are you okay, Liv?"

It wasn't Monsignor O'Connell's voice asking me; it was Special Agent Streeter Pierce's.

"I thought so."

But I wasn't.

Realization had somehow seeped through the cracks of my consciousness, its icy fingers gripping my innards like a wicked disease, twisting my confidence and chilling my bones.

I had knocked my noggin, cracked my corn, and was surprised the EMTs had let me off so easily from their requested hospital overnight for concussion watch. I had bruises and abrasions all over my body from being grated like a hunk of cheese across the catwalk at my family's quarry. I had nearly been killed in the past eight hours—*twice*, if the FBI was correct and Mully's attack at the Firehouse Brewing Company in downtown Rapid City was indeed intended to harm me. But I was fully justified for my involvement in last night's second episode: My younger brother Jens had been accused of killing his fiancée. I knew that couldn't possibly be true.

You'd think, though, that I'd learned to let the experts handle these situations when my employee Jill Brannigan was killed in Colorado a month ago, and I was almost killed because I'd imposed myself into *that* investigation. And, on top of experiencing two near-death situations, somehow I managed to attract the attention of a motorcycle-gang leader in the process, a biker who seemed to be following me every time I looked in my rearview mirror.

I stole a glance in my side mirror and peered into the dark. No motorcycles. Just the headlights of Jens's truck, which Special Agent Stewart Blysdorf was driving, following at a distance.

My jeans had been hacked hurriedly into cutoffs by the EMTs. I had thick bandages on both knees and palms, and my left shin was shiny from an emerging contusion. I pulled the visor down to check the growing lump on my head, only to discover there was no mirror on the visor.

Agent Pierce reached up to the rearview mirror and twisted it toward me.

"That's why we were insisting you let the EMTs take you to the hospital."

"I know, Agent Pierce, but I just couldn't go back to another hospital after being at Poudre for the past month."

"I understand. And call me Streeter," he said.

"Streeter," I repeated, liking the sound of it much better than Special Agent Streeter Pierce. Or Agent Adonis, as I had come to call him. Secretly, in my head, of course. "And thank you for everything else you've done for me, Streeter."

I examined my goose-egged forehead in the mirror and decided I had indeed made the right decision not to go to the hospital. I was going to be okay. Physically. It was my psyche I was concerned about. I pulled my hair back and tied it into a knot on the back of my head, then brushed away the loose strands from my face that my shaky hands had missed.

Without a word, Streeter reached over to flip on the heat to high and laid his warm hand on my bare thigh, just above the bandages.

I sucked in a deep breath and the trembling began to subside.

As we watched the high beams of our headlights sweep across the trees, revealing the nocturnal eyes of wildlife, the vision of Streeter running across the Firehouse bar through the crowd to help me popped into my mind. He was amazing. Then and now.

And his hand radiated heat.

I laid my bandaged hand over his. My nerves calmed, and I began to enjoy our aloneness, driving in the moonlight on winding roads that took us farther away from Rapid City and toward Deadwood.

"Thank you."

"For what?"

"For this," I said, pressing my hand against his. "For calming me down just now. I don't know what came over me. I've never had a reaction like that to anything."

He gripped my thigh briefly before sliding his hand back to the steering wheel. "Well, could it be that you were nearly killed just now? Watched a woman die? Had your bell rung not once, but twice? Were attacked by a biker in a bar? All in the same night?"

"But I got a dog out of it." I laughed and reached down to pet Beulah's head and neck. She grunted in her sleep, content to be warm and safe like me.

"How far do we have to go before the turnoff?"

I had convinced Streeter to swing by Tommy Jasper's house a few miles north of Nemo so I could return the cell phone he'd lent me before Streeter took me to my brother's house in Rapid City. Despite the late hour—more like early morning hour—I suspected Tommy would be awake already, being a rancher.

"We're about there. Tommy's road is easy to miss, so you'll have to slow down and turn on your brights."

"Already on," he said.

I peered out the windshield at the dull wash of headlights. "Lamps must be caked with mud. Not enough in the budget for car washes?"

I could see his kinked grin in the glow of the dashboard lights.

"Well, maybe you'll let me wash your car tomorrow as my way of saying 'thank you' for saving my life. Fair trade, don't you think?" I liked his smile. "And for thinking enough of me to entrust me with this gorgeous bloodhound Beulah, and for thinking I'm capable enough of becoming her handler. You know, I'm no Lisa Henry."

He chuckled, sounding like a failed attempt at starting an ancient lawn mower, which brought a smile to my lips.

Lisa Henry was a special agent who had lost her life in the line of duty. And she was my friend. A college bud. Which is why I never hesitated to accept the responsibility of caring for Beulah.

"Well, Lisa was amazing at her job with the bureau and loved that dog more than anything." His smile waned.

"She loved more than that dog." I didn't know what made me say the thought aloud.

His eyes slid toward me, an eyebrow raised. "The bureau? Did she talk to you about becoming an agent?"

"No, I just meant she talked about you."

"She was a good friend," was all Streeter shared with me. Pointing, he asked, "Is that the waterwheel you told me about?"

I saw the wooden wheel slowly turning from the force of the flowing creek on our left.

"That's it. Tommy's turn is the next right. There."

Streeter slowed and turned off the highway onto the two-track jagged trail that led through the trees. The lights were blazing inside Tommy Jasper's small cabin, and the headlights of Jens's truck washed over us through the back window as Agent Blysdorf pulled in and parked behind us.

"He must be awake already," I said, pulling on the handle and stepping out of the car, Beulah barely stirring. Jens's truck window was open. I shouted: "I'll be just a sec, Agent Blysdorf."

"Bly."

I smiled. "Bly. That's nice."

I wasn't surprised that both agents escorted me to the door, but I was surprised at how quickly they were at my side, stepping up on the porch behind me as I knocked.

I stepped back to wait for Tommy Jasper, knowing he'd offer us all a much-needed cup of coffee, and I pulled the cell phone from my pocket to hand him. But no one came to the door. I knocked a second time and thought back to the dinner we had had together at the restaurant at the Nemo Guest Ranch last night, which seemed like eons ago. Nothing came to mind about anything he was planning to do today, but he had mentioned going to Ernif Hanson's funeral on Thursday, tomorrow.

When I stepped back after knocking—more like pounding—a third time, I glanced in the windows. I was not the least bit apologetic about my meddlesomeness, considering the cabin had no drapes or curtains and my intention for snooping was solely out of concern, not idle curiosity.

I thought I saw something far to the right, down the hall, move. "Is that his boot?"

Both agents flanked me and trained their eyes where I had pointed. Before I realized what was happening, the two were through the door and down the hall within seconds, heading toward the work boot, which indeed still housed Tommy's foot, his body lying supine in the hallway. I just stood there on the porch at the window, mouth agape, until I saw Bly bolt for the telephone in the living room and stab at the number pad, leaving Streeter to attend to Tommy. The garbled sound of Bly's hurried words made me feel like I was trapped in an endless dream of disaster, a veritable Queen Midas situation where everything I touched turned to mold. Or more like Queen Mab, making house calls with my offerings of plague as people sleep.

I snapped out of my stupor when Bly's steely eyes laser-locked on mine. His mouth was still communicating with whomever was on the other end of the line, but his attention was entirely on me. I blinked several times as if to awaken from yet another bad dream. The only thought coming to mind was a comment a coworker made years ago about how Nemo spelled backward was Omen. This was a bad one.

Before I made it through the front door, I heard Bly say, "I think she's in shock. I'll take care of her."

He was beside me in seconds, but I shrugged off his steadying grip as he guided me toward the couch. "I *am not* in shock. I'm just stunned, that's all. Forget about me. How's Tommy?"

Together we walked down the hall where Streeter was crouched beside Tommy, checking his pulse and staring at his watch.

"Is he dead?"

CHAPTER 3

"HE'S STILL ALIVE." STREETER'S growl was all business and implied the word "barely." He turned to Bly and asked, "Did you reach them in time?"

"Yep, they hadn't left yet. They're on their way."

I assumed the "they" he was talking about were the EMTs we had just left fifteen minutes ago at the iron ore quarry south of Nemo. They had been called out there from Rapid City Regional Hospital to attend to me and luckily were still nearby, considering we were at least thirty minutes out of town and another fifteen to the opposite side of Rapid City, where the hospital stood.

Both agents were assessing Tommy, sliding their hands over, beside, and under his body to feel for any injuries, blood and other body fluids, broken bones, wounds, or anything out of the ordinary.

I recognized what they were doing from the annual first aid classes I have to take to keep my MSHA certification current. The Mine Safety and Health Administration, the federal regulatory agency created to keep mines safe for all us workers by establishing work standards and assuring compliance through unannounced site visits, requires that seasoned miners be trained at least eight hours annually. First aid and first response are my favorite parts of training, considering how remote most of our mine sites are and how necessary the skills are in all aspects of life.

"What do you think happened?" I asked, curiosity getting the better of me.

Streeter sat back on his haunches and shook his head. "Can't say. He's unconscious. Maybe he fell, passed out. No obvious injuries. Fully dressed, so either he got up early for work this morning and this just happened or he's been here since yesterday."

I glanced at the brown, snap-button shirt, the cobalt blue and chocolate brown kerchief fastened around his neck, and the Wrangler jeans and said, "Last night. He's been here since sometime around ten o'clock or so."

Both agents swung their heads and planted their questioning gazes on me.

I shrugged. "We had dinner together. He has on the same clothes as he did then. That's when he lent me his phone."

"You've got to be kidding," Streeter said.

"True story," I said. "I gave mine to my older brother Ole. A company phone. Customers use it. And employees. And suppliers. And neighbors around our quarry."

Bly added, "You sure do have a knack for getting all tangled up in everyone else's messes, don't you?"

I thought about this and wondered if it were true. Worse, I worried if it was more like I *caused* the messes. Then a horrible thought came to me. "Oh no."

"What now?" Bly asked.

"The phone. I've had it all night. If Tommy had kept it, maybe when he fell or passed out or whatever, he could have called for help."

Bly snatched the phone from my hand, shaking his head. "No signal. It wouldn't have helped him one bit. Mine doesn't work this far into the Black Hills either. That's why I used the land line."

As Streeter made sure Tommy's airway stayed clear, I babbled on. "He's seventy-two, lost his wife to cancer a year ago. He lives alone. He's fit, strong, but suffers from arthritis. He dropped me off at the quarry around nine-forty or so last night. I remember because it was nearly ten when I stopped at the Lazy S Campground down the road the first time. Tommy would have arrived home about the same time."

Bly scowled at me. "The first time? You didn't tell us that part earlier."

"Well, I was trying to find out where to look for Charlene Freeburg, Michelle's little sister," I explained. "Anyway, the point is I know Tommy ate a hamburger, fries, and drank a Jack and Coke around nine or so. Tommy never mentioned having any food or other types of allergies."

Both men stared at me.

"What?" I said. "Stomach contents. Aren't the emergency personnel people going to want to know all that? Oh, and he's on some kind of medication. Tommy said he wasn't a fan because the medication made his head fuzzy and made him feel really sleepy."

"You talked about his medications over a hamburger?" Streeter asked skeptically.

"Okay, I know this sounds weird, but I only know about the medications because his doctor stopped by and reminded Tommy to take his new pills. He insisted they were critical for his heart. Blood pressure, I think."

"Stopped by where?"

"At the Nemo Guest Ranch. Dr. Morgan had stopped in to buy a bottle of booze and saw Tommy and me eating. We were back near the bar because I needed a couple shots of vodka to calm my nerves after my standoff with Mully and Lucifer's Lot."

Streeter rubbernecked. "Standoff? Last night? What are you talking about, Liv?"

"At the quarry," I started.

Before I had a chance to explain, sirens cut me off and flashing red and blue lights shone through the front window, signaling the ambulance's arrival. The convoy included the vehicles of several other agents, police, and emergency personnel, all parked in a cluster in the clearing out front. The living room instantly filled with a half dozen men and women, familiar faces from the quarry.

Streeter rattled off all the vital statistics he had been monitoring since our arrival, along with the information I had just shared with him and Bly about my dinner the night before with Tommy: the food, the time, the medical details. The EMTs from the hospital had Tommy on a gurney within seconds, hooked to all sorts of gizmos I couldn't identify.

"Geez, can you smell that?" one EMT said as he leaned closer to Tommy's mouth.

Streeter grimaced. "Breath smells fruity?"

The EMT nodded.

"Yeah, I smelled it too. What's it mean?"

The guy shrugged and the other EMTs each leaned down to take a whiff. I overheard Streeter tell Bly to order one of the other agents to take me home where I belonged.

I was getting pawned off, ushered out, and my only interest at that point was in Tommy's well-being. I interrupted Streeter. "I'm going with him."

Too many eyes turned my way.

Bly asked, "Who, me?"

"No, with Tommy." Pointing toward the ambulance parked outside the front door, I repeated, "I'm going with him. To the hospital."

A smile played on the corner of Streeter's mouth, a mouth I desperately wanted to explore tonight. The touch of Queen Midas soon chilled that steamy thought, however.

As the ambulance team ushered Tommy out of the living room and into the night, the driver said, "The hell you are. Unless you can prove you're an immediate relative, insurance disallows you as a passenger. And when I say proof, I'd need the judge himself to tell me you were legit, because we wouldn't believe a word you say, *Mrs. Gilbert Muth.*"

Bly laughed. Streeter covered a smirk with the back of his hand, but I could still see mischief in his eyes.

They were on to me.

I hadn't recognized the team when we were at the iron ore quarry, but I did now. These were the same emergency medical technicians who had helped me recover consciousness at the Firehouse earlier last night when I cracked my skull against a table base. And I talked my way out of a mandatory trip to the hospital by lying, saying I was married to a doctor, implying my brother's friend Gilbert Muth had a medical degree rather than a doctorate in engineering. Busted.

"Damn, how long is your shift anyway?" was all I managed.

"About four hours too long tonight, thanks to you," the uniformed EMT said, giving me a mock salute as he followed his team out the door.

I turned back to Streeter and his conspirators. "I'll just wait here until you're done," I said.

I flopped down on Tommy's couch and ignored their discussions about Tommy's house being a potential crime scene, a cursory investigation being debated, and plans that included extricating me from the scene. My pool of self-esteem unable to fill a teacup at this point, I struggled to hold on to every evaporating droplet as they argued about who was stuck with driving me home.

When Streeter was called into the back bedroom about a medication bottle that had been discovered on the floor—something about Lisinopril—I snuck out the front door unnoticed. Quietly, I coaxed drowsy Beulah out of Streeter's car and into Jens's truck and slipped in behind the wheel, pulling out with my headlights off.

After all, although my self-esteem was damaged, my head felt fine.

CHAPTER 4

"SHE SAID NO."

"Ms. Bergen," he tried again, holding the loaded needle in his gloved hands, a glistening drop clinging to the tip. "I understand how upsetting this must seem to you, and I don't want to appear harsh. But Mrs. Hanson has been on a strict regimen for treatment since she was placed in our care last month by Mr. Hanson, and you don't have the authority to make changes to that treatment."

"Ernif is dead," Elizabeth stated, pulling Helma closer as she sat beside her in the bed. "She has no other family."

Although faint, a smile appeared on Dr. Morgan's aged face. "No one knows that better than me, Ms. Bergen. I've treated the Hansons for years. Decades, really."

"Then you know I'm the closest to kin she has."

"Actually," he began, handing the unused needle and discarded rubber gloves to the nurse, "she hasn't mentioned a thing about you." He perched on the edge of Helma's bed and rested his hickory cane with its big brass ball grip against the metal frame, causing a perfect chime to fill the room. "Neither did Mr. Hanson. Tell me. How did you come to know them?"

His tone was kind, his smile gentle, but Elizabeth detected something accusatory in his eyes and she decided to draw a line. "It doesn't matter. What matters is that Helma does *not* want to be treated for her cancer anymore. She doesn't want whatever it is you have in that needle."

Dr. Morgan bowed his head and sighed. "Hospice emphasizes caring, not curing, Ms. Bergen. Our job is to care for the terminally ill. We are only here to make Helma as comfortable as possible in her final days."

Elizabeth pinned Dr. Morgan with her eyes. "Cure or care, she's not comfortable with any more needles. So whatever you have in that thing to 'comfort' her doesn't matter."

"But it does matter, Ms. Bergen, because unless you can show me proper documentation that you speak—in legal terms, mind you—for Mrs. Hanson, then I will have to ask you to leave."

Trembling, Helma gripped more tightly to Elizabeth.

"Sorry, doc. I'm not going anywhere. You heard Helma. The nurse heard Helma. I heard Helma. She said clearly, 'No more needles.' Doesn't *she* have a voice here? What proof do *you* have that she's incompetent and can't make those decisions for herself?"

Dr. Morgan looked up at Hester Moore, whose resolve on hospice rules appeared to be wavering in favor of Elizabeth's argument.

"Well, I see I'm outnumbered here, and I don't want to cause anyone discomfort or hardship," the doctor said with a resigned sigh, slapping his thighs with open palms. Speaking to all three women, he offered, "So I'll tell you what I'm going to do. I'm going over to the hospital to make my predawn rounds. While I'm there, Hester, will you please review the file and see what forms Mr. and Mrs. Hanson signed? Release, permission, emergency contact?" He pulled out a pocket notebook and started scribbling, and then he ripped the page from the notebook and handed it to the nurse. "Call this number and ask my assistant, Steven, to hightail it into the office and send you whatever he can find in my files on the Hansons. Tell him I said to contact legal and have them recommend protocol on the preferred care for Mrs. Hanson in light of Mr. Hanson's recent, unexpected death." To Elizabeth, he added, "In the meantime, you stay here with Mrs. Hanson and keep her calm."

Elizabeth raised her chin and said, "Thank you. I will."

The nurse shambled out the door and down the hall, appearing to be relieved not to be a part of the debate any longer.

Dr. Morgan eyed Helma. "Mind if I examine you, Helma?"

Helma clung like a barnacle to Elizabeth's arm.

"I don't think that's a good idea. She's still too upset," Elizabeth said.

"Did she tell you why she's so upset?"

"She said she had a bad dream," Elizabeth lied.

Dr. Morgan nodded. "Nothing else?"

Elizabeth shook her head. "Nothing except when you pulled out your medicine bag. You heard her. 'No more needles.'"

His eyebrows buckled. "Irritability is a sign that we aren't managing her pain properly. We switched opioids about a week ago. Morphine was causing her to have nightmares, according to Mr. Hanson. Maybe this new narcotic is ineffective in controlling her pain."

Elizabeth glowered at him, resolved that no matter what he said, she wasn't going to go against Helma's wishes. "No needles."

Dr. Morgan patted Elizabeth's shin. "I know. I hear you. And I heard Mrs. Hanson. But we have other options. We have oral solutions, patches, even suppositories, if she'd prefer."

Elizabeth felt Helma bury herself deeper into her embrace. "She'll think about it."

Dr. Morgan's smile seemed patronizing to Elizabeth. "The nightmares could be caused by the cancer progressing. Maybe if you share the details of the dream with me, I could compare them to what's in her files and determine if the dreams are related to pain medicine or to the lack of pain control."

Elizabeth shrugged. "She was like this when I found her. Out of it. Scared. She just kept repeating 'Bad dream. Very bad dream.' No details. Nothing."

"You know that the worst thing for these patients is to not control their pain. To tough it out."

Elizabeth nodded.

"Very well," he grumbled, then reached into his black bag and withdrew a bottle, shaking out a couple of pills into a miniature paper pill cup he grabbed from the stack on the metal table nearby. "Will you at least allow her to take these sleeping pills?" He rattled two large white pills in the cup. "She needs to rest."

Elizabeth took it and coaxed Helma to swallow the pills.

Dr. Morgan offered a smile that warmed his aging face.

Elizabeth guessed him to be in his sixties, but the cane made him appear older. So did the archaic black bag. As if expecting to make house calls was totally congruent with modern health care expectations. She studied him as he removed the notebook once again from his pocket. She watched as he scribbled his name and several phone numbers on it for her. He tore it from the tablet and handed it to Elizabeth. She scanned the note and stuffed it deep into a pocket.

"If for some reason Mrs. Hanson is unable to sleep or her condition changes, have the nurse call me at the first number. The others are just in case I can't be reached on my personal beeper. Keep a close eye on her and I'll be back in an hour to check on her again. I'm going to see what we can find out about her care and your authority to suggest what's best for her in light of the situation."

"Thank you," Elizabeth managed.

She watched as Dr. Morgan, in his old-fashioned flowing white coat, leather medical bag firmly in his grip, disappeared from the room, leaving her alone with Helma.

"You lied," she whispered into Elizabeth's shoulder. "For me."

Elizabeth realized that Helma Hanson's catatonia had all been a pretense, intended to keep the nurse and doctor off balance. She understood that everything Helma had told her was not the rambling of a crazy, over-medicated hospice patient. It was real.

"I believed you," Elizabeth responded, eyes glued to the open doorway to make sure they remained alone.

She held out her palm to Helma's mouth and Helma spat the two large pills into it. Elizabeth couldn't believe the size of the pills, wondering how on earth they expected tiny Helma to swallow one, much less two. She grabbed a tissue in which to wrap the pills and stuffed them deep into the same pocket that held the note from Dr. Morgan.

Helma patted her forearm and sighed a sweet "Thank you."

Elizabeth remained very still. She felt Helma's grip loosen gradually as her adrenaline rush subsided and sleep washed over her, no thanks to the pills Dr. Morgan had given her. She worried about the effect of sheer terror on Helma, recalling how she had described the man in the dark who tried to smother her to death, and about how Elizabeth had saved her life.

The muted sounds of hospital-related devices could be heard from neighboring rooms. The sky outside was as dark as when Elizabeth had arrived to check on Helma, an instinct she would never quite understand why she had had. And now she sensed her late son's, Scout's, presence buzz by her face, pecking her on the cheek with an angel's kiss, which was soon followed by a tear that spilled from Elizabeth's eye.

Carefully, so as not to disturb Helma, Elizabeth reached into her pocket to retrieve what she needed to put an end to all of this.

CHAPTER 5

ON THE LONG DRIVE back to Rapid City, lost opportunities clouded my vision of what might have been on my anticipated car ride home with Streeter. Our time alone had been sweet but way too short. I didn't even get a chance to see if the obvious spark between us was the ember of a blistering bonfire or merely the chance striking of two flint stones in a rainstorm, fleeting like most of my attempts with men. I realized how little I had needed to fuel such a wild fantasy, relying heavily on Gilbert Muth's musing that Streeter had been consumed with me at the Firehouse last night. Clearly blinded by the glow of the ember, I now felt the chill of truth permeate my reasoning. On reflection, I suspected the concern Streeter showed for me when I hit my head at the pub wasn't born of his infatuation in me, as Gilbert interpreted. It was more likely that Streeter showed keen interest in me because he was concerned I might sue him or the FBI for knocking me into a table, into unconsciousness.

The clouds further darkened my happy thoughts and Mr. Bluebird flitted from my shoulder when I imagined how incredibly pissed off Streeter was likely to be when he found out I had defied them by ditching Tommy Jasper's place in Jens's pickup. Or, worse, maybe he'd be relieved to be rid of me.

Only on nights like this did my choice to live life as a loner feel lonely. As a miner—a quarrier, to be precise—working with dozens of great people, mostly men, at a limestone quarry near Livermore, Colorado, I could count on one hand how often I had boyfriends who lasted longer than a handful of dates. Although I was engaged once, right out of college, I would be lying if I said I was heartbroken when he ended the engagement, accusing me of being married to my work. I've never apologized for keeping my nose to the limestone.

It was nearing a quarter past four in the morning when I tiptoed into Jens's house, expecting to find him and my sister Elizabeth fast asleep in their respective bedrooms. Jens's door was closed and the door to his spare bedroom open. My bedroom. Temporarily. And the one I offered to share with Elizabeth when she called about coming to Rapid City from Louisville, Colorado, yesterday evening.

I felt my way in the dark, discarded my EMT cutoffs on the floor, and motioned as quietly as I could for Beulah to lie down on a pallet of my dirty clothes as her temporary bed, which she obediently did. I liked her already. I felt around for a pair of fully intact (albeit dirty) jeans and pulled them on, roughing up Beulah's ears as she drifted off to sleep. I closed the door to the bedroom so I could use the bathroom without awakening anyone.

I waited for the water to run hot and entertained the idea of sleeping until well past noon, but the dream shattered with the screech of Jens's telephone.

In the split second that passed between reentering the skin I had jumped out of, and quietly snatching the receiver from the cradle to stop the phone from ringing a second time in the nearby office, I recovered my sense and breath enough to whisper, "Hello?"

"Come get me." The whisper belonged to Elizabeth. And she was all business. "I'm at Heavenly Hospice behind the hospital. Park in the southeast corner of the front lot with your lights off. Hurry."

―――――――

It was 4:45 AM when I pulled into the empty lot by the row of hedges, as far from the front entrance to Heavenly Hospice as possible, parking exactly where Elizabeth had instructed. I hadn't questioned her, but on the ride over, I wondered what she had gotten herself into this time. Elizabeth was notorious for getting into trouble—albeit always with good intentions—and even more renowned for how she expertly averted the long arm of the law or formal charges of any kind. But, to this day, I always feel like an accessory to a crime whenever she involves me in her crazy life.

I'm not a superstitious person by nature, but I've found a strange comfort in collecting rocks that remind me most of people close to me. At home, I have rocks on my dresser, each one representing my parents and eight brothers and sisters. Elizabeth is best captured in a chunk of sand, a high-grade silica pure enough to be melted into glass, yet strong enough to keep an oil or water fracture wedged open far beneath the earth's surface to allow a better flow. Sand that is friable, shifting, ever changing, like beaches with every ocean wave, willingly riding every breeze that blows. That is Elizabeth.

I trained my eyes on the front door, expecting her to burst out with guns blazing, yet not having a clue what she would be doing here at this hour. So, I nearly had a heart attack when I heard the passenger door of the truck click open. The overhead light in the truck flicked on and I saw a tiny, aged woman dressed in a navy blue jumpsuit being pushed toward me on the bench seat of the pickup. Seemingly asleep, her itty-bitty frame was being lifted onto the seat beside me by my sister's equally tiny frame. Elizabeth soon appeared beside the frail woman and hurriedly closed the door with a slow, quiet click.

"What are you doing?" My raspy voice sounded harsh even to me.

"Better drive if you know what's good for you," was all my sister said.

I did as I was told, as I always do with Elizabeth. We drove in silence through the parking lot.

"Where's your car?"

"On the other side of the hospital."

"What? That's like only a quarter of a mile away. So why did you call me for a ride? All of a sudden scared of the dark or something?"

As if it were obvious, she pointed at the old woman leaning against my shoulder.

"What, so she's the one who's scared of the dark?"

Elizabeth's elfin facial features morphed into that scary mask I could only describe as Chucky-like. Indignant, controlled, determined. Maniacal. "I couldn't carry her that far. And she wouldn't let me leave her alone, so I couldn't run to get my car and come back for her."

"Who is she, and what are you doing with her?"

"You know Helma," Elizabeth said. "Helma Hanson."

"What? No."

I couldn't believe it. The last time I had seen Helma Hanson was five years ago, at Scout's funeral. Caskets made for babies are the most disturbing, indelible images a person can ever try to erase from memory. But for some reason, I remembered enough other details from that wicked day to recall Helma Hanson's presence at the funeral. I vividly remembered thanking her for everything she'd done for my sister.

When she refused counseling by hospital personnel the day after losing Scout to SIDS, friends suggested that Elizabeth meet a woman who had experience losing a child to SIDS decades earlier and who had a reputation in the community for all her work with women suffering as she had. Just to get everyone off her ass about seeking help she wasn't in the mood to receive, Elizabeth dialed Helma Hanson's number, only to discover the chance meeting invaluable. As it turned out, Helma and Elizabeth became fast friends, and I'd heard a lot about Helma and Ernif ever since.

But *that* Helma Hanson was not this tiny or frail. More like a chubby cherub of a woman. A solid little Norwegian for sure.

"She's dying," Elizabeth said flatly. "Of cancer. That's why she was in hospice."

"So why'd you park all the way over here?"

"I didn't know exactly where she was. Besides, it was outside the visiting hours and my Jeep would have been obvious in the empty hospice parking lot."

"So you knew you were going to bust her out of there before you ever even saw her?"

"No," Elizabeth said, sounding exasperated. "I just knew a posted sign announcing the normal visiting hours wasn't going to keep me from seeing Helma."

I drove around the front of the hospital and through the rows of parked cars until I finally found my sister's yellow Jeep. I pulled in front of it and threw the stick into park. Before I could say a thing, Elizabeth was out the door, starting her Jeep, leaning in to adjust the passenger seat to recline, and retrieving a blanket from the emergency kit in the back to wrap around Helma. With seemingly little effort, she lifted the cocooned Helma and gently placed her in the Jeep, strapping her in and closing all the doors.

Helma never woke.

When my sister came back to close the door of the truck, I asked, "Where are you going?"

"Away," she answered, about to shut the door.

"Elizabeth, please. Just talk to me. I deserve to know why I'm going to jail for aiding and abetting a kidnapping. You owe me at least that much. What's going on?"

Holding the door open, she looked over her shoulder to check on Helma and her head drooped, the spiky mix of primary colors pointing at me like a deadly circus weapon, at once threatening and comical. I thought she might be crying, which would be unusual for Elizabeth, but when she lifted her face to me, I could see in her eyes she was debating whether to talk.

"Come on. Climb in. Helma's sleeping," I urged her.

She nearly had to vault herself into Jens's truck as if the seat were a pommel horse. She clicked the door shut so as not to awaken Helma, her eyes glued to the woman's sleeping form the entire time.

"I've never seen anyone so scared in all my life."

"Scared of what? Of you? Because someone killed Ernif?"

Elizabeth shook her head and her spikes were a blur of colors in the coming sunrise. "No, not that."

"Then what?"

"She said someone tried to kill *her*."

CHAPTER 6

"WHAT? WHEN?"

"Tonight. More like really early this morning. She said someone tried to smother her. She said she blacked out and can't remember much, just that I saved her somehow."

"You saved her?"

"No. Yes. Well, I don't know," Elizabeth said, burying her face in her hands. "It was all so strange. I was driving into town around two thirty, coming up Highway 79 from Hermosa, and something just told me to stop by the hospice, to see Helma before coming over to Jens's house. So I did."

"They don't let people visit at two thirty in the morning, Elizabeth. How did you . . . never mind." I really didn't want to know the answer. "Tell me you called the police."

Elizabeth shook her head. "Not yet. She wouldn't let me."

"So? Do you really think she's thinking all that clearly?" I jerked my head toward the Jeep. "I mean, it seems to me she's out of it."

"I know. But Helma can't remember what happened. Only that she's scared to death and refuses to spend another minute at the hospice."

My skepticism must have been obvious.

"She wants to remember first. Get her head clear. Then she'll let me call the police."

"Call the police anyway."

"She knows she's out of it and doesn't want the police to think she's crazy. You can understand that, can't you?"

"Someone tried to kill her." I could see where she was coming from, considering I had made a similar—wrong—decision not to call the police this week during the Sturgis Rally. Stupidly, I thought I had all the answers, watching a young girl pass out in the heat, assuming as we all do during the Rally that calling 911 might mean an ambulance will respond, or the police. But rarely both. And sometimes neither. Depending on the severity of the emergency. And now I regretted not trying harder. Yet I knew Elizabeth well enough to know I wouldn't be able to convince her she was wrong not to call the police. Just as she wouldn't have been able to convince me I was wrong. I had to try. "Call. The. Police."

"I can't."

I sighed. "Just tell me what happened."

"Well, by the time I got there, it was more like three o'clock. And I snuck past the nurse who was sleeping and simply walked down the long hall, reading the names on the doors as I did. Helma was at the end of the hall, by the emergency exit. Right by where I asked you to park the truck. I snuck her out the back door so they wouldn't know she was gone."

"Okay, so you snuck in and snuck out. No one saw you, right?"

"Not exactly," Elizabeth admitted. She stared out her window to check on Helma. No movement. "I had to protect her from the nurse. And a doctor."

"Protect her? Oh, great. This night just keeps getting better." I thought about my Queen Midas touch and saw another world crumbling into a pile of deep mold.

"Well, she said no more needles, and they were trying to shoot her with some kind of painkillers. Opioids, I think the doctor said."

"The strongest pain killers of all," I said, recalling what the nurses told me while I was at Hotel Poudre Hospital. "Her cancer must be advanced."

Elizabeth nodded. "So I gathered. But she insisted, Boots. No needles."

Only my immediate family calls me Boots. I've made damn sure of that. One time in grade school a boy called me Boots after he heard my sister Frances call me that, and he ended up with a wedgie so powerful his eyes watered for days. I tolerate my family's good intentions in using that nickname, knowing it's in reference to my affinity for wearing steel-toed boots. Not the high-heeled, zip-to-the-knee boots the word conjures. So no one dares sing about this Boots being made for walking unless he or she is prepared to have me walk all over their sorry ass.

"So why is she out like a light? Did she ingest something?"

Elizabeth shook her head. "She pretended to take the sleeping pills her doctor insisted she swallow. We hadn't even talked about that, but she spat them out the second he left. Must have hidden them under her tongue or something. No, I think she's out because she feels safe again. Post-adrenaline rush, I suppose. I'm telling you, this is the closest I've ever been to seeing someone scared to death."

"Because someone tried to kill her," I repeated. "And you believe her."

Elizabeth nodded.

"Maybe it's the medication. Maybe she's hallucinating. Maybe it was all just a dream."

"No. Listen. When I got to the room, she was gasping and choking. I rushed to her bedside and tripped over a pillow that was beside her bed on the floor. She said someone tried to smother her with it. She begged me not to call for the nurse, not to leave her. So I stayed, but I didn't believe her at first. I called for the nurse, and when she came, that only seemed to make Helma more frightened. The nurse had Dr. Morgan paged over at Rapid City Regional Hospital. Apparently, he had just arrived for early rounds. He came over to Heavenly Hospice within minutes, attending to Helma almost immediately. But she wouldn't let him touch her either. Wouldn't let go of me. Actually went into this weird catatonia that kind of freaked me out. But when the doctor and nurse stepped out of the room for a minute, Helma begged me to get her out of there. Before someone tried to kill her again."

"See? You need to call the police. Even Helma thinks it's possible the killer will come back."

Elizabeth sighed.

"Do you think it was one of the nurses who tried to kill her?"

She shook her head again. "I don't know who it was. She said 'he,' so I assume it was a man. Or did she? Maybe she said 'someone tried to kill me' and my mind just equated a killer with a 'he.' All I can tell you is that it was real. To Helma."

"Elizabeth, Helma's probably been heavily sedated for days, weeks. Just look at her. The cancer has all but eaten her away already. She must be on tons of morphine or something for the pain. Are you sure that she's really capable of making major decisions about her life?"

"If you'd seen the look in her eyes, the look I cannot get out of my head, you'd know my decision to help her is the right one. She was so insistent. So clear."

"So you kidnapped her? So she wouldn't ever have to be medicated again?"

"Well, sort of."

"So you rescued her," I concluded.

Elizabeth grew still. Her tiny frame seemed to deflate.

I realized instantly that my comment was hurtful. Everyone close to Elizabeth knew she had become a rescuer ever since Scout's death. She had trained to be an EMT, a fireman, a grief counselor, and, lately, a graphic artist specializing in logos for nonprofit organizations to benefit children. Shifting like sand. When she committed herself to a cause, she was 100 percent dedicated, even dying her hair the appropriate color. Her blonde locks were white when she was an EMT, red as a fireman, blue as a grief counselor, and now every primary color of the rainbow as the artist she is. Her commitment is always so pure, so well intended; Elizabeth is just that way—all heart—and forever trying to rescue others from the pain she experienced.

Elizabeth hadn't saved Scout's life. It was medically impossible. But she believed she could have—should have—beaten those odds for SIDS victims. I sighed. "I'm sorry."

Her stillness was powerful. Reverent. Her voice was small when she asked, "Do you believe in angels?"

"Of course."

"Me too," she said. I knew her thoughts were leading somewhere and her point would be profound. "I fully admit it, Boots. I am a rescuer. Always will be. But is that so bad?"

A smile dawned like the morning sun. "Only if someone doesn't want to be rescued."

"But Helma does."

"Her death may come sooner than if you'd left her at Heavenly Hospice," I said, knowing she'd already thought this through.

"If death is delayed by medicines such that she lives in misery and fear, is it worth it?"

I couldn't disagree with that logic. I tried a different approach. "Her quality of life may drastically be reduced, with more pain than is necessary without those medicines."

"But without choice, is it her life to live?" Elizabeth stared at the yawning doors of the hospital for a long time, then back to Helma in the Jeep beside us. "'To those who have watched a loved one suffer,' Dad always says, 'sometimes death comes as a friend.' I think Helma is ready to greet that friend and wants to go back to her home to prepare."

"To Rochford? Are you serious?"

"She's worried about her bees," Elizabeth said, as if this explained everything.

"Her bees," I repeated, incredulity creeping into my voice. "She said that?"

"Not exactly."

I was spent.

My dad pegged who Elizabeth would become by giving her the Norwegian middle name Eldrid, meaning "fiery spirit." She was all that and more. I had already said too much and knew that once Elizabeth made up her mind, the journey she decided to take allowed no detours. And her mind was made up. All I could do was support her decision.

"I know this sounds crazy, but I had to get her out of there. I need to sort all this out for myself. For Helma's sake."

"You're insane."

It was her turn to sigh. "Probably."

"But you know I love you anyway."

"Even though I'm a rescuer."

"*Because* you're a rescuer. Because you're *you*."

She smiled.

"Call me if you need anything. Anything at all, Elizabeth."

"You finally have your cell?"

"Ole has it. In Fort Collins."

Elizabeth shoved her cell phone into my hand and jumped out of the truck. She retrieved something from the Jeep and tossed it on the seat. "The charger. The cell phone won't be any good where I'm going. No towers, no coverage." She reached in the Jeep again and wrote something on a napkin, shoving it my way. "Helma's home phone. Dial it now on the cell. It's an unlisted number. Got it?"

I punched in the numbers, hit send, and terminated the call. "Why are the Hansons unlisted?"

"Helma told me once it was because she got tired of realtors always calling to ask if they'd sell their ranch."

She shredded the napkin and tossed the pieces in a nearby garbage can, dawn's rays a spotlight on her colorful coif.

"Now what?"

"I've got to go."

"I know."

"Don't tell anyone, okay?"

I shrugged.

And she was gone.

CHAPTER 7

"WHAT DO YOU MEAN she's *missing?*"

"She's not here," the nurse said, pursing her lips.

When Streeter asked for a transfer to Denver a decade earlier, he had reluctantly handed the Crooked Man file over to Bob Shankley. But he never let the murders go in his mind. And now he wanted those murders solved. The motive had eluded him for ten years, and now the news that the dying widow, Helma, had also eluded him caused his frustration level to mount. What secret might Helma hold to understanding what had been gained from Ernif Hanson's death and thus serve as a critical key to solving the other cold cases? And was she even aware that on the prior Sunday a seventy-eight-year-old body—her husband's—had been draped, belly down, on a rock outcropping near their cabin, as though he were a discarded dishrag? Just as in the other Crooked Man cases, Ernif had had the back of his skull crushed in and was left to die.

"But I thought once someone was placed in hospice care, they never left until . . ." Streeter's voice trailed off, his mind attempting to wrap itself around the news about Helma Hanson's disappearance.

"Until they die. Correct," the nurse whispered. "Look, my shift started at eight. Everything was hush-hush by then so as not to disturb the other patients. You can understand the importance of not upsetting all of these people and their families, can't you? So, if you would, please keep your voice down."

"Of course," he mumbled, biting his lip as he thought about his next move.

"I've already told you too much, and that badge of yours doesn't scare me. Shouldn't have said a word to begin with."

He hadn't slept much in days.

"And I appreciate what you've done for me. I promise, it'll stay between me and you."

Earlier that morning, delayed by the discovery of Tom Jasper's unconscious body and with the disappearance of Liv Bergen, Streeter had precious few hours to prepare for the debriefing that he had scheduled back at the bureau for 9:15 AM. En route to the office, he had decided to stop by the Rapid City Regional Hospital to check on Bob Shankley—who had suffered a heart attack the night before—and to talk with Tom Jasper's doctors about their initial assessment of what had happened to him. Which led him to stop by and see Helma Hanson at Heavenly Hospice. All impromptu stops that were making the time frame during which he could prepare for his morning meeting even tighter.

The Special Agent in Charge, or SAC, in Rapid City for the local branch of the FBI's Minneapolis Field Office had suffered a cardiac infarction severe enough to end his career—quite possibly his life—but that was as yet undetermined, according to the doctors. Shank's prognosis wasn't too promising, but Streeter was encouraged when he heard that Tom Jasper's vitals had improved and stabilized and that everything indicated he would eventually regain consciousness.

The nurses assured Streeter they would call the minute Mr. Jasper's status improved or Shank's condition changed. Plus, Streeter learned that Jasper's daughter had been by to see him a few minutes earlier, and their description of her—tall, athletic, striking green eyes, chestnut hair pulled into a pony tail, and "full of piss and vinegar"—sounded a lot like the misplaced Liv Bergen. "A looker," the male nurse had called her. Streeter decided not to burst the nurses' bubbles that the notorious "Liv Jasper" was likely nothing more to Tom Jasper than a friend and, more accurately, a con artist. He anticipated the look on her face when later he'd call her Liv

Jasper in person, maybe just before he formally encouraged her to consider joining the FBI.

Streeter roused himself from his reverie to explain, "I'll need to talk to the nurse who was on staff last night so I can find out what happened to Mrs. Hanson."

The day nurse crossed her arms, hugging her thin waist with a braid of fingers, hands, forearms, and elbows. He studied the nurse's nametag, stared into her golden brown eyes, and said, "I know you have rules, Linda. I know about HIPAA. And without a subpoena you can't give me any information about Helma Hanson. But understand, I am the lead investigator in her husband's murder."

"Not that I'm calling you a liar or anything, but that's not what I heard."

Streeter opened his hands palms skyward and asked, "What did you hear?"

Her pout did nothing for her prematurely aged face, skin leathery from too much sun. Her eyes locked on his.

Streeter waited.

Nurse Linda started tapping a foot impatiently and said, "I need to make my rounds. If you'll excuse me?"

Noting her wedding ring and the locket she wore around her neck that was inscribed with a single word, "Mommy," Streeter touched her arm and said, "You can understand, can't you, what it must be like for her, having lost her only child, her baby, and now having her husband murdered?"

She pulled up short, the fingers of her left hand flying up to her locket and rubbing it like a lucky talisman. "Mrs. Hanson lost a child?"

"SIDS."

She averted his piercing gaze and stared down the hall, as if work was calling for her, torn in allegiance.

"I'm not lying. But I'd be interested to know why you are so sure that I am," Streeter persisted.

Unimpressed by the credentials he flashed her, Linda leaned toward him so none of the other Heavenly Hospice employees could overhear. Her eyes sliding left and right, she hurriedly said, "Because I heard the names of the two agents who *were* here Monday night to interview Helma about her husband's death on Sunday, and your name wasn't one of them."

"Does it help if I told you I know they didn't get anything from Helma Monday night because she was so heavily medicated?" Streeter asked. "Or that the name of the other agent was Bob Shankley?"

She pinned him with her stare.

"Let me guess," he said. "Not your shift? And you don't want to get whoever it was that told you in trouble for shooting her mouth off to you about the FBI's visit Monday night?"

Nurse Linda looked away from him, cleared her throat, and stood a bit straighter.

Streeter pulled out his cell phone and punched in some numbers. He spoke into the phone: "It's Streeter. I'm at Heavenly Hospice. Just tell this nice lady who you are and why I'm asking for help on the Hanson case."

He held the phone toward her but she just stared at it. Finally she grabbed it and held it to her ear, her eyes still darting back and forth to spot any witnesses to her indiscretion. "Who is this?"

Streeter watched and waited.

"No, this is Linda," she said, her eyes meeting Streeter's again, a faint smile growing on her lips as she listened. After a long while, she said, "Thank you, Agent Blysdorf."

Handing the phone back to Streeter, she said, "Okay, he told me about Agent Shankley and said you were the lead investigator. He thought I was Dori, the night shift nurse who was here Monday night when they came to interview Helma."

"Which means what?"

"I'm convinced. What do you need to know, Agent Pierce?"

"Tell me who was on graveyard shift last night, who I should talk to about what happened with Helma Hanson."

"That would be Hester Moore," Nurse Linda said, scurrying behind the desk and opening a locked drawer to retrieve a personnel directory. As she read off Hester's phone number and address, she said, "She probably just fell asleep. She's going to be upset that you woke her up so please don't tell her it was me who gave you that information, okay?"

"I won't."

"Hester won't share much with you, even if you are the lead. She's overly protective of Heavenly Hospice. Been here for something like . . . well, forever."

Out of the corner of his eye, Streeter saw a man hurrying toward them. Nurse Linda dropped her informal tone and injected a more generic line about hospice policy into the conversation as the man stopped nearby.

"Hester Moore?" he asked, laying a file on the counter.

Without even looking at the file, Linda leveled her gaze at the man, clearly annoyed. "What can I do for you?"

The man cocked his head and drew his lips into a taut line. His sour words matched his mood when he answered, "You can tell me if you're Hester Moore."

Streeter didn't think Linda was aware of how instantaneously her posture and demeanor had matched the man's. Feisty.

"And you can tell me why you need to know."

Streeter could see she was struggling to keep her composure. He would have bet money that she had been disciplined at some time for speaking her mind to rude people like this man, but she needed her job and was doing everything possible to appear accommodating while resisting the straightforward answer he was demanding.

Streeter took measure of the man: his hands were soft, his nails well manicured. He was likely in a profession that required an advanced education and an indoor work environment. Streeter estimated him to be in his late forties—the extraordinary care with which his skin and hair were attended to helped shave years off his face. He was impeccably dressed in designer clothes and shoes, odd considering the off-rack retail outlets that dominated this area. Not from around here originally. Probably from a big city. His overall appearance was contemporary. Rich.

"Well, you don't have to be so snitty," he replied, slamming his fists on his slender hips.

It was the first time Streeter detected effeminacy in this otherwise masculine man, amusement in Linda.

Arching an eyebrow and measuring her words, Nurse Linda said, "Hester isn't here. What can I do for you?"

The man sighed and turned his wrist to check the time, bothered by the inconvenience. "Dr. Morgan asked me to bring this file to Hester Moore."

For the first time, Linda's eyes dropped to the file on the counter, as did Streeter's. The label read HANSON, HELMA K.

"Hester's on graveyards. I'm Linda Borrows, head nurse for day shift. So I'll have to do." She sighed. "Who are you, so I can make a note for Hester?"

The man extended a limp hand to her, his fingers long and loose. "I'm Steve Preston, Dr. Morgan's . . . P.A."

Streeter noted Preston's hesitation in describing what he did for the doctor and wondered if it was discomfort in, frustration with, or embarrassment from the title. It was definitely something. For the first time since Preston approached the nurses' station, discourteously interrupting the conversation, he seemed to have taken note of Streeter's existence, his eyes narrowing as he gave him the once-over.

"I'll make sure Hester gets the file when she comes in tonight," Linda said.

Preston continued his visual scan of Streeter while responding. "Don't wait. Read it. It may be helpful in administering care for Mrs. Hanson. By the way, what room is she in? Dr. Morgan told me to check on her while I was here."

"Then you should already know Mrs. Hanson isn't here," Linda said, earning a rubberneck by Preston. "We left a message on Dr. Morgan's cell."

"What do you mean she isn't here?" Suddenly forgetting all about his keen interest in Streeter, Preston was immediately absorbed in Linda's story, the gossip, as evidenced by his body language. He leaned over the counter and covered his lips with the tips of his fingers, whispering, "Did she die?"

"No," Linda answered, unimpressed by his seemingly spontaneous discovery of compassion.

"Then, I repeat, what do you mean she's not here? Has she been moved to the hospital? Did Lowell—I mean, Dr. Morgan—give you the right cell phone number? He always gives people like you *my* cell so I can keep him abreast, and I didn't receive any call."

"I don't know what number we called." Linda shook her head. "And Mrs. Hanson hasn't been taken to the hospital, and yes, we called the number Dr. Morgan gave to us and left a message that Mrs. Hanson checked out."

She offered Streeter a conspiratorial wink, which indicated to him that her use of the term *checked out* was deliberately masking that Helma was actually missing.

"Checked out? This isn't a hotel. It's hospice for pity's sake! What in blue blazes is she thinking?"

Upon hearing the term "blue blazes," Streeter instantly notched up by a few years his estimate of Preston's age. Or, he speculated, Preston had been raised by a grandparent or a much, much older parent.

The man closed his eyes and tilted his head back. "Oh, that's why Dr. Morgan asked for the file. He didn't want her to check out. Wanted to see if he had legal recourse to keep her here, keep her in treatment."

Nurse Linda nodded.

"Where'd she go?"

Linda shrugged.

"Come on," he coerced, offering a rather unsettling grin that he must have thought enticing.

Linda leveled her concrete barricade of a gaze at him again and his charm dissipated.

"Thanks for the help," he said with disdain. "Thanks a lot."

Preston gave a sideways glance to Streeter before walking down the corridor to the main entrance. Streeter and Linda watched as he walked away as if he was on a fashion runway, strutting with confidence and attitude. Streeter was convinced Preston knew their eyes were glued to him.

Flashing Nurse Linda an amused grin, Streeter stuffed the information about Hester she had given him earlier into his front pocket. His fingers resting on the file, he said, "Do you mind?"

"Can't. HIPAA and all," she said, then turned her back and started whistling while she rustled papers on the desk behind her. "HIPAA stands for Health Insurance Portability and Accountability Act, you know." Still facing away from him, she continued to babble away about medical professionals' obligation to assure confidentiality of patient files.

Streeter opened the file and scanned each page quickly. The process of gaining legal access to the file, which he would eventually have to do anyway, was time-consuming and tedious. This way he'd know the contents in a timely manner. He finished gleaning the information he wanted, closed the file, and cleared his throat.

At once, Linda also finished her paperwork and turned.

Reaching across the counter and patting her arm, he said, "Thank you for bending the rules for me, Linda."

Nurse Linda blushed, her fingers flying up to her locket again. "I've really got to get back to work, Agent Pierce."

"Me too."

As he turned to leave, he felt her hand on his arm. "Agent Pierce?"

He bent toward her as she crooked her finger and motioned for him to move closer.

She whispered, "I heard who it was they think took Helma out of here."

"Who was it?"

"I don't know the woman, but her name is Elizabeth Bergen."

CHAPTER 8

BY THE TIME I got back to Jens's house around six, my brother had already gone to work. I went straight to bed, but I couldn't sleep.

Between replays of Tommy being found unconscious and Helma Hanson thinking someone had tried to kill her, my mind would not turn off even though my body was exhausted. So I tiptoed out of my room and headed for the kitchen.

I found the note Jens had scribbled and left by the coffee pot. "Call Mom. Doctor's appointment rescheduled for tomorrow at nine. Nice dog." I smiled at how forgiving a person he was. Not only had I stolen his truck until the wee hours of the morning, but I had brought a dog into his house and let it curl up in the bed with me. And I hadn't even had a chance to tell Jens about what had happened the night before. I would catch up with him when he came home from work tonight for sure.

For now, I could wile away some sleepless hours surfing the Net and sipping my coffee. I went into the den and powered up Jens's computer.

The first words I typed in the search bar were "Crooked Man."

True, I had landed in some bad scrapes because I'd imposed myself into a couple of criminal investigations, but this time I wasn't imposing myself on anyone. I was simply curious and concerned about the welfare of my friend Tommy, my sister Elizabeth, and her friend Helma. It's not like curiosity would get me killed or anything. I wasn't a cat, for pity's sake. Although I wouldn't mind having a few of those nine lives they're rumored to possess.

I narrowed the search by adding "Ernif Hanson" and scrolled through the list of news articles about his murder this past Sunday. The *Rapid City Journal* had three articles related to Ernif and to the FBI's file of cold cases known as the Crooked Man, and an obituary that had been originally printed in Tuesday's paper was in this morning's as well. According to the obituary, Ernif had been preceded in death by his infant son, Steiner, and he was survived by his wife of sixty years, Helma Hanson.

The statistic that jumped out at me immediately was that Helma—the itty-bitty, enfeebled woman I had seen with Elizabeth just a few hours earlier—was listed as seventy-eight years old.

What would possess someone to want to kill a terminally ill elderly woman in hospice, a woman already several frail strides into her final mile of life?

The answer clearly wasn't that someone wanted her dead, but rather that someone wanted her dead *now*.

My mind worked through the possibilities.

First, the most likely reasons someone wanted Helma dead included for financial gain, for revenge, because of mental illness, obsession, for attention, in passion, out of jealousy, for the thrill, out of fear (such as a hate crime), and for self-preservation (such as in self-defense or eliminating someone who knew too much). And because of my recent encounters with Lucifer's Lot, my mind stirred up a variety of gang-related motives for murder, such as initiation, mob contract, professional hit, and gang vengeance. My trailing thoughts were that a murder could be accidental or—as in the case of Helma Hanson—the "attempted murder" was a figment of the victim's imagination.

In light of her husband's murder a few days ago, I thought it best to assume Helma was lucid enough to recognize reality and that someone was actually trying to kill her. If so, my initial reaction of calling the police—or, at the very least, telling Streeter—was the best course of action in my mind. I didn't understand Elizabeth's resistance, but if someone tried to get to Helma, they'd have to go through Elizabeth first, and I pitied the poor fool who attempted that.

Second, I began to narrow the list of motives by testing each one's plausibility one by one, in no particular order.

—If the attempt on her life was accidental, then Helma was safe with Elizabeth.

—I doubted that the attempted murder was gang related because a surprise visit by Elizabeth would have resulted in two dead bodies, not one nearly dead seventy-eight-year-old.

—Helma didn't fit the profile of any hate crime victims, unless elderly or Norwegian Americans had recently climbed onto the list of "at risk" groups.

—If the person had tried to kill Helma for the thrill, the obvious suspect would be a nurse or hospice employee.

—It was difficult for me to imagine someone trying to kill Helma for attention or who might be obsessed with her.

—I ruled out jealousy, unless Helma had been sleeping around with some other woman's husband, which I found hard to believe. And even such a crime of passion was unfathomable to me, given the victim's age and condition and the time of day.

That left me with four possible motives for someone wanting Helma dead. The murderer sought revenge, had a mental illness, would gain financially in some way, or needed to eliminate her as someone who knew too much.

That brought me back, full circle, to my original question: What would possess someone to kill a seventy-eight-year-old woman who lay dying of cancer in a hospice facility? Did the four motives still apply in that situation?

Since Helma was dying anyway, revenge didn't make a lot of sense as a motive, whether the killer wanted revenge against Helma or against someone else using Helma as the punishment. The killer would gain but shallow satisfaction by removing her days earlier than was natural.

If someone with a mental illness had attempted to kill Helma, then her death likely had nothing to do with Ernif's murder. In that event, removing her from Heavenly Hospice was a smart move by Elizabeth.

The idea that the criminal would gain financially was a viable and likely motive for killing both Ernif and Helma, assuming they owned something of value. But that again begged the question: Why would the killer jeopardize his or her freedom by committing a murder when Helma would probably be dead in days or weeks anyway?

The idea that a killer thought Helma knew something incriminating made sense, since there would be a chance she might talk before she died, and that same motive could very well apply to why Ernif was killed. But I had to wonder, what could they possibly know?

What I could not imagine was that there might be two different killers with two different motives, first for killing Ernif and second attempting to kill Helma in the same week. I was convinced the killer was the same person in both cases, assuming Helma's alleged murder attempt wasn't a drug-induced mirage of terror.

I reread every word of the articles about Ernif Hanson, absorbing the facts, making my deductions, and I studied the photos in each article. I found more articles about the cases attributed to the Crooked Man and printed off what little had been provided to the press at the time. I highlighted the names and death dates of the murdered victims. Then I tried to piece together in my mind where the six ranches mentioned in the articles were located.

Poring over the files spread across Jens's small desk, I drank my tepid coffee and started to arrange the newspaper articles and pictures to my liking. I started with the three earliest documented unsolved cases.

Eleven years ago, on July 24, a fifty-two-year-old rancher, Wade Barns, was found dead by his girlfriend, Melinda Hocking. He had been struck on the back of his head, his body discovered in a berry patch behind his barn. No one saw anything. He had no known enemies. The girlfriend was cleared as a suspect, having had a solid alibi, confirmed by dozens of witnesses at a Deadwood casino where she was a dealer, bracketing several hours on either side of the time of death determined by the Crook County coroner. Barns's twelve-hundred-acre ranch was located on the western side of the Black Hills in Wyoming, five miles south of the former small lumber town of Moskee, which had sprouted as a timber bracing and structure supplier for the underground Homestake Gold Mine east in Lead, South Dakota.

On July 25, two years almost to the day after Wade Barns was murdered, Homer Larson, a seventy-six-year-old widower and rancher, was found, barely alive, with the back of his skull smashed in. A neighbor found Larson on his homestead, four miles south of O'Neil Pass on the South Dakota side near the state line. Larson's body was lying in Cold Creek. The article was dramatic in its depiction of Larson's dying words to his neighbor: "Crooked man. Crooked. Crooked."

That was how the case received its name, and it was the point at which the mention of various sheriffs disappeared from newspaper coverage and information from FBI agents became scant. An article three days after the discovery of Homer Larson read: A "first office agent assigned to the Rapid City branch office, Special Agent Streeter Peace"—the typo made me smile—"was named the lead investigator on the Crooked Man cases and was presented with Wade Barns's case and the unsolved Buddy Richards case from the previous year." A sheriff quoted in the article mentioned he believed the three cases—Barns, Richards, and Larson—had enough similarities to suggest a potential serial killer may be involved. No quotes from Streeter "Peace." Studying the articles from that year, I discovered that Buddy Richards, a ninety-year-old retired rancher and widower with a patch of ground about a mile and a half northwest of Deerfield on Castle Creek, was found on August 2. When Buddy didn't show up for the church service in Hill City—the thirty-minute trek Buddy made each week without fail—his concerned preacher went looking for him. The coroner estimated that Buddy was killed by blunt force trauma to the back of his skull on July 26 or 27, although the exact time of death was unknown. Buddy's body was found in the brush behind his barn.

As I read the article, fond memories of Hill City flooded my tired mind. Rides on the 1880s vintage train, the coal-powered locomotive that continues to operate on rail lines throughout the Black Hills for tourists. I remembered Father Shannon quizzing us eighth graders in government class about which city in our county was the oldest—Hill City—and none of us getting it right and wondering how a town of less than a thousand could hold title to such an honor. I also remembered Father Shannon explaining that the draw for settlers to the Hill City area was the Black Hills gold-mining rush, and how red his face became when I countered that tin, not gold, was the single largest mineral extracted from mining claims in that area in the late 1800s and early 1900s. Leave it to me to know mining trivia at age thirteen.

Encouraged at first that maybe the common denominator among these murders had something to do with mining, I recognized a connection between the first and second murders. Wade Barns was killed near Moskee, a town whose lifespan solely depended on the boom and bust of Homestake Gold Mine. Buddy Richards was killed near Hill City, South Dakota's oldest city, thanks to the gold rush. I worked the puzzle in my mind to link mining with the Larson case near O'Neil Pass, but for the life of me, couldn't come up with anything I knew about that area besides snowmobiling.

What the cases did have in common was that all of these victims were older men, ranchers, who were living alone—or, more accurately, the articles made no mention of surviving wives—and all of them died from blunt force trauma to the back of the skull. And I couldn't help but wonder why these men were dying at the end of July each year.

I contemplated whether the unsolved cases could be connected in any way with the recent slaying of Ernif Hanson.

The men weren't married, but Ernif was, though he was living alone because Helma had been moved to hospice care. So, technically, all of the men lived alone at the time of their deaths. They were ranchers. They were old. And the date of death was within a similar time frame. The first three at the end of July, Ernif's on August 4.

I thought some more about those dates.

The first three murders had occurred in the week or two before the annual Sturgis Motorcycle Rally. Could they have had some connection to the event? The Fourth of July celebrations around the Hills were long since over by the third week of that month. Tourists bombarded the Black Hills from Memorial Day to Labor Day, but nothing significant was ever scheduled for the last week of July. The only thing I could imagine was a Rally connection. I cringed at the thought of my close encounters with the motorcycle gangs the past week. And shivered.

I wrapped my hands around the cold cup of coffee as though it would magically warm me. It didn't.

Just then my eye fell on the clippings from the Homer Larson homicide. I had been so intent on reading the article the first time through to find a mining connection that I had not noticed the small photo below the larger one of Homer Larson. The caption beneath the small grainy head shot read: FBI SAC Streeter Pierce, Rapid City Bureau.

I stared at the picture in disbelief, barely recognizing him with all that dark hair. Turning back to the computer, my fingers flew over the keys to find the electronic version of the article. I zoomed in on the photograph and studied every feature of his face. Everything else about Streeter was the same other than his hair, which was now stark white, and the lines around his eyes—or maybe it was something *in* his eyes—which were harder, sharper. Wounded.

I dragged my finger across his picture and had a thought.

Surely the staccato of my fingers against the keyboard matched the irregularity of my breathing as I hurriedly searched the news articles for everything that had occurred after July eleven years ago, well before Streeter took over as lead investigator. The information about the investigation for the two and a half years that followed was scant until an obituary appeared in the *Rapid City Journal*. The obituary that popped up in response to my search of "Streeter Pierce" said it all. That fall nine years ago must have been hell for Streeter. Unrelated to the Crooked Man, within a few months of being named the lead investigator on the Homer Larson case, a replacement was announced for Special Agent Streeter Pierce at the Rapid City Bureau. And Streeter was transferred to the Denver Bureau.

A week after burying his wife.

I stared at the picture until my eyes ached. I drew in a long breath, exhaustion becoming my autopilot. I gathered up all the articles, powered down Jens's computer, and padded back to bed.

I hurt for Streeter, even though I barely knew him. The warm tears soothed the ache behind my eyelids, inviting drowsiness that was as comfortable as a mother's lullaby.

No matter how hard I tried not to think about her, the image of Paula Pierce's beautiful face filled my mind's eye. The black-and-white obituary photo was small, but when I did an advanced search, I found a color photo from a ten-year high school reunion on someone's social networking site. Paula had been tall, thin, athletically built. Striking. Her hair was the color of winter wheat, not auburn like mine. But something in her green eyes resembled my own. And when she was killed, she was twenty-nine. My age.

The image haunted me almost as much as the way she had died.

CHAPTER 9

THE WOMAN SITTING BETWEEN Jack Linwood and Stewart Blysdorf was not Dr. Berta Johnson, the Denver County coroner and frequent adviser to the Denver Bureau, as Streeter had expected it would be.

Streeter pulled up short in the doorway, clearing his throat so that the three whose heads were conspiratorially bent would notice his arrival. "Sorry I'm late. I had to follow a lead this morning."

"We just got here ourselves," Linwood said, rising to his feet and pumping Streeter's hand as if they hadn't seen one another in years.

"We?" Streeter said, glancing over his shoulder at the open doorway. "So Berta's here somewhere?"

Linwood glowered and folded his six-foot-six frame back into the chair beside the gorgeous blonde, whom Bly couldn't stop ogling. "Lemley said absolutely not—Dr. Johnson's needed in Denver. But he did say he'll let her help you from her lab there or if you need her consultation. Telephonically."

Streeter thought that his request to the SAC of the Denver Field Office, Calvin Lemley, to send both Linwood—the best Investigative Control Operations specialist—and Dr. Johnson had been a bit optimistic, but Lemley had offered whatever Streeter needed; he should just ask. So, he had asked.

Streeter frowned and took a seat at the head of the conference room table.

"But the consolation prize is Jenna," Bly said, wide-eyed and nearly drooling.

The blonde stood and leaned across Jack Linwood to reach Streeter, who couldn't help but notice the distasteful expression on Linwood's face as he turned his head away to avert his eyes from the impossible draw of the vast cavern of cleavage she displayed inches from his cheek. Amused that someone had finally evoked emotion from Linwood, the buttoned-down egghead, Streeter let a crooked smile form on his lips, which the blonde clearly mistook for his pleasure in seeing her. As a result, she gave his hand an intimate, lingering squeeze.

"Jenna Tate," she whispered, mockingly introducing herself to Streeter as if this were the first time they'd met.

"Knock it off, Tate," he answered, quickly withdrawing his hand from hers and resisting the urge to wipe it on his pants. "Where'd you find her, Bly?"

"I didn't find her," Bly said, holding up his hands in surrender. "Jack did, lucky bastard."

Jenna tapped Bly on his forearm with her well-manicured nails, saying, "Oh, stop."

Linwood and Streeter exchanged sour expressions.

"Lemley asked me to bring Tate with me. Since you asked for Dr. Johnson and me, he thought you might need two of us," Linwood explained.

She smiled in affirmation.

Streeter studied her briefly, wondering how her expertise could possibly be of help to him. If anything, she might hinder his concentration. The snug, tailored suit, with its short skirt and low-cut silk blouse, was nothing like he'd seen on any other female agent with the bureau. And although stiletto open-toed shoes were not banned in the Bureau's handbook, it seemed obvious to Streeter how they could hinder an agent in apprehending criminals. He wondered if she could manage to draw her service weapon quickly enough with two-inch manicured nails and decided, because of it, he would not want her as a partner in undercover work. Nor would he trust her fully to have his back in a scrape.

"You seem disappointed," Tate said, lowering herself into the chair between the other two agents.

"I am," he answered honestly, which earned him a raised eyebrow, albeit plucked to a perfect arch. "I asked for Berta and you're not Berta."

"Sorry to disappoint," she said, casting her eyes demurely. "But I didn't come to replace Berta, obviously—I came because I heard we have fresh meat. Ms. Bergen, that is."

"I haven't even asked her yet."

"I heard you did."

"Not formally. She accepted the dog, not the job."

"So why am I here?"

They were at an impasse.

"Let's get on with it." Streeter distributed files to each of the three agents. "You have what I have. I'll start with the most recent murder and move backward in time. Ernif Hanson was murdered on Sunday, August 4, on his ranch near Rochford, South Dakota, about fifty miles from here."

He moved to the large map of the Black Hills posted on the wall. With a black marker, he drew a star over Rapid City, indicating the location of the federal building where they were meeting in relation to the dot he marked for Hanson's murder.

"On Monday morning, a hiker on the nearby Mickelson Trail found Hanson's dead body sprawled across a rocky outcrop in a meadow near his house. Hanson had been clubbed in the back of the head with what appears to be the same round weapon that was used in the other murders. He was struck sometime on Sunday and left to die. He was seventy-eight."

Streeter marked three more dots on the map, one northwest of Deerfield Lake, one four miles south of O'Neil Pass near the state line in South Dakota, and one five miles south of Moskee near the state line in Wyoming. "Nine years ago, ten, and eleven," he said pointing at the circles he had drawn. He stabbed at the dot he'd made near Deerfield and said, "This man was still alive and told his neighbor, 'Crooked man. Crooked. Crooked,' before he died."

"That's how the case came to be named Crooked Man," Tate said with certainty.

"Brilliant," Streeter mused to himself. "I was lead investigator for only a few months, but the Crooked Man moniker stuck with all the cold cases."

"Crooked could mean many different things, of course," Tate continued. "It could mean crooked as in the man who killed him was a crook, a
deceitful man. Maybe the victim was referring to a mentally or physically
bent man. Could be he meant a politician. Maybe someone who lived along
Crooked Creek, someone who lived in the township of Crooked Creek in
Pennington County. Someone from Crooked Canyon or Crooked Pine.
Could be someone related to the many businesses in South Dakota that
use Crooked in their name. There's a resort, a campground, an outfitter, a
construction company. I counted dozens."

Streeter remembered that, apart from her vixen façade, Tate was very
good at her job. His request for help must have given her no time to prepare, and he suspected she came straight from headquarters in D.C. or
from the training facility in Quantico, Virginia. Her list of possible mean-
ings, which could eventually become leads, was more robust than the ones
he had considered initially. Tate's talent to think creatively would be useful
to him after all.

"And I found at least two hundred South Dakota or Wyoming resi-
dents with 'Crooked' in their name," Jenna added. "Crooked Man is the
name of a dam in nearby Montana, and it was also the title of a famous
Sherlock Holmes mystery. And there's the Crooked Man at Storybook
Island here in Rapid City, of course. Incidentally, that's a tourist attraction
I'd like to see."

Left momentarily speechless, Streeter was saved by Bly, who offered to
take Tate there while she was visiting Rapid City.

"I actually prefer Storybook Island to Mt. Rushmore," Bly told Tate.

"This isn't happy hour," Streeter said. "We have work to do. Let's go
through this case by case and put together a timeline."

They got to work studying the six case files, including the two that
Bob Shankley had tied to the Crooked Man after Streeter's transfer to
the Denver office—Bobby Daniels and Frank Pelley. Both landowners,
ranchers on homesteads in the Black Hills, confirmed bachelors, and
older than fifty.

Two years after Homer Larson was murdered, Robert "Bobby" Daniels
was found on his 320-acre ranch six miles west and three miles south of
Hill City, southeast of Medicine Mountain. Although the telltale three-

inch diameter wound was found on the back of his skull, he was also found to have suffered a broken leg. His body was found by a concerned relative on July 31, two days after he was thought to have been killed, and was originally thought to have been stomped on the head by a horse, as his body was found in the corral. Once the autopsy revealed the round wound to the skull, the county coroner alerted the FBI. It was quickly determined thereafter that the blow to the head came first, disabling Daniels, and a second blow to the leg, fracturing a femur bone, was also likely not caused by a horse.

Three years after Bobby Daniels was murdered, another elderly man was killed near Deerfield, a seemingly popular place for the Crooked Man. On the hot afternoon of August 6, Frank Pelley, a widower of three years, was found floating in his stock pond four miles southeast of Deerfield Lake, one mile north of Green Mountain. Pelley was a hero to most, allowing neighbors to hunt ducks on his property—known by locals as the Gillette Prairie—rather than making them fight for prime hunting spots on the federally owned lands that surrounded his ponds. Again, a coroner passed on the tip to Special Agent Shankley that the victim had been bludgeoned on the back of the skull before his body was tossed into the pond, the likely murder weapon similar to those used in the previous Crooked Man murders. The coroner also determined that Pelley was murdered on the same day he was found.

———

After two hours of reviewing the facts surrounding each case, Streeter suggested they take a quick break, clear their heads, and start fresh.

When they returned, Linwood said, "Thinking fresh, I want to get back to the thread you were following originally, Streeter. Ignore the Crooked Man reference for the time being. We have six related deaths as you mentioned. Eleven years ago, July 24, Wade Barns. Ten years ago, July 26 or 27, Buddy Richards. Nine years ago, July 25, Homer Larson. Seven years ago, July 29, Bobby Daniels, only he had a broken leg as well. Four years ago, August 6, Frank Pelley. This year, August 4, Ernif Hanson. That's a pretty tight pattern of dates."

"That's what I was thinking," Streeter agreed. "I've asked our people to pull up all deaths— accidental or otherwise—that occurred in the last week of July or the first week of August eight years ago. Only cases where the bodies were found outdoors in the Black Hills on or near the victim's property."

"Let me guess," Bly said, "you found another case, only someone didn't recognize the connection."

"I found a case, but I don't know if it's connected," Streeter explained. "Eight years ago, Greg Schumacher's body was found on Reynolds Prairie. The coroner reported that death was the result of a crushed skull, and he speculated for the press that the wound was caused by an elk's hoof. The coroner wrote it off as bad luck for Schumacher: startling an elk and getting the unfortunate end of the situation."

"And what date was that?" Tate asked, leaning forward with rapt attention.

"July 28. But I was hoping Berta could confirm the coroner's musings on what caused the blow."

"Coincidental that it's at the end of July, don't you think?" Tate asked. "What next?"

"Bly, I want you to stay here and work with whoever you need to to look at each subsequent year and see what you can put together, assuming each year our Crooked Man claims a victim in the last week of July or the first week of August."

"Got it. Jenna can help me."

Streeter shook his head. "Sorry, no. I meant help from Berta's office. Tate, Linwood, and I are going up to the Hanson place to see what we can learn. I want to scour the crime scene myself on this one, go out to the spot where Ernif Hanson was killed. Linwood, I want you to use Beulah, see if she can track any kind of trail from the perpetrator that might still exist."

"Do we have something that the Crooked Man left behind?"

"Nothing but the victims." Streeter paused before adding, "Don't look at me that way. Just humor me. I'm trying to kill a couple of birds with one stone. I know it's a long shot that you'll come up with anything, but I need to see the crime scene with my own eyes. Besides, we need to give Liv Bergen some initial training as Beulah's potential handler before our new recruit leaves for Quantico next month."

"*If* she leaves. Waste of time until she's been offered the opportunity and formally accepted," Tate reminded him.

"She will be," Streeter confirmed without even looking Tate's way. To Linwood he said, "Are you up for it?"

Linwood nodded.

"And Ernif's widow, Helma, disappeared from hospice this morning. I have a sneaking suspicion she went home. I want to talk with her." Streeter looked at the clock. "Eleven thirty. Bly, help Tate and Linwood with directions on how to get to the Hanson place while I call Liv."

CHAPTER 10

"WHAT TIME IS IT?" I asked whoever was calling with such urgency.

"Eleven thirty," the familiar voice answered.

"Morning or night?" I asked, trying to place the voice. Trying to place me. I was known to be a sleepwalker, and clearly I had found myself awakened with a start without knowing how I got from my bed to this room. I stumbled out of my slumber toward the noise, just wanting to make it stop. I was confused about where I was until my eyes adjusted to the light in the room. I was in Jens's house, his den. And his phone had been ringing. Not sleepwalking, just reacting like a dog of Pavlov's to the sound of a ringing phone. Wake up, get out of bed, and move toward the phone. My sleepiness faded.

Relieved, I waited to hear the familiar voice.

"Morning." That voice. The man who gargles with barbed wire. "This is Special Agent Streeter Pierce."

"Such formality," I said without thinking. There was a long pause as I gathered my bearings. A big red dog came lumbering out of my bedroom and stood by the front door. "Just a minute, please. I have to let Beulah out for a second."

I made my way with the portable handset to open the front door when Streeter warned, "Not out the front door."

How had he known? I closed the door and looked around the room, wondering if the FBI had put cameras in Jens's house to spy on him. Or on me. I pulled my T-shirt down to cover my underwear and glanced around the room as I ushered Beulah out back to Jens's fenced yard. "I wasn't going to," I lied. "I put her out back. Why?"

"First lesson in owning a man-trailing bloodhound. Never let the dog roam free or it will track an animal or some scent until it's miles and miles away."

I couldn't ignore the sad eyes of the bloodhound staring back at me as she squatted to relieve herself. I was instantly impatient to do the same and jealous of her. "That's why you called me?"

I opened the door and let Beulah back in, watching as she slowly lumbered back to the bedroom and onto my bed. So much for the pallet I'd made for her last night. I crawled in beside her and stroked her jowly neck.

"Where did you slip off to last night?"

In my drowsiness, I'd forgotten all about ditching him and Bly at Tommy Jasper's house. I was suddenly awake. "To the hospital. To see Tommy."

"You have to stop impersonating people," Streeter said in a low growl.

"Who was I impersonating?"

"Be ready in ten minutes. We're coming by to pick you and Beulah up for your first day officially helping the FBI."

"But—"

He had hung up on me.

Ten minutes?

I sat up in bed, noting in the mirror above the dresser how disheveled I looked. My shoulders sagged with exhaustion, my eyes were rimmed with dark circles, and my hair looked like overwatered monkey grass. I wrestled into my jeans, peeled off my T-shirt and threw on a fresh one and a hoodie, and pulled on my steel-toed boots. After brushing my teeth, I rooted around Jens's room until I found a ratty Post 320 baseball cap, pulling it on over my ponytail. I saved most of my time for rummaging through the refrigerator, which was largely a disappointment. While I started a fresh pot of coffee, I scarfed down a can of Diet Coke and an old burrito still wrapped in a now-soggy Taco Bell wrapper. Keeping up with me, Beulah wolfed down her bowl of high-performance dog food, too, and I decided we'd become good friends.

I envied her for getting so much more sleep than I had. "Oh, well," I thought, "at least I stole a few hours."

My ten minutes were nearly up so I punched in the number of the hospital and asked for ICU. "Hi, this is Liv Jasper. Any change in my dad, Tommy?" The nurse told me he was still unconscious but his condition had been upgraded from critical to stable. I gave the day nurse Elizabeth's cell phone number and told her to call me as soon as he regained consciousness.

The next call was to my mom. I was vague about what I'd been up to, felt bad that I wasn't being totally forthright with her, and told her Jens was doing well. A knock came at the door. I told my mom I loved her and that I'd call her later. I replaced the receiver, took a deep breath, and moved quickly to the door. Swinging the door wide, I was surprised to see two people I didn't know standing behind Streeter at the door.

"Am I under arrest?"

"Should you be?" asked Streeter.

I just stood slack mouthed and wondered who the tall handsome man was and the blonde bombshell beside him.

"You kinda look like a modern-day Mod Squad," I said.

"Are you going to invite us in?"

"Should I?"

"Do you have coffee?"

"As a matter of fact, I do," I said, stepping aside and letting them all in. "Cream or sugar, anyone?"

All of them mumbled something, which I took to mean they liked their coffee black.

"To-go cups, Liv," Streeter called into the kitchen.

"Did he just call her by her first name?" I heard the blonde whisper to the tall handsome man.

So now I'm a *her*. I poked around in Jens's kitchen just long enough to find a couple of Styrofoam cups and filled four of them with what was left in the pot. I brought two cups out into the living room, handing one to the woman first, then to the tall man next. With hands emptied, I introduced myself, "I'm Liv Bergen."

The man responded first, his handshake warm and welcoming. "I've heard a lot about you. I'm Special Agent Jack Linwood and this is Special Agent Jenna Tate."

Her handshake was limp. I noted how fashionably dressed she was in comparison to me and imagined they must think me a hobo. My sinking self-confidence must have been evident because she said, "What a lovely young lady you are, Liv."

I wanted to hug her and punch her all at the same time, throwing me a complimentary bone while treating me like a dog.

Special Agent Linwood said, "Actually, I heard stories about how beautiful you were and I see the sources were, for once, speaking the truth." Something flashed in Jenna's eyes. I smiled my appreciation, and he added, "Call me Jack. I'm going to be doing some basic training in the field for you with Beulah today."

"Thanks. Sounds like fun."

I was aware that Streeter had disappeared. Apparently, when I took off to get coffee, he took off to the back of the house to use the bathroom, I'd assumed. When I saw him returning down the hall, I retreated to the kitchen for two more cups of coffee for him and me.

"Making yourself at home?"

"Just checking."

"On what?"

His answer was merely a grin as he headed for the door, sipping his coffee.

"Do I need to bring anything?" I asked.

Jenna stated the obvious. "The dog."

I blushed and turned back to retrieve Beulah. Getting used to caring for a dog was going to be a challenge.

"I have all the equipment you'll need in the car," Streeter said. "Lisa Henry's duffle bag."

I nodded and went down the hall to the bedroom, yanking on Beulah's collar so she'd follow me, which turned out to be no easy feat and quite embarrassing. "I guess she doesn't want to get up early this morning either," I called out to the agents in the living room.

"At the crack of noon," Streeter quipped. Eventually, Beulah cooperated, and she and I walked through the front door that Streeter held open wide for everyone to pass through.

Jenna opened the passenger door to the car where I'd been sitting last night and started to slide in next to Streeter until he said, "I need to talk with Liv alone about the other case from last night, Tate. Would you mind riding with Linwood?"

The bubbly Miss Tate didn't appear to have minded one bit and slid in next to Jack in the other car, saying she preferred it, although I didn't believe her for a minute. Nor did I think Jack was too thrilled with the decision.

I, however, was thrilled.

I opened the door to the backseat and let Beulah in, watching as she sprawled across the vinyl and fell asleep before I could climb in the front with Streeter.

"Where to, Special Agent Streeter Pierce?"

"Streeter, please," he said.

"But on the phone, you said—"

He sighed heavily. "We're going up to Rochford. I want Jack to work a crime scene with Beulah, see what she turns up."

My gut twisted. "We're going to Ernif Hanson's house?" Right where the fugitives, Helma and Elizabeth, went to hide out this morning. My sister was going to think I ratted her out, for sure.

Streeter's eyes slid my way as he started the car. "Is there a problem with that?"

"Just a minute," I said, opening the door wide before he pulled away from the curb. "I just remembered I forgot something."

Before he could protest, I was out of the car and had dashed inside. After closing the front door, I retrieved Elizabeth's cell phone from my pocket and punched the button for recent calls that I'd placed. The phone rang and rang and rang. No message center. I couldn't warn Elizabeth and Helma that we were coming. Hopefully, they weren't there. I hung up and tried again to make sure I had dialed the unlisted number properly. The phone rang a dozen times before I hung up.

I took a deep breath and bounded out of the house again. I glanced at the car ahead of Streeter's, and Jenna made a finger-waggling wave to acknowledge my arrival. Jack pulled out before I was in Streeter's car.

"Ready now?"

"Uh huh," I said. Holding up Elizabeth's cell, I added, "Forgot my cell phone."

"I thought you didn't have your cell phone."

"I don't. This one's my sister's."

The drive was a long one, made even longer by Streeter's lecture about trust and safety and honesty. I felt guilty for having snuck out last night, but what was done was done. I wasn't sure where the rest of the lecture was coming from. I felt even guiltier for knowing so much about him and his past—it made me feel almost like an unwelcome voyeur—wondering if maybe the lecture about honesty was because somehow he knew what I'd been up to earlier this morning.

About half an hour into the drive, I finally made my peace with him. "Streeter, I'm sorry I left last night. I was just frustrated and feeling like a burden to you. And I was worried about Tommy."

Without a blink of his eye, he said, "Well, I can see why. It's hard to see your dad unconscious like that, Liv Jasper."

"How did you—"

Streeter cut me off. "That, and the stress of aiding and abetting your sister Elizabeth in kidnapping a fatally ill woman from hospice. I can see why you would be so worried."

My heart accelerated at least twice its normal speed. I felt like that eight-year-old kid again who thought she was being so tricky by quietly taking the screen off her bedroom window so she could climb out onto the ledge and from there grab onto a nearby branch. Then she'd shimmy down the tree to go for unescorted walks in the woods to sneak up on different animals and try to catch them. It wasn't like I was doing anything bad. But I knew catching wild animals, like skunks, raccoons, squirrels, snakes, and the like would worry my mom. So I just didn't want her to know. Instead of sparing her the worry, though, I multiplied it because she spied the screenless window one day and found me precariously balanced on the ledge, hovering above the concrete walk below, about to leap and grab the nearby branch.

Only as an adult did I realize the stress I'd caused her. And only now did I remember how my heart raced when she ordered me back through the window off the ledge. Caught red-handed in my secret life as a wannabe Crocodile Hunter or the lesser-known Jim Fowler, catching, snaring, trapping, and handling all sorts of wildlife.

Streeter was about as happy with me, and my seemingly innocent indiscretions, as Sister Delilah had been the time in third grade when I brought a rat snake I'd caught for show-and-tell. It wasn't dangerous. I hadn't meant to cause all the commotion, which never would have happened if she hadn't screamed so loudly when I pulled the eighteen-inch constrictor out of my pencil box.

"That's why you disappeared at Jens's house? Checking to see if I had Helma hidden back there?"

He didn't answer.

"I can't get away with anything around you."

"Better to learn that sooner than later." He tapped my knee with the back of his hand, his knuckles brushing my fingers. "If you're going to work for the bureau, you have to learn to be more honest with me."

I just stared at him in disbelief.

"Did you hear me?"

"Work with you?"

"I said, you'll have to be honest with me."

"Honest?" It was easier for me to wrap my brain around an argument of truthfulness than what I thought I heard was an offer to work with the FBI. With Streeter. "About what?"

"Everything. To start with, where did Elizabeth take Helma?"

"What? Tell me you're joking."

"I'm not. I need to know where your sister took Helma Hanson."

"Not that. About working with you."

"We're hoping you seriously consider being formally trained at the FBI Academy in Quantico, Virginia. Of course, if you do, we'll have to set up an interview, wait for approval, and then expect you to report Tuesday after the Labor Day weekend."

I had forgotten to breathe.

CHAPTER 11

ALTHOUGH DOUBLE THE USUAL number of meeting attendees each month, the lunch crowd that had gathered in the ballroom of the historic downtown hotel was embarrassingly small.

He spotted the empty chair at the head table, the chair he'd worked so hard for, given so much to secure—*his* chair—yet he remained content to stay in the shadows of the balcony overhang for the time being, jotting down names and noting with purpose who wasn't present, eager to extract pounds of flesh for their absences should their excuses be unworthy. Short of a medical emergency or death of an immediate family member, he really couldn't think of a reason that would be excusable.

He kept an eye out for Anthony Burgess, the president and CEO of Nature's Way—one of the fastest-growing international conservancy groups—who was here, in the flesh, sacrificing his precious time to come to provincial Rapid City to applaud the local chapter's conservation success. The Black Hills chapter had the steadiest growth in the entire country both in the number of members supporting the cause per capita and in the acreage dedicated to conservation as a percentage of privately held ground.

Of course, President Grover Cleveland and later President Theodore Roosevelt had paved the way, considering they had conserved most of the

1.2 million acres at the turn of the twentieth century under the auspice of protecting the reserve of trees for much-needed timber. But he suspected that the nationalization—continuing efforts to convert private lands for public ownership as Black Hills National Forest, Badlands National Park, Custer State Park, National Grasslands, and the countless conservancy groups designed to promote these efforts—was a direct result of the 1874 diary of William Illingworth, the photographer commissioned by the U.S. government to document both the Montana Territory and the Dakota Territory for the potential of gold in the Black Hills.

Was it Illingworth or Ludlow who said of the Black Hills, "The first who come will go away rich?" he wondered. His love for learning more about history was rivaled only by his desire to preserve historical sites. But neither was remotely as powerful as his passion for avenging past wrongdoings.

Better for the public to control and protect the possible riches inherent in the Black Hills than to allow the greed of capitalists to ruin them, he believed.

He also believed Nature's Way was naive in making their motto "Protect and Preserve Through Passive Use and Passion." But he did appreciate their latest advertisements: "Be a good son or daughter. Sacrifice yourself for your sustainable Mother Earth." For the past fifteen years of his life, in honor of his own mother's passing, he had been the best son he could be. And his efforts had not gone unrecognized.

He glanced around the ballroom at all of the panoramic photographs displaying the loveliest conserved acreages around the Black Hills. The Pay Dirt Ranch, donated by the Castle family. The Rough Ride Ranch, donated by the Tuttle Estate. The Mystical Pyramid Ranch, donated by the Schumacher Estate. And the land that inaugurated his illustrious career for helping preserve and protect, the Summit Ranch, east of the famous Inyan Kara Mountain, donated by the Crawford family.

He drew in a long, satisfied breath, pleased with his success. And he imagined a new display for next year, the most famous and elusive of all inholdings within the Black Hills: the Hanson Ranch, which he would rename, of course. Maybe it would be "Grizzly Gulch Ranch" or "Bloody Knife Bluff," giving credit where it belonged.

His dream world dissolved at the sight of Senator James Billings, who had just entered the ballroom. What was he doing here? He couldn't possibly have been on the invite list for today. "How had I missed that?" he wondered.

Billings was nothing more than giardia to his fountain of youth, his private property rights agenda and estate tax reduction legislation constantly spoiling what would have otherwise been "done deals." Landowners considered conservation as a means to avoid burdensome death taxes. Without the tax, conservation would depend solely on the landowners' desire to do the right thing for humanity. And that wasn't a sustainable strategy.

Senator Billings was not smart enough, nor had he the gift of vision, to see that lowering taxes for unintelligent, non-worldly, inexperienced benefactors who inherited the land from deceased relatives would likely turn to developments or sale of smaller parcels to maximize their unearned wealth. And it certainly wasn't in the best interest of all to promote the wealth of one, particularly when the one was Junior, the stupid, gun-slinging ranch kid who couldn't spell the word *self-actualization*, let alone achieve it.

And where was the brilliance of this politician, who defended the landowners' rights under flawed logic known as the 1864 Homestead Act and the General Mining Act of 1872? Those acts had rewarded settlers— mostly greedy opportunists after gold, silver, timber, and fur—and continued to be honored to this day. How could anyone support laws that countered the efforts of Cleveland's Reserve Act in 1897 and Roosevelt's National Forest Act during his tenure to preserve the Black Hills in 1909? So what if those laws were enacted twenty-five years later? As Teddy best described the efforts, conservationism was the solution to combat the exploitation of land grabbers at the expense of public interest.

How could Senator Billings sympathize with the tantrums of a few— the loggers, the miners, the ranchers, the outfitters, the hunters—who gushed over the supposed supremacy of "multiuse" land, with the opponents to passive use on public lands just for the development of basic industry, the harvest of our precious natural resources? And to think Billings called them "Nature's Gardeners." How could Billings support the landowners of inholdings within one of our country's most unique and precious national forests? After all, their ancestors acquired that land for nothing through homesteading, a gift from our government off the backs of the good people in this country. Those homesteaders were nothing but squatters.

For the benefit of one at a cost to many.

He watched as Senator Billings worked his way through the crowd, shaking hands, making a beeline for Anthony Burgess. The two men stood near the podium talking and laughing. He gritted his teeth, wanting the polite intercourse to stop. Like a grizzly bear raring back on his hind haunches before an attack, Billings towered over the Nature's Way executive, but he smiled, thinking about how easy it would be to defeat the ferocious beast with a single, well-placed jab to the ribs with a butter knife. Or in the jugular. Or better yet, with one mighty swing, aiming for the sweet spot on the back of the senator's head.

Anthony Burgess motioned for Senator Billings to sit beside him in the empty chair. *His* chair. His blood boiling, his face hot with anger, he took a step from the shadows under the balcony so he could push through the crowd to reclaim the seat at the head table, unafraid to displace the haughty senator.

Just as he did, a familiar hand slipped around his waist and the other gripped his hand. The equally familiar voice whispered, "Calm down. I don't mind giving up the chair to Billings."

He resisted the urge to pull free from his lover's embrace and said, "But I do."

CHAPTER 12

STREETER WAITED FOR LIV'S answer.

This was it. Her first test. He watched her from the corner of his eye, studying her body language. She fidgeted with her shirt.

"Did you say you want me to join the FBI, as in *the* FBI?"

He nodded.

"Full-time?"

He nodded again. She was stalling.

"I have a job. I love what I do."

He said nothing.

"Is there such a thing as being an official FBI agent and handler for Beulah part-time?"

He could feel her eyes on him. He didn't answer her. Instead, he repeated, "Where did Elizabeth take Helma?"

She tugged on her shirt again. She reached down to retie her boots. She repositioned her baseball cap and smoothed her hair, straightening her sweatshirt and sitting more erect in the passenger seat beside him.

Stalling again.

Eventually she said, "I can't tell you. Elizabeth asked me not to say anything."

She was honest, yet remained loyal to her sister and true to her word. The perfect answer.

"Thank you," he said quietly.

Just as Liv opened her mouth to speak, his cell phone rang, jangling her nerves. "I would have thought there wasn't any cell coverage up here," she said as he fumbled with his phone.

"This is Pierce."

He had actually hit the speakerphone and Blysdorf's voice sounded in the car. "Streeter, your instincts were dead-on."

"Bly, a word of caution. You're on speakerphone and I have Liv with me."

"Hi, Liv," Bly said. "Good to know you're alive and well. I was worried after you slipped out last night."

"Hi, Bly. Sorry to worry you like that."

"Well, I'll forgive you, now that you're calling me Bly."

She grinned, her dimple deep in her left cheek, the sparkle in her green eyes brilliant.

"Sneaking around like that causes those of us who care about you nothing but grief," Streeter said.

"You care about me?" she asked, studying Streeter and awaiting his answer.

"We all do," Bly piped in. "Listen, Streeter, like I said, you gave me a dead-on hunch to follow up. I'm finding several cases of strange deaths throughout the Black Hills that were ruled accidental yet might be questionable. A year and a day after Bobby Daniels died, there was an accident outside of Custer at the mica plant—on July 30. No one seems to know what that was all about, but they assumed the guy fell from a catwalk and smashed his skull."

"Let me guess: The wounds were consistent with a fall *except* the one to the back of the head," Streeter said.

"Yes, sir. The broken bones were indeed consistent with a fall from one of the catwalks, but a round wound at the back of the skull was unexplained. They ruled the death accidental."

"Clubbed from behind while he was on one of the catwalks, causing him to fall and break his other bones?"

"Appears so," Bly said. "Dr. Johnson says she would have ruled the death undetermined if she'd been doing the work. And now, seeing the consistencies among the Crooked Man victims, she said she would likely have ruled homicide, based on the skull fracture and contusions on the deceased's stomach and thighs, which would be consistent with someone lifting his unconscious body up and sliding him over the railing."

"And the next year?" Streeter pressed.

"Well, this one is a guess. It's the only one I'm not sure about. Five years ago, on some private ground sandwiched between Custer and Custer State Park just south of Calamity Peak, a man was found crushed, and a horse with a broken neck was found nearby. They think the horse toppled off the peak onto the man, killing him."

"The date he died?"

"Sometime between August 2 and 5. The Custer County coroner was not able to narrow it down any closer than that."

"Why do you suspect that has something to do with the Crooked Man?"

"Just that the dates fit. Dr. Johnson is working that file hard. She says it will take time to confirm one way or another."

Streeter noticed Liv leaning forward, biting her fingernails, hanging on every word.

"And four years ago was Frank Pelley, the floater."

Streeter grimaced at his choice of words with Liv listening, but she didn't seem to be too bothered by it. "And three years ago?"

"August 8, eight miles northwest of Nemo off Nemo Road. Really thick woods in there, but a guy's car was found wedged in a grove of trees. Looks like he was in an accident and no one found him for a long time," Bly explained.

"How do they know it was on August 8 then?"

"Last time he was ever seen alive was that night at the Sugar Shack. Drinking. He didn't show up to work the next morning. It just fits."

"What's the Sugar Shack?"

"A tiny little restaurant southwest of Nemo."

"Best hamburgers west of the river, I swear," Liv said. "Besides the Moonshine Gulch here in Rochford, of course."

Streeter thought Bly might actually be licking his lips. "Did you call Berta? What did she say about that autopsy?"

"One unexplained wound."

"To the back of the head?"

"Right again. Inconsistent with the car wreck, according to Dr. Johnson. Why haven't I met this woman in person yet, Streeter? She sounds like a pistol."

"She is. And she's the best medical examiner in the country." Streeter noticed Liv's gaze slide toward him and wondered if he detected a bit of jealousy. Then he brushed the thought off as wishful thinking.

The theory was indeed playing out as Streeter had expected. Something about the last week of July, first week of August was important to their killer. "Notice the dates, Bly?"

"Yeah, they seem to move forward each year in most cases."

"Most, but not always." Streeter saw a trend with the dates connected to the earlier murders, a year and a day apart almost every year, and wondered if the number 366 had some meaning to the Crooked Man. "Two years ago?"

Bly's voice was breaking up. Streeter wanted to hear the rest so he made a U-turn on the two-lane highway and headed south until Bly's babbling was clear again. Then Streeter pulled another U-turn and eased the car onto the shoulder of the road. The reception was perfect. "Repeat, Bly. Two years ago?"

"Oh, sorry. Thought you could hear me. Two miles south of Nemo. Right where your family's iron ore quarry is, Liv. The neighbor north of you."

"Oh, yeah. I remember. Donny Finch. Someone beat him to death with a baseball bat. That was horrible." She started gnawing away on a thumbnail and then pressed a hand against her forehead. "The rumor was he must have gotten into one of his notorious bar fights, only this time, it was with the wrong guys. A fatal error. They never solved the case, did they?"

"Nope," Bly answered. "Wooden baseball bat was found. Someone obviously was not concerned about leaving the murder weapon behind."

"If the bat really was the murder weapon." Streeter said. "What did Berta say?"

"Wounds were consistent with the bat. Except one."

"Back of the skull?" Liv asked.

"Yep. The bat as a weapon was different from the other homicides, which is why we thought this might be the handy work of a motorcycle gang. Lucifer's Lot, to be exact. More their MO. Lawrence County Sheriff Leonard Leonard suspected it was a gang initiation for a prospect."

"But you think it wasn't?" Streeter asked. "What was the date?"

"August 12, and I doubt it. Dr. Johnson agrees, considering the fatal blow was the one delivered to the back of Finch's skull. A round wound consistent with the other victims' wounds."

Streeter was relieved to see Linwood's car coming toward them. Linwood had obviously figured out he and Tate had lost Streeter and so turned back to come looking for him. As Linwood slowed, Streeter held up his cell phone to show why he had stopped on the side of the road. Linwood drove past them, expertly pulled a U-turn, and parked in front of Streeter.

"And last year?"

"Well, that's a toughie too. I couldn't find any deaths, accidental or otherwise, in the Black Hills except car and motorcycle accidents, which you told me to ignore."

"Right," Streeter said. "So nothing?"

"Well, I did find one just outside the Black Hills, although it appears to have even more to do with the Rally than the rest. Sometime between August 14 and 15, a man was murdered four miles east of Sturgis; one mile south of Fort Meade hospital near Bear Butte. His body was found on the prairie face down, like Ernif Hanson."

"And he'd been struck with something on the back of his skull?" Streeter asked.

"You got it," Bly answered.

Streeter sat staring out the windshield at nothing for a long moment in silence. "Twelve years. Twelve murders. Starting eleven years ago."

"What are you thinking, Streeter?"

"I don't know yet." Streeter said, stealing a glance Liv's way to make sure she was handling this discussion well. She seemed to be. She looked as deep in thought as he was.

"Is there any chance there are murders in other times of the year that might fit this profile?" she asked.

"Good point," Streeter conceded. "Bly, do a little cross-checking on that and make sure I narrowed the search properly. See if Berta has ideas on the weapon used to smash the back of all these skulls. It might be our only chance to tie the deaths together."

"Just so you know, she's already suggesting the wounds on the back of all victims' heads are likely from the same weapon."

Liv couldn't help asking, "Does all this suggest something to you about the murderer, Streeter?"

"It'd be better if we leave that to someone with BAU."

"Which is?"

"Behavioral Analysis Unit," Bly cut in. "But I'm with Liv. So is Dr. Johnson. We want to know what this is telling *you*, Streeter? Instinct?"

"The Crooked Man is patient, kills with purpose, is organized," Streeter said, hesitating. "My guess is you won't find anything outside the time frame that you've already searched, Bly, which would tell me the number of killings hasn't sped up or multiplied."

"Which means what?" Liv asked.

Again, Bly took the lead in answering. "These seemingly fit the definitional classification of serial killing: multiple murders, same time in between each murder, same modus operandi, same killer," Bly explained.

"My gut says it may not be that simple," Streeter admitted. "I can't put my finger on why, but this seems more like criminal warfare."

CHAPTER 13

"**CRIMINAL WARFARE? I DON'T** understand," I said. Criminal warfare yanked my thoughts directly to terrorism, and I just couldn't fathom that type of activity in South Dakota.

Bly spoke up. "Classifications are as important as profiles in narrowing the search for suspects in an investigation. Once more than three people are murdered, the likely classification given will be serial killing, mass murder, or spree. Serial killing normally comes from an organized mind, marked by patterns and an MO that rarely change. Mass murderers are typically disorganized and motivated by anger, and they tend to kill a bunch of people at one time. Spree killings are done by people who have no apparent MO, no pattern, no reason. They simply snap."

"You'll get a crash course during your training next month at Quantico," Streeter said.

He must have noticed that I flinched. The concept was huge, beyond my ability to grasp at the moment, and I needed time to ruminate.

"You said yes? You've decided to go bureau?" Bly said excitedly.

"She never gave me an answer," Streeter corrected him.

"I don't know if I am or not, Bly. It's a lot to think about."

I couldn't imagine life without mining. Without working with my family. Yet the world as an investigator was so alluring, energizing.

"Come on, Liv. You'll love it. We're like one big happy family."

My throat clenched. "I have obligations. At work. To *my* family."

Bly pretended not to hear my objections. "You only have a month to get your affairs in order."

"You make it sound like I'm dying."

I shook my head when I saw the grin on Streeter's face.

"Even if I do decide to join the FBI, Streeter," I began. I couldn't believe what I was saying. I was actually considering the offer. Surreal. "Let me try again. I'm having a difficult time imagining myself making it through the process by Labor Day, let alone getting my affairs in order. I have to be vetted, meet all the criteria, get accepted. And you said I'd need to be interviewed."

"I'll get that arranged for you sometime soon, okay?"

I nodded once and changed the subject. "Take me back to what you said about criminal warfare. I know you sense these murders would be classified as 'none of the above' of the options Bly just outlined, but you think it might be criminal warfare. What is that?"

"Just an instinct. I said I thought a criminal warfare element was in motion here," Streeter said, measuring his words carefully.

"I still don't understand," I confessed.

Bly spoke up, "Think about Lucifer's Lot. You wouldn't call them serial killers, even though a biker or bikers of that outlaw motorcycle club may be organized, patient, kill for a purpose, and likely use the same or similar MOs. They are murdering to enrich a group, which is not quite considered serial killing. It's a definitional thing. Classifications help narrow our search and solve the crime."

"So you think Lucifer's Lot is behind these murders?" I directed my question at Streeter.

"Bly was just using Lucifer's Lot as an example. I'm just saying something with the Crooked Man cases is not quite fitting the serial killer classification here."

"Maybe working Michelle's case all week, shadowing Mully and his motorcycle gang, is influencing you somehow. After all, the blame went to him right away as the killer. And Michelle's murder had nothing to do with bikers or the Crooked Man case, even though she was killed with a blow to the back of her head." I felt the tremors begin in my stomach and thighs as I recalled I had almost been killed the same way. I forced myself to move on. "Maybe the police had it wrong about Donny Finch. About Lucifer's Lot being involved just because there was a baseball bat involved."

Streeter sighed and didn't address any of my points. I wondered if it was because he noticed my legs had started trembling again. "Bly, all these other potential murder victims that you uncovered and Berta confirmed may be tied together by the same murder weapon. Did they generally fit the pattern? Ranchers found dead on their own property, older, living alone?"

"Mostly," Bly said.

"Do me a favor and map what you have so far. See if there are patterns, causality, other than the profile of the victims, choice of weaponry, and dates. See if there's something else connecting these crimes, like the location of the murders, where or how the bodies were placed. And see if you can find a common link, like a ranchers' association, a church group, anything the victims might have in common."

"Check AA," I suggested. He looked at me and his skepticism was obvious. "What? You said these were all older men, loners. We're still a bit old-fashioned out here, valuing our happy hour as the social norm. If they were all widowers, they likely found solace at the bottom of a bottle."

"Okay."

My body had calmed again. Maybe the world of investigations was good for me after all.

"Or check local gun clubs. We also value our right to bear arms."

Streeter stared at me with open curiosity, probably wondering if I was packing under this sweatshirt of mine. To Bly he repeated his earlier instruction. "Check out whether there are any similar unsolved murders that occurred outside the search criteria I gave you before, outside the dates I provided."

"Will do, boss," Bly said.

"Don't call me that. I'm not your boss." Bly couldn't see the grimace on Streeter's face, but it came through just as clearly in his voice.

Bly chuckled.

"See you later this afternoon." Streeter signed off and signaled for Linwood and Tate to move on.

I mulled through the information that Bly had discovered and Streeter had explained. A few of the gaps in the timeline I had pieced together from the news articles had been filled in. But I couldn't seem to follow the elusive thread in dates for the murders. And I could not figure out how Tommy Jasper fit in to all of this.

"What did the hospital say about Tommy?"

"He had a reaction to something."

"His new medication?"

"No, they've ruled that out. The toxicologist suspected it might have been an ingested poison."

"Poison? Ingested when? Over time? Like in small doses or something?"

"No, more like a heavy dose of something wicked, like a reaction to something at dinner the night before."

All I could envision was that juicy burger, but there was nothing wrong with how that meal was cooked or prepared. "Then why aren't I sick? I ate with him, remember. He ordered two hamburgers."

"We don't know yet," Streeter answered honestly. "Like I said, toxicology is working through everything as we speak."

"I'm not a suspect, am I?" When he gave no reply, didn't even look my way, I added, "Do I need a lawyer?"

Streeter didn't answer me.

"Streeter, I didn't poison Tommy," I confessed.

I turned sideways to face him, as serious as I'd ever been. I tried to give him my most sincere expression, only to find myself swimming in the brilliant sea of blue I found my reflection drowning in as he stared back.

"I didn't," I repeated.

"I know that." His eyes shifted back to the road.

"He's going to make it through this, right?"

"His insulin spiked for some reason. All we can do is wait and see," he said, turning the wheel to the right onto the gravel road marked Telegraph Gulch and then onto a trail in the native grasses through a grove of aspen trees.

Jack seemed to know exactly where to go despite the lesser-traveled dirt tracks we were following. Both cars bumped along the packed rocky road through the tunnel of trees. The sparse understory of pine needles, pinecones, and hearty grasses, and the thick canopies of trees blocking necessary sunlight, was a testimony of the determination necessary for survival in the harsh western states.

It was difficult for me to imagine what compelled those who ventured west in a covered wagon to ride for weeks on wooden wheels—no shock absorbers—as they traveled across vast empty prairies and through the hills to settle near the Rocky Mountains and beyond. I wondered what compelled the Hansons to spend a lifetime in this seclusion and concluded they were both brave to take on such a challenge, just as the settlers had. Then I wondered if I could be equally brave and take on a new challenge, the unknown as an FBI agent, or if I was content to remain satisfied with the known. After a lengthy stretch, the trail opened onto a meadow on a bluff, a tiny cabin perched on its far edge.

The instant the cabin came into view, I sat upright and leaned forward, my eyes searching the open areas around the only two structures for miles: one cabin, one barn. I peered beyond the dust cloud and struggled to see past the sheer bulk of Jack and Jenna's bureau-issued car in front of us.

"They must have gone to town," Streeter observed.

"Who?" I said, gaping at him.

"Your sister. And Helma Hanson. Probably preparing for the funeral tomorrow."

"How did you—"

"Listen," he said, cutting me off again, "I anticipated that you'd probably want to stay connected to your family business, work at the quarry from time to time on special projects. The bureau has approved that arrangement. If you say yes, you can work part-time for the bureau."

He paused, letting my silence lie heavy in the air. I was dumbfounded. That would make for a perfect life for me. Rock *and* data miner.

"After the interview, once you are officially accepted, you'll need to wrap up your work and commit to the FBI full-time until Christmas. After that, we can work something out."

I worried the hem of my sweatshirt as I fixed my gaze on the horizon, unable to meet his eyes or find the right words in reply.

"I have a lot riding on this unconventional recruitment of you. My reputation is on the line."

My voice was at once small and confident. "I won't let you down."

"I'm counting on it."

And that was that.

CHAPTER 14

THE SUNLIGHT THROUGH THE stained glass windows of the empty
church offered the pleasant refracted light of a prism, pure and exact. The
air inside felt still and cool despite the blazing heat of the noonday sun.

They arrived at Trinity Lutheran Church half an hour early to dis-
cuss Ernif's service with Pastor Keeley, which allowed Helma plenty of
time to maneuver the steps to the entrance and find a suitable place in
the pews. Much to Elizabeth's surprise, the determined Helma Hanson
walked the entire length of the church to the communion rail and knelt
directly in front of the altar and cross that hung high above it. Elizabeth
marveled at the remarkable recovery and changes in Helma just since she
had left Heavenly Hospice earlier that morning and after only a few hours
of sleep. She was no longer listless or confused, and Elizabeth wondered
if the effects of cancer were waves of clarity followed by confusion or if,
possibly, she'd been overmedicated and her system was now clearing. Only
time would tell, she supposed.

Helma leaned against the rail, laced her bony fingers, bowed her head,
and prayed. She prayed for a very long time.

Elizabeth had quietly made her way to the first pew, uncomfortable
being in a church for the first time since Scout's funeral. Having been so

mad at God for taking the one thing from her that she loved more than life itself, she had no business paying Him a visit in His house, pretending that she'd want to talk with Him for any reason other than to yell at Him, which she did often at the graveyard.

She folded her arms across her chest, refusing to look up at the cross, and instead tried to focus on anything else besides the fact that she was sitting in a church again. She noticed the color scheme, the arch of the wood ceiling, the smoothness of the pews. Being an artist, she appreciated the attention to detail of the stained glass windows, the simplicity in the design for acoustics, and the ornate pipe organ in the loft at the back of the church.

But her eyes continued to be drawn to the tiny woman kneeling at the altar, the streams of color bright on her back and around her head like a colorful halo. This made Elizabeth smile, touching her own spiky halo of vibrant hues.

If Helma could do this, so could she.

Elizabeth reached for the Bible next to the hymnal in the rack mounted on the back of the pew in front of her. The book fell open to the chapter in Mark where she read about Jesus in the temple. She remembered the nuns telling stories about Jesus scolding the money changers outside the temple and how she always felt the heaviness of guilt as she knelt in prayer at church for having three or four quarters tucked in her knee sock so she could stop at Rempfer's, the corner convenience store, after school. She supposed the nuns were trying to tell her to fork over those quarters as an offering at Friday Mass, but Elizabeth refused, thinking that God never intended to have His people give money out of guilt or shame but out of desire, which is what held her steadfast to her refusal to go to church until she was damn well ready.

Rebellion quickly turned to boredom and, flipping a few pages, she started reading the oft-told parable known as the widow's mite. She always thought the nuns were talking about the widow's strength, the widow's "might," because the Catholic school she went to never actually used Bibles in religion class. Elizabeth was left to imagine the words she heard from Sister Bonnie Jean and Sister Gabriella as they explained about Jesus's appreciation for the widow sacrificing all she had for Him. And so, as a child, Elizabeth visualized Wilbur the pig's spider-friend Charlotte at the word *widow*, since catching widow spiders was a favorite pastime, and Mighty Mouse at the word *mite*, conjuring in her mind a very kind, yet powerful spider-woman called Charlotte whose superpowers were used to help everyone she met.

Those childhood images had faded in adulthood, and Elizabeth was reminded of the powerful message the story was intended to convey. Wealthier people paraded into the temple, tossing money in Jesus's name into the collection plate, but Jesus acknowledged only the widow's contribution. Two mites. The smallest denomination of currency from that time, one mite being lesser in value and size than a penny. And the widow gave all that she had, everything to live on, and gave it up for God's sake.

Elizabeth's eyes lifted to take in the image of Helma Hanson, dedicated to prayer at the altar of her God. After losing her own baby, losing her husband, somehow Helma found the strength to pray to Him, the omnipotent, the all-powerful. The one being who could have spared her from her two sacrifices. Her real-life mites. Everything she had in this world.

To Elizabeth, Helma epitomized the widow's might.

It dawned on Elizabeth that the weight of those quarters in her kneesocks was a burden she hefted into her mind, not a burden the nuns shamed her into carrying. The gratification of candy bought over the satisfying clink those quarters would make being tossed into a collection plate.

Nevertheless, Elizabeth wondered if Helma was cursing at God like she herself had done so many times over the past five years. The image of Helma scolding her maker was comical. Elizabeth hadn't realized her laugh was audible until she saw Helma raise her head and turn toward her.

"Sorry," Elizabeth said, holding a finger to her own lips to quiet herself as her voice bounced off the high ceilings.

With considerable effort, Helma pushed her tiny frame off the velvet cushion where she knelt and hobbled to the pew where Elizabeth sat, sliding in next to her.

"I'm so sorry," Elizabeth whispered. "I didn't mean to interrupt."

Helma didn't whisper. "You didn't. I was done. Now, what were you laughing about?"

"Well, I wondered what you were praying about this whole time. Then I wondered if you were bad like me and were scolding God for taking Ernif from you."

Helma giggled. "You scold God?"

"More like yell at Him. For taking Scout from me, mostly."

Helma patted Elizabeth's thigh. "Oh, shame on you. You shouldn't do that."

"I know," Elizabeth said with a sigh. "But He shouldn't have taken my baby."

"SIDS took your baby. Not God. God opened His arms to hold Scout forever so that nothing bad could ever happen to him again. Just like He did my Steiner fifty-five years ago."

A lump rose in Elizabeth's throat. On some spiritual level, if she allowed herself to go there, she understood this. But it was easier to stay mad at God.

"I'm just not ready to forgive Him yet."

"Forgive Him?" Helma said, throwing her head back and laughing.

Her laugh was rich and deep. And contagious. Elizabeth shared in the laughter until Helma's turned into a horrid cough. Elizabeth cradled her shoulders. Skin slipped beneath her fingers' grip, and the bones felt fragile, as if they'd shatter from all the coughing. Helma crumpled into a pile on the pew.

"Are you okay?"

The answer was on Helma's embroidered kerchief—a horrifying amount of blood.

"Never been better, dear," Helma said through the coughs, cradling her abdomen. "My head is clear, my heart is clean, and my spirit is lifted again. I just need a minute."

Her coughing subsided and Helma righted herself in the pew, tucking the bloody handkerchief out of sight and producing a clean one from her pocket.

"How can you be filled with joy? We're here to plan Ernif's funeral. Aren't you angry?"

"I tried being angry once. But that didn't work out so well for me, so I gave it up."

Elizabeth marveled at Helma's attitude, so much stronger, so much better, so good in comparison.

In a voice so small she barely recognized it as her own, Elizabeth asked, "What were you asking God for just now?"

"I wasn't asking for anything," Helma said. "I was thanking Him for everything."

This only made Elizabeth feel worse.

"You spent all your time up there thanking Him? Even after what happened Sunday?"

"Especially after what happened Sunday," Helma said with more conviction than Elizabeth thought humanly possible. "Can you keep a secret? It was Hester who told me. About what happened to my Ernif. You remember my nurse, the one who was there with us this morning at Heavenly Hospice? Hester said Dr. Morgan gave them strict orders not to share such horrible news with me."

"He's your husband. You had a right to know."

"That's what Hester thought. But before you judge Dr. Morgan, understand he was concerned for my health. And he thought I was too far gone to understand, too sick and weak to handle the news."

"But you weren't."

"I wasn't. And now I'm even stronger without all the pain medicine and treatments. Now I can pray and prepare to hold Steiner and dance with Ernif again. Soon." For the first time since Elizabeth first met Helma Hanson, she witnessed a tear roll down her cheek. A tear of joy. Of longing. A woman preparing for the end of her journey in this world.

Goosebumps covered her body when Elizabeth realized that her image of the woman from the parable of the widow's mite had always been someone like Helma. She was the grown-up version of the superhero she'd imagined in girlhood. The adult version, the widow's might, was sitting right beside her. The tiny woman was supercharged with a power that comes from the fuel of faith.

Elizabeth's heart filled with an understanding that had evaded her for years. A peace washed over her that she hadn't felt since Scout died.

"Thank you," Elizabeth said, squeezing Helma's hands in hers. "And I'm sorry."

"Sorry, for what?"

"I saw you this morning. I know you weren't able to keep your breakfast down and that you are suffering from incredible pain. I feel guilty about taking you from hospice because now you no longer have access to whatever will control the pain."

"Don't you understand, dear? I wanted to go home. To die."

Elizabeth was stunned by Helma's directness. She looked at the cross for the first time. "I'm also sorry for not telling you that Dr. Morgan's assistant, Steve Preston, called this morning. He was directed to set up home care with hospice for you. The hospice caregiver will move in with you and take care of you. Around the clock. Whatever you need to be comfortable."

"I have you."

"I mean hospice would allow you someone who could administer something for the pain."

"I don't want to control the pain, sustain life. I just want to live it, to feel everything again, to think clearly for a few fleeting moments like today. I couldn't have made my peace with God just now if I'd still been under the influence of all that medication. I'm trying to thank you. Before it's too late."

"But—"

"But nothing. You rescued me."

Elizabeth's spirits soared.

"And I want to return the favor. I've been keeping a secret—"

"Helma," a man's voice interrupted.

Neither of them had heard him approach, and both women jerked with a start. He strutted around the edge of the pew and stood between them and the altar. He was tall, bald, and quite lean. He wore jeans cinched with a worn leather belt, which Elizabeth imagined was quite necessary to prevent the man's pants from puddling around his scrawny ankles. Tucked into the jeans was a plaid threadbare shirt. His glasses were thick and cloudy from lack of a good cleaning. And because of his crooked nose— clearly a break that was never set—Elizabeth would have described him as a modern-day Ichabod Crane. The broken nose gave him an edginess she found interesting on the otherwise bland-looking man.

"Pastor Keeley, good to see you," Helma said, reaching up around his neck as he bent to give her a hug.

"I tried to visit you at Heavenly Hospice this morning and they said you'd disappeared."

"Not disappeared," she corrected. "Checked out."

"But Helma, they said you hadn't checked out. They've been worried about you. Dr. Morgan's office has called at least three times to see if I've heard from you. In fact, I'm supposed to call them if you show up here."

"Please," Helma said, "don't call them. It would be wasting time. I'm not going back."

"You need to go back and explain," the pastor scolded, eyeing Elizabeth as he did.

"This is Elizabeth," Helma said by way of introduction.

"Elizabeth, nice to meet you," he said, offering his hand hesitantly. "Does Elizabeth have a last name?"

"Bergen."

"Bergen, as in Congressman Bergen?"

"Yep, he's my dad," Elizabeth said.

Pastor Keeley's demeanor instantly morphed from reprisal to acceptance. "Oh, well then, Ms. Bergen. Welcome. Welcome. You're here to help Helma today?"

"I am."

"Then let's get to it."

The pastor went through his suggested order of service for the next day, the scripture selection, and the song selection. He asked Helma some pointed questions about what stories he should and could tell about Ernif. Helma repeated what she wanted for Ernif, explaining his joyous and perpetually happy nature, insisting on four uplifting, joyful hymns.

After a few more arguments over scripture, Pastor Keeley said, "Helma, can I be frank with you?"

"Why, yes."

"It's not like you to argue. You've always been so agreeable."

"Which is all the more reason you should listen to me rather than disagree with my selections for Ernif."

His sigh matched the deeply troubled expression on his face. "Morgan's P.A. told me you're off your medication. You have to go back to Heavenly Hospice. Please. They'll take care of you."

Helma wiggled free from his tender grip and said, "Elizabeth is caring for me just fine. And I will never go back. It's time for me to move on. It's my life to live."

"But the pain—"

She cut him off. "It's my pain to feel. And it affords me an awareness I'll need as I walk my last mile. Alone."

The pastor regarded Helma as she stared at him for a long moment. "Okay. I understand. Well, let's make sure we have the proper send-off for Ernif."

"Then let's move on to what I'd like at my funeral."

Maybe Pastor Keeley was used to hearing such candidness about life ending. To Elizabeth, a startling proclamation about the need to plan one's own funeral should have evoked more of a response from this man than the one she got. Especially in light of the kind, frail woman having just made plans to bury her murdered husband.

But his response was simply, "With Ernif gone, are you planning to bequeath your estate to the church?"

CHAPTER 15

MY HEART WAS RACING.

I hadn't a clue what I was doing, but I was enjoying the heck out of it. With the lead clutched firmly in my gloved hands, I gave the order, "Find."

Beulah stood near the rocks where Streeter said Ernif's body had been found. I was tempted to glance at the gruesome crime-scene photos of Ernif, but told myself to ignore them and focus instead on finding clues through Beulah's keen sense of smell. Standing on the side of the hill, our backs to the Hanson cabin and facing the rock, we would have been looking at the top of Ernif's head. His chest would have been against the rocky ledge, his head drooping chin to neck and hung over the edge of the jetting rocks, his limp arms dangling to either side of him like willow branches heavy with spring foliage. The dark mass of dried blood spread across his thinning gray hair on the back of his head, his skull crushed by an unforgiving object.

What struck me—once I got past the idea that a man was murdered only three days earlier right here where I stood—was how his fingertips had barely touched the top of the hillside grasses, the wind-bent heads of bluejoint just tickling his hands. A weird thought, for sure, but something about that particular photo had made my eyes snap to his fingertips. To the fingernails. Groomed, but longer than I expected. Something about his hands made the scene seem familiar, but I shook it off, attributing the ominous familiarity to déjà vu or to the overwhelming circumstances of my life over the past several weeks.

I wondered if I was thinking of how my eyes were drawn a month ago to my friend Lisa Henry's hands, pleading in their lifelessness to help her.

There was also a strange familiarity about that rock outcropping that I couldn't seem to shake. Yes, I quarried rocks for a living, and of course my mind would naturally underscore the rocks over the other details in the crime scene. But my mind latched onto the image of that jutting outcrop on the grassy hillside as if I'd seen that exact setting before. I didn't think I had ever visited the Hansons before, and I wondered if my hiking and biking trips on the 114-mile Mickelson Trail ever brought me this far north. I didn't think so.

Something about the way this mountain of a man rested where he fell on top of the only outcropping in the entire area tugged at me. The rest of the outcroppings that were visible on hills across the creek offered a cross-sectional view of the sedimentary layers of stone that had been exposed through weathering or breakage from volcanic uplifts over the centuries.

Yet this is where Ernif Hanson took his last step.

I shivered, nearly forgetting about the task at hand. Beulah, I saw, had obeyed my command to find what she could for a scent, which included what appeared to be a preliminary and somewhat lengthy assessment of all the scents that existed at the scene.

Jack, who was standing just behind me, coached in a whisper, "Be patient. She's working."

"How realistic is it that a scent would still be here after—"

My arms were nearly yanked out of my shoulder sockets as Beulah took off from the rock, heading across the hillside and down into the valley. Within a few paces, I managed a downhill face-plant, Beulah pulling my weight easily in a prickly, rocky skid.

"Get up," Jack called. "Don't let go."

I scrabbled to my feet, glad that at least I hadn't heard any snickering. I found it difficult to hold tight to Beulah's lead, particularly with raw palms I hadn't re-bandaged after my shower this morning. I ran as fast as I could to keep up with her.

"Lean back," Jack shouted, running a pace or so behind me. "Be in control of her pace, yet don't squelch her enthusiasm."

"Huh?" I managed between labored breaths.

"Hold tight and lean back without jerking the lead and without stopping her altogether," he repeated. He sounded as if he were standing still, yet I knew he was immediately behind me matching every stride.

I leaned my shoulders back, running on the heels of my boots rather than on the tips of my toes. I imagined myself waterskiing behind a powerful boat and instantly understood the reason not to jerk on the lead, not to stop altogether. To feel the fluid motion of the boat's momentum and to use it to my advantage to stay afloat, rather than to let it overpower me into a belly flop, I leaned backward, allowing my heels the solid contact in the earth and my legs the steadiness of the flow. As soon as I leaned back, Beulah struggled against her harness, moving surely and evenly through the valley toward the bluff where the Hanson cabin perched.

"There you go," Jack encouraged. "You've got it!"

"More like she's got me," I said, trying not to let my strength drain too quickly. "I had no idea how strong she was."

"Stay with it," Jack encouraged as he saw Beulah start her charge up the hill to the cabin. "Maintain as much energy as you can. Let her pull you up the hill to some extent."

I understood what he was saying. I held on with both hands and let Beulah's hard-charging momentum pull my weight up the hill as though she were a pommel tow at a snow-ski resort; I just didn't have the plastic disk to slip between my thighs.

"Encourage her," Jack said, staying close to me.

"Find," I yelled again, loud enough for my bloodhound to hear me. If I had to guess, the lead was nearly fifteen feet long, and Beulah was ahead of me by nearly all of that.

My command encouraged Beulah to charge the last few yards of the hill to the top of the bluff. By the time I reached the top, letting Beulah's strength pull me up the rest of the way, she charged ahead strong and sure, trying to pull me along at her pace.

We had covered a distance of about an eighth of a mile—maybe a quarter mile if the earth were stomped flat—and resisting the dog's power was exhausting. Before I could catch my breath, Beulah was dragging me across the high meadow plateau toward the Hanson cabin, stopping short of the two cars we'd arrived in. She sniffed the air, circling in the grass about ten yards south of where Streeter had parked beside Jack, directly in front of the cabin. She sniffed and circled.

"Give her some slack," Jack coached in a whisper again. "And stay back where you are."

Beulah sniffed and circled again.

"Give her encouragement," Jack whispered in my ear, sending chills down my spine. The good kind. It had been a long time since a man had whispered in my ear.

"Find," I said, my voice quavering.

"More firmly this time," Jack instructed. "Make sure she knows who's in charge."

I cleared my throat, repeating the command in a stern tone.

Beulah looked back at me, circled, doubled back a little ways toward me, and repeated the motion exactly where she had been. Eventually, she stopped in the same spot three times and just stood there, whining.

"Very good," Jack said. "Reward her."

"For what?" I said, totally confused.

"Go on, pet her," he said, nudging me in my lower back with the flat of his hand. It felt warm through my sweatshirt.

I went to Beulah, who waited for me, whining, and knelt beside her, rubbing her ears, stroking her neck, and talking to her about what a good dog she was. I glanced over my shoulder just as Jack was giving Streeter and Jenna a thumbs-up. Jenna leaned against Streeter's shoulder as he studied the ground around the rocky outcropping where Ernif Hanson's body was found. Several times he squatted down, which appeared to me to be his way to avoid being her human crutch, yet each time she found a reason to place her hand against him. As they made it a third of the way up the steep hillside, I could only imagine how she was balancing in those high heels of hers, but still that was no excuse to touch, in my humble opinion. Change your shoes, girlfriend, I thought.

Jack, in his worn Redwing boots, ambled over to me and squatted beside me, giving Beulah a loving rubdown.

"You did a good job."

I wasn't sure if he was talking to me or to Beulah.

Before I could ask, he said, "Come on. Trust, but verify."

He was headed toward the cars and past the cabin into the trees before I could gather the lead and encourage Beulah to follow me. As I walked, I brushed the pine needles and cockleburs off my clothes, my knees and palms throbbing from the freshly opened scabs, and felt the sting of my chin as my glove brushed it. I must have earned myself a new road rash with my face-first fall.

What a mess I was.

We caught up to Jack as he slid down the hill on his boot heels, scrambled up the other side, and walked along another bluff to the north of the Hansons' cabin.

"What are we doing?"

"I told you," he said, offering little by way of explanation.

"You didn't," I protested.

"I did," he said.

I walked beside him, and Beulah caught up to me.

"What did you tell her? When you gathered the lead to follow me?"

I was so confused, I had to think about it for a minute, struggling to remember what I had said to Beulah. "I said, 'Come on.' And she followed me."

"Trailing dogs aren't like most dogs. You want to have only a handful of commands. Three or four one-word commands are about the limit. Nothing more. Don't waste those commands on words like 'sit' or 'beg' or anything else that's useless. When you speak, you need Beulah to do exactly what you mean. I believe Lisa taught Beulah to 'find,' 'heel,' and to react instantly to 'no' to protect the dog from danger."

"So what should I have said to her?" I asked, not wanting to disappoint Jack in any way.

He turned toward me, his dark eyes bright and his face full of energy. "It's not so much what you say but how you move, how you interact with her, when you say it. Like when I told you to reward her. You said all sorts of words that were meaningless from a command standpoint, yet worthy of praise because it was accompanied by you rubbing her ears and hugging her neck. But just now you used 'come on,' patted your leg, and walked away, like you'd given a new command. Other than that, you did great."

"Thank you," I said, happy to have pleased him. "So where are we going? I must have missed something?"

"Trust, but verify," he said, leading me through the edge of the trees where we stood above the jutting rock outcropping, coming back to it from a totally different direction. "If the perp killed the victim here, we want to know where he went after that. Beulah will track from the oldest to the newest scent."

"Oh, so the murderer didn't leave on the Mickelson Trail like the first responders initially guessed?" I asked, watching Jenna in the distance as she hung on Streeter's shoulder while perusing the photos.

"Right."

I fell in line behind Jack, allowing Beulah to trot beside me, enjoying the easy walk. I couldn't help but notice how Jenna was whispering in Streeter's ear like Jack had whispered in mine, but my gut told me Jenna wasn't doing so for professional reasons.

My stomach lurched.

There was no way I could compete with Jenna for Streeter. She was gorgeous. I looked down at myself and thought "hobo" was too kind a word to describe me in comparison. More like "slob." The skinned chin and scuffed knees and palms weren't helping.

"Beulah's what we call an air-scent dog," Jack said. "She trails a scent that comes off the ground and is able to 'wind,' if you will, the scent of skin cells. She's able to distinguish a particular person's scent from all others. Amazing when you stop to think about it."

"Uh-huh," was all I managed, sneaking peaks of the seemingly happy couple to our right as we circled high around them through the trees on the bluff.

"Air-scent dogs are great for finding survivors in collapsed structures or drowning victims, for example. She's also exclusively trained to be what is called a mantrailer, not a bomb- or drug-sniffing dog."

I was barely listening to any of this and hadn't noticed Jack had paused and was watching me watch Jenna and Streeter.

"Where are we going?" I asked.

"We're coming from another direction to start the search over again, just to make sure Beulah picks up the same scent, follows the same trail."

Just then, seeing Jenna press herself against Streeter's arm and rest her chin on his shoulder, I mumbled, "Rats."

"What did you say?"

I realized I had better rise above my fog of discouragement and get to work. Quickly. And I had better start paying attention to the job at hand, which was to learn everything I could about this bloodhound.

"I said 'rats.' Like doing tests on lab rats? The findings must be repeatable, consistent."

The noise he made was not quite a chuckle, but I wasn't sure what it was. "Not quite like that. To have a dog's trail be admissible as evidence in court you cannot direct the dog or lead the dog in any way. So if the dog comes to a door, you have to go through it. If a dog comes to an obstacle of any kind, you have to wait until the dog goes over it, through it, under it. Whatever it takes. You cannot lead the dog around it or the evidence of the trail will be thrown out as inadmissible."

"What if we hit a barbed-wire fence or something?"

"You cut it and worry about repairing it later."

"What do you think of Jenna Tate?" I heard myself ask, but could not believe I did.

"She's okay," Jack said unenthusiastically. "A bit too accommodating for my tastes, but her talents have a place, I suppose."

"Her talents?" I asked, staring at Jenna and wondering how in the world she made her tight miniskirt, clingy silk blouse, and impossibly tall stiletto heels appear congruent with the woodsy, natural outdoors.

"That," he said, pointing at the two on the hillside below us. "She walks around like she owns the place. Her confidence has turned many confessions."

"Oh," was all I could think to say.

"Come on," he said, motioning for me to lead Beulah over the bluff's ridge and down the side of the hill toward Streeter and Jenna. "Let's see if she can do it again."

I hoped he wasn't referring to my undignified face-plant.

CHAPTER 16

SHE WAS ANNOYING THE living daylights out of him, hanging on him and chattering in his ear as if that would change his mind about her. The games most women played annoyed him. He was not the least bit flattered. Women like Jenna Tate saw Streeter either as a conquest or a means to make another man jealous. He wasn't sure which it was with Tate, considering their past, but he suspected she had a thing for Jack Linwood, who tended to have an equal repulsion for women who played games.

Jenna Tate was accustomed to getting her way. There was no mistaking her intentions as she rubbed those massive breasts of hers against the back of his arm. And his annoyance with her was heightened when she mentioned what a "sweet little doll" Liv Bergen was. Realizing those would be the last words he would have chosen to describe Liv, yet how accurate Tate was, made him smile.

He heard the noise behind them and looked up over his shoulder. Linwood came crashing out of the trees, skiing on the heels of his leather work boots to avoid unnecessary steps, followed by Beulah and Liv. Linwood looked happy. It struck Streeter that he'd never actually ever seen Linwood smile before, but a hint of one played on the corner of his stern lips as Liv sidled up beside him on the final paces to the spot where Hanson was killed.

"So?" Streeter growled.

Linwood's eyes danced, his dark skin glistening with a thin layer of perspiration. Liv avoided his eyes, which caused Streeter to pause.

"We want to try it again, to be sure," Linwood said. "But I definitely think our Crooked Man parked right up there." He pointed across the valley to the west, up toward the cabin on the high meadow plateau above them.

"So he probably knows the Hansons," Streeter concluded.

"Looks like it."

"Or the Hansons were just being neighborly," Liv suggested. "It's kind of the code of the West to welcome strangers way out here in remote places like this. No matter who drives up, it's natural to invite them in for coffee."

"But there's no doubt he parked up there," Streeter said to Linwood, ignoring Liv.

He wasn't sure how to deal with his feelings about her. He felt betrayed somehow, seeing how much fun Liv was having with broody Linwood while he was thinking of nothing but her, despite Jenna Tate practically throwing herself at him. He and Liv hadn't dated or even talked about a relationship, but it seemed to be unspoken that a mutual infatuation had indeed bloomed between them. His claim to Liv was unfounded, his jealousy ridiculous.

"Beulah loses the scent up there. The spot where she stopped is not directly in front of the cabin, so she wasn't trailing Ernif Hanson's scent, unless he didn't come from the cabin, which was doubtful. His old truck is parked in the barn, so he either had to come from the cabin or the barn. But Beulah went to neither place."

"Could be he got a ride in with someone. Or maybe she followed Ernif's scent as he was carried to the ambulance," Tate suggested.

Linwood shook his head. "Ambulance went out that way." He pointed down the valley to the south and up the side of the hill. "And, it's unlikely Beulah would trail from newest to oldest scent. She's too good a mantrailer for that. From what Lisa Henry told me, Beulah went out of her way to follow from oldest to newest scent in the order of how someone walked, even if it meant backtracking on the same trail."

"You mean that if I was trailing someone who was walking, dropped something and didn't realize it for a quarter mile, backtracked until he found it, and then moved on to where he was heading, Beulah would actually follow that exact path, doubling back and then moving forward again instead of moving on to the freshest scent?" Liv asked as she removed her gloves and stuffed them in her back pocket.

"That's exactly what I'm saying. She's good. And she never strays from her job to trail every step her target takes."

"Helps when we're trying to establish the exact sequence of events. Not all bloodhounds will do that." For the first time, Streeter noticed Liv's freshly skinned chin and reached to touch her cheek, tilting her head back to examine the wound. "What happened?"

"I didn't anticipate how strong Beulah would be when we started the search. I lost my footing and she drug me for a stretch."

"But you didn't let go?" Streeter asked, looking down at her raw hands. She shook her head.

He tilted her head this way and that, not wanting to let go. "You'll live." He resisted a smile. She didn't.

"So what do you know about the track she followed from the rock to the bluff?" Liv asked, her ponytail poking over the strap of the baseball cap, which was pulled low to shade her freckle-spattered nose.

Streeter had never stopped to consider the age difference that had become obvious to him as he studied her youthful face, the energy in her long-legged step, her sinewy, toned arms as she readied Beulah for another trail. Liv had removed her hooded sweatshirt. Her flimsy T-shirt was clinging to her boyishly athletic figure with a thin sheen of perspiration. He couldn't avoid comparing her to Tate. And he liked what he saw.

Streeter wondered if Liv herself had noted the age difference and if she'd therefore discarded any notion they'd be anything but coworkers for the bureau—he a lifer, she a potential new candidate. If she knew he'd be turning thirty-nine soon, she'd probably think of him as a fatherly figure. She couldn't be a day over twenty-five or twenty-six. Or maybe she just appeared young, her smile coming so frequently and easily. And the freshly skinned chin made her appear childlike.

"The scent Beulah followed was most likely the killer's. She followed it away from the rock, not toward it," Linwood explained.

"It wasn't Ernif's scent she was following, because his freshest scent would have ended at the rock. Or at the ambulance door, which was parked right there," Streeter further explained, pointing down the hill about twenty yards. He watched as Liv's eyes scanned the meadow.

As she studied the valley below, her mind likely piecing the story together, Streeter realized she was noticing—probably for the first time—the matted grass in the distance at the base of the bluff to the far south, just beneath the two-track ruts that precariously led off the bluff into the meadow. The area of matted grass was on the flat as far from the north fork of Rapid Creek and the Mickelson Trail as possible before the steep grade of the hill leading to the bluff on the far south. But it was also as far from this rock on the north side of the grassy meadow. He wondered if she was intelligent enough to piece everything together without knowing all the facts or if it would even dawn on her that the crime scene technicians would have had to park somewhere and had to choose a spot that wouldn't contaminate the crime scene.

"So Ernif never ventured away from the rock, at least not leaving a fresher scent than where he ended up when he was killed," Streeter continued. "Speculation would lead us to believe that the trail was of the killer, or someone who would have left the scene of the crime."

"Why couldn't it have been the trail of one of the technicians who scoured the crime scene?" Liv asked, squinting at the area in the distance.

Atta girl, Streeter thought.

Tate was the one to answer Liv's perceptive question this time. "We're trained to protect and preserve the crime scene. No one who is a professional would have parked up there. They would have parked in the designated spot, which was over there, based on the photos," she said, pointing to the area Liv had been scanning a few moments earlier. Tate stepped closer to Streeter. "Right, Street?"

It took everything in him not to shrink away from her.

"Right," Linwood finally answered. "Our killer probably parked to admire the view of the creek and trail below rather than to visit the Hansons; just look at how far away the vehicle was parked from the cabin. Maybe our killer initially thought the place was abandoned, so Ernif's presence surprised him. Maybe our killer intentionally parked where he did. Hard to tell."

"Well, either way, it doesn't really matter. There's not much to go on," Tate said, scowling at Liv as if it were her fault that the dog didn't turn up a smoking gun.

Streeter defended Liv. "But the trail she's establishing is something. The killer moved from Hanson's body down into the valley, up the hill, and onto the high meadow by the cabin, stopping at the same point each time. Likely a car. Consistent."

"Follow us this time," Linwood suggested. "Plus, you'll get to see how Liv is a natural at this."

Linwood sounded nearly giddy, something Streeter would have believed impossible before today. Jack Linwood was the most serious, stodgy professional in the office, second only to the buttoned-down Special Agent Phil Kelleher, who also found himself enamored of Liv's charm when he was asked to stay with her in Fort Collins during the DeMilo murder case. Streeter watched as Linwood stood at Liv's shoulder, preparing her for the search. He didn't like the way Linwood being so close to Liv made him feel, and he averted his eyes, pretending to study the crime scene photos again, pretending not to care that Linwood was taller, younger, and more handsome than he was.

When Liv commanded Beulah to "Find," the trio took off across the hillside in no time. Streeter started after them in long strides, with Tate teetering on her heels, clinging to his shoulder like a repugnant, prized parakeet.

This wasn't at all how he had intended to spend his time during a delayed stay in Rapid City, a blonde leaning against him as he watched Liv traipsing happily along with another man. All Streeter wanted to do was solve the Crooked Man crimes and get back to Denver.

Quickly.

CHAPTER 17

Thursday, August 8, 7:45 AM

I WAS MOTIVATED.

Yesterday had been a good day for Beulah and me. And today was going to be even better.

Jack and Jenna had given me a ride home from the Hanson ranch because Streeter had decided to head back to Rapid City early. By the time I was dropped off at Jens's house on Teepee Street, he was home from work, waiting for me—and so was dinner. He had prepared a pheasant under glass, a dish Mom used to make when we were kids. A delicious one from last spring's harvest of ring-necked pheasant, served with wild rice and mushrooms. Absolutely exquisite.

I spent the entire evening catching up with my brother. We gorged ourselves on the home-cooked meal while Jens peppered me with questions about what had happened at our iron ore quarry the night before—or, more accurately, early that morning—when the FBI closed in on his fiancée's killer. I was able to shed light on any shadows of doubt that remained in Jens's mind about anyone believing he was responsible in any way for Michelle's murder. I assured him how much she really had loved him and how willing she had been to set herself free from the past in order to share her future with him. After a lot of tears and beers, agonies and apologies, I filled him in on why Elizabeth never showed up at his house and how he was stuck with a big old red bloodhound as a houseguest instead.

After dinner, and with Beulah curled up beside me, I started reading a great book about mantrailing with bloodhounds that was in Lisa Henry's equipment bag. I fell asleep around nine. I didn't wake up until seven, when Beulah nudged me to take her outside. Ten glorious hours of dreamless sleep. I wasn't sure if my deep sleep was attributable to all the exercise from working with the dog or if it was from the peace in knowing my brother was going to not only survive but eventually thrive.

Although Jens went in to work at his normal five o'clock in the morning, he told me the night before that he'd stop by at twenty minutes after ten to take me to the funeral, so I had plenty of time. Idle hands and all.

My heart was pounding and my hands were gripping the lead tightly. Beulah's harness was cinched and her eyes were pinned on me, awaiting the command, ready to work.

Cooperative—albeit reluctantly—Nurse Hester Moore stood near the doorway, her thick arms folded across her ample breast as her wary eyes scanned the empty hallways. "Better hurry up."

From what I had learned last night reading about mantrailing, and from my brief and exhilarating experience with Beulah in the field yesterday, I decided first thing when I woke up to go to Heavenly Hospice. See if I could learn anything more.

Hester had told me Dr. Morgan had already been in, and the other doctors would be making rounds shortly after the shift change at eight o'clock, and she wanted me out of there before anyone from administration saw me. I had promised her I'd make it quick.

Standing next to the empty bed in the sanitized room where Helma Hanson had been staying up until yesterday morning, I quietly and firmly told Beulah, "Find."

She was sitting on her haunches, droopy eyes moving back and forth between Hester and me. She seemed confused.

Again I instructed, "Find."

There my beautiful bloodhound sat, staring at me.

Hester let out a heavy sigh. "Woman, if you don't get moving, I'm going to lose my job for sure."

"Find," I said one last time, and Beulah rose to her feet. She circled the bed and around the room slowly, lazily. Twice. Three times. Six times.

"Come on, Beulah. Find."

I tried not to sound as embarrassed as I was. I don't know what I was thinking. I'd only worked with Beulah once, so assuming she'd know what I was expecting from her in this hospital room was a bit of a stretch. I hadn't even given her a scent to track. There must be thousands, including Hester's, which is probably why Beulah kept looking back to her. My hope was that she would revert back to the scent she trailed yesterday, track Ernif's killer, and confirm that Helma's attacker was one and the same.

As she circled and circled and circled, I noticed Hester turn her wrist and crane her neck to scan the hallway.

"What's the procedure when someone leaves? Do they scrub the room as well as change the bedding?"

Hester leaned against the doorjamb. "From floor to ceiling. This is hospice. Most people who check in never check out, so you can imagine the regulations we have to comply with in between patients."

I could. I imagined the floors, the walls, the ceilings, everything being wiped down with something like ammonia, although I couldn't detect the scent of clean. With Beulah's sense of smell being millions of times more accurate than mine, I could understand her confusion with me asking her to detect and trail a human scent—a scent I hadn't even provided a sample of for comparison—in a place that had been wiped clean with a chemical that must be overpowering her nose.

All I could hope is that she would know I was talking about the same scent she had picked up yesterday, since Streeter and Jack both thought the scent she had followed must have belonged to the killer.

"Find."

I noticed Beulah's circling had widened to include parts of the room away from the bed where we first started, and just as she inched near Hester by the door, she lifted her head higher and suddenly charged past the nurse and down the hallway. The lead slammed tight against the doorjamb opposite to where Hester stood, and her eyes popped open wide and a strange noise escaped her startled lips. I suspected that the twang of the lead being pulled taut made her wonder if Beulah's strength could have put her in a full-body cast if she'd been standing in the wrong place once Beulah sniffed the killer.

I struggled to keep pace with Beulah as I trampled out the door, swept away in Beulah's current with Nurse Hester nothing more than a mere boat fender as I bounced off her.

Apologetically, I called over my shoulder, "Thank you, Hester."

Beulah led me in the opposite direction from the door where I had waited for Elizabeth the morning before and toward another remote exit down a different hallway. Just then a nurse emerged from a room and met Beulah head-on. She screamed, dropping the clipboard she'd been carrying, and it clattered to the floor. Beulah was undeterred.

Over the noise, I heard moans and mumblings from the patient rooms as we passed and Nurse Hester coming our way yelling, "Everything's okay, Naomi. I'm on it," to the startled nurse. To me Nurse Hester scolded, "Now get out of here. No dogs allowed!"

Bless her, Hester Moore had creatively invented a way to justify why I was trouncing through hospice with a dog without drawing attention to my real mission. I'd have to send her chocolates later to thank her.

Luckily for me, Beulah headed straight for the exit at the end of the hall and pulled up short at the closed door. I pushed it open and reminded her, "Find."

She was still on the scent, sure and confident. I followed her across the small parking lot, up over a hill to the south, and through a meadow I guessed to be about twenty yards to the nearby housing development. We ended up in an apartment complex parking lot where Beulah confidently led me through the nearly empty lot to a row of cars farthest away from the housing unit and stopped.

"Find," I encouraged, but she didn't budge.

Beulah stood with her head high, her legs as rigid as a statue's. I walked toward her, yet she remained rigid. I bent down and hugged her, telling her what a good girl she was, and only then did she relax and sit back on her haunches.

I believed I had just followed the footsteps of a would-be killer.

I believed Helma's story. Who else but the one who tried to smother her would have been in that exact room and walked directly to this parking lot? Heavenly Hospice had plenty of parking at all hours of the day, so if the trail were that of a visitor, it would have led to a parking spot in their lot, not here. And if the trail were that of an employee who lived at these apartments, I imagined that person would walk from the apartment complex through the field to the hospice's back parking lot, but not to a car parked in a lot this far away. It just wouldn't make sense. And wouldn't that same employee have to clock out first or check in with a supervisor somewhere in hospice, which would have led Beulah through that room before heading to the door? Instead, Beulah made a beeline from Helma's room out a back door. And it wasn't the trail of Elizabeth or Helma, the only other two, to my knowledge, who had snuck out.

And what other scent, absent any guidance from me, would Beulah follow other than the one she followed yesterday? If not the same scent, certainly the strongest. And the scent she had just followed had to be recent given the amount of deep cleaning that occurred in the hospice facility.

I plopped down on the curb of the nearly empty parking lot and ruffled the folds of loose skin on Beulah's neck. "Good girl. You are such a good girl, Beulah."

As Beulah nuzzled my neck and I hers, I noticed light from the morning sun skip off something lying in the grass behind her. It looked like a tiny bottle cap or something. Curiosity got the best of me, so I rose to my feet, Beulah close on my heels, and stooped to pick up the odd-shaped coin. It was silver and smaller than a penny. It bore an embossed image of a man who resembled John F. Kennedy, and all I could make out was the word "George."

I stuffed it into my pocket, deciding this had been a good day and this was my lucky coin.

═══════

On the way back home, I stopped by Black Hills Bagels on Mt. Rushmore Road and bought a cup of deep-roast coffee with real cream and a fresh, hot bagel with a slice of tomato and a light smear of cream cheese to go.

I rewarded Beulah with an extra cup of her dog food and a stew bone I found in Jens's freezer. We both sat on the back porch enjoying our spoils—Black Hills' version of my favorite food, rivaling that of Gib's Bagels back home in Fort Collins. Our meal finished, Beulah decided it was time to take a nap. I padded off to the shower.

Within an hour, Jens had picked me up and dropped me off at the front of Trinity Lutheran Church while he found a parking spot. I walked into the sanctuary and the first person I saw was Streeter. My breath caught in my throat; I was overwhelmed at how incredibly handsome he looked in his custom-fitted dark blue suit and surprisingly contemporary tie, which screamed couture. The lines of his wide, muscular shoulders and chest highlighted his narrow waist. His piercing blue eyes were alive and mischievous beneath his thick shock of white hair, his rugged face cleanly shaven. I wanted to reach over and touch his cheek like he had done to mine. His smile was brilliant, and the moment that passed between us powerful. I imagined that despite all my missteps in life, God was finally rewarding me for my good intentions by freezing time, allowing me to live in eternity right now, right here, staring at this man.

Before I could take one step toward him, however, Jenna Tate was at his side, tugging on his arm with urgency so that he might follow her down the hall toward the offices—a cruel reminder that earthly rewards really aren't the Good Lord's thing. To drive home the painful realization that I had no right to expect such blessings, I couldn't help compare my simple black dress and practical pumps with Jenna's impeccable fashion. She was wearing what I would have sworn was a Dolce&Gabbana three-quarter length black dress—surprisingly modest for Jenna. And I could recognize those $900 raspberry Christian Louboutin Lady Peep patent leather platform pumps anywhere—the same ones I almost bought myself before deciding to pay down the mortgage on my house instead. Side by side, Jenna and Streeter appeared to be the hottest "it" couple on the red carpet, totally unaware of their admirers stacked dozens deep beyond the rope line, anxious to catch a glimpse.

I compounded my earlier fantasy once I witnessed what I could have sworn was an expression of apology on Streeter's kissable mouth as he succumbed to Jenna's urging to escort her. And I satiated my frustration of inferiority to Jenna by reminding myself that I didn't have to be feeling so generous as to accept his apology, implied or otherwise.

I met Jens in the vestibule and we signed the guestbook. We stepped to our right to get out of the flow of patrons making their way into the church. We watched the acolyte attempt to light candles near the altar on the opposite end of the church, the pews filled with onlookers. Ernif's casket was to my right and behind it a closed door, which I knew from childhood was the money counter's room. To my left was the rack where parishioners hung their coats and the hall leading to the offices for the pastoral staff.

"Considering you have Michelle's funeral to endure tomorrow, it was nice of you to be here for Elizabeth's sake," I told Jens.

As if the mention of her name had conjured her, Elizabeth was suddenly at my elbow, motioning me to follow her. I saw her disappear into the money-counting room behind Ernif's casket.

"I'll catch up with you," I said to Jens.

I poked my head through the door and saw Elizabeth sitting next to Helma Hanson. The woman who Elizabeth had pushed toward me in the truck more than thirty hours earlier was not the same one sitting before me now. No way. This woman appeared healthy, strong.

"Hi," I said, waggling my fingers at them.

Elizabeth rose and I hugged her tight. "Your hair looks amazing."

The spikes of color—formerly blue, red, orange, green—that tickled my nose as I squeezed her were now gold and brown.

"Thank you," she said. "Helma did it for me last night."

Both women snickered.

"I'm Helma," the tiny woman said, rising to her feet and gripping my hand.

Based on the handshake, I guessed she was freakishly strong like Elizabeth and that people continuously underestimated Helma Hanson, like I had.

"Nice to meet you again," I said, surprised by how different she appeared since yesterday morning in the parking lot of hospice. "I'm Liv. I was the one who drove the getaway car for you and Elizabeth from Heavenly Hospice yesterday. And I met you at Scout's funeral a few years ago."

"Oh yes," Helma said. "Now I remember. Only, I thought I heard someone call you something else."

I frowned. "Boots. That's what my family calls me. Because I hated dresses as a kid."

Helma scanned me from head to toe. "Doesn't look like that's a problem for you anymore, dear. No, I was thinking your mother called you something else."

"Genevieve," I said in unison with Elizabeth.

"My baptismal name," I added.

"Mom doesn't like the nickname Boots and refuses to call her by her Norwegian middle name, Liv," Elizabeth explained. "We all have a saint's name as our first and a Norwegian name as our middle name. It was the compromise of our Irish Catholic mother and our Protestant Norwegian father."

"How clever," Helma stated. "Isn't life all about compromise? What's your middle name, dear?"

"Eldrid," Elizabeth said.

"Fiery spirit," Helma said. "That's what Eldrid means in Norwegian."

"And 'Elizabeth' is the patron saint of widows," I said before thinking.

"Aren't I lucky?" Helma smiled, hugging Elizabeth. "I'll call you Liv. That means life, you know. Great name. Liv Bergen. Life as a mountain dweller."

"Thank you," I said. "Look, I hate to intrude, and I know you have a sad good-bye facing you, but this can't wait. The reason I came early was to warn you that the FBI is looking for you. I was out yesterday at your cabin with them, Helma, and luckily you weren't there."

"You *told* them?" Elizabeth employed the same unmistakable ass-kicking tone she used to unleash on me when we were kids.

"No, I was working with them on the crime scene."

"What?"

"Long story. Listen," I pressed, trying to use my own urgent tone to get Elizabeth to focus, "they're here. They know you busted Helma out of hospice and they have questions for her. I didn't tell them anything, Elizabeth."

As if on cue, the door swung open and in walked Streeter and Bly. All three of us froze, probably looking guilty as hell.

CHAPTER 18

"I'M TELLING YOU, STREETER," Bly said, pacing the length of the conference room. "You were right. I chased down several different patterns and eliminated nearly all of them except the one you suggested might be *the* pattern. You told me to test the connection between the murders as to timing. I checked all the deaths in western South Dakota and eastern Wyoming that occurred every year during the last week of July, first week of August. There is definitely a pattern."

Streeter took a seat by Linwood, having opted not to return to the chair at the conference table where he had been sitting before he got up for coffee. Tate had once again taken a seat beside him, and he wanted no part of it. Now, seated opposite Tate, Streeter could study without interference the digital map that Bly had been working on.

"How much time do you have before you go back undercover in Sturgis tonight?" Streeter asked. As he did so, he marveled once more at how much Bly looked like the motorcycle gang members the two of them had been tailing the previous week. Special Agent Stewart Blysdorf looked nothing like FBI in his ratty blue jeans, his filthy leather vest with the Serpent's logo and rocker on the back, his matching domer—which barely contained the fly-away black and silver curls brushing his shoulders—and the nasty beard he hadn't shaved for weeks. He looked like he'd beat the living daylights out of anyone who stared cross-eyed at him. His undercover garb was so convincing not even the Serpents would question if he were genuinely one of them.

"About an hour. But I've got time to explain all this," Bly said, looking at Linwood, "just like I heard that you made time at the funeral to run interference for Helma Hanson with the hospice staff and Dr. Morgan."

"Seemed to be the right thing to do."

Tate narrowed her eyes. "What was that about?"

"It seemed as though everyone was against Helma, trying to get her to go back to the hospice facility when she clearly said she didn't want to be there," Linwood said.

Streeter turned toward Bly and grumbled, "Just get on with it."

"Okay, hear me out." Bly resumed sliding back and forth in his biker boots, chains rattling, as he paced across the tile floor at the head of the conference room table. On the wall behind him was projected a GIS forest service map of the Black Hills he'd been studying and marking that day: One overlay showed in green all of the federally owned lands and a second overlay showed in white all of the privately owned grounds. "Twelve deaths, twelve years. All a bunch of old farts. Youngest was fifty-two. Average age, seventy-five. All confirmed bachelors or recently widowed. All living alone."

"Maybe we have one of those rare female serial killers. A black widow," Tate interjected.

Streeter heard Linwood mumble, "Let him finish."

Bly was animated.

His wild eyes were glued to the map as he explained. "Slogging down beer after beer with a bunch of criminals I'm pretending to be buds with isn't conducive to the focus needed here, but let me show you what I've found so far. There's something here, Streeter. Something." He stabbed at each crime scene, marked on a third overlay with an ominous black cross, and said, "First death—at least that we know of—was July 24. Second, July 26, maybe 27. Third, July 25, the only murder out of sequence. But maybe it was out of sequence precisely because the murderer was new at this. Maybe he wasn't as organized at the beginning."

As Bly pointed to each murder site in the subsequent years, he announced the date of the death. "July 28, July 29, July 30, sometime between August 2 and 5, August 6, August 8, August 12, August 14 or 15, and then 'Bam!' August 4."

Streeter noted the pattern made by the series of black crosses and saw that the murders had initially occurred on the far western rim of the Black Hills in Wyoming and were progressing east into South Dakota.

"Out of sequence," Tate said.

"That's right," agreed Bly. "August 4 is back out of sequence. What is that?"

"If you're right—that the murderer simply had a killing out of sequence because he was new to the game, hadn't planned all that well—it wouldn't explain why he was out of sequence twelve years into his killing game," Tate continued.

"That's right." Bly paced, staring at the map. Paced and pointed at the second and last murder locations. "Out of sequence. Why?"

"It does seem more than coincidental that the murders progressed each year by a day or two," Linwood suggested. "Does it speak more to opportunity? Do those days all fall on the same day of the week or something?"

Bly turned on his heels and jabbed his finger at Linwood excitedly. "That's what I was thinking. But even if this early one, the third murder, was in sequential order, the days of the week are all over the place."

"What about the day-and-a-year concept?" Streeter asked.

"Three hundred sixty-six. Right. I tried that too. It's just not right. And I even considered a pattern if our Crooked Man was an accountant, using a three-hundred-sixty-days-a-year concept, thirty days each for the twelve months. That doesn't come to anything either."

"Thorough, aren't you?" Tate asked, drumming her long fingernails against the polished table.

Bly smiled, apparently believing Tate's question was a compliment. Annoyed, Streeter summarized: "So, you're saying there's no pattern in the days other than that they fall chronologically or sequentially in most cases."

"Right, right!"

"Then why are you excited, Bly?"

"Because it made me think differently. I couldn't find a pattern in the days our guy chooses so I started to look at a different pattern. Look."

He turned to the laptop and tapped on the keyboard. A fourth overlay appeared on the map; it depicted a large orange triangle with corners at the first murder on the western edge of the Black Hills south of Sundance, Wyoming, connecting to the murder near Custer, South Dakota, at the mica plant, then to one of the last murders east of Sturgis, South Dakota.

"Do you see that?"

All three agents gaped. Streeter finally asked, "See what?"

"Oh, come on, guys. How does someone go around killing people every year for twelve years and never once, *never once*, end up having the body dumped on federal land? Look at all that green in this triangle. Over a million acres of federally owned land and this guy, who seems to be all over the Black Hills, hasn't left a dead one behind, yet, on anything but private land. Doesn't that seem strange to you?"

Streeter pondered the question. He hadn't noticed how long he had been silently thinking about Bly's observation until a frustrated Bly chimed in, hand cupped to his ear, "Crickets. That's all I'm hearing right about now, folks."

"Bly, I see what you're saying," Streeter began, "but I just don't think it necessarily means anything. After all, the private landowners are the ones being killed."

Bly stood with a hand firmly planted on his hitched hip. "Well, I expected something like that out of these two, not knowing anything about the Black Hills, but you, Streeter? I expected more out of you."

"Help me out," Streeter said, studying the triangle on the map.

"The easiest way to get rid of a dead body is to dump it somewhere on all this federal ground you see in green. Hell, the body might never be found, with all the mountain lions and coyotes out there. On the flip side, the best way to get shot in the Black Hills is to step foot on this private ground you see in white. Everyone who lives in the Black Hills knows that too. Yup, we still cling to our guns and our Bibles, particularly on these inholdings of the Hills, because these guys are constantly battling the trespassing hikers, hunters, and outdoor enthusiasts who claim they mistook private ground for public ground, if you know what I mean."

"So you're thinking it's notable because probably only ten, maybe fifteen, percent of all that ground in your triangle is private, yet all these men died on their own property, on private ground, in the Black Hills," Linwood summarized.

"Except for the guy at the mica plant, which I just can't figure out yet, but otherwise, it's exactly what I'm saying." Bly took a seat beside Tate, who was still drumming those fingernails, only faster. Clackety-clack, like a runaway train. "Even the motorcycle gangs know there's plenty of ground where you can bury a body in the Hills. We lose, on average, one young woman each year during the Rally. They're counted as runaways, but who knows . . ."

"And what you're saying is that the twelve victims may have known the murderer? Or at the very least, felt safe enough not to have pulled a gun on him or her, assuming the person was trespassing?" Streeter asked.

"Well, yeah, doesn't that all seem to fit nicely here?"

"Good job. We need to think about all this, Bly," Streeter said, plowing his fingers through his hair. "Did you have time to look into any connection among all the men through associations they were members of?"

Bly nodded. "Didn't find much, though. A few belonged to AA, like Liv suggested, and all but one owned a gun or several guns. Most had a current membership in one wildlife federation or another, like Ducks Unlimited, Pheasants Forever, or the Elk Foundation, and all of them belonged at one time in their lives to at least one of those organizations. And most attended church, all except two. Not the same denomination, but they were consistent. Other than that, I didn't find a common thread."

"Did you find any deaths of similar nature during other times of the year?"

"Nothing."

"No names jumped out at you after going through the files?"

"I'm leaving that to you, Streeter," Bly said, pushing the stack of the twelve case files toward the temporary SAC. "I'm tied up tonight," he added, ogling Tate. "Or at least I'm hoping to be."

Tate rolled her eyes "Puh-leeze."

"No need to beg," Bly said with a wink.

"This is all good work, Bly," Streeter said. "I know you've got to take off soon, and I don't want you to lose an opportunity to nab a top tenner." Streeter patted the stack of case files. "I know what I'll be doing tonight."

"Do you want me to go up to Rochford to talk with Helma Hanson alone this evening and leave you to work the files with Tate?" Linwood asked.

"No," Streeter answered—a bit too quickly. "I'd rather go with you. Tate, why don't you stay here and take a crack at cross-referencing names. See if you can find any connection among the victims that Bly might have missed. You can debrief us when we get back."

Standing to leave, Bly snickered and added, "Unless you'd rather ride in the bitch seat on my hog tonight, baby."

"Still a pig," she muttered, gathering the files and pulling them toward her as if she'd just won the last hand of an all-in poker game.

"See you, Bly," Streeter said as the door closed behind the undercover agent with a bump. "Look, I'm not sure how Tom Jasper fits in to all this, and I don't want to jump to conclusions, but he fits the profile of the victims. Older man, owns land in the Black Hills, somewhat remote, recently widowed, owns guns, ranch land."

"Probably just a coincidence. Jasper's skull was never smashed," Tate said.

"Unless we interrupted something."

"Back to motive. Maybe someone from a conservation group like Nature's Way is our killer," Tate said.

Streeter shook his head. "Unless I've missed my mark, I really doubt Nature's Way recently adopted a motto of 'Conserve or Die.'"

For the first time in years, he found Tate's laugh in response amusing, not annoying. It was definitely *not* what Streeter had expected. And for the first time since she had arrived in Rapid City, her face brightened. She's a lovely woman when she drops the vampish façade, Streeter thought.

"But it fits," Linwood said, studying Bly's map. "Bly might just be onto something, Streeter. We don't have a motive, but who's ending up with this land? The state? United States Forest Service?"

"I checked years ago with the first three murders to determine motive. I recall that one was contested and the other two land holdings were going to be put up as estate auctions."

"And now we have nine more to add to the original," Tate said, tapping the pile of files.

"These men don't have any families; they lived alone or were widowed," Streeter answered. "Maybe they donated their properties to the Elk Foundation. Or Ducks Unlimited. Maybe there's someone out there who stands to benefit from their deaths." Streeter studied the sites marked on the map and added, "Let's make a trip to the courthouse before we head out to Helma Hanson's house. Maybe you're on to something, Linwood."

"It's a long shot," Linwood admitted, "but what about Dr. Morgan? His legs are crooked."

"I interviewed him early on years ago. He had opportunity," Streeter said. "We need to see if he has an alibi for Sunday when Ernif was killed. I'd sooner believe his physician's assistant, Steve Preston, was the murderer than Lowell Morgan. I don't remember Preston being in the picture ten years ago, but maybe we need to check him out. I don't think he's a local."

"How come?" Tate asked.

"Just a hunch. Set up an interview with both of them for me, will you, Tate?"

"Sure."

"And with Keeley," Linwood said.

"The pastor?" Tate asked.

"Did you see that nose of his?"

"Busted."

"Crooked," Linwood suggested. "Maybe a dying man would call him a Crooked Man. Another long shot, but maybe he's arranging for bequests, preying on the widowers."

"Great thought," Streeter said. "Set something up with Keeley too, will you Tate?"

"That will cost you a dinner," Tate teased. "Besides, Jack promised Liv we'd meet her at the Firehouse for dinner at seven."

"Who's we?"

"All three of us."

Streeter was shaking his head. "Not a good idea. I wasn't comfortable discussing business the last time we were in public."

"Oh, come on," Tate said, diving into the stack of impossibly thick, detailed case files. "We were isolated. The bar was loud and no one could hear us. We have to eat. You owe us that at least."

Streeter frowned. "Seven is going to make it tight."

"I'll cover the courthouse work for you," Tate said.

"Still, it's an hour and a half up and another hour and a half back from the Hanson place."

"That will give us plenty of time to work through a motive," Linwood said.

"Having no motive at the moment, the money trail seems a good place to start," Streeter said.

"I bet land in the Black Hills, especially those properties surrounded by Forest Service, sell for quite a fortune."

They do, Streeter thought. "Linwood made a good point earlier. We should be finding out who stands to profit after Helma dies."

CHAPTER 19

AS I DROVE, I tried to remember all the faces at the church, wondering if it were true that criminals often returned to the scene of the crime or attended their victims' funerals. I assume that's why Streeter, Jack, and Jenna attended—to be on the lookout. I hoped I'd learn all those secrets during my sixteen weeks of training at Quantico and in D.C. That is, if I got accepted.

At the church, Streeter supported Helma's decision to go home to die and never mentioned Elizabeth's role in breaking her out of Heavenly Hospice. And at the cemetery, as Helma and Elizabeth awaited the arrival of Ernif's casket, a throng of concerned people lobbied Helma to return to hospice care, including Dr. Morgan, his physician's assistant, and Pastor Keeley. I didn't like the way a couple of other guys seemed to be eavesdropping on the conversation, particularly when I found out from Jack that they were Nature's Way employees. Vultures, I thought. They didn't desist until Streeter stepped in and politely yet firmly told them all to respect Helma's decision and to honor Ernif by providing him an interment argument free.

Helma remained stoic, tight-lipped the entire time. She appeared at once strong and weak as she stood graveside at the cemetery. I wondered if Helma could feel the progression of the cancer as it attacked her vital organs, raiding healthy cells one at a time. I wondered if she had recovered enough memory, now that she was out of hospice, to recall threads of truth about who tried to kill her early yesterday morning. Regardless, the finality of Ernif's death—truly gone from this world—must have hit her hard, in a way she might not have anticipated.

I'd pay her a visit later to make sure both she and Elizabeth were all right. Meantime, I'd received a message that Tommy Jasper had regained consciousness, and I was struggling to find a parking spot at Rapid City Regional Hospital. Parking spaces everywhere in town were at a premium during the Rally, because for every resident that lived in Sturgis, nearly a hundred visitors descended on the town on two wheels. The surrounding areas, like Rapid City, were destined to absorb the overflow from Sturgis busting at the seams with all those bikers.

After parking across the street at Our Lady of Perpetual Help (the Catholic Church known simply as The Cathedral to locals), I crossed the intersection and trekked through the lot, only to be nearly backed over by a car pulling out of a parking spot. The driver was too preoccupied, craning his neck in only one direction, to see me directly behind him. I almost didn't recognize him behind his shades until I saw that nose of his just as I jumped clear of his path.

Then I thought about Jack's whispered comment to me during Ernif's funeral about Keeley's nose and wondered if he was right about someone relating his appearance to the name Crooked Man. Pastor Keeley had the most crooked nose of anyone I'd ever met. Crooked nose, Crooked Man? Seemed like a stretch.

I made my way through the lobby and up the elevators to see Tommy. The badge pinned to the nurse's uniform announced she was Sandy.

"How is he, Sandy?" I asked the familiar looking nurse in ICU.

She scowled. "He's awake. And he's asking for you, Ms. *Bergen*."

She had spoken my name with an implied curse. She was outing me on my lie about being related to Tommy Jasper, more specifically on me telling her my name was Liv Jasper. I closed my eyes. When I opened them, she was still frowning at me. "I'm sorry for lying. He's a dear friend, and I know with HIPAA rules and all you'd have never called me when he regained consciousness. I'm kinda like his daughter, if that counts."

I was lying again. Sort of. Tommy and I just met for the first time this week. But I wasn't lying about considering him a close friend. Sandy unfolded her arms and placed her hands on her hips.

She surprised me by saying, "That's what he said."

Her smile was barely there, but there nonetheless.

"Thank you, Sandy," I said, folding my hands in prayer as if mine had just been answered. "Which room?"

"That one," she said and pointed to her right.

I slipped into the room and saw Tommy smile, tubes protruding from every orifice.

"How do you feel?" I asked.

"Like the runt pig at feeding time."

"You can stand to miss a meal or two."

His smile grew. "Ow, my lips are chapped and cracking. Don't make me laugh."

"I didn't." I fished out the new Burt's Beeswax jar from my pocket and tossed it to him.

"What's this?"

"Put it on your lips."

"I am *not* wearing lipstick."

"It's not lipstick." I snatched it back from him, broke the plastic seal, and grabbed his hand. "Here. Dip your finger in this and spread it on your lips."

He did. "Feels all tingly."

"It'll make your lips feel better."

"Thanks," he said as I handed him the tiny jar. His smile faded as quickly as it had come. "What are they saying, Liv? Tell me the truth. These nurses are saying I have to wait for a doctor to explain what happened to me and that it might be hours from now before a doctor will show up."

"They're running everything through toxicology. They think you were poisoned." He wasn't nearly as shocked as I was to hear that news. In fact, it seemed obvious to him.

"*That's* why my stomach hurts so bad. Gawd damn tree huggers," he growled.

"Tree huggers? What are you talking about?"

"Those pantywaist girlie-boys from Nature's Way. They've been up to my place no less than a dozen times in the past couple of months, trying to convince me to bequeath my property to them when I die. That Rowland Cowen keeps saying that I've got no one. That I can't take it with me when I die. So why not be the hero and give it to them? Good for nothing son of a bitch."

I smiled. "If I wasn't mistaken, I'd think you had an opinion about these guys."

"I told them to go to hell, that I wouldn't put a damn conservation ease-ment on my place if it was the last thing I'd do. Not over my dead body."

"Speaking of dead bodies, I just came from Ernif Hanson's funeral."

"Yeah, I heard. Pastor Keeley was just here."

My breath caught. "Here? What for?"

"To visit me. He said he was just checking on how I was doing."

"Did he touch anything?" I jumped to my feet and inspected the tubes and bags strung up on the racks around his bed, hoping to spot any sign of tampering, sliding my fingers along each stretch of tubing to feel for dampness that ought not to be there.

"What are you doing?"

"How do you know Pastor Keeley?"

"Oh, just from being around. A lot of folks know Keeley. He hangs out at the bars on occasion, looking in all the wrong places for believers to fill his collection plate, I suppose." Tommy tried to laugh at his own quip but coughed instead, gripping his stomach. "Don't make me laugh."

"I didn't." Alarms were sounding so loudly in my head Tommy's voice sounded distant. "Does Keeley ever make it up to Nemo?"

"Yup. He comes up to the bar now and then. He was there when you and I had dinner. He was over at the bar talking to Doc Morgan's boy-friend while we were talking to the Doc."

"No kidding," I said, concerned. I almost missed the "boyfriend" com-ment altogether.

Tommy chuckled, coughed, made a move toward a glass of water on his bedside tray. Before I could even think why I did it, I snatched it up, along with the pitcher, and poured the contents of both down the sink in his bathroom, refilling each with fresh water.

"Hey! What was that all about?" Tommy asked when I handed him his cup.

"An ounce of prevention or something."

"You think Keeley poisoned my water just now?"

"Why would he?" I shrugged.

Tommy sipped from a straw and set the cup back down.

"Hell, someone's trying to kill me. And maybe it is Keeley. Maybe he's trying to get his hands on a big fat donation to the church at my death."

"Ya think?" I said. "And what was that about Dr. Morgan having a boyfriend? I didn't know Dr. Morgan is gay."

"Well, he doesn't advertise it or anything."

"Then how do you know? Did he tell you that?"

"No, but he takes that fruity assistant with him everywhere he goes."

"That's not nice."

"What's not nice?"

"Calling someone fruity."

"Have you met him? And he's a carpet jumper, to boot. Flirting with other men. Like the Nature's Way boys and Keeley."

"Pastor Keeley's gay?"

"Fruity. The whole bunch. And who cares if I called someone fruity? Didn't you hear me? Someone's. Trying. To. Kill. Me."

I reached in my pocket and handed him my lucky coin. "Here."

"What is it?"

"My lucky coin."

"Oh, so that was you."

"What was me?"

"You were the one who left a coin on my tray. See?"

He moved the pitcher of water and slid the remote aside to reveal a tiny coin with King George's head. "A sixpence, like yours."

"Oh," I said, suddenly realizing this was more than coincidence. Two identical strange coins. The killer must have dropped the coin in the parking lot where Beulah had led me. And must have intentionally left the coin on Tommy's tray. "When did you find this?"

"Right before you got here."

"Anyone else been by?"

"Not that I know of. But I've been napping on and off all day."

Keeley, I thought.

"Okay, so maybe these coins aren't so lucky. Sixpence, huh? Do you mind?" I said, pointing to the coin on his tray.

"Keep it. It's yours."

I pulled a paper towel from the dispenser in the bathroom and picked up the tiny coin by the edges, neatly wrapped it in the paper towel, and stuffed it in my pocket.

"Okay, so I've got to go now. I want you to be very careful, and don't drink or eat anything that visitors bring you, okay? And quit spreading rumors about people being gay—"

"Fruity."

"—About Dr. Morgan having a boyfriend just because he has an employee tagging along with him," I said, glad I had stopped by when I did.

"For drinks after hours at a bar?" Tommy chuckled, then coughed. "Seriously. Check my water well, Liv. Maybe whatever it is they were trying to poison me with *is* in the water."

CHAPTER 20

ELIZABETH KEPT AN EYE on Helma. She had said she was fine, plenty strong after the funeral, but Elizabeth wondered if it were true. Helma hadn't eaten. She said very little on the hour-and-a-half drive home to Rochford. She was determined to show Elizabeth the bees, to gather honey. She *needed* to gather her honey. Today. Hadn't felt like it after all the errands they'd run the day before.

Elizabeth didn't question her logic.

Helma assured Elizabeth that the bees they kept were Caucasian, the very nicest of bees. Ernif, she said, wore neither the protective suit nor the veil, and he put on a pair of plain old leather work gloves when he worked around the hives—and proudly claimed to have never been stung once. But Ernif insisted that Helma wear the protective gear, just to be safe. Elizabeth donned the oversized protective equipment and ventilated gloves, the smell of new leather confirming Helma's assertion that Ernif's equipment would be like new.

As they walked to the first set of hives, tucked in the protective row of trees lining the meadow, Elizabeth was struck by the vibration she felt in the air.

"There must be millions of them," she said, more to herself than to Helma.

"I haven't the foggiest idea." Helma was checking the apiaries. "We maintain only two hives here. Ernif uses the barn where you parked your Jeep for their wintering, rather than shipping them off to California. We heat the barn and put the hives on opposite ends of it. Everyone told us that wouldn't work, but each spring the hives seem to maintain their numbers. Grafting queen cells or splitting hives isn't necessary that often. We have plenty to do with the bees we have."

"How many bees in a hive?"

"Each hive, we're guessing, has about thirty or forty thousand female workers and about three to four hundred males, what we call drones."

"Great odds if you're a male bee," Elizabeth said, trying not to show how startled she was by the sheer number of the bees she and Helma were working with. "Do they ever swarm and attack, like on TV and in the movies?"

Helma chuckled. It was the first time Elizabeth had seen a lightness of spirit return since before the funeral. "As I said, these bees are very gentle. Bees have races, just like us humans. And as a race, this particular bee is among the gentlest in the world. And winter hearty, like us Norwegians."

She chuckled again, waving her hand gently so she could peer inside the cells under the cover. She motioned for Elizabeth to join her. Pointing out each feature, Helma explained what she was looking for, how she determined the bees' good health, and what she would expect to find with healthy breeding cells. She explained how she and Ernif had determined that for maximum honey productivity and colony health they opted to use two ten-frame full-depth boxes each divided three ways. Helma pointed out how the top section was divided into three sections, each consisting of a brood frame loaded with bees. She extracted one brood frame and handed it to Elizabeth.

"Don't be scared," she said, her eyes twinkling mischievously through the black netting.

"I'm not," Elizabeth said, shaking like a leaf beneath the oversized suit. She wished she had a little of the widow's might to draw from.

Elizabeth took the panel and studied the cluster of bees, amazed by their tolerance of her. She listened to every detail Helma shared with her about what to look for with a new queen bee's brood pattern and how to judge the expected honey production based on that pattern. Pulling out the honey super, Elizabeth's eyes widened.

"When do you harvest the honey?"

"In the fall. Right before we move the hives into the barn, preparing the bees for winter. That would be September, dear. You have a lot to learn between now and then," Helma said with a steady gaze.

Elizabeth knew what Helma was saying to her. Helma wasn't going to live that long and she needed Elizabeth to take over. At least for this fall.

Unexpectedly, Elizabeth was fascinated, and before she knew it, the sun was setting.

On their way back to the cabin, Helma asked, "What are you thinking?"

"My mind is racing," Elizabeth admitted. "My hands are shaking I'm so excited. I never dreamed bees could be so exhilarating."

Helma smiled. She turned her face to the clear blue sky above, the clouds tickled pink and purple by the setting sun behind them. "And what do you think of this place?"

"Oh, Helma, I can see why you and Ernif fell in love here. And stayed in love your entire lives. It's magical."

"I'm glad you think so," she said, nearing the porch.

As they stripped off and folded the apiary protective gear, Elizabeth held up the tin can and asked, "When do you use this thing?"

"That's a smoker," Helma said. "It's a safety tool, of course, should the bees decide to swarm unexpectedly, but mostly it's to protect the bees themselves. When we move around cells and brood frames and feed dividers, we don't want to hurt our bees. If we smoke them, they move away for a bit so we can work quickly without any harm coming to them."

"Good," Elizabeth said, setting the smoker on top of the heap of gear.

"What do you think your husband would say about this place, you caring for bees and all?" Helma continued, her eyes fixed on Elizabeth's.

"Michael has supported me in every endeavor. And, of course, I told him I'd be here helping you indefinitely."

They moved into the cabin, hungry and tired, both flopping onto the couch with a glass of lemonade.

"Hand me that leather satchel, dear," Helma said. "The one you found in the chest."

Elizabeth did. As Helma opened the satchel, Elizabeth glided into the kitchen and started cooking dinner. She noticed Helma sitting on the couch, reading the papers that were in the satchel in between bouts of coughing and folding over as she held her waist. She had become so still, Elizabeth thought she'd fallen asleep.

When she saw Helma put the papers down in her lap, Elizabeth asked, "Hungry?"

They ate heartily and enjoyed the view from the living room window of the meadow beyond, deer and elk alike gathering to eat as the sun set. A large red fox skirted the edge of the meadow, something Elizabeth would have missed entirely if not for all heads turning in its direction.

"This is spectacular. Is it like this every night?"

"Just about," Helma said with a playful grin. "See why I said you rescued me?"

Elizabeth nodded, her smile fading. "By the way, what happened at church today when that man came up to your side when we were about ready to leave? You don't care much for him, do you?"

"I do not. He's too eager to please."

"How well do you know him?"

"Met him a time or two. Annoying young man who works for Nature's Way. Name's Rowland."

"The conservancy group?"

Before Helma could answer, both women turned at hearing a car approaching. The herds of deer and elk scattered. At first Elizabeth stiffened, her mind snapping to combat readiness until, in the fading late afternoon daylight, she could see it was one of the cars the federal agents had driven at the cemetery. She couldn't remember which one. "It's the FBI."

"Elizabeth," Helma said, grabbing her arm as she stood to clear the dishes. "Before they get here, I need to ask you something."

Elizabeth put the plates back on the coffee table in front of the couch and sat beside Helma.

"Do you remember Peter Pan?"

Elizabeth cocked her head, her mouth opening and closing like a guppy's, not quite sure what to say. She wondered if the cancer had started to affect Helma's mind. Or if this was the lingering effect of withdrawal from all the medicine she was on in hospice.

Before Elizabeth could answer, Helma said, "The Lost Boys were something, weren't they? Always having fun, on a big adventure. Do you remember the Lost Boys?"

Elizabeth nodded slowly.

"We have lost boys, you and I. Scout and Steiner. But they needed Wendy. And Peter."

Helma extracted some yellowing sheets of paper from the satchel and handed them to her. Elizabeth turned on the lamp and saw the diagrams and drawings, one sheet covered in financial computations.

"What is this?"

"The plan Ernif and I drew up for this place. For the lost boys," she said as she dumped the satchel upside down to shake out the balance of the contents. Among a few sheets of paper and two pens, a single tiny coin dropped onto the coffee table.

Helma gasped. "He found a crooked sixpence. I remember."

CHAPTER 21

WHEN I WALKED INTO the Firehouse, I immediately saw my brother Jens and his childhood friend Gilbert Muth at the same place they'd been two nights ago. Involuntarily, I stole a glance over my shoulder to make sure I hadn't been followed by Mully again. On the opposite side of the U-shaped bar, over by the beer vats encased behind glass, my brother sat at the end closest to the kitchen. The pane of glass directly behind him had not yet been replaced, and I wondered if the owners would be sending me a bill for that. Or if the FBI would have to spring for the cost.

Gilbert's arms were flailing like a fool's as he told some story with great passion and animation.

Jens was nursing a beer, and I caught his eye almost immediately. He raised one finger off his beer glass as an inconspicuous signal acknowledging me but so as not to alert Gilbert to my arrival. I had told Jens I was meeting the FBI team here for dinner, and I suspected he was a bit overprotective of me at this point. Gilbert, who obviously picked up on my brother's supposedly secret signal to me, gave me an A-OK sign in approval of how I had dressed and fixed my hair, then puckered his lips at me and pointed upstairs. I suspected his motivation for being here was for sheer entertainment.

I flashed Gilbert a thumbs-up—though I was tempted to flip him the bird—and a smirk that had "smart-ass" written all over it, and made my way through the bar and up the steep stairs to the seating area above. For what I thought would be a quiet weeknight, even with the Rally still in full swing and it being summer, the place was packed with thirsty patrons. And as I neared the top of the stairs, I realized the place wasn't short of hungry customers either. The second floor restaurant loft area was jammed with diners.

And Gilbert was correct.

Sitting near the railing overlooking the bar, Jack Linwood was seated at a table, the chair across from him vacant. Just as I hit the top step he stood up, gentleman that he was, and waited until I arrived at the table for four. I assumed I'd be dining with all the agents, including Streeter—who was the intended target for Gilbert's earlier puckering—but I wasn't quite sure who had actually made it. The place being ass to elbows deep in people, whoever was already with Jack was sitting behind the beer-guzzling, appetizer-munching football enthusiasts who had their eyes glued to last fall's game replays on the televisions dangling above the bar below, which meant a perfect eye-level view for those on the second floor.

As I drew nearer, I saw an empty chair next to Jack and the back of her head, the long blonde hair unmistakably Jenna's. Crap, I thought. I would be sitting beside Jack and across from Jenna, of all people. I had no chance of getting to know Streeter better tonight. I smoothed my silk tunic top over my skinny jeans, walking confidently in my open-toed platform Louboutin knockoffs—boysenberry—as if I were on the runway.

Jack pushed my chair in for me as I swept my recently-washed-curled-teased-and-generously-sprayed hair away from my carefully made-up face, keeping my eye on the open flame of the candle in the center of the table, unwilling to imagine the humiliation of having all that hairspray burst into flames. "Thank you, sir."

"I could do without the 'sir,'" he grumbled, returning to his seat.

"I didn't mean . . ." I guffawed, noticing the mocking expression on Jenna's face and the budding grin on Streeter's. "I just meant how refreshing it is to be with a gentleman."

That made Streeter's smirk disappear.

"I know what you meant," Jack said. "And thank you."

"So, what is this? A double date or something?" I asked stupidly.

The mix of answers came at me all at once.

Jenna definitely said, "Yes."

I think Jack said, "I wish."

And I'm pretty sure Streeter said, "Hell, no."

Before I could get clarification, the waitress was asking for drink orders.

After she took our order and as we scanned the menus, I asked, "Where's Bly?"

"He had to work," Streeter said, his words sounding kinder than the look he gave me. He seemed unhappy to be here, uncomfortable. I wondered if I'd done something wrong, if I'd spent too long preparing my makeup and hair or picking out my clothes intending to impress, only to disappoint him somehow. My impression of his sourness was confirmed when he added, "Let's just eat and get out of here, back to work."

"Party pooper," Jenna said, leaning into Streeter and reaching under the table to deliver what I presumed was a grip to the thigh. At least I hope it was his thigh.

Streeter's eyes moved to mine. I felt the burn in my cheeks.

"Streeter and I just returned from a visit with your sister."

"Which one?" I asked Jack, a habitual response to people mentioning one of my many siblings.

"Elizabeth. How many do you have?"

"Six."

"Six," Jack repeated, his eyes lingering on mine longer than necessary. "You have six siblings?"

"No, eight siblings. Six sisters."

"And where are you in line?"

"I'm seventh of nine. I have two brothers. One older. One younger. The younger one is sitting right there at the bar," I said, pointing over the railing.

"Fascinating."

Streeter cleared his throat. "We had an interesting visit. Helma was showing Elizabeth some historical artifacts the Hansons had found over the years on their ranch, discarded during Custer's Expedition in 1874."

"What kind of artifacts?" Jenna asked before I could.

"Horseshoes, nails, shell casings, buttons, stirrups. All sorts of cavalry keepsakes."

"Helma and Ernif had a saddle with the letters 'G-A-C' hand-tooled into the leather," Jack added.

"What does G-A-C mean?" Jenna clasped her hands and rested her chin on them, gazing at both men as they spoke. I realized for the first time her interest in them was not unlike mine. She found both men mesmerizing.

I sighed, realizing I had no business thinking either of these men would ever be interested in me. They were handsome, intelligent, hardworking, and clearly had plenty of women interested in them. If Lisa Henry and Jenna Tate were any indication of what FBI women agents were like, fat chance that I'd ever measure up. Both women had the look of supermodels and the brains of professors.

Streeter's voice was soft and rough. "The assumption is that the saddle belonged to General George Armstrong Custer."

"Fascinating," Jenna said breathlessly, repeating the word Jack had used to describe my family.

I peered around her and down the crowded aisle, searching for the waitress and hoping she'd bring me a beer. Quickly. No such luck.

"However did they come to that conclusion?" she said, hanging on his every word.

"I asked the same thing. Helma said there were a lot of pictures taken during that expedition. And lots of field notes."

Filling in the gaps, and receiving an equally attentive gaze from Jenna as if I were invisible, Jack said, "The cavalry chose campsites in the Black Hills during the expedition based on the fresh water from the creek and the food source. I bet there were dozens of deer and elk in that valley for the cavalry to feed on for days. Still are. We saw dozens of them this evening when we drove up."

Streeter continued, "Helma said there are several pictures that show Custer and his men camping in that valley. And one photo shows him with his horse and the saddle. She had a copy of the photo and showed it to me."

"And is it Custer's saddle?" Jenna asked Jack.

"I think it is, but I'm no expert."

"Interesting," Jenna said with a sigh, moving closer to Streeter as she did. "Must be worth a fortune."

"Priceless," Jack said.

"To die for?"

CHAPTER 22

THROUGHOUT DINNER, STREETER, JACK, and Jenna talked about what each one had discovered thus far and the interviews Jenna had scheduled for the next day. I listened attentively, resisting the urge to ask questions or pipe in with my thoughts. It gave me a chance to study them, to understand how the brilliant minds of the FBI agents worked: how they reasoned, deduced, induced, and even speculated about motive, causality, psychopathy, profile, and forensics. I was engrossed by their discussions and realized how little I knew about investigations. The conversation settled primarily on the motivation of the killings and the commonality of the implied behavior at the crime scene.

I could tell the agents were not talking as freely regarding specifics as they'd like, and I assumed it was because we were in a public setting, although we were tucked in a corner of the restaurant's balcony nearest the rail with lots of noise rising from the bar below, not a single person able to make out a word we were saying. But as they talked, eyes flicking over at me occasionally, I began to wonder if my presence was what made them resist identifying places, stating names, and specifying probabilities.

By the time we finished dinner, mine the crazy good three-cheese baked pasta and Jenna's the Asian salad with seared tuna—which pretty much says it all—I was feeling pretty puny. That is, until they discussed Streeter's game plan for the next day.

"There's a public meeting tomorrow at nine at the Ramada Inn. State legislators, in conjunction with Nature's Way, are to present their opposition to legislation proposed by State Senator James Billings to require time limits on any conservation easements in this state," he announced.

"That ought to be fireworks," Jack speculated.

"But it gives us a good chance to observe Mark Goodsell, the state director for Nature's Way, in action," Streeter said.

"And Rowland Cowen," Jack agreed.

"And since we're staying at the hotel where they're conducting the meeting, we can get up early, work over breakfast together, and make the meeting in plenty of time," added Jenna. "See them all in action."

"Good idea, Tate," Streeter said.

I felt a tug somewhere when Jenna emphasized the words *get up early,* as if they'd be sleeping in the same room—the same bed, even?—sliding her gaze across both men as she did. But the mention of Nature's Way suddenly made me remember my conversation with Tommy.

"Did you check his well?" I heard myself ask.

"What well?" Jenna asked, annoyed by my interruption.

"His water well. Did you test the water yet?"

"Goodsell's or Billings's?" Jack asked.

"Tommy Jasper's. You're following the lead Tommy gave you that Nature's Way was hounding him for his land, right?"

From their startled expressions, I knew I had made another huge mistake; I was a lemming who had once more followed speculation straight off a cliff. I had jumped to the conclusion that their visit with Tommy had led them to investigate the Nature's Way angle.

"Actually, we were following the money trail. The land left behind by most of the murdered ranchers ended up being owned by Nature's Way," Streeter explained. "What did Jasper tell you that he didn't tell us?"

"He thought that someone with Nature's Way might have poisoned his well. He specifically mentioned suspecting Rowland Cowen had done it.

"And not to impose or anything," I blathered on, "but Tommy also said Pastor Keeley had visited him today, and he was at the Nemo Guest Ranch the night I had dinner with Tommy, the night he got sick." Noting their blank expressions, I quickly added, "I didn't see him because Keeley was at the bar with Dr. Morgan's assistant."

"Steve Preston?"

"Yes, the P.A. But I don't think Tommy's right. I think it might be Pastor Keeley who's the Crooked Man. Look," I said, fishing the neatly folded paper towel from my back pocket. "It's a sixpence. I looked it up online. It's a British coin, not worth much. Silver from 1960."

Unless I was mistaken, Streeter's eyes widened with recognition.

"So what does this have to do with Pastor Keeley?" Jenna asked.

"Someone left it on Tommy's tray just before I got there, and on my way in, I saw Pastor Keeley speeding out of the parking lot. Tommy told me Pastor Keeley had just visited him."

Streeter stared hard at the coin and at me. "Why do you think this had anything to do with the Crooked Man?"

"Too much of a coincidence, I suppose." I reached into my front pocket, straining a bit because I had changed into my tight jeans, and fished out the other coin. Unwrapped. "I'm sorry I touched this. I wasn't thinking, I guess."

"Where did you get it?"

From the tone of his growl, I would have sworn Streeter was angry with me.

"I . . . I woke up early, so I decided to take Beulah to Heavenly Hospice to see what I could find." All three agents leaned forward, almost in unison. "I started in the empty room at Helma's bed."

"You found this at Heavenly Hospice?" Jack asked, exchanging a glance with Streeter.

"Not exactly," I said. "It took Beulah awhile, but I think she finally picked up the scent and followed it out one of the back doors, through the parking lot, across a meadow, and into the apartment complex lot nearby."

"And that's where you found the coin?" Streeter asked.

I nodded. "But I didn't think about it being evidence. I just thought it was something someone had dropped accidentally."

"And you were right, only the someone was the killer," Jenna said.

I could see the disappointment on all their faces. "I'm sorry I touched it. But maybe Tommy's coin has prints."

"Did you confirm the trail at the hospice?" Jack asked.

"No, I . . ." I could feel my cheeks burn. I had really screwed this up in an attempt to help. "The nurse, Hester Moore, told me I had a small window of time to conduct my search. And during my search, we startled some other patients and nurses when Beulah stormed the halls, so Hester covered for me by telling me to take the dog out and never come back. I had told her I didn't want anyone to know what I was doing."

Studying their faces, I added, "I screwed up again, didn't I?"

The mix of answers came at me all at once.

Jack definitely said, "No."

I think Streeter said, "Not hardly."

And I'm pretty sure Jenna said, "Hell, yes."

CHAPTER 23

Friday, August 9, 7:19 AM

IN THAT THIN TRANSITION between sleep and wake, brilliant thoughts come to me with clarity and purpose, only to disappear with the morning dew, as elusive as gripping a moonbeam in pitch black to illuminate my way back to it. Sometimes, if I'm incredibly lucky, I'm left with a shadow of an image that stays with me for days.

It was one of those moments. A lucky Friday.

The shadow of an image indelibly printed on my waking mind in that magical transition was a connection. A faint, yet tangible, link between something Streeter said last night at dinner and the image in my mind from the photos of Ernif Hanson's body. A connection between what is Helma Hanson today and what was Ernif Hanson Sunday.

I lay in bed trying hard to grip that moonbeam, to wave it all over that clear, purposeful picture that was vivid in transition and like smoke to me now. A connection. What was the importance of the connection? What *was* the connection? What thought came to me in my dreams as I culminated all the activities from the day before and validated them against my life experiences?

I pressed the heels of my hands against my eyes and saw grass tickling Ernif's long fingernails, his hands covered in heavy hair. More like fur. That's all I could manage. Rolling over, I hugged Beulah around her thick neck, eliciting a grunt of appreciation before she nodded back off to sleep. I wondered if my thoughts of fur had something to do with the mongrel sharing my bed these days. I told myself to fall back asleep, to try and recapture the moment that was forever lost.

But I couldn't.

I was up for the day. And if I had any doubts, reality pried the door wide open to wakefulness once I remembered that Michelle's funeral was at nine o'clock. As much as I wanted to attend the public meeting about the controversial proposal for conservation easements, I wanted more to be with my brother, to share in his grief, and to stand beside him as he endured the regrettable, painful task of burying his fiancée.

My schedule may be overloaded at times, but my loyalties are never confused. Family always came first.

I rolled out of bed and caught a whiff of the lovely coffee Jens was brewing. I padded out the door and down the hall to the kitchen, where I poured myself a cup and then went out and pulled up a lawn chair to join Jens in the backyard.

"Nice jammies," he said, sipping from a Vikings coffee cup.

He was referring to my pink camouflage pajama bottoms. Pink was not a color often found in my wardrobe.

"What's with the Vikings? I thought you were a Broncos fan?"

"I am. Michelle is the Vikings fan."

"No accounting for taste. After all, she had a thing for you too," I said without thinking.

"True," he said with a snicker. "Had. Right. Past tense. Michelle *was* a Vikings fan. Not is. Just can't get used to this."

"Hey, sorry."

"No, really," Jens said, "you're the only one who treats me normal these days. Thanks, Boots."

A whimper sounded from somewhere behind us, and I turned to see Beulah's sad, droopy eyes staring at me from behind the screen door.

"Oh, crap!" I sprang to my feet and spilt coffee on my pajama bottoms. "Oh, ow, shit!"

Jens laughed as I hopped around in my bare feet, avoiding the hot coffee running down the front of my leg as I shook out my pants. He laughed even harder with every swear word I launched.

Beulah looked amused, her head cocked to one side as she stared at me, the urgency to relieve her bladder long forgotten. I opened the screen door and she took off into the backyard as I took off to the back of Jens's house to my bedroom, shedding my wet pajamas, pulling on my jeans.

Jens was still chuckling as I returned to my lawn chair with a fresh cup of coffee.

"What's so funny?"

"You. I keep trying to imagine how bad your vocabulary *would be* without your annual New Year's resolution to stop swearing."

"Natural born sailor," I said, sipping as I watched Beulah amble back over to me and flop down at my feet, asleep before her head ever hit the ground. Rubbing her side with my bare toes, I asked, "What do you think of her?"

"I think she's beautiful. Like you."

Nothing in the world could have stunned me more than those two words. Like you. I loved my brother, and early on in our lives we had worked into a banter that suited us. But complimentary words this direct were never a part of our repartee.

I was stunned silent.

"Agent Streeter Pierce stopped on his way down after dinner, bought a beer for me and Gilbert, and told me everything," he said, staring off at the Dinny perched high above Dinosaur Hill that split Rapid City in two. "The story about what happened Tuesday night was a different version than yours. His version would suggest you were something of a hero that night."

Still I said nothing.

"I believe Agent Pierce's version, by the way." Jens drained the rest of his cup, pushed himself off his lawn chair, and padded off across the back porch to the kitchen.

I heard the screen door squeak shut. I had spared Jens most of the gory details of Tuesday night, opting instead to tell only the pertinent facts of solving the case, leaving out a large part of my involvement. I wasn't sure how he was going to digest all the details I'd left out. I decided I'd apologize profusely and promise never to lie to him again.

Before I had the chance, he emerged from the back door carrying the pot and pouring me a fresh cup of coffee. "That's why I think you're beautiful. You're always thinking of others before yourself."

I brought the cup to my lips so Jens wouldn't see the smile he had put there.

With an audible sigh, he groused, "But you could have gotten yourself killed. Then where would I be today? Burying *two* people I love. Oh, man, how am I going to get through all this?"

I stewed.

"But before you start getting all masochistic on me, beating yourself up for what might have happened," Jens continued, "let me thank you for what you did for me. And for Michelle."

The phone rang.

Beulah lifted her head for a moment and then lay back down fast asleep. It was hard for me to believe this dog was such a workhorse in the field. I wouldn't believe it if I hadn't seen it. And I was already madly in love with her.

Jens pushed himself off his chair a second time and slipped into the house.

I laid my head back on the chair, enjoying the sun's warm fingers as they massaged my cheeks. Beulah's red coat felt warm as I kneaded her fur with my toes. I could overhear my brother's conversation and knew, just by the tone in his voice and the words he chose, it was one of my sisters he was talking to. Whichever sister it was, Jens was assuring her with words like "no problem" and "I understand." I assumed he was reassuring Frances, since she was the only one I knew who couldn't make it to the funeral today. Noah, her son and our nephew, was still in the hospital after an infection he had had earlier in the week.

But I was surprised when I heard the squeaking springs of the screen door and Jens telling whoever it was, "She's right here."

He handed me the phone. Elizabeth's voice sounded urgent. "Boots, listen to me. Helma's in bad shape. I can't come to Rapid this morning. She needs me. It isn't good."

"What's the matter? The cancer?"

"No, that all seems to be okay. For now." Elizabeth was whispering, I assume so as not to let Helma overhear her. "You have to come. Please."

"Not until after the funeral," I likewise whispered into the phone. "Not until I know Jens will be all right."

I thought Elizabeth would protest. But she didn't. "I understand. I wish I could be there too. I just can't leave her. And as long as you're up here by nightfall, that's okay. But plan to spend the night, okay?"

I was confused. Elizabeth wasn't an alarmist, nor did she tend to exaggerate, but I didn't want to ask too much in case Jens could hear me. "Do you need me to bring something?"

"Bring a gun. Or two."

"Why? What? Damn it, Elizabeth, what's happening?"

After a short pause, I barely heard the words she murmured. "Someone tried to break in to Helma's house last night."

CHAPTER 24

GOING TO DINNER HAD been a mistake.

The most obvious reason being the hours wasted could have been spent sleeping. The handful of hours Streeter stole in sleep weren't nearly enough. Other than Liv's revelation about the coins and her account of how Tommy suspected Nature's Way had poisoned his well, dinner had turned out to be less productive than he'd hoped. Having to measure every word in case a nearby diner might overhear made the discussion of facts clumsy. Tate had been insistent about not having food brought into the bureau conference room again for them. Considering she mentioned several times that she wanted to see the damage Streeter and Bly had caused the other night at the bar in the Firehouse, her persistence to eat at the popular local restaurant a couple of blocks down the street hadn't surprised him. Her obsession with food did. He knew firsthand how much Tate liked to play, accusing him of being dull from his obsession with work. But Streeter had been surprised by Linwood's support of Tate's suggestion. Of all people, Linwood had been the most like him. All work.

In fact, Streeter relied most heavily on Linwood for anything from Investigative Control Operations for this reason. He never said no, never had outside obligations, always found time to accommodate Streeter, except for the few occasions when Linwood had to take the quickest flight back from his curious trips, never explaining where he'd been off to. No need to. It was personal. And private. Something Streeter appreciated and respected.

And so Streeter agreed to go out to dinner. For Linwood's sake. Because of his departure from everything Streeter knew about him.

What men liked about Linwood—what Streeter liked about him—was that he was all business.

Although fairly new to the bureau, Linwood established himself quickly as the lead in Investigative Control Operations, the go-to person for everything difficult and urgent with cases.

And the business at hand was solving the Crooked Man murders.

Last night, he had directed Tate to get a guard posted outside Tom Jasper's hospital room. She was to explain to him the FBI had decided to err on the side of caution but was not necessarily worried about his well-being. Then Tate was to stick to Pastor Keeley like glue and find out what his connection to all of this was.

Streeter had directed Linwood to go through the bureau inventory archives to see if any mention was made about a coin or coins—specifically a sixpence—being found at any of the crime scenes. It would have been easy to overlook such small and insignificant evidence, particularly since the initial research showed that the coins Liv had given him were not unique, valued only because of their silver content, which was worth a measly buck and a half at current rates. But, given that Helma Hanson remembered the man who had tried to kill her reciting the nursery rhyme about a Crooked Man, Streeter believed the sixpence had significance. Likely, the murderer's calling card.

Streeter studied every file regarding the Crooked Man again, trying to poke holes in Bly's conclusion that a pattern did indeed exist among the victims and in Berta's suggestion that the wounds among all the victims were similar enough to have been caused by the same weapon. Each murdered man was a private landholder within the publicly owned national forest except the one east of Sturgis on the plains. Each was murdered within a year and a day or two of the previous victim. Bly had found no other murders in the last few days of July or early days of August that repeated the days, and he worked hard to find deaths in the days not yet accounted for by the known deaths, but he continued to try. And Linwood had been right to follow the money.

According to Tate's research the day before, each murdered man's ranch ended up being owned by Nature's Way or with a conservation easement placed on the land by them.

All but two properties.

Tate reported that the helpful clerk at Crook County confirmed that Wade Barns's twelve-hundred-acre ranch, now known by local hunters as "Eden," was owned by the Elk Foundation. She found on the Elk Foundation's website that the ranch was so called because of the abundant wildlife peacefully inhabiting the pristine meadows situated alongside rolling hills and rocky outcrops, and because of the plentiful fresh water from both Soldier Creek and Cold Creek that snaked through the grassy fields. The clerk also informed Agent Tate that the Elk Foundation was the benefactor of the estate due in no small part to Barns's girlfriend, Melinda Hocking, who hired a probate lawyer to convince the judge there was no possible way Wade Barns had prepared a last will and testament, let alone left his property to any charitable organization other than the Elk Foundation. Furthermore, Hocking claimed, any document to the contrary was a forgery—particularly the deed allegedly signed by Barns to Nature's Way that surfaced days after his death.

So passionate was Hocking's plea—and she having no vested financial interest in the outcome—the county judge hired a handwriting expert who concluded that Wade Barns's signature may indeed be a forgery or, at the very least, may have been written under duress. The county clerk recalled the case in such detail because so many of the locals applauded Hocking for taking on the daunting task of fighting the system with nothing but piles of lawyer bills to show for her efforts. So the ruling by the judge was a compromise: The Elk Foundation would own the property, and the would-be beneficiary under the questionable document would have the naming rights for the ranch, a suggestion made by the thwarted recipient. The name "Eden" was given to the ranch by none other than Mark Goodsell, program director for Black Hills Nature's Way.

When Tate had asked the county employee why no formal charges were ever filed against Nature's Way or Mark Goodsell, the woman explained that the judge determined Goodsell had nothing to do with the phony document because he himself suggested the land go to Hocking's preferred benefactor, as long as the land would never be developed, a condition to which the Elk Foundation agreed. Goodsell's willingness to not fight for the land and Hocking's confirmation of Goodsell's claim never even to have met Wade Barns satisfied the judge that there was no malicious intention or apparent connection between Mark Goodsell and the questionable last will and testament.

The other property that never ended up in the hands of Nature's Way was Frank Pelley's ranch located northwest of Nemo, South Dakota, encompassing Green Mountain. The popular man had executed and notarized an unrecorded deed dated on the first anniversary of his wife's death, and he kept the deed in a lockbox that was discovered during the probate process. Pelley had left his ranch to Saddleback Ranch, a private group-care center established nearly a century ago by a Christian church to help troubled boys in South Dakota find a better life. When the news of this generous bequest was publicized in the *Rapid City Journal*, the largest local area newspaper, an anonymous benefactor donated an undisclosed sum of money to establish a wildlife preserve on the Pelley place, disallowing any hunting or permanent structures from being erected. A compromise between the donor and the Saddleback Ranch management was to create an outdoor campus to educate the boys about nature and the environment.

Streeter was convinced that the Nature's Way tie to the remaining ten properties where the owners were murdered was definitely too coincidental to ignore. And the motivation was obvious. Nature's Way would want to protect and preserve the inholdings for the national forest. But he still held firmly to his belief that it was highly unlikely this revered and admired organization would ever go to such an extreme as to murder for their cause. Nature's Way had no history of ecoterrorism, had never resorted to illegal means that he was aware of to further their cause after exhausting legal avenues. The FBI had dozens of watch list groups who threatened and destroyed in the name of furthering their cause, but to Streeter's knowledge, Nature's Way was never one of them.

But he couldn't deny the pattern. And he couldn't ignore his instinct that the murders were connected in some way to criminal warfare, which would fit with an overly exuberant supporter of a conservation group.

Streeter finished shaving, buttoned up his pressed white shirt, and tucked in his shirttails before securing his khaki pants and belt. He slid the folder with his summary notes and key files under his arm and headed to the elevators.

Spotting Linwood and Tate safely tucked at a table in the back corner of the deserted restaurant, he walked up to the table and said by way of greeting, "Bly lifted a top tenner last night at the Rally. The Worm. So I told him to go home and get some sleep."

Coffee poured and breakfasts ordered, Streeter pushed his tableware aside and spread his files out in front of him. "We have an hour. So let's start with your report, Tate. Well done."

"I agree," Jack said. "Thorough."

"Thank you," Tate said, reaching into her purse and retrieving some papers. "What I didn't include in the report was this."

She slid a single sheet over to Streeter and one to Jack. Streeter studied the list of names.

"I went through all the files again and cross-referenced names that were common to all or most of the murder cases."

"There are at least two dozen names on this list," Jack said, his eyes wide.

"Thirty-one."

"That's a lot of coincidences," Streeter thought aloud.

"Not for a small town. Everyone knows everyone around here. People shop at the same places, eat at the same restaurants, drink in the same bars, attend the same churches, get care from the same doctors."

Streeter had hoped to narrow the list of suspects and was disheartened by the lengthy list of names the victims had in common. He noted that eight of the twelve victims had knowledge of or some connection to two-thirds of the people on the suspect list. All of those murdered knew eleven of the people on the list, which seemed the likely names to focus their investigation on. He scanned the column of names and found that, just like the victims, he knew at least half of the names personally: FBI SAC Bob Shankley, Rapid City Mayor Ken Vincent, Pastor Keeley, Dr. Morgan, Nature's Way's Mark Goodsell and Rowland Cowen, and Lawrence County Sheriff Leonard Leonard among them.

But the very first name on the list was the one that particularly caught Streeter's eye.

Garth Bergen. Liv's father.

Streeter thought about all this for a moment.

"Good job, Tate. Really good job," Streeter summarized. "What about your assignments last night?"

"Mr. Jasper is as snug as a bug in a rug with his round-the-clock guards. Rapid City's men in blue were more than eager to help."

"And Keeley?"

"He's a freak. I'm still working that angle."

Streeter paused, considering whether or not to pursue that odd choice of words and opted not to. The waitress arrived with breakfast.

Streeter used the interruption to redirect the discussion. "Linwood?"

The Investigative Control Operations specialist's face brightened as he pushed a single sheet of paper from his files toward each of his fellow agents. "I found references to a rare coin, a small coin, a modern mite, and a sixpence in several files from various investigators. From my count, I can tie what is likely a sixpence to six of the twelve cases. Eight where a coin might have been found. Liv's a genius."

"An accidental genius," Tate corrected, snapping off another bite of bacon as she stared at the list.

"So the Crooked Man is leaving a calling card. I wonder . . ." Streeter broke off his statement, deciding that he needed to check something out first to gel his thought before sharing it. "Let me shift gears a minute and tell you what I want each of you to do for me during the public meeting this morning. Linwood, you stick to Anthony Burgess, who flew in from D.C. to help fight the proposed legislation. Tate, you sidle up next to Rowland Cowen."

"He's the guy that works for Mark Goodsell?"

Streeter nodded. "Assistant program director. He was the guy at Helma's funeral who tried to talk with her at the interment and who Elizabeth Bergen nearly punched for trying."

"The tall drink of water? The one with curly red hair?" Tate said, spooning out the last of her yogurt parfait.

"That's the one."

"Am I an agent?" she asked. "Or a tease?"

"Start by being interested in him as a person. Like you don't know him."

"A tease it is," she said. "Ah, something I do well."

Streeter appreciated her honest self-assessment, and for the first time, he thought it might be sadness he recognized in her tone.

Before he could speak, she added, "Always the tease, never the bridesmaid."

Linwood's eyes softened, probably sharing the same thought as Streeter: They ought to give Tate a break.

Streeter was about to offer Tate a sympathetic response, but she started laughing at her own joke. "And who will you be flirting with, Streeter?"

"I'm going to focus on Goodsell. His name keeps coming up. And from what I hear, Goodsell serves up conservation easements as faithfully as a Catholic priest administers communion wafers."

CHAPTER 25

SECOND FUNERAL IN THAT many days.

Both caused at the hand of murderers.

It was hard enough for me to see my sister Elizabeth hurting for her friend Helma at Ernif's funeral yesterday, but today was even harder. Jens lost his fiancée and I lost my future sister-in-law. Worse, Michelle wasn't even thirty. At least Ernif had lived a long, full life.

The Cathedral is ginormous, the ceiling so high I swear heaven's on the floor just above it. My entire family crowded into the first five pews across from the single pew filled with Michelle's family, the Freeburgs. My oldest brother, Ole, came back home from Colorado a day early, and I gave him the biggest bear hug I could muster. I was about to talk shop, ask him how everything was going in my absence, until his six little girls encircled our knees, crowding me out for long-awaited hugs from their dad. Couldn't say that I blamed them, and work could certainly wait. Ole handed me my cell phone and said we'd talk later. Our sister Frances had caught an early morning flight from Denver, leaving Noah in the care of my brother-in-law, Gabriel, and I had time to catch up with her when I picked her up at the airport after dropping Jens off at The Cathedral early.

The funeral was well attended, and the priest expressed as much real emotion and compassion as was humanly possible for someone he really didn't know that well. During the service, I imagined what Streeter and the others were doing at the public meeting, knowing their real mission was to follow the thread that somehow might tie the Nature's Way to the Crooked Man murder cases. Then I wondered if Jenna Tate was sitting next to Streeter and formulated a very unpleasant thought about her, for which I quickly asked God for forgiveness. I was in a church, after all. I saw the gorgeous blonde in my mind's eye, her voluptuous body shorter than mine, but with many more curves in all the right places. Her makeup perfectly applied, my minimal efforts—a little mascara and slash of lipstick—barely noticeable. Her fingernails, perfectly manicured, mine rough and unpainted, my hands more easily slipping into leather work gloves than a manicurist's paraffin treatment.

I looked down at my hands, folded neatly in my lap, thinking how much they looked like a workman's and how accurate my mother was in warning me that one day I would wish I had taken better care of my skin. I was embarrassed at how I had let my mind drift, and when I asked God to help me focus, eyes closed to the funeral world around me, a vision flashed into my mind from my dreams. Ernif's hands dangling dangerously close to the bluejoint, the native grass bowing to the breeze. And then, for an instant, I saw a claw. Ernif's fingernails morphed back and forth in quick succession from neatly cut to clawlike; then the image left me altogether.

I barely noticed the breath I had drawn, but it must have been audible since my sisters Frances and Agatha, each sitting on either side of me, delivered a synchronized jabbing to my ribs with their elbows. My daydreaming about a picture—the photo of General Custer with the famous Black Hills grizzly bear he shot—and its connectedness to the earlier gold rush trivia I had laced into some of the other murder cases led me to wonder if the Crooked Man might have gold as a motive. My recollections of the murder sites that Streeter, Jack, and Jenna rattled off last night were thin, but my desire to grasp them had pulled me all the way through communion to the recessional. I was grateful it had; I really hate funerals.

The parish hall fixings were fabulous, as always, and my heaping plate kept me fueled for all my condolences and family hugs, which ended nearly an hour later.

Elizabeth—hard to miss, even in this crowd with her spiky bee-colored hair—had just arrived and was giving Jens a long hug. I waited until he had finished talking to her to flag her attention, but she already had a bead on me. Of course, I was easy to spot considering I had taken up my usual post next to the dessert table.

"You made it after all. So Helma must be feeling better?"

"Better than earlier this morning, but not as good as yesterday. She's hanging in there. I came to get a gun from you."

"Couldn't wait until tonight?"

"Nope."

"You're sure someone tried to break in last night?"

"Came right through the front door. Helma has no locks, so I'd moved the couch in front of it. I heard the scraping of wooden legs across the floorboards when somebody tried to push through. I grabbed the first weapon that came to mind—the bee smoker—and blasted the intruder where I assumed his face was in the open doorway. Afterward, I flicked on the lights all over the house. The door was left open a crack."

"No one was there? How'd you know it was a man?" My heart nearly stopped when I realized the threat against Helma—and against Elizabeth—was very real.

"Because I heard him screaming like a schoolgirl as he ran through the woods. Apparently, as he beat a hasty retreat from his breaking and entering, he knocked over one of the beehives and the bees must have swarmed him. Probably scared the shit out of him. It was definitely a guy, and I assume he had parked out on Telegraph Gulch Road."

"What did he want?"

"I already told you. To kill Helma."

"I'm calling the police," I said, pulling out the cell phone she had given me and dialing a nine and a one before she folded her tiny hands over mine.

"I've already called. They said they'll come up and take a look around but that there's really nothing they can do but file a report. They're so busy with higher priorities this time of year. So I told them not to bother."

"What exactly did they say?"

"They told me to take Helma and relocate, if possible."

"Then come stay with me at Jens's house. Or at Mom and Dad's house."

"Helma won't leave. They said if we stay, we should be prepared to defend ourselves. The officer asked if I had a gun. I do, but I didn't bring any with me when I drove up from Colorado. So here I am."

"How about letting me talk with the FBI?"

"Fine with me. But in the meantime, give me a gun. And your dog. They said intruders hate dogs."

"Does Helma have anything of value, Elizabeth? Something that someone might want to steal?"

"Maybe the saddle," Elizabeth said. "A historical piece that Helma thinks would go at auction for a bunch of money."

I remembered Jenna's comment about Custer's saddle being worth a lot if authentic.

"I've heard about it. The one belonging to General Custer. I'm telling the FBI," I repeated, stuffing my face with another brownie, trying not to admit to myself how worried I was about these two women.

"Fine, but you know I'm limited. Helma doesn't want to be taken away from her house again. And she's pretty upset about the bees. I'm headed to the lumberyard now so I can repair the pieces that broke. It's the only thing I could offer to do to calm Helma down."

"Is she still refusing to take medication?"

Elizabeth nodded.

"Not even for pain?"

"*Especially* for pain. Says the pain medication makes her head fuzzy. Which reminds me," Elizabeth said, suddenly digging in her pocket and then handing me a wad of tissue. "This is what Dr. Morgan tried to force Helma to swallow. Maybe it's something."

"You think Dr. Morgan is the one trying to kill Helma?"

"I don't know who's trying to kill Helma. I'm just saying check it out if it helps in any way." Elizabeth sighed, her tiny frame looking weak with grief, something I hadn't seen before and something I knew better than to believe. Weak wasn't even in my sister's vocabulary. "I need to go back. I shouldn't have left her alone this long, but she insisted. And I need your gun."

"You left her alone in the house? After someone tried to break in last night?"

She leaned in close and whispered without moving her lips, "She's in the back of my Jeep. She insisted."

My jaw dropped and I stared at my sister. "Are you kidding me?"

"No, I have to go. I need a gun."

I locked stares with her. "You're just going to sit there with her until she dies?"

Elizabeth cocked her head and stared at me like I'd just spoken Swahili. "If I don't, who will? Besides, the bees need me. Any progress on Ernif's murder investigation?"

"You tell me," I replied. "What's Helma saying? And what's with the bees?"

"She's not talking much. She remembered the rhyme."

"What rhyme?"

"Didn't the agents tell you? Helma said the guy recited the Crooked Man nursery rhyme while he choked her."

"That's just sick."

"Yep." Elizabeth was studying the crowd, her eyes skipping from person to person as if she was trained to spot the anomaly and gun him down if he made a move for my plate of brownies. "I heard Pastor Keeley ask if Helma intended to bequeath all of her belongings to the church."

Pastor Keeley again.

"And what did Helma say?"

"She ignored him. Thanked him for following her instructions for Ernif's funeral—which he didn't—and for hers—which he probably won't."

I grimaced at the thought of Helma planning her own funeral.

"I believe her, Boots. Someone really did try to kill her. And someone definitely tried to break in last night."

"I believe her too," I said, opting to say nothing about my exercise with Beulah at the hospice and finding the sixpence, which made a whole lot more sense now that Helma remembered that her attacker recited the nursery rhyme. "Any ideas who?"

"Don't know, but I'll bet dollars to donuts it's one of the names signed in the guest book from the funeral yesterday. Tell your FBI friends to start there," Elizabeth said, her statement like a hiss escaping her pursed lips.

"They're already on it," I said, remembering Jack mentioning something about it at dinner the night before. "With the fog of medications being lifted, I'm surprised nothing earth-shattering has come to mind for Helma, like who would have wanted her husband dead?"

Elizabeth sighed almost imperceptibly, acting like I hadn't even asked the question.

"I mean, who the hell would want to pop off an old man like that? And who would want to pop off a woman in hospice destined to die soon anyway?"

"Pop off? Really?" Her impish grin fit her waiflike features, and for a minute, I could almost hear her saying "Top o' the mornin' to ya" and doing a happy jig for me in some curly-toed elfin shoes. "I think what you meant to say was pop or knock off, but not pop off."

"Okay, so I'm a little overwhelmed and losing my words," I said, draining my plastic cup of red punch to wash down the chocolate. "But you know what I meant."

"You meant *killed. Murdered.* Who would want to have Ernif Hanson killed? Who would try to smother Helma?"

"Right," I said, my eyes starting to spin from the rush of sugar.

"Helma isn't sure. But if she were a betting woman, she said it must have something to do with Nature's Way."

My stomach flipped.

That's exactly what Tommy said and where the money trail was leading the FBI. Streeter was on to something.

"Is that what the FBI told you guys yesterday?" I asked as casually as I could muster without giving myself away.

"What? You got cloth for ears or something?" Elizabeth said, her cheeks blossoming with frustration. "I said *Helma* thinks it must have something to do with Nature's Way. A couple of those federal agents who were at the funeral stopped by the house last night, but Helma never told them anything about the Nature's Way people. She just told me."

"Why doesn't she think it might be Pastor Keeley?"

"Are you kidding? From what I could tell, he's scared of his own shadow."

"Doesn't mean he's not our killer."

"I'll bounce that idea off Helma."

"Why would she think it might be Nature's Way?"

"On account of her tossing them out on their ear the last time they came over for coffee to talk about what the Hansons planned to do with their land when they died in light of their not having any offspring." Elizabeth's cheeks were in full bloom by the time she finished her explanation.

I hadn't seen her that mad in a long time. "She said Ernif was always too polite to run them off. But she wasn't. She finally got tired of their repeated visits, asking Ernif and her to consider their responsibility to help Nature's Way protect critical habitat for the Black Hills, and the importance of preserving the north fork of Rapid Creek."

"Is there gold in Rapid Creek?"

"There's gold in every creek in the Hills," Elizabeth said. "But hear me out. The last time those Nature's Way guys were at the Hansons, Helma said they implied Ernif may not be able to handle living alone out here, rattling around in the house by himself after she died. This was right before Helma went into hospice. She said she'd had enough, telling them they ought to be ashamed of themselves, trying to scare old folks like that."

"And did they get what they wanted? Are the Hansons leaving the land to Nature's Way when Helma dies?" I knew the answer was no, but if Streeter was right about the connection, it may make some sense if they had.

Elizabeth leaned into me, looking over her shoulder and around the room as she did, before whispering, "Hell no. But they don't know that. If they did, can you imagine the harassment she'd be getting from them right about now? As it is, she told them if they promised never to come back to their house, even to visit Ernif after she died, they'd leave the place to Nature's Way in their wills."

Elizabeth pulled away from me as another gaggle of young women approached us, all of them briefly acknowledging us as they headed toward poor Jens. Poor *eligible* Jens.

"Is one tall with curly red hair and the other shorter, kind of balding?" I was thinking of the two guys I'd seen in the cemetery eavesdropping on Pastor Keeley, Dr. Morgan, and the P.A.'s discussion with Helma about going back to hospice.

"Yes. Helma pointed them out to me at the funeral."

I wondered if, after hearing that discussion, they thought Helma had finally caved and gone back to Heavenly Hospice. "Where do you park?"

"What?"

"When you're up at Helma's house, where do you park your Jeep?"

"In the barn. Where Ernif used to park his car. She insists. Why?"

"I'm wondering if whoever broke in assumed Helma was in hospice. Especially if your Jeep was nowhere to be seen."

"You don't believe me. That someone is trying to kill Helma."

"I'm holding out hope that this is all a horrible coincidence."

No time to take chances.

"You know where the key to Jens's house is hidden. My SIG is loaded. It's on the bed in the guest room, under my pillow. Help yourself. Get a box or two of ammunition from First Stop Gun Shop while you're here downtown. I didn't bring any except what's in the clip."

"Thanks. And the dog?"

"I'll bring her tonight."

"Eat something," I insisted.

"Gotta go." She leaned back toward me and said, "It's hard for me to even imagine what would happen to Helma if Nature's Way thought she had changed her mind or if they found out she never intended to leave the ranch to them."

I leaned into her and asked, "And if they thought Helma was dying of cancer and Ernif was the only one standing in the way of owning the only privately held ranch with the north fork of Rapid Creek? Can you imagine what they'd do?"

"Yeah, that land's worth a chunk of money."

"Because it has the headwaters of Rapid Creek?"

"That, and it's where Custer shot his bear."

CHAPTER 26

STREETER HAD BEEN CORRECT.

Based on the comments they made at the mic, some of the supporters of Nature's Way were definitely like religious fanatics. A few were near tears as they pleaded with politicians not to pass the legislation. Proponents of limiting the term of conservation easements and opponents arguing the need for perpetual advocacy to protect nature and preserve life volleyed buzzwords as if lives depended on their wordsmith skills. Sustainability, diversity, global, non-confrontational solutions, pragmatism, advocacy, survivability, transparency. All were words with political undertones that suggested an inordinate amount of fairness offered by one side, yet blatantly ignored by the other, veiled in a sugary sweet civility that made rational people's teeth ache.

Streeter hadn't been this uncomfortable since the time his grandmother dragged him to a holy revival in the southern backwoods against the advice of his uncle, a dedicated Baptist preacher who accused the snake charmers of being demonic. Being just eight years old, Streeter didn't quite grasp the content of the argument, only that both sides were passionate about their religious beliefs and willing to battle like warriors to defend and protect.

Ranchers and private-property advocates railed about their distrust in the government, accusing conservation entities such as Nature's Way of being an unregulated, unfettered arm of the federal government, acting on behalf of the Forest Service to acquire more public lands. An equal number of conservation specialists, supporters, and environmental organizations benefiting from the concept of conservation easements argued the need for such intervention, the voice for diminishing wildlife populations and endangered species.

Streeter, who had sat in a chair against a far wall so he could study the crowd, noticed Rowland Cowen and Jenna Tate, heads bent in conversation as they stood along the back wall of the crowded room. Tate had laughed at several apparently witty statements Cowen made, her manicured finger-nails resting on his arm. She was doing her job exceedingly well.

Because so many in the room wore uniforms, Streeter studied the subtle differences between the Game, Fish, and Parks employees and the National Forest Service employees who all remained expressionless and quiet as the public continued their rants for both sides. He estimated the civilian attendees outnumbered the federal employees three to one in the ballroom now jammed to the fire marshal's two-hundred-occupancy limit.

Streeter's eyes flicked back to Jack Linwood and noted the agent sit up a little taller in his chair. Streeter followed Linwood's laser-lock stare to where the CEO of Nature's Way was just rising to his feet. Cameras started flashing as Anthony Burgess made his way to the microphone in the center aisle with long, purposeful, and confident strides. A shooter for KNBN repositioned himself for better television footage for their nation-ally syndicated nightly news. The popular CEO's decision to speak out against South Dakota Senator James Billings's controversial legislation to disallow perpetual easements had attracted several news crews from around the country. The crowd of reporters seemed to have made the sub-committee more uptight than they already were about the controversial legislation. As one East Coast reporter put it, Burgess's appearance in this "podunk town out west" was critically helpful to battle an "ugly outbreak in the war against stupidity about environmental challenges."

The new religion, Streeter thought.

And just as he had, a man edged up beside him and whispered, "Didn't expect to see you here. Whose side are you on?"

Streeter didn't answer; instead, he simply folded his arms across his chest and focused on the man who commanded the room's attention, ignoring Pastor Keeley. But Streeter wanted to know Keeley's answer to that exact question.

The crowded room hushed as Burgess gripped the mic. He introduced himself, spelled his name, and lingered on every word in his title. The consummate spokesman cleared his throat, demanding an audience he already owned.

"More of our world than ever before is at risk of losing natural habitat and unique species to mankind's wicked hand," he began in a tone of despair and pity. "The challenge our generation faces is ominous and of overwhelming magnitude. Conservation easements are but one shield by which we can defend ourselves from the continuous destructive forces mauling the delicacy of nature. We need to understand nature, be more like nature. Forgiving and bountiful. We need to be part of the solution, not lend a hand to the battering ram we know as progress. I ask that you not succumb to fear mongering by those who are not as educated about the importance of a balanced ecosystem, who defile the very life on which they depend. The breast of Mother Nature from whom they suckle. Please do what is best for everyone, even those like Senator Billings, who do not understand what's truly best for the good people of South Dakota. Preserve and protect it. Forever. In perpetuity. Please, don't limit that protection to an arbitrarily defined number of years."

Half the room erupted in cheers. The other half grumbled. The expressionless federal employees sat still and remained quiet. Neutral. The panel of subcommittee members stared at the crowd, eyes probing face after face, searching to measure the strength in the political winds as effectively as holding up a licked finger to detect a stirring breeze. Burgess bowed his head, a gesture of implied humility, and retreated to his seat.

A bowlegged man in a soiled beaver skin cowboy hat and a threadbare, button-snap shirt sauntered to the microphone. Ignoring the cheers and applause for the previous speaker, he spoke his piece. Streeter heard Keeley talking but couldn't distinguish the words amid the cheering crowd; besides, Streeter wanted to hear what the cowboy had to say, so he ignored the pastor again. The cowboy was at least thirty seconds into his speech before the crowd quieted and listened to what he had to say to the subcommittee.

"And it's been in my family for more than five generations. So what business is it of mine to predict what will be needed five generations from now? Who am I to say I have all the answers for the coming generations?" He paused to shift the dip of snuff from one side of his lip to the other and to hitch his britches up a little higher as he shifted his slight weight from one cowboy boot to the other. "I'm so glad my great-great-granddaddy didn't decide for me. Times have changed. Even in the ranching world. What was needed then is no longer needed now, and what we need today wasn't even thought up back then. In perpetuity is just that, folks. Endless. Forever. Who am I to decide for anyone but me what forever should look like?"

He lifted his soda can and spat as the other half of the crowd—Dakotans who looked like they worked the land for a living—erupted. Anthony Burgess appeared stoically respectful, Mark Goodsell's jaw muscles were working in overdrive, and Rowland Cowen looked like he'd just taken a swig from the cowboy's can.

The spokesman for the subcommittee warned the crowd to quiet down and gave the cowboy notice he had only a minute left to speak.

The cowboy leaned into the microphone after wiping his mouth on his sleeve. "Don't need a minute. Only takes a second to remind people like Mr. Burgess that God created heaven and earth for us. To sustain life in his image. I work the land, and I can't say what my great-great grandkids will need to be able to grow to feed this world, but I sure as hell hope there's some acreage left to raise a cow or two."

Amid the deafening sound of both cheers and boos, the cowboy strode back to his seat and repositioned his hat to the back of his head, a signal that he'd completed the business he'd come to do. Streeter grinned, knowing it probably took every ounce of nerve that old cowboy had to speak in public—probably the first time he'd ever done it—but he wasn't about to show how unnerved he'd been by the experience.

The next person at the microphone was a woman who added, "The federal government already owns thirty percent of the land in this country, almost all of it in our western states. How much is enough?"

Cheers and boos.

The fiery, frizzy-haired woman at the opposing microphone argued, "I wish that percentage of publically owned land was even higher. What's the point of land being owned privately if we continue to put up parking lots and high rises on that land?"

More cheers. And more jeers.

After another twenty minutes of repetitive testimony, Streeter felt Keeley lean into him and whisper, "Agent Tate said you want to talk with me. And she tried to pin me down to a time, but my schedule isn't always my own, if you know what I mean. We finally set something up for Monday, but I don't know if I can wait out the weekend to find out what it is you need to know from me. Do you have some time now perhaps?"

Streeter glanced at the long lines at the microphones, estimated it would be another hour and a half of testimony, and caught Linwood's eye, nodding once toward Keeley to signal his intentions.

"Sure," he said, stepping quietly out of the room and around the corner to the lobby.

Keeley motioned to Streeter to follow him out to the parking lot for privacy. Without a word, Streeter followed.

When they'd settled on a spot, the pastor stuck out his hand and shook Streeter's with great gusto. "We haven't formally met. I'm Patrick Keeley."

"Special Agent Streeter Pierce."

And that was the extent of Streeter's side of the conversation.

To say Keeley was a talker was an understatement. A gusher, more like. It was as though Keeley was in a confessional pouring out his soul, confessing every misdeed he'd ever done—getting a speeding ticket, doubting his sexual orientation, shoplifting a disposable razor from the Nemo General Store, entertaining impure thoughts, as well as every misgiving he'd ever had about his career as a pastor. Was it truly his calling? Fifteen minutes into this rant, Streeter intuited this was not the Crooked Man. Patrick Keeley, unless suffering from a serious split personality disorder, would never have the ability to take another person's life, let alone kept it a secret. Keeley had even described how he broke his nose when he fell off his friend's handlebars, landing face first on the curb, and refused to have it set, frightened to death by all the blood and terrorized by the thought of having his nose re-broken to set it straight. At age ten, Patrick won the argument with his mother and doctor only by screaming until he was blue. To this day, the pastor admittedly hated doctors, although he said he might consider a visit to Dr. Morgan's if only to see Steve Preston again, promptly admonishing himself for having such thoughts about another man.

God love him, Streeter thought. Patrick Keeley couldn't possibly be the ruthless killer of all those men. Too weak. Weary from listening to all this information, Streeter yearned to be back inside listening to the repetitive testimony at the public meeting.

Afraid Keeley's confession would never end, Streeter decided to wait until Monday to find out if Keeley knew all the victims and if he had alibis for the times of the murders. He finally interrupted the pastor by asking, "Why did you ask Helma to bequeath everything she owned to the church?"

"What? I did what?" Keeley exclaimed. He was so startled by the question, he actually fell silent. For a couple of seconds. "I ask everyone about their plans for bequeathing to the church. It's my job. I have trouble keeping my job as it is. The rumors, the backbiting. The elders are constantly on me to ask every parishioner their intentions for tithing in life and memorials at death. It's my job, and for now, I'm trying to keep it. Although I'm hanging on by the skin of my teeth."

His eyes were sad. He had settled back into his comfort zone of self-deprecating confessions, so Streeter decided to hit him straight on. "Did you kill Ernif Hanson?"

CHAPTER 27

"OH MY LORD!" KEELEY said, gripping his chest with his boney fingers. "What? You think *I* killed Ernif?"

His breathing became sporadic, labored. He sat down hard on the sidewalk and fished out an inhaler from his pocket. Streeter stood watching, wondering what to do with this shored fish. Toss him back or fry him?

"Did you?"

"No. No! I swear!" Keeley's face was the pallor of a fish's underbelly. "I would never . . . I could not . . . I am a man of God, for crissakes."

Streeter was sure he didn't realize the irony in his statement.

"Where were you? Sunday."

"At church. All day. I had two services that morning, and I married a couple at three in the afternoon. I never left the church until five and then I went out to the country club for the reception."

Dozens, if not hundreds, of witnesses. With a three-hour roundtrip, he would have had no time to disappear and return. This was definitely not the Crooked Man.

Streeter told Keeley he'd see him on Monday, encouraging the pastor to think hard about who might want to see the Hansons dead and who would benefit. Streeter left him alone on the sidewalk. Weeping.

Streeter caught Linwood's eye the instant he returned to the ballroom and noticed Tate was absent. A quick scan of the crowd told him the tension had intensified. He settled in and counted the number of people still waiting to speak to the subcommittee. The lines were decidedly shorter.

A tiny, shriveled man hobbled to the microphone in the aisle farthest from Streeter and said, "Conservation easements are nothing more than creating public lands for a select few, which forces all of us to pay more in taxes to support the already bloated government."

The ruckus after the old man's message gave Streeter plenty of time to study faces in the crowd. He noted one of the men dressed in olive drab pants and a khaki shirt—the familiar green and gold crest of a tree sandwiched between a U and an S on the pocket—fidgeting as he stood near the door along the back wall. His professionalism ebbing, the pudgy ranger's face contorted as he shifted his weight from hip to hip in the exaggerated manner of a soldier being told to stand down against his instincts, whose urge was to jump into a war zone with guns blazing. Several of the chubby man's coworkers were clearly irritated with him, noting as Streeter had the blossoming red blotches on his flabby cheeks.

An older man, similarly dressed but commanding the chubby employee's attention in the way that only an authority figure can, casually made his way over to the angered Forest Service employee and leaned in to speak with him. The subordinate folded his arms over his expansive waist, screwed his face a little tighter, and made a hasty exit, the older man leaning against the wall by the door in his place.

Streeter caught Linwood's eye, and with a quick jerk of his head, he directed his peer to follow the pudgy Forest Service man and find out what he was so upset about.

Another man, slight but wiry, pranced down the side aisle closest to Streeter. The crowd quieted to hear the bespectacled egghead at the microphone say, "Although the missions of the one thousand eight hundred land trusts in this country vary, all of us want to see the protection of watersheds, habitat, open space, working forests, and historic sites. If we don't, who will?"

"Ranchers," several shouted at once.

"Farmers," a woman cried.

The messenger of hope, now crestfallen, scuttled back to his chair.

The leader of the subcommittee attempted to quiet the unruly crowd, but a chant, "Billings, Billings, Billings, Billings," erupted in a low, coordinated rumble that drowned out his words. When the crowd's movements increased in concert with the volume of jeers and hisses, the leader shouted into his microphone, announcing the abrupt end to the public meeting, and ushered his members out a side door. He ducked around the doorjamb just before a chair was hurled toward the empty head table.

In the panic that ensued, the room emptied quickly as people rushed to avoid getting caught in a brawl. Streeter shadowed Mark Goodsell, who ducked out the side door behind the retreating subcommittee, and followed him down the hall and into an empty meeting room.

Goodsell snapped on the lights and drew in a long breath of relief. Suddenly realizing that he'd been followed, however, he raised his arms as if to protect himself from being slugged.

Streeter stood still and quiet until the startled Goodsell lowered his arms.

"Mr. Goodsell, I'm Special Agent Streeter Pierce."

"With the FBI?" he said, releasing an exasperated breath. "Geez, you scared the living crap out of me."

"Sorry," Streeter said, extending a hand and shaking Goodsell's vigorously.

"That got a little rough in there," Goodsell said. "Those people are crazy."

"Those people?"

"The extremists. Those crazy loons backing Senator Billings."

"You know it was the kid wearing the T-shirt that said 'The Only Way Is Nature's Way,' the same kid who called Billings a bobblehead fascist, who threw the chair, don't you?"

Goodsell stared back at him, at a total loss for words.

"Not exactly a Billings backer."

"But it did get rough in there," Goodsell managed. "And he was probably defending himself. He's not one of our employees or anything. It's not like we can control every supporter's behavior."

Streeter nodded.

"Hey, what interest does the FBI have in Billings's legislation?"

"We don't," Streeter explained, watching as Goodsell finger-combed his thinning hair, straightened his shirt, and assured himself that his already-tucked tails were safely stowed inside his belted pants. He was visibly gathering his composure by the physical act of collecting himself.

"Then why are you here?"

"I want to know how you benefit from Ernif Hanson's death."

CHAPTER 28

AFTER ELIZABETH LEFT, I snuck off to the hospital, which is catty-corner from The Cathedral.

They had already moved Tommy out of his fifth-floor room in ICU. When the nurse told me where they had moved him to, I laughed. The only open beds available during the motorcycle rally were in the maternity ward. I made my way down to the second floor with a grin I just could not suppress.

Before searching for the room number I'd been given, I couldn't pass up the opportunity to ogle the newborns through the heavy window of the baby ward. Eventually I found Tommy's room, showed the guard my ID, and poked my head around the open door to see a man—not Tommy—curled up on his side, sleeping. I tiptoed past his bed and around the curtain. Tommy was propped up in his bed, arguing with a nurse about how much he hadn't eaten from his lunch tray.

"Just open me a can of beans and I'll eat that instead. They must have cans of beans in the kitchen, don't they?"

"Mr. Jasper," said the nurse, a sturdy woman who was standing with her hands on her wide hips, "I can't do that. Just eat your lunch. Please." Her pink scrubs looked as if Mother Goose had regurgitated cartoon animals and white daisies everywhere.

"Why can't you do that? All I'm asking for is a can of beans. Green beans. Just give me a fork and the can. Hell, I don't even need a fork."

"A can of green beans in the kitchen here is as big as me. Now eat your lunch and quit complaining," she said, ending the argument by shoving a thermometer in Tommy's mouth and wrapping a blood-pressure cuff around his arm.

Tommy finally noticed me and gave me a wink. The cuff inflated and beeped. The nurse looked up at me briefly before documenting all his vitals.

"Don't all the patients in this wing get ice chips?" I asked her. "Bring him a cup of ice chips and he'll never complain again about the food you bring him."

She chortled, removed the cuff, and hurried off to help the next patient, mumbling, "I might just do that if he's still here for dinner."

"They're busting you out already?"

He frowned. "If I do everything they tell me I have to do, they'll release me. And I'm not about to give you that list. Let's just say that's why I was asking for the can of beans."

"Oh," I said, feeling the heat rise in my cheeks.

He played with his food, pushing it around his plate with the fork. "Eating solid foods is on the list, but I don't know if I'd call pears and peaches a solid food."

"But what I hear is that any fruit starting with the letter 'p' will help you with the other thing on your list that starts with a 'p'."

He looked up at me, his expression wary. Then he shoveled the food into his mouth in three big forkfuls. Without chewing.

"Look, I told the FBI about your water well. They said they'd test it."

For a brief second, he eyed me. "So that's why I have police standing guard outside my room? Because of you? That's not exactly what the blonde told me."

"Special Agent Tate?"

He ignored me and finished the entire plate of food that the nurse had left on his tray. Then he drank the entire pitcher of water, slurping every drop, as I stood at the foot of his bed waiting for some signal to proceed with our chat.

Tommy wiped his mouth and pushed his tray aside. He stabbed at a series of buttons, his bed subsequently folding, bending, and reclining in all sorts of motions before the frosty nurse returned—apparently in response to one of the many stabs. "What?"

He looked at his tray as though it were a dead skunk lying next to him, and she quickly retrieved it, giving me a nod as she said, "Good job, Mr. Jasper."

Tommy folded his arms across his chest after straightening the blankets, suddenly aware of his vulnerability, and jerked his head toward the chair by the window. "Want to sit?"

"I can't stay long," I said, making my way to the leather rocking chair/recliner/makeshift-bed-thingy that is found only in hospitals. I fished in my pocket, my fingers lighting on the wad of tissue, which made me remember to call Streeter about the pills Dr. Morgan had tried to make Helma swallow. Then I fished some more, pulled out a napkin-wrapped treat, and handed it to Tommy. "Lemon bar. From the church."

He unwrapped and ate it greedily. "Lemons don't begin with a 'p', but I'm mighty grateful to you. This is the tastiest thing I've eaten since our dinner Tuesday night."

"Are you feeling better? You look better. And I'm surprised they're considering letting you go so soon."

"I feel better. Enough to squeal like a mashed cat about letting me go home," he said. "That agent stopped by early this morning to tell me my water is fine. Not poisoned after all. So I told the nurse I want to go home."

"Which agent? Streeter?" I noticed my heart seemed to race at the mention of his name.

"No, the fuzzy-faced one. Agent Blysdorf."

"And your well wasn't poisoned?"

"No, but something was."

"Well, whatever it was, you sure seemed to get over it quickly. Maybe it was just a simple case of food poisoning," I offered.

"If it was, they don't think it was from the food at the Nemo Guest Ranch, since I'm the only one who seemed to get sick."

"But you're still convinced you were poisoned somehow."

"I am sure I ate something that didn't agree with me," he said, rubbing his stomach through his hospital gown and gathering up the thin blankets puddled in his lap. "All I know is that I felt like an old dog that was fed tainted meat by an angry neighbor accusing me of sucking eggs from his chicken coop."

That made me laugh.

"Hey, that reminds me," Tommy continued. "You need to go pay a visit to the Widow Aker south of my place, just outside of Nemo. You know that little white farm house in the meadow to the northwest of where the road to Vanocker Canyon heads to Sturgis?"

"Yeah, I know exactly the place you're talking about. Why do I need to pay Mrs. Aker a visit?"

"'Cause she might know a thing or two. Tell her you came to see me and I told you she shared a secret with me about Nature's Way. That I asked her to tell you about it."

"What made you think of that?"

"Feeling like a poisoned, egg-sucking dog."

I heard the rattling of papers and the tap of a cane as the now-familiar man made his way around the curtain. "You old goat. I heard you're complaining, as usual."

"About time you showed up," Tommy said. "Liv, you remember meeting Dr. Morgan from the other night, don't you?"

"I do."

Before I could stand and extend my hand to him, he slipped the head of his cane between the bars of the bed, whipped the clipboard of data from the holder on the wall, and studied Tommy's progress. Without looking up, he asked, "Your sister is Elizabeth, am I right?"

"Yes."

"She convinced my patient to leave Heavenly Hospice and I'm worried about her unnecessary suffering." His quick glare at me was unmistakably reproachful.

"I've heard nothing but good things since Mrs. Hanson's been home," I lied. "And my sister didn't convince Helma. It was the other way around."

"Mmm," he grunted. "Well, her suffering is inevitable in the advanced stages of the cancer that's ravishing her body."

"It's still her choice, isn't it?"

Dr. Morgan studied me again, only with a more lingering stare this time. His traditional white doctor's frock was open, revealing a monochromatic earth-tone suit and vest beneath, a button-down, perfectly pressed white shirt, and a Windsor-knotted brown tie covered in an array of North American songbirds. The bright white coat and shirt matched his thick hatch of hair. In that moment, a stark image came to my mind. Something from my childhood. Something at Storybook Island.

"You sound just like your sister," Dr. Morgan said.

"Thank you," I replied, knowing he hadn't meant it as a compliment.

"Have you managed to keep any food down?" he asked Tommy.

"So far."

"Any bowel movements?"

Tommy's eyes slid over toward me and I cleared my throat. "And on that pleasant note, I'm out of here. I'll see you later, Tommy."

Out in the hallway, I whispered to the police officer guarding the room to keep an extra-vigilant watch on Dr. Morgan, since he had been a suspect early on, and to keep that information confidential.

I know better than anyone how loose lips can sink ships, but I felt a lot better when the officer ducked into Tommy's room, his hand resting on the butt of his gun.

CHAPTER 29

THE MAGIC OF STORYBOOK Island intensified with every visit. I had been going to the free park for as long as I could remember, and I loved the life-size statues of storybook characters to touch, feel, and climb on and around, which made my mom's bedtime stories come alive for me. Humpty Dumpty, Mother Goose, Winnie the Pooh, Robinson Crusoe, Noah's Ark, the Cat in the Hat, the Three Little Pigs, and my favorite, the Littlest Angel—along with just about any other lovable character imaginable—watched over me as I played on the slides and swings, in the maze, on the train, and by the water.

Every child's dream.

I had called down to the bureau asking to talk with Streeter, and Jack answered. He transferred me to Streeter's cell phone. All Streeter said was to meet him at Storybook Island since I was only a few blocks away at Jens's house.

I found Streeter sitting alone on the bench near the Littlest Angel in the toddler park, watching kids play. I wondered if this was where he came to think when he was in Rapid City.

"Watching children play gives me strength when I feel too tired to chase the bad guys," he said when I sat down beside him on the bench.

I stuffed my hands into my jean jacket to ward off a chill as the sun dropped in the sky. We sat in silence for a long moment.

"I read the articles about what happened to your wife."

I studied his face as he watched a gaggle of toddlers bounce around like pinballs from the tiny slide to the tic-tac-toe games to pirate ships to monkey bars, my mind constantly pairing parents to children as they did.

"She loved children. She used to come here just to watch them play." After a very long moment, he said, "You remind me of her."

"I'm sorry about that."

"I'm not."

I wrapped my arms around his shoulders and pressed my cheek against his. Streeter hesitated before reaching around my waist to hold me. More like crush me. He was holding on for dear life, and he didn't seem to realize his own strength. Neither of us said a word. Neither of us moved. Eventually, I freed him from my embrace and sensed he didn't want to let go.

I was about to say something when he asked, "Why did you call?"

"I was . . . I wanted to . . ." I was at a loss for words at the abrupt change in his demeanor.

He looked at me briefly, pain evident in his eyes, and said, "I don't like talking about it."

He drew in a ragged breath and rose from the bench. "Come on. I want to show you something. We can talk on the way."

I told him I had stopped by the federal building earlier and given Jenna the tissue-wrapped pills that Dr. Morgan had tried to administer to Helma on the morning someone tried to kill her, just in case he might be the Crooked Man and had tried to poison her with the pills. I confessed what I told the guard outside Tommy's room. I told him everything Elizabeth shared with me, including the part where Helma thought maybe Nature's Way might be behind Ernif's murder and how someone had tried to break in to her house the night before. I told him what the police said and how I had given Elizabeth my gun. I told him I planned on spending the next two nights at Helma's cabin before returning home to Fort Collins on Sunday. I told him about the grizzly bear and how the photos of Ernif's body made the image come to mind and that Elizabeth told me the Hanson ranch—the rock—was the actual site where it had happened.

"I wonder if the sites are all tied together somehow with gold as the motive," I said. "You know how gold prices fluctuate. And with this economy and all, maybe as the gold prices have skyrocketed, someone wants to have access to the best creeks to pan for gold."

"That's a thought," he said, "but a couple of the ranches don't have creeks."

"But maybe they have gold mines on the ranches. Almost all of the inholdings of the Black Hills were established through homesteading, which normally was done along the creek beds or through mining claims."

His pace slowed. I wondered if I'd said something wrong.

"It's just a thought."

He grabbed my hand and gave it a squeeze. "A good one."

We walked past the entrance to the park and along the path I'd always taken as a kid. And, suddenly, there he was.

Just off the path on the right stood the image of a man in a topcoat the color of milk chocolate, a matching top hat, tan knickers, white kerchief and stockings, and dark brown shoes. His hair was thick and white, poking beneath the brim of the hat. I had remembered this imagery when I saw Dr. Morgan this afternoon. The character at Tommy's hospital bed, leaning on a cane dressed in browns and whites, had indeed been familiar. Right in front of me was the character who reminded me so much of Dr. Morgan, the character from the nursery rhyme, outside his crooked house.

Who had walked a crooked mile.

Wearing a crooked smile.

That little statue made me goosey. A shiver skipped up my spine, and Streeter wrapped his arm around my shoulder and led me to a bench facing the character set.

"The Crooked Man," I said, sitting as close to Streeter as I dared.

"In Dr. Morgan's likeness. This, and his connection with the earlier victims, made him soar to the top of my suspect list ten years ago."

I waited a beat, hoping he'd give me the current status. But he didn't volunteer it. "And now?"

He sighed. "He's on the list. With you finding the sixpence and Helma Hanson remembering that her attacker recited the Crooked Man rhyme, I am confident there's a connection. But my instincts and experience tell me it's not Dr. Morgan."

"Let me guess. Dr. Morgan was Homer Larson's doctor, right?"

"And Wade Barns's doctor. And Buddy Richards's doctor."

"And Ernif Hanson's doctor."

"Several of the murder victims relied on Dr. Morgan."

"Your instincts and experience tell you that a dying man's words of 'Crooked Man' have no connection with a doctor—*his* doctor, who is physically bent, crooked if you will—who has a storybook character in his image at a well-known tourist attraction in the area," I summarized. "Huh. Go figure."

"I didn't say there was no connection," Streeter said, leaning back and arching an eyebrow as he assessed me. "I said my instincts and experience tell me he's not the murderer. And I didn't say that your observation has no merit. This Crooked Man at Storybook Island might very well be the reference Homer Larson intended with his dying words."

"So how does all that fit in?" I asked, more confused than ever.

"That's what we need to find out." Streeter turned his attention to the setting sun, his eyes staring off to the west. "Clearly, Dr. Morgan is a key link. But another common link seems to be that nearly all of these properties somehow ended up being owned by Nature's Way, either through donation or fire sale purchases from estates."

"How did it go today? Did you meet with some of the people at Nature's Way like you'd hoped?"

"Mark Goodsell is cooperating. He's appalled at the seemingly nefarious connection, and he's defending the intentions of Nature's Way with unparalleled righteousness."

"And do you believe him?"

"I do," Streeter said simply.

"And what about Pastor Keeley?"

"I don't think Keeley's our Crooked Man."

"How can you be so sure?"

"Tate doesn't think so based on her observations and discussions with him. I talked with him today. My instincts say it's not Patrick Keeley we're looking for."

"Is that a gift or something?"

"What?"

"Your ability to meet people and size them up. Being a human lie detector. How's that working for you?" I said with a smile.

"Truthfully, not so well," he said, returning the smile. "I tend to quickly eliminate potential suspects like Dr. Morgan or Pastor Keeley and narrow the field in my mind before all the facts, findings, and lab results are in, but I really shouldn't do that, considering the consequences."

"And have you ever been wrong? About your instincts? Once the findings and facts are all weighed?"

His eyebrows buckled and his expression was wildly erotic, although I had no doubt he hadn't intended it to be.

"Think. Ever?"

"Never," he finally concluded.

"Then you're not wrong to use the gift of intuition."

"Unless I get too comfortable relying on it rather than basing decisions on the facts."

"But from the sounds of it, you do base your decision on the initial facts. You use your intuition to narrow your focus on where to spend time early on in an investigation, using the subsequent facts to actually take action against the criminal, and it seems to pay off," I said, leaning toward him, eager to hear more about what made him tick.

He leaned in toward me. "Is everything in your world so clear to you?"

"What do you mean?"

"I've worked with people for many years who've never pegged me as quickly or as easily as you have. I'm impressed."

His smile was genuine. His closeness was rich. Normally I would never allow a man this close to me unless I was much more familiar with him than I was with Streeter. But I resisted the urge to create more personal space, enjoying the warmth and friendliness emanating from him. I didn't sense he was flirting; he was just comfortable with me.

"Well, some say that's my gift. Reading people. So I understand on some level."

He leaned back, leveling his eyes on me. "That, I believe."

"So tell me how you think this whole Nature's Way connection fits?"

"I don't know," he said, dropping his eyes to the map he had pulled from his back pocket. "The connection is too hard to ignore, but the idea of Nature's Way being behind multiple murders just to secure land holdings is preposterous."

"But wouldn't that fit your concept of criminal warfare?"

He nodded. "Certainly."

"As does the concept that the U.S. Forest Service might be behind the murders to secure strategic inholdings for the Black Hills?"

"Exactly," Streeter said. "And after meeting the key players today for both organizations, I must say the idea is even farther fetched than it was before I met them."

"Trust your instincts," I said. Watching him plow his fingers through his hair, I wondered what it would feel like to run my fingers through it. It was short and spiky, but I imagined it thick and soft, and wanted to ask him to grow it just a little bit longer so I could grip it for dear life while I was beneath him.

"That's the best idea anyone's shared with me today," he said, startling me with his words. For a minute I thought he'd read my devilish and unprofessional thoughts about him. Then I realized he was talking about my statement encouraging him to trust his instincts. "But I just can't shake the strong suggestion that Nature's Way is involved somehow, even if not directly."

"What about Dr. Morgan as a connection?" I asked. Streeter smiled at me, a smile so genuine a rabble of butterflies took flight in my stomach. "What if you are wrong and he is the Crooked Man?"

"If I'm wrong, eight men were killed because I didn't throw him in jail when I was working the case," he said matter-of-factly. "If Dr. Morgan is killing these men, what is the motive?"

I knew he was testing my ability to reason, to use logic to solve cases—in other words, to become an agent—and to assure himself he made the right choice by suggesting me for training at Quantico.

I shrugged. "It just bothers me that he looks so much like this creepy statue."

"That's because it was created in his image. Actually, in his grandfather's image. Bly and Tate followed that line of thinking too. And I told them what I learned when I was first on this case. Dr. Morgan actually donated that set to Storybook Island decades ago, asking the set creator to design the statue to look like his grandfather, but to make the figure misshapen, or crooked, to mirror his own body, which I assume is a birth defect of some sort."

"You're kidding me. And you're still convinced that the victim saying 'Crooked. Crooked man' before dying was not referring to Dr. Morgan?"

Streeter scowled. "True, Dr. Morgan did not have a solid alibi back then, during the time Homer Larson was killed. That has always bothered me."

"But it never deterred you from believing he wasn't the murderer?"

"To kill a man—to kill several men—by striking them dead takes a great deal of strength."

"And Dr. Morgan can barely stand up without the use of his cane," I speculated, picking up on Streeter's reasoning.

Streeter nodded. "I wondered years ago if he'd used the cane to club his victims, and even asked him to let us do some tests with it. He cooperated fully, and the ICO analyzed the forensic evidence and compared the shape of the handle with the wounds."

"No match?"

"Not even close. The handle was flat and square."

"His cane's handle is a brass ball now."

"I noticed. Right size too. Exact match, to be precise. Again, Dr. Morgan has been very cooperative."

"So why haven't you arrested him?"

"Because he isn't our murderer."

His statement hung in the silence that followed like the magical mesh that separates me from the ominous shadow I believe to be a priest in dark confessionals. Believing without question that the mesh allowed me anonymity while I confessed my deepest darkest sins to a man I was supposedly encouraged to put my eternal faith in as the conduit to God. In childhood,

I wasn't very good at not questioning the premise. And I hadn't changed much after all these years, but I have learned to time my questions better.

"So, where do you go from here?"

"Well, I'm not dismissing the connection to Dr. Morgan entirely. But instead of focusing on who did or did not commit the murders, we'll work this from a different starting point. Follow the money. I want to find out who the anonymous donor was on the land with a secret deed that hadn't been recorded, the one where the murder victim left it to Saddleback Ranch."

"Mr. Pelley's place."

"You knew him?"

"More like I knew *of* him. My dad knew him well."

"Any chance he'd know the anonymous donor?"

"My dad? Probably. He knows just about everything that happens around here, especially when it comes to something that benefits the community or the state of South Dakota. Do you want me to ask him?"

"Mind if I call him directly?" Streeter asked, leaning in toward me again.

A warmth spread in my stomach like a shot of chilled vodka after a long, stressful day.

"Help yourself," I offered.

He inched closer, his mouth closing on mine.

CHAPTER 30

I DON'T KNOW HOW long we'd been kissing, but I felt Streeter pull away from me and then coldness fill the void he left behind. It was the most intense, toe-curling kiss I had ever had, and I didn't want it to end. When I finally opened my eyes and remembered where I was, the bench was empty. I looked around and saw that Streeter had moved in closer to the character set.

I heard the clip of high heels heading down the sidewalk in our direction and instantly understood.

"Well, howdy, howdy you two."

I knew the voice belonged to Jenna Tate before I ever turned to look, her southern accent never sounding more annoying than it did to me at this very moment. I was surprised to see Jack Linwood following, the pair taking up positions on the bench on either side of me.

I had heard only one set of footsteps, not two. I wondered how much these two had witnessed. And I realized I didn't care. But I suspected Streeter did.

Jack's eyes lit on mine and he asked, "How are you? Rough day, having to attend funerals two days in a row."

"Worse if it had been my own, right?" I said, a bit surlier than I cared to admit.

I had never felt so robbed in my life. For days, I had been anticipating a moment alone with Streeter. So, focusing my anger on Jenna for interrupting us was easy. But seeing Jack made it harder for me to be angry. A lump rose in my throat and I shoved it back down into my heart where it came from, embarrassed that I'd somehow become all girlie.

With his back to the three of us, still facing the plaque near the Crooked Man, Streeter asked, "In South Dakota, do ranchers use stiles?"

"Cattle guards and wire gates are more the norm," I said.

"What's a stile?" Jenna asked.

"When ranchers fence areas for cattle, they build a wooden structure, or stile, like a gate or a ladder or a tiny maze, that humans can maneuver through, but no way could a cow work its way through," I explained.

"So a ranch with a wooden stile might be unique in the Hills?"

"I suppose. Why do you ask?"

All three of us sat on the bench staring at Streeter's back as he read from the plaque. "There was a crooked man who walked a crooked mile. He found a crooked sixpence against a crooked stile. He bought a crooked cat, which caught a crooked mouse, and they all lived together in a crooked little house."

He turned to face us but not before Tate said, "The sixpence."

"That's why we never found sixpence at the other four sites," Jack said.

Streeter held up three new evidence bags, each containing a coin. "The coins were still embedded in the wood of the stiles at each of the other sites. I had our tech team scatter to find and retrieve them today. You found the first eight coins on or near victims who didn't have wooden stiles on their ranches."

"Oh my word," Jack said. "You're brilliant."

Streeter joined us on the bench. "I wouldn't say that."

"But that's eleven. What about the twelfth?" Tate asked.

"Helma found a sixpence in her satchel where she and Ernif kept some blueprints. Ernif must have been showing the murderer the plans for the Saddleback Ranch idea on Sunday before he was killed, which tells me he was familiar with the person. The murderer must have slipped the coin into the satchel then," Streeter said.

"But Homer Larson was the third to be murdered. The one who said 'Crooked Man.' So the murderer must really be a crooked man, don't you think? Do you still believe Dr. Morgan is innocent?"

"I never said he was innocent. Could be the victim in his blood-loss delirium was simply repeating the nursery rhyme the killer had recited. Let's talk about the plan for tomorrow. What are you thinking, Jack?"

"I need to take Liv and Beulah to Nemo to do some field work. I'm thinking we can meet back in Rapid City at eight, have breakfast, and be up there by nine thirty or so."

Not only was I planning to spend the night with Elizabeth at Helma's, I had also told Mrs. Aker I'd meet her at eight, and her house was near Nemo. But I didn't want to tell any of them why I was meeting with her. Not yet, anyway. Tommy had confided in me, alone. He could have told the rest of them, the FBI, but he didn't. He told me because he trusted me. I couldn't violate that trust, and for all I knew, Mrs. Aker had nothing to tell me but more speculation and gossip. I had to meet with her alone first, to see what her story might be about.

"I'm sorry," I piped in, "but I told one of our Nemo Quarry neighbors I'd meet her at eight at her house, but I could take Beulah with me and meet you guys wherever you're going after that."

"On a Saturday?" Jenna asked.

Streeter cleared his throat. "How about if we wait for you over at the Nemo Guest Ranch for breakfast?" he said. "We have some people that we need to talk with anyway, and this would be a perfect opportunity."

"I set up an appointment for us to meet with Dr. Morgan at his office at seven tomorrow morning," Jenna said.

Miffed, I guessed it was normal for FBI agents to work on Saturdays, but not normal for quarriers. Go figure.

"He's one of the people I was referring to that we need to talk with," Streeter answered, seemingly more exasperated than I was that we had been forced to get back to work.

"I'm sorry if that's too early," Jenna apologized. "The physician's assistant told me it was the only time Dr. Morgan was available."

"Steve Preston," Streeter said. "Yes, I met him at Heavenly Hospice."

"He's kind of a prick."

I liked Jenna's frankness.

"What do you have on him?" Streeter asked.

"I did a little digging." Jenna plucked a file from her Gucci purse and thumbed through the pages, reading from one sheet. "Steve W. Preston was born in Rapid City fifty years ago to Loren and Cynthia Williams Preston. Cynthia died during childbirth. It appears Steve moved with his father to Loren's hometown of Baltimore, Maryland, when the boy was about five or so, and they lived with Loren's parents. I lost track of Loren, though. Young Steve attended school at Goddard, then St. Paul's in Concord, a prestigious boarding school, the Ivy League version for K–12."

"What did his father do to afford that?" Jack asked the question that came to my mind too.

"I think it was his grandfather who had all the money. Appears he was in the financial services industries, a self-made multimillionaire. Left a trust fund for his grandson, Steve." Jenna scanned her notes for where she left off. "An honor student, Steve Preston easily gained acceptance to Princeton where he pursued a chemistry degree. Went on to get a physician's assistant certification but stopped short of going to medical school. He was hired by Dr. Morgan to be his physician's assistant seven years ago."

"Seven years ago. Hmm," Streeter mumbled. "Well after the Crooked Man killings began. What did he do after college?"

"He worked in research for Camden Pharmaceuticals."

"So how'd he end up in Rapid City, South Dakota?"

Jenna shook her head. "Beats me. Looks like he quit his job and drifted for fifteen years, became a wanderer, never settling anywhere permanent until about eight years ago, when he made Rapid City his residence."

"Why would a man with a chemistry degree from Princeton, who inherited a fortune from his parents, choose to live in Rapid City and work as a physician's assistant?" Streeter was looking at me when he asked Jenna his question.

She plucked more papers from her file. "Well, let me tell you what I found out about Dr. Morgan and see if the information jives with what you know from when you were the case agent years ago."

Her fingernail dragged down page after page, and I couldn't help but notice both Streeter's and Jack's rapt attention as she licked her finger before turning each one. "Dr. Lowell Morgan was born fifty-four years ago and was raised in Rapid City by his mother and maternal grandfather.

He lives modestly, still claims his mother's house as his primary residence. His grandfather died when Lowell was a boy, his mother when he was a teen. Comes from a long line of doctors. Lowell was an only child. Also attended Princeton. Also independently wealthy and doesn't need to work. Never married. No kids."

"Maybe Preston and Morgan met in college? They were only four years apart at Princeton," Linwood suggested.

"Both about the same age," Streeter conceded, "yet Morgan appears to be a decade older than Preston. Preston dresses in designer clothes, while Morgan's wardrobe is practical clothing in neutral colors. Morgan is humble and kind, Preston pertinacious and proper."

"Maybe that's what attracted them to each other. The odd couple," I added. In response to their confused looks, I said, "What? I heard they were boyfriends."

Jack stared at me. Jenna's jaw dropped.

Streeter asked, "Where did you hear that?"

I shrugged. "Local folklore. They were at the bar together the night I had dinner with Tommy at Nemo. But so was Pastor Keeley. I don't know, does it matter?"

"Yes," the three of them said.

"Okay, Tommy said that Dr. Morgan keeps it a secret but that most people know Steve Preston is more than just his assistant. And a bit of a slut."

Streeter was still. He was thinking. Hard. I was sure of that. "Jenna," he finally asked, "did Steve Preston mention if he'll be at our meeting with Dr. Morgan tomorrow morning?"

"He said he'd have a fresh pot of coffee and homemade sweet rolls for us."

Streeter approached us, and Jack and Jenna rose from the bench. I did the same.

"Liv, meet us at nine thirty tomorrow morning at the Nemo Guest Ranch after you get breakfast on your own, okay?"

"That will work."

"What I need you to do tonight is to protect Helma Hanson. I know you gave your sister your SIG Sauer, but do you have another weapon?"

I nodded. I wasn't going to Rochford empty-handed. I had my dog. And my Smith & Wesson revolver.

CHAPTER 31

MRS. AKER'S HOUSE WAS like so many ranch houses in the Black Hills. Built around the turn of the century, it was in bad need of a coat of paint, but it was sturdy, designed to keep the wind and cold out in the winter, the heat out in the summer. Her round, soft face reminded me of a tiny hoot owl. Her eyes large, lids slow to open and close, she peered around the door as it creaked open, and then she welcomed me inside, cats rubbing up against my legs and hers the instant I stepped off the porch into her house.

The odor inside hit me like a fist, the distinguishable stench of a humungous litter box. She must have owned about a dozen cats, although I really couldn't count them as several darted in and around the stacks of magazines, boxes, canned goods, jars, and garbage strewn about the floor.

It didn't take a degree in psychiatry to tell that Mrs. Aker was a hoarder. It wasn't so debilitating that she was buried in her own used diapers or anything. More like an organized and excessively frugal saver. I recalled that Tommy had called her the Widow Aker, which led me to believe she was likely living on a fixed income—or no income at all—and had to live like a squirrel just to survive. I guessed her to be nearly a hundred and wondered if this house had been her parents' homestead, also common among the folks here in the Hills.

"Have a seat, sweetie," she said to me, inching her way past the folding table next to the only uncluttered place on the couch and motioning me toward the buried rocking chair.

I shooed away the cat that was curled atop a pile of knitted blankets, and it hissed at me for doing so. Mrs. Aker chuckled as she scolded the feline, then started talking to all of her cats as I moved the items one by one from the chair to a spot on the floor, one of the only areas left that still allowed a path of escape to the door should I need it. I sat in the rocking chair across from Mrs. Aker and watched the cats gather around her on the couch, one by one.

Even though they still moved and snaked and curled and scampered quickly, I opted to try to count tails. My estimate of a dozen was a fraction of the cats I counted now, and I stopped at twenty-two, realizing it was a lost cause. All that mattered was that Mrs. Aker clearly was a compassionate, lonely woman who enjoyed the companionship of cats.

"Was this the house you grew up in?"

"It was. My grandparents moved to South Dakota in the late 1870s. My grandfather was one of General Custer's cavalrymen, an officer actually, who was sent back to Fort Abraham Lincoln with the photos and findings in the fall of 1874, two years before General Custer led his men to the Battle of the Little Bighorn. My granddaddy collected my grandmama and all their belongings from the tiny town across the Missouri River from Bismarck and settled here because he remembered the area so fondly."

"Lucky for him he wasn't one of the men who ended up a statistic on the battlefield of Custer's Last Stand," I said, remembering that so few had survived that bloodbath.

"Indeed," she said, settling back on the couch and letting a particularly friendly cat settle onto her lap as she stroked it gently with her gnarled fingers. "And luckier still that no one had yet settled here in the valley he loved so much. My granddaddy used to tell me stories about how the cavalry played baseball in the big field right by your quarry. And before he died, my daddy told me that somewhere in the archives historians mention this valley in all the expedition diaries, and that in one particular man's diary—I believe it was Captain Ludlow's—he mentions my granddaddy telling him that he wanted to stay right here for the rest of his life. And he did."

"That is amazing!" I said, feeling the goose bumps rise on my arms. Something about the connection to history always made me feel so insignificant yet at once real and important in the overall plan for humanity. "I just can't believe how great a steward you and your family have been to the memory of your grandfather and the sacrifices he made."

"Well, not such a great steward, I'm afraid." The sadness that overcame her was like a death mask, permanent and final. "You mentioned Tommy Jasper sent you. How do you know him, dear?"

"We met and became fast friends a few days ago. He found my brother's fiancée's body by Box Elder Creek on Monday morning. Did you hear about that?"

"No, but that is awful. Your brother's fiancée? So she was a young lady like yourself?"

"Afraid so. Even younger, actually."

"And Tommy found her?"

I nodded. "He told me to tell you that he was rushed to the hospital early Wednesday morning. He was in ICU until yesterday morning. They moved him into a regular room and he hoped to be released yesterday, but I'm betting he doesn't go home until today or tomorrow."

"What happened?" Her face was concerned but not overly alarmed.

"We found him unconscious in his house. The doctors said if we hadn't found him when we did, he would have died. But they were able to stabilize him quickly once they got him to the hospital. They think he ingested some poison."

Her face melted into a mess of frustration, pity, and anger.

"He said I should tell you that although the FBI tested his well and concluded it was not the source of the poison, he thinks Nature's Way had something to do with his illness and that you could shed some light on why he thought that." I had saved that mouthful for the right moment and was now greatly concerned the words would cause her to drop dead on the spot.

Mrs. Aker sat deathly still, all color draining from her wrinkly cheeks. Her arthritically crippled fingers lay still on the cat, but they must have tightened, based on the cat's reaction of rolling over onto its back and clawing and biting at Mrs. Aker's hand, which she jerked away with a startled look.

"Bad kitty," she scolded.

"Mrs. Aker, are you okay?"

"I'm fine, sweetie. I was just deep in thought."

I could hear a clock ticking loudly somewhere, but beats me what good it would do if Mrs. Aker couldn't see its face, buried beneath everything.

"Do you know why Tommy Jasper would have sent me to you?"

"What's your interest in all this, dear?"

"I'm working with the FBI. One of their agents—my friend from college—was killed in my house a month ago, and circumstances led them to believe I'd be a good handler for her mantrailing bloodhound named Beulah. She's trained to trail scents, to track criminals and victims, and provide the FBI with backstory at crime scenes." I hadn't heard myself summarize where everything stood on this subject before now, and although I thought I did an adequate job, I somehow felt Mrs. Aker wanted more so I provided it. "And I kind of have my eye on one of the agents."

This brought a smile to her sad face. "I thought there might be more to the story. Lovely. True love and all the memories you create will keep you warm long after that loved one dies."

"How long ago did your husband die?"

"Oh, I never married, dear. I was a schoolteacher." The look on my face made her chuckle. I only felt confused. "The love I was referring to was my cat Waffles. I had him since he was a kitten and he lived with me for over thirty-four years."

"Thirty-four! Wow, that must have been like a hundred and fifty in human years or something."

Again, she laughed at me.

"Seriously, cats don't usually live that long, do they?" I asked, calling her out even though she was a hundred years old.

"Sure they do, dear," she said. "Cats can live even longer, depending on how well they are cared for and, of course, depending on their genetics."

Based on my doubtful expression, which I did not try to conceal, she added, "Waffles wouldn't have lived much longer, it's true, but they didn't have to kill him the way they did."

"Kill him? Who?"

"Nature's Way."

"Nature's Way killed your thirty-four-year-old cat?"

"Well, somebody did," she said, coaxing the bad kitty back onto her lap and petting it lovingly.

"Why do you think it was Nature's Way?"

"I had been talking with them about preserving the Aker homestead. My daddy and granddaddy never would have wanted the ranch developed, and I have no one to leave it to. So I'd been asking if they would buy the ranch."

She stroked the bad kitty's fur, the others looking on, and I would have sworn they were jealous.

"They said they didn't have money to buy the ranch, but if I was willing to put a conservation easement on the place, I would no longer have to pay taxes to the county and they would look for a friend of Nature's Way to buy the ranch with a conservation easement on it."

"That's how that works? They don't buy property?"

"Well they do, if the ranch is important enough or big enough to attract donations. But they said this wasn't of significance and the size was too small to attract much attention." Her aged lips pursed at the words. She looked up at me and said simply, "I told them it was important to me."

I offered her a smile. "Of course it is."

She sighed, the bad kitty jumping off her lap and another taking its place. "They said that if I put a conservation easement on the place, they'd find a buyer to donate money to buy the land for Nature's Way. I agreed. But when I got the paperwork, I told them I would not sign the agreement unless they struck the language stating they could at any time trade my family's ranch for more strategic conservation land in the future."

"Well, doesn't that defeat the purpose of you trying to protect and conserve your property against future development?" I said.

"That's what I said to them. They told me it was boilerplate legalese and that every conservation easement had that type of language. They recommended I just ignore it, that it wasn't important. I told them if it wasn't important, they should strike the language."

"Good for you," I said, thinking one for the widow, zero for Nature's Way.

"We went around and around, and I finally just struck a line through the language with my red pen, initialed the change, and signed the agreement. When Mark Goodsell and Rowland Cowen came by that afternoon to tell me they found a buyer for my ranch, I handed them the modified agreement and told them I would sell the land under two conditions: one, that I would have the right to live in the house until I died, and two, that they had to initial the agreement with my modification."

"You go, girl," I said, excited by her spunkiness.

"They returned in a week and told me the buyer accepted the terms, as did Nature's Way, under a counter condition that I no longer allowed cats in my home, due to their destructive nature to the delicate populations of birds in the Black Hills."

"What? That's the least of the worries. Your cats were more likely to be eaten by a mountain lion up here or a bobcat if you didn't keep a sharp eye on them when they went outside anyway."

"That's what I told them," she said, adjusting her shriveled body on the couch. "So I told them no. The next day I found Waffles. Dead. So now, instead of having one cat, I have thirty cats."

"And it wasn't old age that killed the cat?"

"Sweetie, old age doesn't nail a cat to a tree after breaking its spine in two places."

CHAPTER 32

PRESTON'S EXPRESSION WAS REVEALING.

Streeter noted how instantly the P.A.'s initial hostility morphed to alarm then to worry and finally settled into annoyance as he recognized Streeter as the same man he'd seen at Heavenly Hospice three mornings ago. He suspected Preston was irritated about having to awaken early enough on a Saturday morning to open Dr. Morgan's office by seven, brew coffee, and greet the FBI when he should have had the day off or at least been allowed to sleep in after a long week. Streeter could understand that. And the alarm and annoyance were also explainable, considering the unfriendly—even hostile—behavior Preston had demonstrated toward Nurse Linda the other day, Streeter having witnessed the entire event. But that sliver of worry sandwiched in between the two changes of expression is what bothered Streeter. Remorse, yes. Embarrassment, maybe. But worry?

Preston's annoyance propelled him into action as he scurried to retrieve coffee for Streeter and Tate, which gave Streeter time to look around.

Dr. Morgan's practice was housed in a converted residence, nothing more than hallways and tiny rooms barely large enough to fit the reclining medical tables for the patient and single stool with wheels for the doctor. Preston had instructed them to come in through the street-side entrance, which opened up into a waiting area large enough only for nine narrow chairs to line the three walls, with two chairs side by side in the middle of the area. Streeter speculated this had formerly been the living room, the nearby receptionist's area the kitchen, which is where Preston had disappeared to a minute ago.

As Streeter wandered through the halls, poking his head in dark rooms, Tate whispered, "Where are you going?"

"Just looking."

He sensed her shadowing him as he looked in each of the four small examining rooms, opened a door to a bathroom with nothing but a commode and a sink, and then looked into a final room in the back, which was bigger than the rest. The room contained a partner's desk in the center of the room and two chairs facing one another across the desk. The left half of the desk was completely clear of items other than a computer monitor and two pens lined up like soldiers, and the right half was covered with stacks of papers, journals, and magazines, not one sliver of wood showing beneath the catawampus mounds.

Streeter didn't need to scan the certificates hanging on the wall behind the messy desk to know this was Dr. Morgan's office. The medical journals lined neatly on the shelves behind the desktop helped give it away. As did the nature of the work—appearing at once organized and in complete disarray—that branded the curious Dr. Morgan. Streeter had no doubt this is where Lowell Morgan spent the lion's share of his time.

"What's that?" Tate said, pointing at the photo on the wall to the left of the office door as they turned to leave.

"Looks like somewhere here in the Black Hills," Streeter said, realizing the landscape indeed looked familiar. He looked closer, studying the meadow surrounded by pine trees, with what looked like an old homestead in the near distance; just the roof and part of one wall were visible beyond the tree line. Streeter was leaning forward to study the building closer when he heard the shuffle thump of man and cane coming down the hall toward them.

"Agent Pierce," Dr. Morgan said upon entering his office, extending a delicate yet strong hand to the special agent in charge.

"Dr. Morgan, this is Special Agent Tate," Streeter said, stepping back so the two could meet.

Gripping her hand in his, Dr. Morgan asked, "Do you have a first name, Agent Tate?"

"Jenna," she said. "Do you?"

"Well, yes, it's Lowell. But I'm sure you already know that as well as where I was born, what score I earned on my medical exam, and even what size and brand of boxer shorts I buy," Morgan said, shuffling past them both and sitting down in the chair on the right side of the desk. "Diffidence doesn't suit you, Agent Tate. And I don't believe for a second that Agent Pierce hasn't described in great detail all the reasons why he believes I am responsible for the Crooked Man murders and how he continues to search for the smoking gun that doesn't exist in my possession."

Streeter resisted the urge to smile as he saw Tate blush. Morgan motioned them to the other side, and Streeter pulled the chair out for Tate as he sat on the edge of the credenza behind the large desk.

"Dr. Morgan, you're confusing admiration for diffidence. I'm honored to meet you after hearing so many wonderful things about your medical marvel from all the people we've interviewed since I've started helping Agent Pierce with this case," Tate said as she leaned back in the chair opposite the doctor. "Besides, if I thought you were packing a smoking gun, I'd be the first to frisk you."

Dr. Morgan's wry smile was quick. "Then it's my loss for not possessing it."

Streeter hadn't heard him come down the hall, but Steve Preston instantly filled the doorway, clearing his throat. Handing Tate and Streeter each a cup of coffee, Preston asked, "Forgive me for interrupting, but would you like coffee?"

It took a moment for Streeter to realize he was asking Dr. Morgan, considering Preston's eyes kept probing his and Tate's faces as he spoke.

"Thanks, Steven. That would be lovely."

Preston retreated, and Tate took the opportunity to ask, "Physician's assistant *and* personal assistant?"

"He's attentive," was Dr. Morgan's reply. "Now, Agent Pierce, what's this all about?"

"You've been cooperative. We appreciate that," Streeter began. "But I've told you before. I'm struggling with the fact that you knew all these people who were murdered. And I told you I don't believe in coincidence."

"And I've told you, this is a small town. There are a lot of people who know all these men who've been murdered."

"Not a lot, but some. That's true," Streeter said, watching as Preston returned with Dr. Morgan's coffee and a plate of sweet rolls he placed in the middle of the desk.

Glaring at Tate as he walked around Dr. Morgan, Preston propped himself against the credenza behind the doctor, just as Streeter had behind Tate. Squaring off. "It's just that not all of the names on the list who were acquainted with all the victims have a cane with a brass ball that exactly matches the wounds."

"What?" Preston popped to his feet, nearly spilling his coffee. He rushed to Morgan's side to his defense and placed his hand on one of the doctor's shoulders. "Lowell, what is this about?"

Morgan patted Preston's hand. "I didn't want to upset you. It's nothing. And Agent Pierce knows it's nothing or he would have arrested me years ago."

"That's true," Streeter said, realizing that these two men definitely had a connection beyond a customary doctor-assistant relationship. It dawned on him that Tate was probably sitting in Preston's chair, on Preston's side of the partner's desk. And he realized Liv had relayed a reliable rumor, it appeared. "But you must admit, it's curious."

"Now just you wait a minute," Preston straightened, pounding his fist on his hip. "Dr. Morgan is the kindest, gentlest man I've ever known. He's in the business of saving people's lives, not taking them."

Streeter remained still. He willed Tate to do the same.

"There, there, Steven," Dr. Morgan said, rubbing Preston's elbow as he spoke, almost in a fatherly way. Maybe the rumors were wrong after all, the relationship between the two men horribly misinterpreted. "Calm down. I'm fine. Really. This is just the cat and mouse game Agent Pierce and I have settled into all these years. Agent Shankley wasn't nearly this persistent, and I have to admit, Agent Pierce, I've rather missed our discussions about the Crooked Man. Tell me, who is the latest victim?"

"Your patient. Ernif Hanson."

Streeter watched Morgan's face twist into repulsion. "Oh, of course. I should have known. Oh dear. I'm sorry. I didn't make the connection."

Tate leaned forward, spilling her large breasts across the desktop. "You don't read the papers? Listen to the news?"

"I'm afraid not," Dr. Morgan said. "I truly didn't know. Forgive my trivial question in such a serious matter."

Streeter registered actual remorse and sorrow in Dr. Morgan's expression.

"It's not you who should be apologizing, Lowell," said Preston. "It's them. The nerve, accusing you of the cold and heartless murder of patients who were already dying. What kind of investigators are you, anyway?"

"Dying?" Streeter asked.

"You didn't know?"

"Ernif was dying?"

"He had testicular cancer," Dr. Morgan admitted. "He chose not to tell Helma."

"You mentioned patients, plural, who were dying." Streeter leveled his gaze at Preston.

"I just . . . what I meant was . . . they were old. Of course they were dying. Eventually."

Streeter wondered if maybe something else was going on here. Maybe he had miscalculated and Dr. Morgan had been involved all these years after all. But the doctor's motive bore something of a Kevorkian intent, a belief that terminally ill patients had a right to choose whether they lived through the suffering or committed suicide to avoid it.

"Dr. Morgan, do you believe that the Crooked Man victims over all these years somehow brought this on themselves? That they intended to commit suicide yet somehow made it look like homicide?"

He pondered that question, setting his coffee cup down and tapping his forehead with the tips of his fingers. "No, I don't think so."

"Why not?"

"Who would benefit from that?" he said. "None of them, except Ernif, had living relatives. Normally, patients who might have suicidal tendencies in those situations eventually find life is indeed worth living, even if in pain. And those who do request to be overmedicated—which, incidentally, I am happy to oblige, short of overdose—would only opt for a homicidal solution such as the Crooked Man delivers if they had insurance policies that would benefit the living and precluded payout should the investigation rule the death a suicide."

Lowell Morgan was as matter-of-fact as Streeter would have expected. He had no reason to believe the doctor was the Crooked Man or involved in any way. But Streeter wasn't convinced about the younger P.A.

"Preston, what about you?" Streeter asked.

"What about me?"

"Do you believe in a patient's right to die?"

"Of course. What I don't believe in is the right for federal agents like you to badger a man to death, which is what you've been doing to Lowell for years."

After a moment of silence, Dr. Morgan once again patted Preston's arm and suggested, "Steven, why don't you let me talk with the agents alone, please. I don't want you to be upset."

Preston pursed his lips, shoulders sagging. He took a step away and then turned on his heels and resumed his seat on the credenza next to Streeter.

"All right, then stay," Dr. Morgan said. "Agent Pierce. You know I didn't murder these people. But what is it that keeps bringing you back to me?"

"Several factors don't fall in your favor. You knew all the victims. The head of your cane is consistent in size and shape to the wounds discovered on all the victim's skulls. And you never had strong alibis. Early on, you had none. If only you had alibis."

Preston's head dropped, his chin resting on his chest. Dr. Morgan's brows buckled.

Dr. Morgan's words were measured as he said, "Do you have time to give me dates? After all, we're here in my office, and at least I could consult my calendar to see if we can figure something out."

"Let's start with Sunday when Ernif Hanson was murdered. Where were you that afternoon?"

Preston sighed heavily, staring down at his Italian custom leather shoes with fancy tassels. "This won't help. You do so much alone, Lowell. Outside of work, I mean. Just because you won't have alibis for when these horrible murders took place, you shouldn't let these agents steamroller you into thinking you should help them. Lowell, you need to stop talking with these people and hire yourself an attorney. Please."

Streeter saw Morgan weighing his options to help the FBI at the risk of alienating Preston. Accordingly, the special agent in charge took a different tack. "Okay, maybe we can change gears. Dr. Morgan, have you ever collected coins?"

CHAPTER 33

MY TIRES WERE CRUNCHING across the gravel parking lot of the Nemo Guest Ranch by 8:50. I had a good forty minutes to gorge myself on one of the hearty breakfast platters this place was famous for, plus buy a heaping pile of eggs and ham in a "to go" box to apologize to Beulah for smelling like Mrs. Akers's cats. This being the last official day of the Sturgis Motorcycle Rally, the gravel lot was littered with bikes and trailered bikes, more people than I was used to seeing in this sleepy little town, even for a Sunday morning before church or on the first day of hunting season. There were absolutely no parking spaces left, and I had to park across Nemo Road at the fire station and walk back to the restaurant.

It was also packed, yet I didn't see a single familiar face at the tables in the front dining area, let alone anyone who wasn't wearing leather. I quickly hustled to the back room, surprised to find Jack Linwood alone at a table for four between the fireplace and the pine tree growing through the middle of the bar and out the roof. Although the Black Hills heated up to a healthy eighty degrees this time of year by the early afternoon, the mornings were still a bit chilly after cool nights, and locals appreciated the warmth from an early morning log fire.

Jack looked fresh and alert, eager to see me.

"Morning, Jack. What are you doing here alone?" I said, sliding onto the chair across from him. "Where's the rest of the posse?"

"We had a late night last night. And the meeting with Dr. Morgan this morning led Streeter down a different path. He called me and told me to offer you his apologies for bailing out on trailing today."

"No problem," I lied. Big problem. I was hoping to spend my last day in Rapid City—at least a couple of hours of it—getting to know Streeter better. My plane left tomorrow, and I would be back to work at the quarry and plant by four o'clock to wade through stacks of mail, messages, and email. "And Jenna? Is she in the bathroom?"

I looked over my shoulder, expecting to see her clipping toward us, gracefully trying not to get her spiked heels caught in the knotholes of the saw log flooring.

"I haven't seen her since Streeter took her back to the hotel last night. I stayed behind to help coordinate the priorities for the lab. I assume she went with Streeter to the interview with Dr. Morgan this morning and will be working with him today."

I felt the blood rush from my face, frustrated that I once again misread the signs. He'd picked the southern belle, not me.

"Are you okay?" Jack said, his finger lightly touching my wrist.

"Oh, just hungry I guess," I said, forcing a smile to my parched lips. "And in bad need of a good cup of coffee."

"How did it go last night for you at Helma's? Any trouble?"

"No, I stayed up most of the night sitting in the recliner in the living room. Nothing happened. So maybe Helma can die in peace now."

"Maybe. Thanks for the medication that Dr. Morgan tried to give Helma, by the way. It might prove to be useful after all."

That perked up my spirits. "What did you find?"

"Not sure yet. We have a few more tests to run."

We enjoyed a hearty breakfast, he choosing eggs over easy, no breakfast meat, and wheat toast, and me choosing eggs and biscuits soaked in sausage gravy. We waddled out of there by a quarter to ten and over to his car, me carrying my offering to Beulah. "Hop in. I'll park over by your truck and we'll ride together in it."

"Where are we headed? I never did ask last night," I said, jumping in beside Jack in the bureau-issued car.

"We're going to do a little bit of trailing. Confirmation for our files, just in case."

"Confirmation of what? In case of what?"

"I need you to have Beulah work the crime scene for Michelle Free-burg's case, just in case someone cries foul with the recorded confession," he said, sliding his dark eyes toward me. Jack so resembled the grown-up version of Disney's Mowgli that when a lock of thick, straight hair fell across his forehead, I had to resist the urge to brush it off.

He pulled in beside my truck, gathered his equipment into a duffel bag, and tossed it in the back of my truck while I let Beulah out to do her business and eat her breakfast. After loading her up into the truck, I slid in behind the wheel, turned the key, and asked once more, "Where to?"

"The Lazy S," he said, loading a digital video camera with a fresh memory stick.

I swallowed hard and pulled onto Nemo Road, careful not to plow into or over a bunch of bikers as I did. I quickly drove the two miles south, turning into the Lazy S Campground just past the turnoff to our family's iron ore quarry. The first thing I noticed was the crime scene tape over the door of the deserted campground. I parked where Jack directed, unloaded Beulah, and strapped on her working harness and lead, which instantly stimulated her energy and interest.

We were so far away from the door of the campground I wondered what Jack was doing, until I saw a woman's tennis shoe in an evidence bag. He handed me the camera, showed me how to operate it, and told me to point the lens at him.

The button switched to on, I swung the camera upward and steadied my arm as he recited his name, bureau office association, date, time, and location, as well as stating my full name for the record and Beulah's. "We are going to allow the bureau-trained canine trailer, Beulah, to verify our speculation and the murderer's recorded confession that murder victim Michelle Freeburg willingly followed her murderer from this location to the place where she was struck on the back of the head and left to die five and a half days ago."

I continued to hold my breath to further steady the camera as Jack lifted the bagged tennis shoe up to the camera lens.

"This is a shoe taken from the victim's body. I am holding the sealed evidence bag close enough to the camera lens so that the evidence document number can be clearly read by the viewer and so that the seal can clearly be determined to be unbroken."

Again, I took a deep breath and steadied my hands, focusing on the lettering on the front of the bag and the paper seal. After several dozen seconds that stretched a lifetime, Jack removed the bag and motioned for me to give him the camera.

Jack continued with the recording and the commentary. "Liv Bergen, handler for bureau trailing dog Beulah, will instruct the dog to find. Based on the recorded confession, we expect the dog to circle the parking lot, pick up the victim's scent at the door of the campground, round the building to the back, go through the fence, across the meadow and creek, and follow the tree line north and west to the area where the victim was struck and killed."

I stood listening to Jack not knowing what to do. Camera still recording, pressed to his left eye, Jack handed me the evidence bag. "Liv Bergen is going to break the seal and set the bag on the ground at Beulah's feet."

I did exactly as he told me. Then I stood, Beulah staring at me as I did. Jack pulled his face away from the camera, which he kept steadily focused on me, and mouthed, "Go ahead. Go." Then he offered me a wide smile.

I readied the lead in my hand, knelt beside the evidence bag, and firmly told Beulah, "Find."

Without lowering her head, she sniffed the air a few times as I repeated the command, "Find. Find."

She walked slowly across the parking lot, making wide circles with her nose high in the air, her steps hesitant, but persistently in circling motions.

"Find," I repeated, letting out more of the lead and noticing Jack recording her every move. I turned back to Jack and asked, "Don't you think after all the people who have trampled across this crime scene and after nearly six days, the scent would be—"

All of a sudden, like a bullet from a gun, Beulah took off toward the door, turning sharply to her right and around the building, dragging me along for the ride. Beulah zipped along the building and across the back of the lot to the barbed-wire fence, not hesitating as she ducked beneath it. Then she headed through the grassy meadow to the creek. I dove under the barbed wire before she pulled me clean through it, commando crawling on my belly across the rocks and weeds, afraid to cause a problem in the chain of evidence somehow. I could hear Jack close behind me, stepping easily over the barbed wire fence with his long legs, never taking the lens off Beulah, who was far in front of me.

I scrambled to my feet once completely clear of the fence and trotted behind Beulah as she plunged down the creek bank and through Box Elder Creek and up the other bank. I nearly fell ass over teakettle when my steel-toed boots bogged down in the creek bottom, and then I lost a toehold on a slippery, mold-covered rock. Beulah trotted along at a healthy clip, her nose high in the air as she followed Michelle's scent across the meadow to the tree line, then turned left along the edge of those trees, following the creek upstream.

I glanced over my shoulder, careful not to lose my footing, and saw Jack following along with the recording camera. I could see his lips moving but couldn't quite hear what he was saying over the noise of my clomping wet boots and heavy breathing. I vowed that if I were going to be any good to the FBI, I had to get into shape. No more sausage gravy and homemade biscuits in the mornings for me. I'd have to settle for sliced tomatoes or a piece of fruit. And maybe just an occasional slice of veggie pizza.

Beulah pulled me along the rocky ground of the tree line headed directly for the corner of the fence and big rock where Tommy Jasper had found Michelle's body earlier in the week. After the long mile or so to the rock, Beulah pulled up short for just a second, then trudged back over the creek, ending up on the bank exactly where Michelle's body was discovered, baying wildly at the spot. Her legs stiffened and her nose to the sky, she sounded the alarm that she had found her mark.

Over the howling, Jack was explaining to future viewers how Beulah had indeed ended up at the exact location where Michelle Freeburg's body had been found and that the trail Beulah followed was consistent with the murderer's recorded confession. Again, Jack pulled his face back away from the camera and grinned. "It's okay. Go congratulate her. Reward her."

That part was easy. I rubbed Beulah's loose skin and soft coat, telling her what a good job she had done, how proud I was of her, and what a great dog she had been. I hadn't noticed that Jack had long since turned off the camera and was squatting beside me, admiring me admire the dog.

"What are you grinning about, Jack?" I said, burying my face in Beulah's neck.

"You," he said. "And believe me, there's not a lot that gets me grinning these days."

"Ah, that's not good for you. Life's too awesome for anyone not to be grinning all the time," I said, happy to see his face light up with such a big smile.

"Depends on the anyone," he argued.

"Well, let's just say the 'anyone' is you. What would stop someone like you from smiling all the time?"

I was surprised to see his grin disappear, his eyes avert mine. He rose to his feet and walked away. I scratched Beulah behind the ears one last time before I, too, rose to my feet and stood beside him.

"What did I say?"

He ignored me, busying himself with the gadgets on his camera. I gathered the lead and removed Beulah's harness, assuming our training and confirmation was concluded.

Halfway back across the meadow to my truck, confused by what had just happened, I decided to tell Jack about my visit with Mrs. Aker. When I got to the point of Waffles being nailed to the tree, back broken, I realized how ridiculous I must have sounded, suggesting there may be a connection in light of the Nature's Way's involvement and bullying tactics.

"And serial killers always start with torturing pets, don't they?" I said.

Jack managed a hint of a grin.

"You are something," he said, holding down the barbed-wire fence at the Lazy S Campground and letting me step over it, then stepping over it himself before lifting the lower wire and calling Beulah to him.

"What do you mean I'm *something*? Like a science project gone bad kinda something? Moldy bologna in the back of the refrigerator drawer kinda something?"

I had my answer when he turned to me and kissed me hard on the mouth.

"That kind of something."

CHAPTER 34

FINISHING UP AT THE Pelley place earlier than he thought he would, Streeter decided to pull in to the Lazy S Campground as he drove by on Nemo Road to find out how Linwood's trailing exercise with Liv was going.

Until he saw them kissing.

He floored the accelerator and headed straight back to Rapid City—green blurring his vision. He was angry with himself for misreading all the signs he thought he had read in Liv's body language, in her captivatingly sea green eyes, in her kiss yesterday.

But clearly he'd been wrong.

Although it pained Streeter to think about, he had to admit that he had seen the way Linwood's eyes lit up whenever he talked with Liv. And, Streeter conceded, Jack Linwood was tough competition. Linwood was taller than he, maybe six foot six or so. What impressed Streeter was his ability to carry himself off as invisible while possessing the appearance that he was a force to be reckoned with, a formidable adversary with intelligence, strength, and endurance. A picture-perfect representative of the FBI's image. He had thick black hair, dark olive skin that suggested he had at least one grandparent who was East Indian—maybe Sri Lankan—and huge black eyes that gave the illusion they possessed the power of seeing through people to their core. To their soul. It was difficult not to be any-thing but honest with Jack Linwood.

Streeter physically shook his head to clear the image of his rival. He would not waste another moment thinking about Liv or entertaining any thoughts of seeing her or having any relationship with her other than work. Or at least he would not admit that he did.

Linwood's grin when he and Liv finally arrived back at the office said it all.

Streeter avoided meeting their eyes and jumped right into the debriefing of the research, interviews, and investigations each agent had undertaken.

"The connection among all the murders does indeed point to Nature's Way," Streeter concluded. "So good job, Bly, for spotting the pattern and, Tate, for following through at the courthouse on deeds."

"And let me tell you, it's not like these counties made it easy for me," Tate said. "Nothing is electronic. Everything had to be pulled manually. Both in South Dakota and in Wyoming—except here in Pennington County. I had to convince a few supervisors to let me go through the files yesterday and today."

"Public information means people have a right to see it, but it doesn't mean the local governments have to make it easy for them to see it," Bly said, lacing his fingers behind his head and leaning back in his chair, propping his feet up on the conference table. "Especially if you're not from around here."

"That doesn't make me feel all that welcome," she said, looking over toward Bly, then folding her arms.

"It's not about you, darling. It's about protecting privacy and constituents."

"Oh, I understand that. But *one* constituent is slaughtering widower ranchers like they were fresh meat at the packing plant."

"I spent hours grilling Mark Goodsell yesterday and again this morn-ing," Streeter volunteered. "He was cooperative and even made all his peo-ple come in this morning so I could talk with them too. It's none of the Nature's Way people, although Rowland Cowen isn't what I'd call inno-cent. What did you find out about him, Tate?"

She actually blushed. "A lot. He's definitely not innocent."

Streeter wondered what Tate had to do to pry out personal informa-tion from Rowland Cowen. She had absented herself for several hours during and after the public forum the day before, she and the assistant program director for Nature's Way nowhere to be found while he and Linwood interviewed Goodsell and Burgess, respectively.

Streeter pushed aside the question of how she got him to talk and focused instead on what she had learned. "What's his motivation for working for Nature's Way?"

"Well, he loves nature, maybe because he was an asthmatic kid from inner-city Chicago. He's the oldest of three and has had to help with the family business since he was about ten years old. His family owned a dry-cleaning store and he resented it—and his parents—throughout his entire childhood. When they died tragically in a car accident, he and his siblings sold the business, split up the cash, and went their separate ways. He's thirty-four, never been married, into kinky sex. He moved to Rapid City, which he calls—not so affectionately, I might add—Hicksville, when he was twenty-two, just after being hired by Nature's Way."

"Twelve years ago," Streeter said.

"One year before the murders began," Bly noted.

Tate raised her eyebrows. "Oh, and did I mention he has a boyfriend? Seems the rumors are true. Steve Preston is a player. Both Rowland Cowen *and* Dr. Morgan consider him their lover. I bet neither knows what Preston's really up to. And just in case you're wondering, Rowland swings both ways."

Streeter was, but he didn't want any more details about how she knew that for certain.

"I don't care about his sex life. Is he capable of murder?"

"Capable of a lot of twisted activities, but capable of these murders? I don't know. I think our Crooked Man is more patient, more organized than Rowland Cowen. If Cowen is capable of murder, it would only be in a fit of rage. Never planned."

"Could you see him getting angry enough to kill a cat, break its spine, and nail it to a tree?" Liv asked.

They all turned to stare at her.

Once she explained the story, Tate said, "Yeah, I could see Cowen doing that to get back at Mrs. Aker in a fit of rage."

"More the spree killer type?" Liv asked.

"You're paying attention. Good." Tate continued. "By the time the meeting ended in that ruckus, Rowland and I were coming back from the

Ramada Inn. He told me to give him a minute in the parking lot. Ended up head bent with a U.S. Forest Service employee named Brett Appleton. They were both mad as hell at Billings, ready for any and all fisticuffs over the limited terms of conservation easements. In fact, as I approached them, Brett was squealing like a feral hog with a tit in a ringer over the tongue-lashing he'd received from his boss for not containing his emotions at the hearing."

Streeter thought back to the young man he'd seen by the door, fidgeting and fussing over every public speaker in favor of Billings's proposal. The man whose older supervisor finally had to ask him to leave. "Is Brett Appleton blond, mid-thirties, on the heavy side?"

"Looks like he's never missed a meal and maybe picked up a few extras in between," Tate said.

Linwood took that as his cue to make his contribution on the subject. "The supervisor who sidled up to him when Appleton couldn't contain his emotions is Drew Morley, the Forest Service ranger for the Mystic District. Good guy. I chatted with him before acting on Streeter's signal that I follow Appleton outside. Morley handled the situation well. He said he told Appleton to contain his emotions and remain neutral or to go home and cool off. Appleton stormed off, saying, 'They're all idiots in there. All I'm trying to do is protect this world from idiots like that.' For a minute there, Morley confessed, he thought Appleton was going to punch him. That's how out of control he was. Based on what Morley told me, there was obviously no need for me to trail Appleton to get his side of the story."

"A potential suspect?" Streeter asked.

Tate shook her head. "Too volatile, out of control. Again, although I think Brett Appleton and Rowland Cowen are militant environmentalists prepared to go to battle against anyone who doesn't share their opinions, neither is controlled or organized enough to be our Crooked Man."

"To plan acts of criminal warfare," Liv said.

"Exactly," Streeter said.

"But then we still have this crooked cat," Liv repeated.

Again, Streeter noticed everyone staring at her, the room going still.

"Seems we might have a definite theme going on. But I'm wondering why the cat was killed rather than Mrs. Aker if this was the handiwork of the Crooked Man?" Liv said.

"Tate, you mentioned Rowland's penchant for twisted sex," Bly said, raising an eyebrow. "Could twisted be perceived as crooked? Would someone consider Rowland Cowen a Crooked Man if, for instance, he performed a twisted sexual act on a rancher's wife? Or his goat?"

"Geez, Stewart," Tate said, moving away from him as she did. "You are one sick puppy."

"But is it possible?"

Tate glared at Bly, then looked over to Linwood and Streeter for support. "Well, I suppose. Rowland Cowen could very well be into goats or other barnyard animals."

"Crooked." Bly raised both eyebrows.

"Twisted," Tate argued, dragging out each syllable to make her point.

"What about the national guy? Berglund?" Bly said. "Could he be our Crooked Man?"

"Burgess. Anthony Burgess," Streeter corrected. "I met with him too. He flew out yesterday afternoon, but not before he emphatically demanded that Goodsell cooperate until this was resolved. In fact, he insisted that Goodsell open up all Nature's Way's files to us so we could see what we wanted."

"And did you? See what you wanted?"

"Not everything," Streeter frowned. "Tate's right about one thing. I'm waiting on a call from the secretary of state's office in Pierre on some information about certain companies that are big donors to Nature's Way. With it being Saturday, the governor had to make some calls to get people into the office to look for it."

"You know the governor?" Tate asked.

"No, I just picked up the phone and called him."

"This is South Dakota," Bly added. "Full access to our leaders."

"Actually, Garth Bergen gave me his number along with some ideas on who might be financially supporting Nature's Way and who might have anonymously donated for the Pelley place."

"Let's get back to my trip to Frank Pelley's place this morning," Streeter said, clearing his throat and avoiding Liv's eyes. "I found a plaque dedicated to Camp Saddleback Wildlife Preserve. See for yourself."

Streeter dimmed the lights and typed on the computer keyboard, bringing up the projection of a photograph of a large engraved brass plate mounted on the side of a small log cabin. The sign read:

NOTHING IN LIFE COMES AS EASY AS SHOOTING DUCKS ON A POND.

AND THOSE WHO THINK OTHERWISE WILL EVENTUALLY MAKE A

MISCALCULATION AS BIG AS THE BATTLE OF LITTLE BIGHORN.

"What in the hell kind of twisted dedication is that for a bunch of troubled boys?" Bly said, reading the sign again.

Tate added, "That's it? No name, no other indication who this person is or why they wanted this land?"

"Just Mark Goodsell's testimony that the only requests the anonymous donor made were that the wildlife preserve restrict hunting and that this sign be posted," Streeter explained.

He was as baffled as they were, which was why he had wanted to stop by earlier at the Lazy S and bounce ideas off Linwood and Liv before returning to Rapid City. The Pelley place was just up the road a few miles, and his hope had been that three heads would be better than one. But then three heads were trumped by four lips.

"What's the Battle of Little Bighorn reference got to do with anything?" Tate asked. "Was that battle fought here in South Dakota or something?"

"Nope," Bly answered, sliding his riding boots off the table and righting himself in his chair. "Eastern Montana."

"And why was it mentioned, for Pete's sake?" Linwood asked.

"Wasn't the Battle of the Little Bighorn also known as Custer's Last Stand? Where the Native American tribes joined forces and wiped out the U.S. Army? My history isn't that good," Tate admitted.

"Not wiped out," Liv began. "About a third of the 7th Cavalry Regiment of the U.S. Army was killed by the Lakota Sioux, who called on the Arapahoe and Northern Cheyenne to help them. That's where Chief

Crazy Horse earned his fame. And Custer's Last Stand is the nickname for the Great Sioux War of 1876."

Streeter was impressed with Liv's knowledge of the area, her expertise in a variety of venues seemingly endless.

"Wasn't there some rumor about Custer being scalped or something?" Tate asked.

Bly snorted. "Other way around, missy. The soldiers' bodies were found mutilated, stripped, and scalped as a matter of practice, but General Custer's body was basically untouched, scalp left intact."

"Out of respect," Tate concluded.

"No, not out of respect," Liv added. "The Indians considered Custer crazy, and scalping a crazy person released the evil spirits."

"So, let me get this straight," Tate said with an exaggerated drawl, showing she was focused more on the case than on hiding her southern roots. "Someone is murdering old, lonely ranchers each year and their land is ending up being owned or controlled by Nature's Way, for the most part. And one of the few properties that didn't end up in the Nature's Way inventory, the Pelley place, happens to have a sign referencing how hard life is and not taking anything for granted or you'll end up like Custer. Did our anonymous donor mean that you'll end up dead or insane?"

"Or did he mean that if you aren't careful, you might find yourself underestimating the enemy?" Streeter asked.

Tate pushed herself away from the table and started pacing the length of it, crossing behind Bly as she did. "And what does Custer have to do with Nature's Way? Or with Camp Saddleback? Do you suppose Saddle- back Ranch was started by Custer? Or started *in* Custer, South Dakota?" Tate asked.

Liv shook her head. "Saddleback Ranch isn't that old. It started about eighty years after General Custer was killed. Has turned into a summer camp for wayward kids so they can experience things like fishing, hunting, camping, rodeos—typical activities for Dakotans—while the counselors try to instill values in the campers through Biblical teachings."

"Whoa, whoa, wait a minute," Tate said, stopping across the table from Bly. "Did you say rodeo? As in *ranch* rodeos?"

Bly's eyes shot to Tate's like polarized magnets, their thoughts merging as quickly as their gazes. "Ranch? All the murder victims owned a ranch. A connection?" Bly offered.

Tate resumed her pacing, holding Bly's gaze. "Childless ranchers who fished and hunted, mostly churchgoers, being murdered, their land ending up in Nature's Way. Except one."

"Two."

Linwood caught on. "Pelley secretly donated his ranch to a Christian camp for wayward boys. Unbeknownst to the murderer?"

"Then, some anonymous donor imposed himself into that transaction," added Streeter, picking up the thread.

"Commemorating his donation with the scolding words not to hunt the ducks," Tate said, "or you'd end up dead like Custer."

Streeter nodded. "Could be. It would explain why the donor forced a 'no hunting' rule on Camp Saddleback, steering the outdoor activities to benign wildlife activities such as hiking and observation, all passive experiences."

"Experiences more compatible with Nature's Way line of thinking than with that of typical Dakotans, whose philosophy and heritage reflects the rugged westerner, living off the land," Linwood observed.

"Eating the food you harvest, hunt, catch, or kill," Liv said, letting the last word hang over the room like a smothering blanket.

The room became still.

After a long, quiet moment, Tate concluded, "Do we really think our anonymous donor might have some connection to the Crooked Man murders?"

Streeter's computer sounded a message alarm. He moved quickly to the keyboard and clumsily stabbed at the keys to pull up the message, everyone seeing the projection on the screen as he did.

"Renee? From the secretary of state's office in Pierre?" Tate read.

"Info about the two anonymous donors," Streeter said. "Here are the names of the members for the two LLCs. One was owned by Willis and Claudia Lipscomb, and the other by Tex Crawford."

Streeter turned to Bly, who shrugged and said, "Never heard of them."

Streeter closed the message and mumbled, "I'll call Garth Bergen again and ask him if he knows these people. I need to call him anyway."

"Good idea. Congressman Bergen knows everyone around here," Bly agreed.

They all looked at Liv. "You won't get an argument from me."

"And if he knows them, find out what each anonymous donor's fascination is with General George Armstrong Custer," Linwood requested. "Seems to me there's something more here in the foreboding dedication at Camp Saddleback than a simple reference to Custer's Last Stand."

"Incidentally, what were they fighting over?" Tate asked.

"Who? Custer?" Bly said, his eyes flicking over her face as if touching every square inch of it, which made Streeter uncomfortable for some odd reason.

"Yeah, I mean I know settling the west was challenging and the Native Americans were supposedly vicious toward them as they moved west, but what was the Battle of the Little Bighorn about?" Tate said.

Linwood cleared his throat, and Streeter would have sworn his olive cheeks blossomed and his dark eyes narrowed.

"The Indians viciously fought to protect their homes," Bly said, "just like I would if a bunch of soldiers came to occupy mine. But a couple years before that, the Indians left Custer and his men alone, never once waging war."

"Publicly, the battle was to protect settlers moving west from the escalating dangers from angered tribes," Liv added. "In reality, the battle was fought by the army to capture the Black Hills. The Indians fought to defend the sacred center of the world, the place of the gods to the Sioux."

"I thought the battle was fought in Montana," Tate said. "And what was happening two years before that?"

"Custer's Expedition," Liv said.

Confused, Tate stared at her for an explanation.

"Since 1868, when the government signed a treaty granting Paha Sapa, the Black Hills, to them, the Native Americans left the U.S. soldiers alone as long as they embarked on missions of knowledge or science. Custer's Expedition, six years after the treaty was signed, was all about gathering information about the Black Hills."

"And?" Tate asked, impatient for the conclusion everyone else had already made.

"And the U.S. soldiers largely left the Native Americans alone until they shared with the brass back at headquarters what they found during the expedition."

"Then all deals were off," Bly snorted.

"So what did they find?" Tate could hardly contain her curiosity.

"Gold."

CHAPTER 35

GOLDEN HONEY POOLED IN the center of my plate, all that remained of the four fresh homemade biscuits smothered in Hanson honey I had just eaten. I would have licked the plate, too, if I didn't think my belly may burst. I laid my head back on the couch cushions and watched the herds of deer gather in the field of gold. The sunset seeped through the ring of pine trees just like the honey had dripped from the tines of my fork as I shoveled in every morsel. I would have stretched out across the couch had it not been so tiny. Most of the furniture in the living room was designed for itty-bitty people like Helma and Elizabeth, and I tried to imagine Ernif lowering his lumbering body onto this couch, his knees, like mine, towering above the coffee table when he sat. I suddenly realized that the one large recliner in the room was probably reserved for him.

That's where I'd spent last night, barely sleeping a wink. Nothing happened, which made me think that my idea might be right: that whoever had broken in thought the house was empty.

While Elizabeth assisted Helma in the bathroom, I scuttled over to the comfy recliner and stretched out. Beulah followed me and curled up beside the chair. I stretched out and turned my head sideways to watch the elk slowly moving in the shadowy tree line, waiting for the sun to set, signaling their turn at the wheat grasses that carpeted the meadow. Thick as they grew in the Black Hills, the pine trees allowed easy sighting of animals as they ambled through the light and shadows of the woods. My eyes automatically scanned the area when I saw several of the deer turn their heads toward the far southeast woods touching the bluff. A mother coyote and her two pups were avoiding the herd of elk looming in the shadows and skirting the meadow. Cautiously, she stole several glances over her shoulder as she led the pups to the water below. I knew if I sat here long enough and resisted the urge to close my heavy lids, slumber as thick and irresistible as the honey I had devoured, I'd see all sorts of nature's wonders in the beautiful Black Hills.

I thought how lucky Helma and Ernif were to live here. I also thought how ironic it was that they raised cattle most of their lives, yet as they reached their golden years, the couple sold off the cattle and turned to the bounties of golden honey for their subsistence. My heart ached for Helma as I suddenly understood the depth of her loss with Ernif's death. And I wondered if she also felt relief—maybe even joy—knowing Ernif was spared from a destiny of living lonely had he survived her.

I wondered if I would ever share such a love with someone as Helma had with Ernif. I'd tried a few times, and all of them were men I could live with, but not one of them was a man I couldn't live without. So I'd keep searching. My mind drifted to earlier today, when Jack kissed me. He then asked me out on a date, but when I hesitated, he suggested we meet for brunch somewhere between Denver and Fort Collins, neutral ground, to prove his intentions were pure. Jack's kiss was nice, but Streeter's was exhilarating. But he hadn't asked me out on a date, and I stayed up all night wondering why not.

I watched one of the does inch closer to the porch, her eyes pinned to mine just as Jack's had been earlier, willing me to smile, to say yes.

"Boots, come here, will you?"

I jerked upright in the recliner with a sudden motion, startling the deer, which scampered off across the meadow to join her herd. Beulah lifted her head, the skin around her eyes sagging. She had worked hard today and deserved to sleep. Uninterruptedly. I scratched behind her long ears until her head fell back to the floor in a deep slumber. I quietly tiptoed down the hall to the bedroom.

Helma was propped up in her bed, eyes closed. Elizabeth was at her side, cooling her forehead with a wet washcloth.

Without opening her eyes, Helma asked, "Did you enjoy the biscuits?"

"Loved them," I said, trying to study both women's faces. Elizabeth was usually easy for me to read, but right now I was confused. Knowing Helma was nearing the end of her life, I would have expected Elizabeth to be sad, concerned. But her expression revealed a contentment I hadn't seen in a long time. "Where did you find the energy to bake biscuits?"

Helma laughed. And coughed. Elizabeth brought a glass of water to her mouth. She drank and drew a few labored breaths before settling in under her covers. "Elizabeth made those biscuits."

"What? Elizabeth?"

Elizabeth arched an eyebrow. "I can cook."

"No, you can't."

"I taught her all sorts of things this week," Helma said, Elizabeth dipping the cloth into the icy water, ringing out the excess, and returning the cloth to Helma's tiny forehead. "We've been working hard. She learned how to maintain the water well pump, how to harvest honey, how to care for my bees, how to read the blueprints on building a bunkhouse and headquarters for the lost boys, how to mend a fence, how to dress out a deer, how to cut a whole chicken, and how to make homemade biscuits."

I wasn't sure if I had heard correctly, but it seemed to me Elizabeth had been busy learning how to run this place. I could envision Elizabeth dressing out a deer, mending a barbed-wire fence, and cutting a whole chicken, but caring for bees or baking biscuits? No way. Not Elizabeth.

"Close your mouth, dear," Helma said, a tiny giggle escaping her petite frame.

I hadn't even realized I was gawking. "Sorry. I just can't imagine Elizabeth rolling and kneading dough. Or tenderly caring for bees."

"What? I'm good with the bees. I can be tender."

"As tender as an alligator."

Helma laughed. "Oh, you girls remind me of how my sister and I used to quarrel. I miss her."

"When's the last time you saw her?" I asked.

"She died fifteen years ago," Helma said, the lines of her mouth curling into a pair of parentheses unique to a smile. "I'll be joining her soon. My sister, my mother and father, my husband, and my baby. All together again. Very soon."

I glanced at Elizabeth, who offered me a sad Mona Lisa smile. Then she closed her eyes and rolled her head, rubbing her neck with one hand as she still held the washcloth to Helma's forehead with the other.

Helma sighed. "It won't be long now. Thank you for staying with me last night. And tonight. Elizabeth says you have questions for me, before you leave for Colorado tomorrow."

Under the thin blankets of her bed, her tiny frame appeared childlike, fragile, yet that image was deceiving because I knew she still had strength in those hands. She patted the bed, inviting me to sit beside Elizabeth so we could talk. The bed springs groaned beneath my frame, and for an instant, I thought the box spring might collapse, the mattress slide off with my load. Or worse, that Helma and Elizabeth would bounce off the mattress, reminding me how I used to send Elizabeth and Frances skyward on the teeter-totter, two flying leprechauns to my giantess. But of course that was only in my mind, and I reminded myself that Ernif must have weighed sixty or seventy pounds more than me. Helma was used to living around a giant.

"Go ahead, dear. Ask anything you'd like."

I had her tell me again about what she remembered about Tuesday night, or rather Wednesday morning, when someone tried to smother her at Heavenly Hospice. And everything she recalled since. I also asked her to recall what she knew or heard about Sunday, when Ernif was killed. Oddly, as an hour passed, I noted how Helma's mind was very clear on every detail of her life from six weeks ago and earlier, became unclear during the time since she was diagnosed with cancer and through her taking medication for the pain, then clearer again this week as she weaned herself from the pain medication. Make her pain go away? Or make *her* go away? When I pointed this out to her, she agreed that the pain medication made her head quite fuzzy, but that it did make her pain go away. And my mind lost its footing on that slippery slope again, wondering if Dr. Morgan had indeed overmedicated Helma to keep her out of the picture, under control.

"Would you prefer to be on the medication as the pain worsens?" I asked.

"Please, no," she said simply. "I know how painful it will get, but I also know that my mind will not allow me to suffer that which I can't handle."

"She'll black out when it gets too intense," Elizabeth said. "Already has a few times."

I had no idea the body and mind worked in such harmony to protect.

Eyes shut, she said, "I'm clear that as the man was trying to squeeze the life out of me as expertly as Elizabeth is ringing the water from that rag, it was your sister who saved my life."

I smiled at Elizabeth.

Helma's lips pursed. "There was a crooked man who walked a crooked mile."

"He said that? While he was smothering you? That's just sick."

She nodded.

"Do you remember the man's size at all? Was he tall and lean like Pastor Keeley? Big and sturdy like Nurse Hester Moore?" I asked. "Or tiny like Dr. Morgan?"

"None of the above," Helma said. "He was just . . . average. But I just can't place the voice with a face."

"Do you think the man who tried to kill you had any connection to the person who killed Ernif on Sunday?"

"I do. And I told the FBI the same thing last night."

"Special Agent Pierce speculated that the Crooked Man used a different MO to deflect attention away from himself as a suspect," Elizabeth said.

"Who do you think would want you and Ernif dead? Who would benefit from your deaths?" I asked.

"No one."

"A distant relative? A coveting neighbor? A greedy pastor?" I pressed.

She shook her head. "Pastor Keeley asked if I was bequeathing anything to the church. I told him no. So what would he have to gain by our deaths?"

"What if someone is trying to steal your saddle?"

"Oh that's silly," Helma said. "Anyone with half a brain would know we're out with the bees most of the day, rarely locking our house. I was in hospice for a month and Ernif was in town visiting me daily. If someone was trying to steal the saddle, there was plenty of opportunity without having to kill us."

She had a point. It still came back to who would benefit from them both being dead.

"Helma, did you and Ernif have a will?"

She shook her head again.

"So all your belongings will revert to the state and be disposed of at their choice?"

She shook her head again.

"Helma, that's impossible."

"Not if we gave all our belongings away in life rather than in death. Then there's no need to have a will."

Helma was so serene and still, I assumed she had fallen asleep.

"She gave it away?" I mouthed to Elizabeth.

"*They* gave it all away," Elizabeth replied. "Both of them. All of it."

As Helma's chest rose and fell in the steady rhythm of a deep sleep, Elizabeth motioned me to follow her out of the bedroom, quietly closing the door.

"Gave it all away? Everything?"

Elizabeth nodded. "They both signed a deed on this property and just hadn't recorded it yet."

"Is that legal?"

"Yep. The danger in not recording a deed is that the owner could sell a property twice. And the first person to record it at the courthouse owns the property. But there's no danger of the Hansons selling it twice."

"Crazy," I said, trying to make all the puzzle pieces fit in my head. "So, someone killed Ernif. And someone tried to kill Helma. If it wasn't for the inheritance, what was the killer's motivation? Was it because the Hansons knew something, heard or saw something?"

"I don't know. But I do know they haven't told a single soul that they already gifted their land and house in life. Except me. So maybe the killer thinks their property is still up for grabs."

"Or maybe you aren't the only exception. It would make sense they told whoever it was that now owns this place. Maybe whoever they gave this place to had to wait until both of them died to move in and decided to move it along." I saw Elizabeth open her mouth to respond, but the thought that came to my mind leapt from my lips. "Oh that's right! I meant to ask you and Helma in there. When she told me about teaching you how to cook and dress out a deer. Something about building a bunkhouse for the 'lost boys.' What was that all about, and does it have anything to do with the murderer's motivation?"

Elizabeth perched on the edge of the couch and patted the cushion next to her. I folded myself up in the sliver of space remaining, drawing my knees to my chin as I watched her splay a bunch of papers across the coffee table. Numerous sketches depicted the exterior and interior of two enormous buildings, both constructed of massive logs. The first set of sketches was of a bunkhouse with lots of beds, several bathrooms, and a nearby well. The second set of blueprints was for a sizable building that housed a gathering hall, a mess hall, and an educational center. In the main gathering room, the windows faced east, overlooking the bluff to the valley and creek below. A large circular indoor fire pit was surrounded by various styles of benches, chairs, and stools; a ground-view sketch showed how the hood of the fire pit would hang high enough above the fire to allow people to face each other as they sat in a circle.

My breath caught. "Amazing!"

"Isn't it?"

"Where is this place?"

"Here. In the future," Elizabeth said. I stared at her slack jawed. "I'll tell you all about the gift the Hansons have made to Saddleback Ranch for the lost boys. If you just close your mouth, dear."

"To the Saddleback Ranch? That's the new owner? Maybe it's someone there who's responsible for killing Ernif and trying to kill Helma. The Saddleback Ranch was involved directly with property on one of the Crooked Man cases. Maybe someone there is in a hurry to inherit this land, get started on the new place for lost boys," I speculated, my mind racing.

"They know nothing about this."

"How do you know that? Maybe the Hansons never told Saddleback Ranch, but maybe the new owner did. Where's the deed? I need to see the name on the unrecorded deed. That just might be the name of our killer. Of the Crooked Man."

Elizabeth frowned and handed me the single sheet of paper. I read the deed. The name was clear.

Elizabeth Bergen Elston.

CHAPTER 36

STREETER INSISTED ON HAVING dinner brought in to the office.

Garth Bergen had confirmed that Willis and Claudia Lipscomb, an elderly couple with no relatives to inherit their fortune made from a local car dealership, were law-abiding, upstanding citizens from Piedmont, just north of Rapid City. The reason they donated anonymously, according to Garth, was that they were raised to believe that the act of giving money, in and of itself, wasn't charitable; only by giving out of love, with no recognition for the gift, could it be considered truly charitable. To the Lipscombs, being recognized for their charity negated the godliness of the act. Liv's father also told Streeter that the couple donated anonymously, and in large quantities, to many of the organizations in the communities of western South Dakota.

Garth responded to Streeter's direct questions with refreshing efficiency and candidness, professing that there was absolutely no way either Willis or Claudia Lipscomb would or could murder another human being. When Streeter read Garth the dedication plaque from the anonymous donor who helped Saddleback Ranch with Pelley's bequeathed land, the elder statesman unequivocally discounted even the most remote possibility that the Lipscombs were involved in that donation, stating it sounded nothing like them with its reproachful, negative tone.

The only thing Garth could come up with about Tex Crawford was a vague recollection of someone over in Wyoming—maybe in Gillette or Sundance—with that name. But he admitted the memory was old, from a decade ago or more. Streeter was impressed by the depth of Mr. Bergen's knowledge about what made these people tick and thanked him for his contribution to the investigation.

Streeter had assigned Tate to research everything she could find out about Tex Crawford, Rowland Cowen, and Brett Appleton. Streeter asked Linwood to read through the files that Bly had scoured to see if there was a pattern or any other connection they might be missing, this time through the lens of the suspect being involved with Nature's Way, with the U.S. Forest Service, or as the anonymous donor.

Truth be known, Streeter wanted time to storyboard—to lay out his assumptions, theories, and findings and start working backward through the timeline. He couldn't argue with Tate's assessment that neither Brett Appleton nor Rowland Cowen had the discipline or patience required for the annual and methodical killing of selected individuals. Streeter focused all his attention on two assumptions: The murderer, The Crooked Man, was the anonymous donor known as Tex Crawford, and there was a connection with and significance to his reference to Custer's Last Stand and shooting ducks on a pond. And each time Streeter replayed the scenarios, he put a different face on the Crooked Man—Rowland Cowen, Brett Appleton, Mark Goodsell, Dr. Morgan, Steve Preston, Pastor Keeley, Anthony Burgess—to see if it fit. He likewise added a faceless name to the list, the anonymous Tex Crawford.

Sitting alongside Linwood in complete silence for what seemed like hours, Streeter went forward and backward through the case files looking for references related to any combination of the words Tex, Texas, Crawford, Custer, Crooked Man, and ducks on a pond. Something niggling on his conscience bothered him so much he aborted his file search and instead began a cyberspace search of differing phrases. His Internet search led him to Custer in the Black Hills in 1874, and Streeter started reading everything he could about the famous expedition. Liv had been correct; the mining laws of 1872 sparked interest in finding gold in the Black Hills, even though the land had already been given by treaty to the Indians. Treaties offered, signed, broken, ignored: The spoils of all the wars of the late 1800s between the U.S. government and the Native Americans continued to be debated, contested, and disputed more than a century later.

Just as Streeter's eyes landed on a map of Custer's 1874 expedition through the Black Hills, Tate burst into the quiet conference room and shouted, "He died! Was murdered."

"Who?" Streeter asked.

"Tex Crawford. He was shot at his ranch south of Sundance twelve years ago, six months *before* he filed for status as a limited liability company known as Godly Garden LLC. Tex Crawford was already dead." She was waving some papers in the air as if that explained everything.

Streeter was thinking about what Garth Bergen had said, his mind sliding back to someone of the same name who lived in Sundance or Gillette, Wyoming, not in South Dakota. Probably why he remembered the name, since murders were not all that common in this area, especially a shooting.

"Tex Crawford must be a fairly common name. Maybe it's a son. Or a different Crawford altogether," Streeter surmised.

"I checked. There are no Tex Crawfords in Wyoming or in South Dakota. Lots of Crawfords, nothing even remotely similar to Tex as a first name," Tate explained.

Linwood looked up from his files. "Maybe it's a nickname."

"Possible, but hear me out. On a whim, I called over to the clerk at Crook County and she made a special trip into the office. Guess who Tex's widow eventually sold the ranch to?"

"Nature's Way," Linwood said.

Tate nodded. "And I checked out the date. It fits. There might be a thirteenth victim of the Crooked Man. The *first* victim."

"The date?" Streeter asked, moving toward his map on the wall.

"July twenty-second. The year before what we thought was murder number one on July twenty-fourth. Wade Barns's death eleven years ago."

"Thirteen, not twelve," Streeter said, finding Sundance on the map. "Show me where he was killed, Tate."

She walked over to the map and located a spot twelve miles south of Sundance on Highway 585, and then she slid her finger three miles due west of the highway to the famous landmark known as the Inyan Kara.

"Right there."

Streeter noted that Tex Crawford's murder location was west of where Wade Barns had lived. That put it within the pattern of murders falling later in days and locations moving from west to east from year to year. "Thirteen murders," Streeter repeated. "In thirteen different years starting twelve years ago."

"And get this," Tate said. "Do you know what that ranch is best known for, why Nature's Way wanted to buy it from Tex Crawford's grieving relatives? Because Custer's name and the number seventy-four is carved at the summit of Inyan Kara."

"Custer's 1874 expedition?" Streeter asked.

"Exactly. And one year later we have Wade Barns's ranch eventually landing in the hands of Nature's Way via a forged document, remember?"

"Until the girlfriend Hocking fought back," Linwood reminded them.

"The Elk Foundation ending up with the ranch and Nature's Way with the naming rights." Streeter was following Tate's logic and didn't need convincing that Tex Crawford's death had been at the hands of the Crooked Man.

"Right again," said Tate. "And they named it Eden. Get it?"

Streeter noticed that Linwood was staring at Tate as intently as he had been. Neither got the importance.

"Eden," she repeated, as if they would grasp the notion once she repeated it. "Don't you get it? Tex Crawford is shot to death, murdered. Nature's Way buys the ranch from the family. Some South Dakotan benefactor, who wants to remain anonymous, files for an LLC with the name Tex Crawford as the sole member and names the newly formed corporation Godly Gardens LLC. Then six months later, Wade Barns is found dead. Murdered. Eventually, after a legal tug-of-war, Nature's Way settles for naming rights. And they call his place Eden. Get it? The Garden of Eden? Adam and Eve? Created by God?"

"Godly Gardens," Linwood repeated.

"Shows premeditation," she added. "If this is our killer."

With certainty, Streeter knew Tate was on to something.

"Same Godly Gardens that donates a boatload of money to the Pelley ranch, right?" Tate said. "Years after Tex Crawford is killed, donated by an LLC whose sole member is *named* Tex Crawford? A coincidence? I think not."

"And if our Godly Gardens' Tex Crawford is the Crooked Man, it means the same man who demanded the ominous plaque on the Pelley place—"

"Was the same man who clubbed Frank Pelley and left him to die in his stock pond. Easy as shooting ducks on a pond," Tate concluded, finishing Streeter's thought.

"This changes everything," Streeter said.

"And nothing," Linwood said. "We still don't know who assumed Tex Crawford's identity."

"True, but at least we know it's highly likely that our Nature's Way donor and anonymous benefactor, Godly Gardens LLC, a.k.a. Tex Crawford, is also our Crooked Man," Tate said.

"Likely," Streeter repeated.

"Crooked because he's stealing the land from the ranchers and somehow getting it into the Nature's Way inventory?" Linwood asked.

"And is it possible that Nature's Way would know nothing about this?" Tate asked.

"Possibly," Streeter guessed. "The donor may want to see the land protected by Nature's Way—or the gold that's on the land to be owned by the conservation group—but, unlike the organization, is willing to do anything to accomplish the goal."

"A rogue soldier for the war on conservationism," Linwood summarized.

"Exactly," Tate said. "You said it all along, Street. These murders feel more like criminal warfare. And that's what it appears to be. Criminal warfare with the spoils of war going to Nature's Way or to any other conservation group as an alternate plan."

"This doesn't prove anything," Linwood warned.

"No, but it may help us narrow our efforts," Streeter said. "Having heard all of this, what jumps to mind for you after studying all the files you reviewed, Linwood?"

"What comes to mind is the fight over Wade Barns's ranch. Remember, Nature's Way stepped aside and let Elk Foundation own the ground. The reason they didn't pursue criminal charges against Nature's Way for the forged document was because they insisted the land go where Hocking wanted it to go . . . *if* they were given the naming rights. I wonder why naming that ranch 'Eden' was so important? Tate, why would you think the anonymous donor had anything to do with the name? All we heard is that Nature's Way insisted on the name 'Eden.' And if Nature's Way is not involved with the murders, why would you associate 'Eden' with our killer?"

"It just fits. The Garden of Eden is God's original garden, the garden of all gardens. So the name Godly Gardens and Eden must be tied, right?"

"Not necessarily," Linwood said. "But what you asked of me, Streeter, was what jumps to mind after poring through the files and after hearing Jenna's information about Tex Crawford being shot. I find it quite telling that Godly Gardens LLC, the same entity that insisted on that horrible dedication plaque for Camp Saddleback, was created six months *after* Tex Crawford's murder *by* a Tex Crawford."

"We need to follow the thread that may exist in the naming rights since that seemed to be important in the Wade Barns case."

Streeter nodded in agreement. "Okay then, you two pay a visit to Mark Goodsell tonight. Find out the names of all the ranches they have under easement or under deed. I'm going to keep working the files. Meet back here as soon as you're done."

CHAPTER 37

Sunday, August 11, 12:37 AM

IT WAS MIDNIGHT BY the time they called it quits and headed back to the hotel.

Streeter was in the shower when he heard the knock on his door. Sliding on his khaki pants, commando style, and shirtless, he opened the door. Before he could refuse, Tate pushed through the opening and ducked under his bare arm, raking her fingernails across his ribs as she slid around him.

He stood at the open door, refusing to give her the satisfaction of closing it, and asked, "What do you want, Tate? It's late. I'm tired."

"I want to know what you've got against me?"

He frowned. "Nothing. You're a bright, talented agent. You've done a good job on this case."

"I mean, what have you got against *me?*"

He felt her beside him pushing the door gently closed and sliding the bolt into place. He clenched his jaw and stood rod straight in response.

"Come on. All work and no play makes Streeter a dull boy," she said, pressing her breasts against his bare stomach. He could feel her skin, warm and soft, through the sheer fabric of her camisole. Her nipples erect, she pressed against him and he nearly groaned with a pleasure he didn't want to feel. He reminded himself that raw sexuality between the two of them was what started their failed relationship last time.

"I prefer dull," he said, unbolting the door and opening it wide.

Tate ignored his rebuff, bumped the door closed with her firm buttocks, and pulled him into her. Her lips were on him as she drew his face down to hers, her tongue hot and sweet as she pressed her hips against his thigh. At first he didn't kiss her back. Then an image of Liv kissing Linwood flashed in his mind's eye and he slammed his body against Tate's, grinding hard against her as she moaned, pulled his hair, and wrapped her legs around his waist.

Before he realized it, she was fumbling with his zipper.

Something deep in his subconscious snapped. Stepping back, releasing her from her pinned position against the door, she clung to him like a koala bear on a bamboo pole, staring at him as he straightened.

"What is it?"

"We can't do this, Tate."

"Why not?"

"We work together."

"So?"

"I'd only be doing it for the sex."

"So what's new?"

Their history reminded him of a particular obstacle at Paris Island. What the Marines at the boot camp referred to as The Crucible. A virtually impossible obstacle to overcome.

"Get out, Tate. We both need sleep."

After an interminably long silence and without another word of protest, Tate left.

━━━━━━

After a long, cold shower, Streeter regrouped and caught his second wind, opting to study the list of names Linwood and Tate had retrieved from Mark Goodsell earlier that night. He took the list of the ranches donated, or purchased by Nature's Way from—unless otherwise noted—the murder victims or their survivors, and added beside each the date and the name of the man who had been murdered there.

Year 1   Tex Crawford, July 22, Summit Ranch

Year 2   Wade Barns, July 24, Eden (Named by Nature's Way)

Year 3   Buddy Richards, July 26, Survivors Ranch

Year 4   Homer Larson, July 25, Freak of Nature Ranch

Year 5   Greg Schumacher, July 28, Mystical Pyramid Ranch

Year 6   Bobby Daniels, July 29, Left to Chance Ranch

Year 7   Chris Night Hawk, July 30, All That Glitters Ranch

Year 8   Maurice Castle, August 2 through 5, Pay Dirt Ranch

Year 9   Frank Pelley, August 6, Camp Saddleback (Not Nature's Way)

Year 10   Steven Tuttle, August 8, Rough Ride Ranch

Year 11   Donny Finch, August 12, Ballpark Ranch

Year 12   Evan Drummer, August 14 or 15, Hot Dry Breath of Prairie

Year 13   Ernif Hanson, August 4 (TBD)

Streeter jotted down his thoughts on the investigation. Thirteen murders in thirteen different years starting twelve years ago, nearly twelve months apart to the day. Different methods of death, but likely all related to the Crooked Man, based on the murderer's calling card of a sixpence left at each crime scene. All ranchers, most widowers, most without anyone to inherit their property. Eleven of thirteen owned, controlled, or named by Nature's Way. An unusual coincidence with a tie to General Custer on a handful of the ranches. The first, Inyan Kara, with "74 Custer" carved in the rock at the mountain's summit. Another with the ominous dedication plaque at Pelley's property. A third, the artifacts from the expedition, and the original GAC saddle, found on the Hanson ranch.

None of this made sense.

He looked at the clock. One thirty in the morning. He needed to get some sleep, yet Streeter didn't feel the least bit tired. He decided to go for a walk. He pulled on a T-shirt, slipped on shoes, and grabbed his room key.

Thirty minutes later, as he returned through the lobby, something in the gift shop window caught his eye. He moved toward it, staring at the cover. Before the desk clerk, who was also the night manager, could unlock the door and retrieve the book for him, he knew it held answers he'd had questions about concerning the thirteen murders and the tie to Custer. The book was *Exploring with Custer: The 1874 Black Hills Expedition,* by Ernest Grafe and Paul Horsted.

Within twenty minutes, Streeter punched in Jenna Tate's number.

"Can you come back to my room? Please?"

CHAPTER 38

WHEN THE TOE OF his shoe snagged on a thick twig underneath the tangle of thatched grasses, he cursed under his breath. Nearly spilling to the ground, he caught himself on a nearby pine branch, and used it to pull up and steady himself. In the pitch dark, he had forgotten how limited his sense of feeling had become, because he relied so heavily on his sense of sight in daylight. He thought he knew the woods well enough to pick his way through the trees along the meadow, using nothing but the starlight to guide him through the shadows. So far, he'd been able to maneuver around rocks, through the trees, and over the downed timber without incident. But, he noted, when he walked over flat, clear ground with no obvious obstacles, he tripped up, which reminded him how important it was to remain aware and alert at all times, not just when conditions called for it.

Staying aware and alert had allowed him up to now to accomplish everything he had achieved. Taking advantage of every opportunity to embrace his legacy, regardless of any obstacles in his life or any controversy that had lingered from his ancestry. Once and for all he would right the family wrong, set the record straight. He came from a long line of compassionate and capable professionals, not careless butchers and killers, like some people, whose family legacy was neglect.

His mind drifted back in time when he heard the story about a boy—not much older than he was when he heard it—who experienced a horror on a night like this.

Not quite the bedtime story most fathers tell their sons, but one his father told him—an impressionable seven-year-old—during visiting hours one Sunday shortly after a jury convicted him to life without parole. His father's foreboding tone that day should have alerted him to the corroded spell his story would cast on the rest of his life. Particularly since he never saw his father again. Alive.

———

"The boy said he had been awakened by a blood-curdling scream. His mother, having heard nothing of the sort, assured him it was probably a rabbit that got trapped by a coyote. But he didn't believe her and had to see for himself." His father's voice was low and hushed, like he was sharing the darkest of secrets with him.

"He slipped on his boots and snuck out the window wearing nothing but a nightshirt. He carried a buck knife in one tiny hand and a slingshot in the other. He crept through the shadows of the woods. To find the coyote. See him gnawing on the bones of that rabbit with his own eyes. But somewhere deep in his heart, he knew he wouldn't find that coyote. Or the rabbit." He wanted to ask his father why it was so important to him to spend their precious visiting hours this week on such a scary tale.

"When he reached the crest of the rolling hill between his house and the pasture where they kept the horses, he saw it and knew. He told his innocent eyes to look away, his young feet to run back to the house and get his mother. She'd know what to do. She always knew what to do. She'd had all the answers for him, even after his pops had died in a tragic lumber mill accident."

His grandmama was off talking to the warden or someone about his father today and she had left him all alone. With his father. With the rest of the prisoners and their families. Only, the story was being told just for him.

"Instead," his father continued, "his feet defied him and moved steadily toward the shadowy figure in the middle of the meadow beneath the flagpole, the crescent moon shining like a spotlight in the final act of a Broadway musical. The horses had disappeared into the trees, keeping their distance from whatever rested against the single tombstone in the middle of the meadow, the memorial he'd mowed, pulled weeds from, and cared for his entire young life, just as his pops had taught him to do."

He wondered if there was any way that the families sitting behind them or at the end of the table where he and his father sat could hear this conversation, scared that he might be the only one who could. And that no one would believe this frightening story of a boy not much older than he.

"As he crept toward the figure, he dragged his feet through the grass, feeling for the familiar bump and tumble of rocks, his eyes pinned to the lump on the headstone. Each time his toe struck a sizable rock—big enough for his slingshot but not too big to fit in the leather pouch that was the sling—he scooped it up and shoved it into the pocket of his nightshirt. When he came within a few yards of the headstone, he laid the buck knife at his feet, slipped a rock from his pocket and placed it into the sling, aimed and shot at the mass near the headstone. The rock hit his target with a sickening thud, causing the mass to moan."

He wanted to tell his father to stop, slam his tiny hands against his ears and scream so he couldn't hear the rest of the story.

"He scrambled to find the buck knife, his knees and fingers trembling. But the monster in the moonlight hadn't charged in his direction, hadn't awakened and sniffed him out, didn't move an inch. Holding his knife out in front of him, he crept forward on his tiptoes, step by step. Lifting his knife high above his head, he readied himself in case the shadowy figure leaped up at him. His little arm trembled as he approached, the weight of the rocks felt reassuringly heavy in his pocket."

His father's eyes were wild and excited.

"Father, stop. Please."

He didn't. Wouldn't.

"Just as he approached the lump that was draped across the famous headstone, his eyes were drawn to the ground. The grass he had mown just two days earlier was covered in a sticky dark substance that left a familiar smell in his nostrils, taste on his tongue. Like when he and his granddaddy and pops would dress out a deer, careful not to get the innards on their clothes or near the meat they butchered."

"Please?" His voice sounded so small.

His father's smile was cruel. There was no way he could stop him from telling the story. "He took one squishy step onto the patch of mowed grass and froze. The figure draped across the headstone was not a deer, but a man. And the groaning was unmistakable. One of an injured man. A man in great pain."

"Stop it."

His father's eyes grew even wider. "'Boy. Come,' the man groaned. He stood staring at the man, trying to reconcile the familiar voice with the body folded over the headstone as if he'd collapsed on it. 'Boy?' It was definitely the voice of his granddaddy. But his granddaddy was strong and tall, not weak and helpless like this man."

"Visiting hours are almost over. I'm going to find Grandmama."

His father reached across the table and gripped his arm. "The boy's mind told him to run and get his mother," the father continued, "but again his tiny feet defied him, taking three short steps to the headstone, where the man turned his face to him. 'Granddaddy?' The man smiled. 'Help. Help me.' The boy asked, 'How?' The man took several labored breaths and motioned for the boy to come closer. He took a hesitant step forward, dropped his slingshot in the sticky grass, and touched his granddaddy's head. 'Grab my arm. Roll me off.' He heard the labored breathing, knew his granddaddy was hurting, but was still too scared to let go of the knife and do what his granddaddy had told him to do. What if he was not his granddaddy? What if this was a ghost?"

He felt like crying. But his father didn't stop.

"Maybe this was all a bad dream. Or like in Little Red Riding Hood, maybe this was a coyote dressed up like his granddaddy. And he was the rabbit. About to get eaten. 'Boy,' his granddaddy coughed. In that instant, the eight-year-old boy abandoned his childhood, dropped his knife, and yanked with all his strength on his granddaddy's arm until he managed to make his granddaddy's body tumble to the ground onto his back. His granddaddy passed out from the pain. But not before he howled like a madman. Seeing his granddaddy's innards strewn across the headstone and beside him on the mowed grass, he screamed in horror."

He peed his pants. Right there in the prison cafeteria, the visiting area for families.

"His granddaddy's feral howl echoed through the hills. His mind's eye forever locked on the deep, dark gash down the middle of his granddaddy's belly. Dressed out like a deer. The sticky grass. The smell."

His father didn't notice the sour smell of urine, the tears that streamed down his cheeks, the pleading in his eyes. Instead, he continued his story.

"He stood there screaming until his throat ached, the sound gone, replaced by sirens as a fire truck and an ambulance picked their way from the road across the meadow to the headstone. Dawn was breaking by the time his granddaddy was strapped onto a gurney with leather belts, the emergency team shoving his granddaddy's innards back into the cavity of his body before they moved him. His mother never thought to cover his eyes, just his mouth, as he stood as rigid as a two by six. Screaming."

His father pinned him with an icy stare that nearly froze his young blood.

"That's the story he told in court. That got me here, boy. Do you understand?"

"Yes, sir," he said that day. The last words he ever said to his father.

Years later, he tracked down that boy. Asked him questions. Told him he read about the case. Never told him who he really was, who his father was, how he'd committed suicide in prison all because of his testimony in court that day. When he was a boy not much older than himself.

And the boy he tracked down, who was a college student eager to unburden himself of his boyhood woes, explained that it wasn't until he took an American history class in college that he learned the significance of that headstone and why his granddaddy was killed the way he was, dressed out like a deer, left to die a painful death. His mother had never told him that her paternal grandfather, his great granddaddy, was the medical officer blamed for the death of the soldier whose grave he tended to all those years. His mother never told him that his great-granddaddy was dubbed "the butcher"—never shaking the horrible moniker—because two soldiers died of dysentery while under his care during Custer's Expedition, a slow and painful death.

Since then, he had explained that the significance of his family's allegiance to that particular piece of ground and the sacrifices his family had made in an attempt to rewrite history compelled him to overcome all his obstacles and pursue a life of self-actualization. For his great-granddaddy's sake and for the preservation of his family's good name. So that his grand-daddy hadn't died in vain. As unpleasant as it was for him to witness his granddaddy's suffering, good had come of it because he worked hard his entire life to be the most caring, compassionate person he could be.

Tsk, tsk. Forgive him if he didn't shed a tear or two over such a sad story. *His* story was a sad one, too. And that boy's granddaddy was the cause of him becoming an orphan, was the reason he had to listen to that awful story at such a young age. How he found out his mother had died during childbirth while in the care of the other boy's granddaddy. And how he came to understand why his father committed suicide instead of being committed to a psych ward for the rest of his life.

As if the motivation for vindicating his parents' deaths wasn't enough, he had used every image from his father's story to propel him to perform each vile act, like the one he was creeping through the woods to do tonight. Much good would come of this too.

It was *his* family who'd be vindicated, *his* daddy who would not die in vain. Forget about the butcher's family. Better yet, remember them with rage and disgust. For centuries to come. He had spent a lifetime studying, planning, and preparing. He memorized events in history, studied police procedurals, invested countless hours in courthouses to exact his revenge. Even interviewed a serial killer on death row to authenticate a concocted MO. And the time was near to enjoy the fruits of his lifelong labor.

He stepped out of the shadows and shuffled toward the cabin, duck-ing beneath the window to catch his breath. He slowly rose to peek in the picture window and saw the familiar living room of Helma and Ernif. No movement, no sound, no light.

He glanced at his watch and saw that it was nearing three thirty in the morning. The sun would be stretching its warm tendrils across this meadow within the hour, so he mentally calculated his next moves, know-ing he'd likely find the imp known as Elizabeth in the spare bedroom down the hall on the right and Helma in the master bedroom at the end of the hall. He decided to take out Elizabeth first, then Helma.

Redemption.

Although he had no beef with Elizabeth, she hadn't left Helma alone since. He should have completed the task on Wednesday morning when he had the chance. But this was less messy, more in line with what the Crooked Man would do, he thought. Besides, he needed that final piece of ground, his final offering to set the world back on its rightful axis as far as his family was concerned. Then he would take his final revenge. He would kill the last descendant of "the butcher" who started all this. *His* family would finally be vindicated. Heroes. While *their* family name would rightly strike a synonymous chord with the careless, neglectful drunk and butcher who started all this.

Helma Hanson's battle with cancer had been valiant, but her war with the disease was almost over now. Her and her husband's time had come. It was time for those with a greater purpose, a common good that would come from the few who reached self-actualization and were striving to achieve more for all those who would never be capable of attaining it for themselves.

Beyond one, for many.

And he would not allow cancer to do the job he was destined to do— destined since that day he visited his father in prison. Destined since he heard the horrifying story of how a boy, just a bit older than he, had landed his father behind bars. And six feet under.

The door was not locked, just like on Thursday night, and the couch would still be pushed against the door. Only this time, he knew to be more careful, more patient. He twisted the knob slowly, pushing the door open millimeters at a time so as not to make a single squeaking sound. Careful to tiptoe around the couch, across the floorboards, willing himself to be light-footed, he found himself standing beside the open door of the guest bedroom, as silent, still, and unnoticed as a shadow.

He heard breathing, the sounds of slumber.

Waiting for his eyes to adjust to the darkness in the house, no starlight creeping in to this bedroom, he readied his weapon, knowing he would be bedside in two or three quick steps. He drew in a deep breath and placed one foot in the room, stepping on something that wriggled beneath his feet and yelped in pain.

A dog.

The dog growled and chomped at him in the dark, biting through his pant leg and latching onto his anklebone. He let out a muffled cry and ripped his leg free from the dog's teeth, swinging in the dark with his weapon until he felt the vibration through his palms as he landed a solid thump to the dog's body. The dog yapped and growled between whimpers. He heard two women rustling in the dark, one fumbled for the lamp switch, cursing, "Where's my gawd damn gun?" while the other one yelled, "Stop or I'll shoot!"

He hadn't expected a gun. Or a dog. Or more than one woman in the bedroom. He only saw one vehicle by the house. A pickup truck, which he assumed was Elizabeth's. He hadn't accounted for this. For killing three women. Despite his plans to the contrary, and ignoring the command to stop, he clumsily retreated in the dark down the hall, holding his breath with each labored step on his bleeding ankle. He pitched the couch easily away from the door, swung it open wide, and exploded onto the front porch. He heard the dog howling and baying behind him, a woman yelling at the dog to stay. He saw the lights snap on throughout the house, which helped him find his way more easily in the dark outdoors. He hurried for the cover of darkness in the trees and shuffled quickly through the woods, avoiding the beehives, out to Telegraph Gulch Road where he had left his car parked in the ditch.

He drove off with no lights, using the starlight to guide him until he was at a safe distance down the dark, desolate highway. He pulled over under a street light in Hill City and raised his pant leg to assess the damage. His sock was soaked, his shoe full of blood.

And he cursed under his breath.

CHAPTER 39

"WELL, THAT WAS WORTH being awakened at two fifteen in the morning," Tate said, yawning and stretching as she rose from Streeter's bed.

Streeter watched as she ran her long fingernails through the blonde hair, fluffing and primping in the mirror, securing her flowing locks with an elastic band at the nape of her neck. Even with no sleep and little primping, Jenna Tate remained drop-dead gorgeous.

"I agree," Linwood said, pushing off the bed and away from the scatter of papers and heavily tabbed book. "How did you stumble across this?"

"I went for a walk to clear my head," Streeter admitted, leaving out the part about Tate's earlier visit.

"At two o'clock in the morning?" Linwood said.

"Sometimes I have trouble sleeping," Streeter said, glancing over at Tate.

Tate strode across the room and opened the hotel door wide, propping it open with a chair. Turning back to the two, she said, "Afraid they might get the wrong room and I won't get my coffee."

Soon afterward, the hotel server greeted the three and wheeled the cart into the room. On it were two pots of coffee and three plates of eggs, sausage, toast, and hash browns, a platter of fruit and cheese, and three bowls of oatmeal. They all thanked the server, Tate stuffing a tip into her palm before closing the door behind her.

Linwood whistled. "That's a lot of food."

"Tate, do you eat like this every morning?"

"Only when I work all night and haven't had any sleep." She poured three coffees, grabbed a plate, and sat cross-legged on the bed. Around mouthfuls of food, she asked, "So every date and name matches a day of travel for Custer's Expedition?"

"Right," Streeter said, stabbing a sausage with his fork and eating half of it. Chasing it with coffee, he explained. "Tex Crawford was shot on July twenty-second near Inyan Kara. His ranch was sold at the widow's urging to Nature's Way and was called Summit Ranch because of the famous carving of General Custer's name and year of the expedition on the mountaintop. Not so unusual. Alone, this murder would seem to have the most natural tie to the Custer Expedition reference. That tie turns ominous, though, when placed in the context of the 1874 Custer Expedition. A man was shot on that same day, July twenty-second, in a scuffle that was attributed to—and I quote—'a lippy Texan' who apparently deserved it. A bit of a stretch by itself, but as each murder is analyzed, it all fits."

"Tell me again," Tate insisted.

"Let's stick with how we can prove my theory based on the first murder. Then everything else will fall into place.

"Tex Crawford is shot. Six months later, an entity known as Godly Gardens is created as a South Dakotan LLC by a Tex Crawford, who doesn't seem to exist. No one found in South Dakota with that name. And the only one nearby named Tex Crawford, from Sundance, Wyoming, has been dead for six months by the time of the filing."

Pouring everyone more coffee, Tate added, "Our killer, most likely."

"Speculation," Streeter said. "But if we prove that whoever is murdering all these people was the one to start this entity, then the prosecutors have a conviction with malice aforethought."

"Premeditated. Which stands to reason, considering every single one of the thirteen murders was planned for a specific date," Tate said. "Even the first. Although I'm still thrown by the Crooked Man's use of a gun, a weapon so alarmingly different than the one used in the other murders."

"The first murder may have been accidental," Streeter speculated.

"Second year, next murder, Wade Barns, July twenty-fourth," Linwood said, spooning oatmeal from the bowl. "Eden, because when Custer's men rode through that part of the country, they likened the area to the Garden of Eden, so full of berries, rocky outcrops, and lush valleys."

"Left a clue for us by leaving Wade Barns in the raspberry bush," Streeter said.

"Mouth stuffed with berries," Linwood added.

"Not a ranch that Nature's Way ended up owning, but I bet if we pursue handwriting analysis on the forged document and compare it to the Crooked Man's, we'll find a match," Tate said.

"He got smarter after the second murder," Streeter said. "Changed up the MO by making it look more like an accident, but used the same weapon and didn't force the issue of leaving the land to Nature's Way with forged documents."

"That we know of," Tate added.

Streeter nodded.

"Third year, Buddy Richards. Murdered on July twenty-sixth near Deerfield Lake, which is where Custer and his men encountered their first Indian in the Hills. They were surprised the Indians didn't try to kill them. Hence, Survivors Ranch."

Linwood was gnawing on a piece of toast, flipping through the compiled notes. "Fourth year, Freak of Nature Ranch, which was Homer Larson's property, with Cold Creek running through it. Freakish indeed, because Custer's scientists mentioned it was the sole creek they'd ever seen where the supply of water increased only to have the size of the creek grow smaller."

"They probably weren't aware of the porous nature of the limestone around here and the many sinkholes in the creek beds throughout the Black Hills," Streeter said. "And this murder was out of order by date. Homer Larson was killed July twenty-fifth. The year before, the murder was committed on July twenty-sixth."

"But the dates and places do coincide with the Expedition diaries," Linwood said, flipping through the tabs.

"My point is that the Crooked Man got smarter and planned better as the years passed."

"Fifth?" Tate asked, polishing off the last of her breakfast platter and moving to Linwood's untouched plate of eggs.

Linwood read from his notes. "Greg Schumacher, July twenty-eighth, Mystical Pyramid Ranch."

"Oh yeah, that's the one where the pyramid of antlers was piled up in the middle of a prairie," Tate said, wiping her fingers on the linen napkin.

"We almost missed this one," Streeter said. "Schumacher was first thought to have been an accidental death, gored by an elk while mending fence along Reynolds Prairie."

"But after Bly suggested it might be part of the Crooked Man case, Dr. Johnson confirmed the head wound was consistent with the previous cases," Linwood reminded them.

"Right," Streeter said, draining his coffee. "And Berta's initial assessment was that this was no accident. Based on the location and depth of the wounds, she concluded the man was first stabbed in the face with a set of antlers, then clubbed on the back of the head and skewered again in the chest with the same set of antlers."

"Bad luck," Tate said. "And sixth?"

Linwood flipped through pages in his notepad, having more difficulty finding this case. "Bobby Daniels, July twenty-ninth, Left to Chance Ranch. This one was outside Hill City near Medicine Mountain. It was here that one of Custer's soldiers shot a deer, then was kicked by a horse, leaving the soldier with an injured leg."

"And he left his injury to heal by chance?" Tate asked, popping a sausage in her mouth.

"No, his name was Lieutenant Chance."

"Left to Chance Ranch. Clever," Streeter said. "Make sure we get Berta to pull up that particular autopsy and see if she can determine if Daniels's broken leg was caused by the same weapon that was used on his skull."

"Got it. Seventh murder was Chris Night Hawk, July thirtieth, All That Glitters Ranch," Linwood said, thumbing to the next page on his pad. "He was the guy who worked at the mica plant and owned a small place along French Creek, one of the major gold discoveries in the Black Hills by that expedition team."

"And finally we know why this one was killed at the mica plant. The killer was taunting us. Mica glitters," Streeter said. "Liv was on to something there too. She thought that someone might be accumulating properties with gold potential."

"Who would have guessed that the reason was for historic preservation of land that was significant because of the exploration *preceding* the gold rush?" Tate added.

"Eighth murder, year eight, was Maurice Castle, near the same area as Night Hawk," Streeter said. "Sometime between August second and fifth, Castle was found crushed by his horse. The Pay Dirt Ranch."

"Remember, this one was left as an accidental death until Bly connected the dates and Castle's head wound was compared with Night Hawk's and others," Streeter explained. "Definitely the same weapon as the one used in the Crooked Man cases, according to Berta."

"What did all that have to do with Custer's expedition?" Tate asked.

Linwood looked up over his pad of paper at her. "Everything. During that same time period, they had one of their men nearly killed when a horse toppled over him in the same area, just south of Calamity Peak."

"You're kidding, right?"

"No," Linwood said, flipping more pages. "Ninth murder, ninth year, Frank Pelley, August sixth, which we know well by now. Land gifted by Frank Pelley to Saddleback Ranch, and an anonymous donor read about his good deed and offered more money to establish a wildlife preserve as long as no structures other than Pelley's original cabin were ever constructed. And that weird dedication plaque was mounted."

"But this is where the strongest tie exists between the donor and the murders to date," Streeter said. "It was here, on Frank Pelley's land, one mile north of Green Mountain, southeast of Deerfield Lake on what is known as the Gillette Prairie, where General Custer himself was quoted as saying, 'I will knock the heads off a few of them,' referring to the ducks that were swimming around the pond. Historians say Custer was mocked for being a bad shot, and on that day—after making such a bold proclamation about some ducks on a pond—he proceeded to shoot again and again, missing over and over."

"Oh dear," Tate said.

"And remember the dedication? 'Nothing in life comes as easy as shooting ducks on a pond. And those who think otherwise will eventually make a miscalculation as big as the Battle of Little Bighorn.'" Linwood was reading from his notes again. "Our killer was mocking Custer but also mocking us. For not figuring out who he was."

"Like the trail of sixpence. Our killer is extremely intelligent. Subtle. Yet he was practically posting a neon sign saying you're too stupid to catch me," Tate said ruefully.

"And he's right," confessed Streeter. "I missed it."

"*Shank* missed it, Streeter," Linwood corrected him. "*You* were in Denver by that time, remember? And you were only on the case as lead investigator for months before . . ."

"It was my case," Streeter said. "I should have tried harder. Maybe so many people wouldn't be dead."

Tate walked over to where Streeter sat and started rubbing his neck and shoulder muscles while he ate. He didn't resist.

Linwood continued. "Tenth murder, tenth year, Steven Tuttle, August eighth, Rough Ride Ranch."

"We almost missed this one, too, if it wasn't for Bly seeing the pattern of dates and finding it," Streeter said. "Eight miles northwest of Nemo. Our killer was trying to stage what happened back in 1874. One soldier was so scared of being scalped by Indians, he got his wagon stuck between some trees, and he nearly whipped his mules to death trying to force them to pull him out of there."

"So the Crooked Man lured our drunk Tuttle to the same spot, somehow got Tuttle's car wedged between two trees, and smashed in his face, his head, and his windshield for good measure?" Tate asked.

"Probably used the same weapon on the windshield as he had on Tuttle's skull."

"Dr. Johnson said Tuttle's facial injuries were consistent with hitting the steering wheel," Linwood reminded them.

"It would have been easy for the Crooked Man to slam a drunkard's face against the steering wheel, rendering Tuttle unconscious, before staging the car, delivering the fatal blow to his skull, then smashing up the windshield to make it look like an accident," Streeter asserted.

"And how in the world did Stewart Blysdorf figure out that a drunk found dead in his car jammed between two trees wasn't just a typical DUI accident?" Tate asked.

"He noticed the pattern and filled in the holes, which led us to the autopsy reports and the same type wound, unexplained, from what appeared to be a round weapon," Streeter reminded her.

"My hero," Tate sighed.

"Mine too," Streeter said. "So be nicer to him, will you?"

"Maybe," Tate said, stepping away from Streeter and placing all the breakfast plates onto the cart. As she wheeled it out the door, she called to Linwood over her shoulder, "Eleven?"

"Donny Finch, August twelfth, Ballpark Ranch, near the intersection of Norris Peak Road and Nemo Road. Donny was beaten with a baseball bat. Though it wasn't a bat exactly," Linwood corrected himself. "Dr. Johnson agreed with the conclusion that Donny Finch was beaten about the body with the bat left behind at the scene. And she's asked for the bat to be pulled from evidence to retest for DNA or fibers. But she said the bat was inconsistent with the wound to the back of the skull."

"Of course," Tate said. "Why the bat, then?"

"The soldiers played ball in what they called Genevieve Park back in 1874."

"So you're telling me our murderer brought in a weapon and a bat when he killed Donny Finch? Why would he do that?"

"I believe the weapon of choice has a purpose," Streeter said. "The rest of the tools he brings in, like the bat, are tools to stage the crime scene, to emulate the story of Custer's expedition. He's crafting a message. He is smart enough to leave clues yet evade capture. Brilliant, really."

"Murder twelve was Evan Drummer, August fourteenth or fifteenth, Hot Dry Breath of Prairie. Evan was found spread eagle on his property, fried to a crisp by the sun, which meant the blow to the head hadn't quite killed him. His ranch was near Bear Butte, east of Sturgis. One of Custer's men, Ludlow I think, called that area a hot dry breath of prairie, which is what Nature's Way named the ranch."

"And the thirteenth murder was Ernif Hanson," Tate said. "Killed on August fourth. And it doesn't match when Custer was on that property? It's out of order?"

"I can't think of an explanation as to why Ernif was killed on the fourth instead of the seventh. But I understand why the murder was out of order with the rest. Where Custer killed the grizzly is the most recognizable event of Custer's expedition. If he had killed Ernif in date order, he likely believed we would have understood the connection of the killings to the 1874 expedition long before now. And if it wasn't for Liv remembering the photo of the grizzly bear on that same rock in 1874, I might not have pieced this together. But if Liv recognized the location, other locals might, too. So he waited until the end."

"How are you so sure this is the end?" Linwood asked.

"Because," Streeter said, reaching for the book on the bed and thumbing through it. "Hot Dry Breath of Prairie. August 14 and 15 were the last days of Custer's expedition in the Black Hills area before heading back north to the fort. Plus, the Hanson place was the crown jewel of locations. This is not only the headwaters for Rapid Creek but also a historically memorable site. Our killer knew that. Actually staged the body accordingly. Liv said the photos of Ernif reminded her of Custer's grizzly bear. Ernif was murdered on the very rock where Custer allegedly shot a grizzly bear. The most famous picture and lasting memory from Custer's expedition in 1874. Dated August seventh."

Streeter held up the book for Tate and Linwood to see, the grizzly bear on its belly, flopped across the jutting rock outcrop on the side of the hill, with Custer and some of his men standing nearby. Then Streeter lifted the picture of Ernif Hanson, splayed into the same pose on the same rock.

"If he had committed this murder in order, our killer might have been caught before he completed all his planned murders. I think this murder was planned to be the last. Other than the incidental smothering of Helma Hanson on the morning of August 7."

"I didn't see how that was related to the Crooked Man because it's such a deviation from the others. But now I see what you were saying about your instincts," Tate admitted.

"Instinct, and I believed Helma Hanson's account about the other night," Streeter said. "It explains everything. Our killer knew Helma's days were numbered, considering she was in hospice, but he wanted her to die on August 7. An extremely symbolic day for him."

"Plus, he dropped the sixpence the night he tried to kill Helma," Tate said.

"Probably accidentally."

"He was leaving us calling cards at every murder scene. You think Helma's safe now that it's the tenth?" Tate asked.

"I think she's been safe because she's had the Bergen sisters stay with her. And because we instructed Liv to stand guard. But we need to get more people up there today."

"Unless we miss our mark, the Crooked Man is probably upset he missed his opportunity to commemorate the seventh by killing Helma, but he'll likely just wait for the cancer to finish her off," Linwood speculated. "Don't you agree?"

"I'm not sure."

"All these murders, the names of the ranches, tie to Nature's Way," Tate said.

"Without question," Linwood said.

"We need to get some answers from Mark Goodsell," Streeter said. "Now."

CHAPTER 40

"I'M SUING FOR ENTRAPMENT," Cowen barked at Tate.

Mark Goodsell had spent nearly an hour cajoling his direct report, Rowland Cowen, to return to the conference room.

Cowen remained unapologetic for his childish tantrum about Jenna Tate betraying him.

"Entrapment is when someone like me from law enforcement induces someone like you to commit an illegal act that you would otherwise not have done," Tate said.

Cowen's face reddened when Tate conceded he would have a valid complaint if South Dakota law prohibited two consenting adults from having sex. Tate even went so far as to shamelessly admit she had enticed him to have sex with her.

"But I wouldn't have done that if I'd known," he protested.

"Wouldn't have done what?" Tate said, not the least bit embarrassed. "Had sex with a woman?"

"No, I mean yes. I mean, what does sex have to do with anything? Do you see that?" he asked, hands lifted like he was surrendering to Streeter. "She twists everything. She's evil."

"You didn't think I was evil when I had your hands bound behind your back, wearing only my underwear while I spanked you," Tate added.

Streeter knew Tate well enough to see that she was not telling the truth, only trying to get Cowen angry and frustrated.

"That's not true. None of it. What I mean is she tricked me into talking. We never even had sex," Cowen spat, ignoring Goodsell's suggestions to calm down.

"So you wouldn't have sex with a woman?" Tate goaded. "Just men like Steve Preston?"

"Leave him out of this."

"Does Dr. Morgan know how close you and Steve have become?" Tate pressed.

Streeter marveled at Tate's techniques, knowing she was renowned in the bureau for being the best at setting up just such an interrogation.

"Oh, man. I wouldn't have said anything bad about Morgan, or Senator Billings, or South Dakota, or all the rich people around here too cheap to pitch in a few bucks to save the environment. I wouldn't have said I hate miners, loggers. You tricked me into saying all that!"

"Don't forget the ranchers," Tate said. "Didn't you call them . . . stupid cows?"

He stood at the table, his cheeks a deep crimson, the cords of his neck bulging.

"Rowland, sit down and shut up. Now!" Goodsell demanded.

He did.

Goodsell sat beside him, a purple vein popping from the translucent skin of his forehead. "Let's move past this. We're here to help, so let's hear what you have for us."

Streeter powered up the wall-mounted screen along with his computer. The slideshow flashed from picture to picture, one by one, showing the thirteen bodies found bludgeoned, gored, or crushed to death. The series started with the second murder, committed twelve years earlier, and went up through Monday morning's discovery of Ernif Hanson. The series ended with the first of the thirteen murders, that of the smiling cowboy in his middle fifties. The photo showed him wearing a dark brown beaver-skin cowboy hat, sweat clinging to his forehead. The man, sporting a five o'clock shadow, was sucking on flowering wheat grass and looking off into the distance to the camera's left, his right.

"This man was shot twelve years ago. Recognize him?"

Both men, who'd been grimacing and trying to avert their eyes from the previous photos, leaned forward and studied the man. Streeter genuinely believed they had no clue who this was.

"Does Tex Crawford ring a bell?" Tate said, the question directed at Cowen.

Cowen's netted eyebrows relaxed, his eyes widened. "Summit Ranch. In Sundance. I remember hearing about this guy."

"Who is he?"

"A legend. He got shot. Papers said he was known around Sundance as the Lippy Texan. Someone shot him one night and they never did figure out who did it."

"Did you shoot him?" Tate said.

"Go to hell," Cowen said. "I wasn't even here."

"Until eleven years ago," Tate said. "Yeah, I already heard that."

Seeing Cowen was about to speak again, Goodsell jabbed him in the ribs.

"And Nature's Way bought Summit Ranch," Streeter said, flipping back to a picture of Wade Barns, the fifty-two-year-old rancher found lying on his back in the middle of a berry patch. "Does this look familiar, Mark?"

Goodsell leaned forward, elbows on the conference table, his eyes squinting to study the photo. "Who is he?"

"You should know," Streeter said. "You battled over owning his ranch for nearly two years."

Goodsell squeezed his eyes shut. "Eden."

"Yep, Eden," Tate mimicked.

Goodsell opened his eyes and shot a glance at Tate before leveling a stare at Streeter. "Look, that was my first year here. The former director was promoted into the Utah territory and I was told to clean this one up. Hocking was relentless. Said her boyfriend hated Nature's Way and would never have bequeathed his ranch to anyone besides the Elk Foundation."

"Who named the ranch?" Streeter pressed, noticing Linwood making notes, as he was instructed to do, about his observations of Goodsell and Cowen.

"I . . . I don't know," Goodsell said, hesitating for a few seconds. "We did. Nature's Way."

"Who within Nature's Way?" Streeter asked.

"I don't know. I'd have to look back in the files." Goodsell closed his mouth and glared at Streeter. "Hey, wait a minute. That's why you were asking for a list of all the names of the ranches we've conserved, isn't it? What's this about? Do we need lawyers?"

"You tell us," Streeter said, folding his arms across his chiseled pecs and holding Goodsell's stare. "Do you want to continue to cooperate or do you want to place a call to your lawyer?"

Goodsell held up his hands in surrender. "I've got nothing to hide. I'll cooperate. You?"

He had turned to Cowen, who turned a sickly shade of gray as his face drained of all color. "Go to hell, Mark. I didn't kill any of these guys. And I didn't have sex with *her*," he declared, jabbing a finger in Tate's direction.

"Then let's continue, shall we?" Streeter said.

Before Streeter could click to the next photo, Goodsell asked, "What's that in his mouth? I swear, I've never seen these photos before in my life. No one ever showed me . . . no one told me about this."

"They're berries," Tate said flatly. "Someone stuffed Wade Barns's mouth full of raspberries. After he was dead."

"Jesus," Goodsell said, grimacing as his eyes stared at the photo projected on the screen.

Cowen's formerly ashen face now turned as red as the berries.

Streeter moved on to each successive photo. "Buddy Richards, Survivors Ranch. Homer Larson, Freak of Nature Ranch. Greg Schumacher, Mystical Pyramid Ranch. Bobby Daniels, Left to Chance Ranch. Chris Night Hawk, All That Glitters—"

"Stop," Goodsell interrupted, looking as if he were going to be sick. "Just . . . just wait a minute. These are all Nature's Way ranches."

"And they're all Crooked Man cases," Streeter announced.

"Oh my word," Goodsell whispered, the color in his face now draining. "The list of the names. Of the ranches. Oh my word, oh my word, oh my word."

Cowen's head drooped.

"*Do* any of these men look familiar to either of you?" Streeter said, volleying his accusing stare between both men.

Goodsell remained quiet, his lips pursing into a tight line. His eyes slid over to Cowen.

"Screw all of you!" Cowen exploded, his eyes red and on the verge of tears. "I didn't kill these guys. I just knew a few of them who were toying with the idea of donating their land to Nature's Way. That's it. I was doing my fricking job!"

"You were doing your fricking job with a bunch of ranchers, the cows," Tate said, folding her arms and pinning Cowen with her stare. "What about the Widow Aker's cat?"

"That cat was ancient!" he shouted. His eyes widened. "I—"

"You what?"

Cowen cut his eyes toward Goodsell, who glared at him.

"You killed the Widow Aker's cat and nailed it to the tree. To scare her. To punish her. Didn't you?"

Goodsell fumed. "What have you done, Rowland?"

Cowen's eyes softened with the realization of what he'd just said, incriminating himself without knowing it. His demeanor morphed from anger to contrition. "I swear to you on my father's grave I did not kill these men."

"But you did kill the cat."

He dropped his eyes and wept. "I didn't kill any humans."

"Who did?" Streeter pressed.

Cowen genuinely looked perplexed, as did Goodsell. Goodsell leaned forward on the table and growled, "I haven't a clue, but we're here and we're not leaving until we've helped you any way we can to find the bastard who's doing this. Right, Rowland?"

"Right," Cowen stammered, tears trailing down his reddened cheeks.

"Let me tell you one thing, Agent Pierce," Goodsell said, his eyes fixed in earnest. "This is *not* what Nature's Way is about." He was pointing to the gruesome photo of Chris Night Hawk's body sprawled on the concrete floor of the mica plant near Custer, his arm and head twisted at an unnatural angle. "We believe in our cause, but we're not militant."

"If you ignore the torturing and killing of cats," Tate said.

"We're not murderers. Do you understand?"

"Someone is," Streeter said simply, holding his stare. After several beats, Streeter turned to the screen and resumed clicking through the photos. "Maurice Castle, Pay Dirt Ranch. Steven Tuttle, Rough Ride Ranch.

Donny Finch, Ballpark Ranch. Evan Drummer, Hot Dry Breath of Prairie. Ernif Hanson. And what were you going to name *his* ranch?"

Goodsell stared at Streeter blankly.

Streeter clicked to the electronic map. "Here are your ranches. Where the murders took place. And the names of the victims." He was pointing at the labeled flags at each location. Then, dragging his finger along the red line that connected them all, Streeter said, "All of your newly acquired ranches, names, and dates of the murders by the Crooked Man coincide with the travels of Custer's expedition in 1874 and an event that happened on the exact same day of each murder."

Closing his eyes, Goodsell's expression filled with sorrow and remorse. And what Streeter thought might be recognition.

"Oh no."

Cowen started bawling like a baby. Goodsell lowered his head.

"If not one of you, then who is the resident expert on Custer's expedition?" Streeter pressed. "Who's been suggesting the names for the ranches?"

Goodsell shook his head slowly. "No one at Nature's Way. No one, I swear."

"How can you be so sure?" Streeter said.

"Because there's only one other man I know besides Cowen who knew all these men," Goodsell said, his face filling with pain and shock. "Only one man who's a self-proclaimed expert on the 1874 expedition by General Custer."

"Is it the same man who named each of these ranches?" Streeter asked.

"He's the one who gave us the recommendations, yes," Goodsell said, squeezing his eyes shut as if not believing the horror that was unfolding in the truth.

"Who is he?"

"A friend."

"We need a name."

"Dr. Lowell Morgan."

CHAPTER 41

"**SHE DIDN'T HEAR A** thing last night," Elizabeth said, whispering to me as she poured us both a cup of coffee.

"How in the hell did she miss all that commotion?" I asked. "Beulah growling and barking and baying. What in the hell is going on?"

"That's what I've been trying to tell you. Someone is trying to kill Helma. That's why I asked you to stay the last two nights. I had your SIG. You had the revolver. I needed backup. Michael's coming today and bringing an arsenal."

"You need more than a couch and a couple of guns. You need to call the police again. Or call Streeter," I said.

"And say what? That the crazy bastard who tried to kill Helma at Heavenly Hospice has been sneaking around here the last few nights? I can't prove anything. And you know it."

"But this time we have the blood to prove it. DNA. Look," I said, pointing at the drops of blood on the wood floor leading to the door. "Beulah got him good."

"And he got Beulah good," Elizabeth reminded me. "You need to take her to the vet. She might have a broken rib."

"Her rib's not broken, but I do need to take her to the vet. I called down to the animal hospital in Spearfish. They're standing by. But I'm not going until I know you're okay. I'm not leaving you until Michael gets here."

"He won't be here until this afternoon," Elizabeth said, lighting on the couch and wrapping both hands around the coffee cup. "And you have a flight to catch."

"I'm not leaving. Not until I know you two are safe. And Beulah's okay." I sat down beside her, pushing the coffee table away to give my legs room. "Look, let me call Streeter. Please. He'll know what to do."

Elizabeth shook her head, raising her pleading eyes to me. "Don't you see? Helma is dying. They'll take her from here. I promised I wouldn't let that happen. She wants to die in her bed."

I set my cup down and took hers as well, wrapping my hands around her hands. She was shaking. "Elizabeth, you've done everything you could for Helma. She's not safe here. You're not safe here. It won't do any good if you're killed by some whacko who's got this obsession with Helma."

Elizabeth lowered her eyes.

"And what about the plans?" I added. "How can Helma depend on you to fulfill her dream if you go and get yourself killed? What about the lost boys?"

This did the trick. Instantly, I saw Elizabeth's spine straighten, her hands steady. She looked me dead in the eyes and said, "I'm not going to get myself killed. That's why you're here. To help me."

"Well, I could have been killed too. And now Beulah. Elizabeth, listen to me. Whoever is doing this hasn't given up. He's tried to get to Helma three times. You don't want her to die this way."

"I don't want her to die at all," Elizabeth said, tears pooling in her large eyes. She swiped at them with the back of her hand and skittered off to the kitchen with her coffee cup.

I followed her, holding my cup out for her to refill. "I don't want her to die either. And I don't want you or Michael hurt."

She set the pot of coffee down and leaned against the counter.

"If the same guy that broke in here last night is the one who killed Ernif, then he's one really badass murderer," I said. "He's killed a lot of people, sis. He won't think twice about going through you—or Michael—to get to Helma. Do you understand?"

Her head drooped. "I understand. But Helma has asked me to do everything I can to let her die in peace here at home. In her bed," she repeated. "Do *you* understand?"

I nodded.

We both heard the moan and darted toward the back bedroom. I was a step behind Elizabeth, who swung open the door and stopped short, me ramming into her, both of us staring at an empty, disheveled bed. My heart raced and the thought of us arguing in the kitchen about what to do, leaving Helma alone in her bedroom, vulnerable to whomever had been trying to get his hands on her, shamed me to the core. We were too late. She was gone.

Elizabeth must have been thinking the same thing, staring at the lacey curtains dancing in the slight breeze from the open window, gawking at the empty bed along with me.

Neither of us took a breath or moved until we heard a faint moan again. Like conjoined twins, Elizabeth and I scrambled around the bed and found Helma sprawled on the floor in the tiny space between the bed and wall with the open window.

With one swift movement, Elizabeth had Helma back on the bed and was smoothing the gray strands of hair from her frail face.

"This is why we're calling Streeter," I said with conviction. "The FBI can help us. Helma can stay here and they can protect her."

Elizabeth ignored me and asked, "Helma, are you okay?"

Her moan was faint, barely audible. Elizabeth bent down, her ear against Helma's lips.

"What? Doctor? Are you saying Dr. Morgan?"

Elizabeth looked at me, motioning for me to listen, and I did.

"Tell me, Helma. Tell me again," Elizabeth said, leaning into her once more. "Definitely Dr. Morgan. I heard Dr. Morgan this time."

"Maybe it's the pain. Maybe she needs the medicine now, Elizabeth." I lowered my voice. "Maybe it's . . . maybe it's . . . time." I mouthed the last word.

I watched as Elizabeth expertly tucked Helma into her bed covers, adjusted her pillows, and placed a new cold compress against her forehead. "She has a fever."

Based on the heat I felt rising in waves off of Helma's skin when I bent close to decipher her mumbles, I agreed with Elizabeth. It was indeed a fever. What I didn't know was if that was a normal occurrence with someone dying from cancer. From her moaning and the grimaces she made as she lay in the fetal position, wrapping her thin arms around her waist, I suspected she was in far more pain than was necessary.

"Elizabeth," I said, moving closer and putting a hand on her shoulder. "She's in pain."

Elizabeth swiped at her eyes again and whispered, "I know."

"She needs Dr. Morgan," I said, hoping against all hopes that Streeter's instincts were right and he was not the Crooked Man. Otherwise, I was inviting a murderer into Helma's home. To kill her.

"I know that too."

"You don't have to take her to the hospital if you don't want. They can't make you."

"I doubt if Dr. Morgan makes house calls, especially after the way I treated him. And especially all the way out here," Elizabeth said.

"Only one way to find out."

Elizabeth sighed. "Okay. But let's call Dr. Morgan before—"

"No!" Helma's eyes went wide and wild, her body stiffening under the covers before she lost her grip on lucidity and drifted back into her world of confusion and pain.

"No?"

Elizabeth's eyes filled again with tears as she comforted Helma. She dipped the cloth in the bowl of ice water and twisted and draped it across her forehead. "She's burning up. Get me something for the fever."

I stumbled backward out of the room and fumbled in the bathroom cabinet for Tylenol.

Helma had drifted off into a deep sleep, her chest rising and falling laboriously. Elizabeth propped her up, popped three pills into her mouth, and forced her to drink water. "That should help, Helma."

Helma's eyelids opened slightly and a small smile came to her weak lips.

Elizabeth lowered her back onto the pillow and tucked the covers close to her chin. "Go to sleep. Rest."

With Helma enveloped in a sweat-soaked sleep, Elizabeth's shoulders relaxed.

"You okay?"

"Hell no," she said.

"What do you want to do?"

Elizabeth studied Helma's face, watched her chest rise and fall, rise and fall. "Call Dr. Morgan. See if he'll come. Helma comes first in all this. And I can't stand seeing her in this much pain. After that, call the police or the FBI or whoever you think we need to call."

"Deal."

"What time is it, anyway?" she asked.

"Eight thirty."

"Will you stay with me? At least until the FBI or Dr. Morgan arrives? Even if you reach them, no one will get out here until ten thirty or eleven. Ten at the very soonest."

"Elizabeth, if I have to catch a later flight, it won't be the end of the world. Besides, I'd feel more comfortable if I waited around until Michael got here."

I was relieved to hear what I thought was genuine concern in Dr. Morgan's voice when I told him about Helma. Lately he'd been attending the early service at church but said this morning he'd duck out early, head back home, grab his bag with what he believed Helma might need for medication, and be up at the house before eleven. I thanked him, ended the call, hesitated, and dialed the number of the man I most trusted with a plea for help.

"Can you help me? I'm up at Helma Hanson's house with my sister Elizabeth. Someone tried to break in to the house again . . . yes, again."

CHAPTER 42

WHEN THEY KNOCKED ON the door at Cliff View Lane off Nemo Road, Streeter really hadn't expected Dr. Morgan would answer. Without waiting long after the second knock, he directed the SWAT team to bust through the door and clear the house. Finding everything inside the home neat as a pin, organized and spotless, Streeter suggested they break into teams and search more thoroughly.

After finding nothing except some suspect unlabeled bottles of pills amid numerous labeled bottles—two were marked Glyburide and Lisinopril, carelessly spilt on the kitchen counter with pills that all looked identical, which were bagged and tagged by Linwood for Dr. Berta Johnson to analyze—Streeter stepped outside to draw in a deep breath in the morning sun, the flag waving in the slight breeze catching his eye to his left.

He recognized the scene as the same one in the photo hanging in the doctor's office.

Streeter looked in the opposite direction, to his right, and spotted the roof of an old homestead over the hill. He walked toward it, realizing the homesteaders had likely settled on the downhill side, just over the hill's edge, as protection from the winds and snows, maybe even from the Indians who fought to regain their land. The house was still in fairly good shape, although the wood had weathered to a dark gray.

The door opened with a creak and the house, although dusty from being unused, was not filled with the cobwebs and mouse droppings he would have expected to see. Someone had been keeping the place fairly tidy, despite it being vacant. And ancient. The fireplace was the focal point in the living room, and on either side of the front room were hallways leading somewhere back in time. Streeter took the right first, the hall leading to a detached kitchen, which Streeter imagined was designed such that if the stove caught on fire, the rest of the house wouldn't burn down, an old southerners' trick to building homesteads. He also imagined that whoever settled this place likely came here after the Civil War. The kitchen was filled with original hardware, a potbelly cast iron stove, and handcrafted cabinets.

On his way back through the hall and into the front room, Streeter noticed for the first time a branding iron hanging above the stove. He pulled it down and studied the markings. Then he went left, down the short hallway that led to three rooms and a bathroom, which had more modern plumbing and fixtures than the rest of the house. He imagined that if he wandered out back, he'd find the original outhouse; modern plumbing must have come only within the past fifty years or so.

One room was tiny, a child's room, everything still in place from the furniture to the comforter to the toy cars and blocks. On one wall, he saw a photo of a woman with her son, his legs in braces, his arms braced in crutch-like apparatuses. On the bottom of the photo was written in ink, in perfect cursive writing, a single word.

Polio.

Dr. Morgan wasn't crooked because of a birth defect. He was crippled from a disease. From polio. And it made sense why he related so well to the storybook character the Crooked Man. And why he likely found a passion for healing. Not only was he from a long line of doctors, as Tate had described, he had suffered from a childhood disease that was entirely avoidable in today's world with proper preventative shots. He wondered what had made his parents decide not to allow him to take the polio vaccine, particularly in light of his coming from a long line of doctors.

In the bedroom nearby, larger and clearly designed with a woman's touch, Streeter noted the lacey spreads, an ancient brass headboard, a wooden chest on the floor, and an ornately beaded lampshade on the bedside light. A sepia photo on the wall in an ancient frame depicted a woman in a high-collar dress, her hair pinned into a bun of the time, a demure smile on her face as she sat beside a man in a suit, a ruffled tie around his neck. She was holding a bouquet. A wedding photo.

In the bedroom across the hall were a large, heavy dresser, a simple bed and spread, and an old black leather bag resting on a stand in the corner. Streeter stepped into the room and pulled the curtains back so he could read the certificates that hung on the wall. He surmised that the man who lived in this room had also lived in this house as a boy and had graduated from all these universities at the turn of the century, a proud accomplishment for that time.

One shadowbox indicated that this man's grandfather had been in the Civil War, and just as Streeter suspected, he fought for the Rebels. Another shadowbox appeared to contain the belongings of an officer who had been in the 7th Cavalry Regiment of the U.S. Army, also a doctor, likely this man's father. Streeter inferred that the man who built this house was likely the medical officer who settled on this land after Custer's expedition, maybe even after the Battle of the Little Bighorn.

Streeter wondered what would induce the medical officer to choose this site to homestead. What would compel him to load up his family in a covered wagon and leave their southern home to travel across the rugged countryside and settle here? Especially after he had lost nearly three hundred fellow cavalrymen—some his friends—on the wicked battlefield of the Little Bighorn. Then Streeter remembered the flag waving in the distance. And the book he had read. And the photograph of this very place that Dr. Morgan kept in his office. This appeared to be the very ground where the doctor in Custer's regiment buried the second soldier he had lost to dysentery during the expedition.

Streeter opened the top drawer of the dresser below the shadowboxes and found a newspaper clipping from fifty years ago. The cover story was about a seventy-nine-year-old local man, a beloved retired doctor known for making house calls, whose grandson found him disemboweled and left to die on his property. Streeter's eyes scanned across the lines of yellowing paper, landing on the name of the alleged killer taken into custody. The reporter said that the man had boasted about killing the doctor for taking his wife's life during childbirth five years earlier. The alleged killer was quoted as saying, "He's a butcher. Just like his daddy was a butcher. From a long line of butchers and drunks." It had been determined, the story went on to say, that the suspect was not mentally competent to stand trial.

The suspect's picture that accompanied the article was the face of a young man Streeter was sure he had seen before, but he couldn't put his finger on where. He studied the photo, held it under the light for a closer look, and then closed his eyes to make his mind conjure up where he'd seen that face.

Streeter replaced the newspaper article for the crime scene technicians to bag later, closed the dresser drawer, and exited the house. Again his eyes landed on the headstone beneath the gently waving American flag and his thoughts returned to the soldier who had died of dysentery and to the animosity so many of the soldiers' accounts expressed toward the regiment's medical officer during the expedition.

Then, recognition clearly registered on his face. "Oh no . . . how did I miss that?"

Streeter took off at a sprint and ran through the meadow toward the flag. He knew what was inscribed on the headstone beneath the flag before he ever reached it, recognizing the small memorial from the book. Private James A. King. The second soldier to die from severe diarrhea. But what he didn't know was that Dr. Morgan would still be alive, propped up against the headstone.

The stage had clearly been set to resemble a suicide: the gun lying at Dr. Morgan's right side, the bullet wound in his abdomen, not his head. It reminded Streeter of the way in which women typically shot themselves in suicides (even though guns were generally rare in female suicides): into the body, not the head. A gut shot like this one would mean a slow, painful death. Just like the way Dr. Morgan's grandfather had died.

Streeter dropped beside Dr. Morgan, pressing his bare hand against the wound.

"No . . . stop." Dr. Morgan's breath was ragged. "Too late."

"It's not too late," Streeter said, whistling through his teeth—the pitch high, the volume even higher—as if calling in the hound dogs. He saw movement from the house, agents running from all directions toward them, and he turned his attention back to Dr. Morgan.

"Why did you do this?"

"I didn't."

"Why did he do this to you?"

"He's not well," Dr. Morgan managed to say. "Go easy on him."

"The ranches. For Nature's Way. You named them all," Streeter said, realizing Dr. Morgan's time was fading. Fast.

"No . . ." Blood bubbled from the corner of his mouth. "He did."

As the agents tramping across the meadow drew nearer, the pieces all fell into place in Streeter's mind. "He staged this to make it look like you murdered all those people, then killed yourself because we were closing in on you," he said with pity in his voice.

"Hurry . . ." Dr. Morgan's eyes closed, his head lolled to his shoulder.

Streeter barked orders to the others and motioned to Linwood and Tate to follow as he ran through the meadow toward his car.

"Come on! Let's go! Before we're too late."

CHAPTER 43

I ADMIRED DR. MORGAN'S obvious dedication to his patients. Why else would he be willing to drive his fancy Cadillac so fast across the rough dirt trail as to create the rooster tail now curling high enough to be noticeable for miles? Clearly he wasn't overly protective of his expensive car like so many rich people tended to be, parking their vehicles in the last row at grocery stores or mall lots just to avoid a possible ding from a car door being opened nearby.

"Elizabeth, he's here!" I called down the hall as softly as I could so as not to wake up Helma. She had awakened in fits and starts throughout the morning, mumbling about Dr. Morgan, which we both took as a plea for help.

I opened the door and greeted him. "Hi, Dr. Morgan!"

Only it wasn't Dr. Morgan.

Admittedly, I was relieved. No more would I have to wonder if Streeter's instinct was right or wrong about Dr. Morgan being the killer.

"I'm Steve Preston, Dr. Morgan's P.A. He was called to the hospital on an emergency and asked me to come up here to attend to Helma."

"I remember you. You were at Ernif's funeral with Dr. Morgan," I said, noting how firm his grip was as we shook hands. "Well, thanks for coming up here. We're so lucky that Dr. Morgan is willing to send you so far out of town to make a house call. Especially after everything that's happened."

"Oh, nonsense," he said, offering a smile and making his way through the door. "Anything to help Helma. You know that."

Elizabeth emerged from the back bedroom down the hall and, having heard the conversation, reached for his hand and said, "Steve, nice to meet you. I'm Elizabeth. We've spoken on the phone several times."

He shifted the black medicine bag to his other hand and gripped Elizabeth's tiny hand in his and said, "Elizabeth. Dr. Morgan sent his apologies. I know I've been annoying. But we do care so much about our Helma. How is she doing?"

"Not well."

It might have been my imagination, but he seemed to be studying her as if under a very intense light to detect the faintest rash, twitch, discoloration, movement, tells. He pinned her with his gaze, and Elizabeth held up to the scrutiny, allowing him to search every feature, every inch of skin with his probing eyes.

"Let's get something straight, Steve. Like I told you on the phone, Helma's not going back to Heavenly Hospice. And she doesn't want hospice to come here. This is where she wants to die," Elizabeth stated with conviction.

"It is indeed," Steve said with a smile. "So let's let her die in peace, shall we?"

The relief that washed over Elizabeth's face was evident. "Thank you. For coming. For helping."

"My pleasure."

He followed Elizabeth down the hall. I hung back to close the door and brew another pot of coffee. Before I ever got the front door shut, I heard Beulah start to howl, from the tips of her paws to the top of her lungs. I rounded the corner of the hallway and saw Elizabeth and Steve Preston jerk with a start at the sound and huddle close to the hall's opposite wall to avoid Beulah, who was baying like there was no tomorrow. I could barely see her nose, so high was it stuck in the air, as she stood in the spare bedroom howling away at Steve. He, in the meantime, had positioned the medical bag like a shield, ready to whack Beulah with it if she came any closer.

Although Jack had told me Beulah wouldn't bite, I was afraid she might, and for the first time since I'd met my bloodhound, I was scared to approach her. But I figured it was better me than Dr. Morgan's physician's assistant, so I lunged at her, hugging her close around her neck and slamming the spare bedroom door shut with my foot, trying hard to calm my canine buddy without further injuring her.

"What's gotten into you, Beulah?"

Beulah lifted her face to me, then turned to the door and howled, whimpering in between howls as she tried to bite at her sore ribs. I knew a rib or two was probably badly bruised, and I wondered if the intruder had kicked her last night or hit her with a baseball bat or a cane, perhaps. Whatever he did, I wanted to do the same to him.

I calmed Beulah down by petting and scratching her ears, humming to her as I did so she'd fall back to sleep. And heal. We had a long trip ahead of us after visiting the vet, and I was not happy about putting her in a kennel for the plane trip home, afraid she might get hurt even worse.

Beulah settled in on my lap, whining and whimpering between growls at the door, and I wondered what she had smelled on or from Steve Preston to get such a rise out of her. He was a little prissy; maybe he used offensive cologne or something. Eventually Beulah fell asleep and moved her head off my lap onto some of my dirty clothes heaped on the floor. Her baying had spooked me, so I double-checked that I had my Smith & Wesson tucked firmly in the holster my brother-in-law Michael had made for me. I wore it, unseen, under the loose unbuttoned boyfriend jacket I wore over my T-shirt. I opened the door and listened for any noise from behind me, wondering if more odors were wafting in that would excite or alarm Beulah. All I heard were Elizabeth and Steve whispering in Helma's bedroom.

I tiptoed down the hall to the living room and saw that the door had blown open in the slight breeze. For a second, I found my heart in my throat, wondering if what Beulah had smelled was actually the intruder from last night. Had someone followed Steve Preston into the house while we were distracted by Beulah's howls? I slipped the gun from its holster and held it close to my chest as I went around, checking in every nook and cranny in the bathroom, the living room, the kitchen, and the porch. I even walked outside and circled the house, keeping my gun cocked and ready at all times. When I came under Helma's window, I heard Dr. Morgan's assistant humming as he tended to her.

There was no howling, so I knew that Beulah was still asleep—or at least that whatever smell had bothered her was gone. I looked off into the trees and thought I saw something move. So, off I pranced on my steel-tipped toes and stood, very still, with my back against a tree. I heard nothing but the breeze in the branches, and after several minutes, I realized that the wind through the trees must have created the movement I had seen. I relaxed and walked back toward the house across the meadow, stuffing my pistol in the holster.

The wind carried with it the pleasant melody Steve Preston continued to hum. I started to hum along as I walked through the back door, when suddenly it dawned on me that he had limped when he walked down the hall to Helma's bedroom. A limp I hadn't noticed him having at Ernif's funeral. "Oh shit!"

I pulled out my gun, my hands shaking. That's why Beulah was howling. Steve Preston was limping because Beulah had bit his ankle last night. That could have been the reason Helma was mumbling Dr. Morgan's name. Maybe she remembered. Maybe she was trying to warn us. Just like Homer Larson was probably trying to tell his neighbor that the killer was the assistant to Dr. Morgan, only all he was able to say was Crooked Man.

And maybe I was wrong.

I tried to think, but sheer terror kept getting in the way. Why in the world would Steve Preston kill these people? Wasn't he sworn to some kind of Hippocratic oath as a physician's assistant? Or was that only for physicians? Mrs. Aker and Tommy Jasper knew Dr. Morgan and surely would have also known Steve Preston, but he was invisible, just an employee of Dr. Morgan's. Tommy Jasper had said Pastor Keeley was talking with Steve Preston at the bar that night at Nemo when I had dinner with Tommy. But I didn't see him then. Preston was always there, but no one ever noticed him. We noticed Dr. Morgan. Preston could easily have poisoned Tommy without anyone noticing.

And Beulah tried to warn me. She recognized Steve Preston's smell from last night. But I didn't recognize her warning.

A potentially fatal error.

My hands shook like a leaf as I crouched and duckwalked down the hall, keeping low and balanced. I no longer heard any humming from the bedroom. In fact, I heard nothing. No breathing, no movement. All was still.

As I passed by the guest bedroom, I quietly turned the doorknob and pushed open the door, pleading to Beulah telepathically to open her eyes and help me. She didn't. I lowered myself into a full squatting position to cover the final few steps to the open door of Helma's bedroom and nearly cried when I saw Elizabeth's feet sprawled on the floor in the tiny space between the bed and the wall where we'd found Helma earlier this morning.

I remembered from a self-defense training course I'd taken not to lead with the gun when entering a room or it would simply be knocked out of my hands and used against me. So I held the Smith & Wesson close to my chest and opted, instead, to poke my head around the door to see where Steve Preston had gone.

Just as quickly I pulled my head back with a swift motion. I felt a gust of air blow against my face and heard the startling thwack of wood against the doorjamb. And I saw the brass ball at the end of a cane two inches from my head.

A cane exactly like Dr. Morgan's.

Where in the hell did he get the cane? I wondered. Preston must have gone back to the car to retrieve it at some point. Probably while I was off listening to the breeze among the pine branches. Jeez!

Preston had just swung a mighty blow through the doorway to strike me dead with the brass ball. What saved me was my duckwalk, since he had aimed his swing high, intending to hit me in the chest as I came in. What hurt me was my duckwalk, because I wasn't as balanced and stable as I would have been if I were standing with both feet firmly planted. I landed hard on my backside, my pistol skittering across the hardwood floor out of reach.

I crab walked backward down the hall grasping for my pistol and saw Preston emerge through the bedroom doorway. He swung again, only this time the cane came straight down and through the floor of the house between my knees, narrowly missing me. It was obvious the P.A. was strong—and much more agile than he would appear or his limp would suggest. My fingers landed on the cool steel of my Smith & Wesson just as Preston flashed me a crooked grin. Not taking my eyes off him, I fumbled to get off a quick shot. He lifted his cane high over his head and lurched forward with a lumberman's chop, the big brass ball landing an inch from my side as I rolled against the wall. I righted myself and tried to level the gun on him, but not before he delivered a thwack to my hands. The revolver was pounded from my grip and skittered behind me.

Again, I scrabbled backward on my hands and feet, gluing my focus to his maniacally mesmerizing eyes, as clear blue as the thin skies of heaven.

"He bought a crooked cat," I screamed. Preston checked his swing in mid-stride.

"What did you say?" His lips were twisted into a curious grin and he was limping toward me, pinning me with those eyes.

"There was a crooked man who walked a crooked mile," I said inching backward, knowing I had no purchase but to buy some time. "Who bought a crooked cat, right?"

He cocked his head and took a step toward me.

I was a dead girl.

CHAPTER 44

I MIGHT AS WELL admit it. There was no way I was finding my gun and no way I could roll out of his reach this time. All I had left was the gift of gab.

"There was a crooked man who bought a crooked cat," I said, feeling myself gaining courage as I did. I always knew the power of prayer, but who knew the power of nursery rhymes?

"Waffles, the cat. Mrs. Aker's cat. You smashed his back and pinned Waffles, the crooked cat, to a tree outside Mrs. Aker's window, scaring her into signing the deed over to Nature's Way."

"Clever girl," he said, taking another step toward me.

"Cruel man," I replied. "Bullying people the way you do."

I poked and prodded with my fingers, hoping they'd land on the gun before the brass ball of his cane landed on my skull. I imagined that's what had happened to Elizabeth and I whimpered. I thought about giving up, but if there was a chance that Elizabeth was still alive, I owed it to her to try to stay alive and save her.

He raised his eyebrows and smiled. "Not me. Rowland Cowen killed her cat. Took nothing more than a sympathetic ear, a comforting blow job, and a catty plan for revenge—pun fully intended—to get his motor running."

"Why did he kill Mrs. Aker's cat?"

"Because I told him to. He was already seeing red, he was so mad at the obstinate widow."

"And why didn't you kill her?" Keep him talking, I said over and over in my head.

"She didn't have a terminal illness like the others. Convincing Lowell to buy her ranch was enough. He's the one who donated all that money. I still have all my money and now I'll have everything in his estate too."

"What?" My mind wasn't keeping up with him.

"Lowell bought the land. It was at my urging, of course. I convinced him to buy Frank Pelley's place as well."

"You? How?"

"*How?* You're not such a clever girl after all. You haven't figured that out yet, have you?"

He stepped toward me. "Figured what out? That I'm not a clever girl?"

"That I'm *not* just Dr. Morgan's assistant."

I knew Tommy was right about the men being partners, but I had to make sure Preston thought he had the upper hand.

"You're brothers?"

He threw his head back and laughed. "Oh, that's rich. You are naive, aren't you?"

It gave me just enough time to edge back a few inches from him.

"We're lovers, not brothers, you stupid girl."

"So why are you doing this?"

"Because you and your sister irritate the living shit out of me."

"No, I mean why are you killing people?"

"For the land. For revenge. For redemption."

"Why? You owe me that at least. All this land. What's it to you?" I said, slowly moving beyond his cane's reach even though I knew it was futile.

"What's it to *you?*" he asked, resting the cane on his shoulder for a moment, his arms weakened from the earlier exertion, no doubt, which encouraged me to lengthen our discussion.

"What's the story? You love to tell the story," I sang, mocking the Christian hymn I had heard him humming earlier.

This pulled him up by the short hairs. He scowled at me and said, "You wouldn't understand. I did nothing but help all these people by guiding them in their journey and honoring them with a lasting legacy that will stand the test of time."

"Bullshit. All you did was cut their lives shorter than God intended."

"What do you know about God's intentions?" he spat, glowering at me and gripping the cane again with both hands.

"Then you tell me. What revenge? What redemption?"

"My revenge is that everyone's lasting memory of Dr. Morgan will be that he was 'the butcher,' just like his granddaddy."

"You did all this to frame your lover?"

"Actually, it's quite the opposite. I *became* his lover ten years ago so that I could frame him for slaughtering more than a dozen people. He hired me seven years ago, and I only moved in with him this year. I've successfully planted a long history of him murdering people using a cane exactly like his," he said, waving the hickory weapon above his head. "Killing people so he could steal their land and hog all the glory. Pretty effective so far, don't you think?"

"But no one suspects Dr. Morgan of these crimes," I said, truly confused by his plan.

"They will after today. You see, he knew all the murdered victims. I made sure of that detail. He's the anonymous donor of the Pelley Place, Camp Saddleback. I put him up to that too. He named all the ranches donated to Nature's Way. Actually, all my brainchildren, but he readily accepted my suggestions." His eyes were wild. "And although no one knows this yet, he committed suicide today, confiding in me what he had done all these years. Me—the bereaved assistant. See how nicely that all came together?"

"But why redemption?"

"To make sure my daddy didn't die in vain."

"Who's your dad?"

"Shut up!" he shouted suddenly, his cane slicing through the air and landing in a thud by my hip. "The important thing is the work we did to conserve historical places, right? We meaning Nature's Way and I. Not Lowell Morgan and I."

His eyes became beady when he recognized the confusion on my face.

"And the great Dr. Morgan will be remembered as 'the butcher,' a drunkard, careless and neglectful, just like his ancestors. You know his granddaddy killed my mother? During childbirth. And my daddy spent his last years of life rotting in prison just because he paid the old doctor a visit and gave him what he deserved."

"Which was what?"

"A cut to the gut and slow death, just like my mama suffered at his hands, 'the butcher' that he was."

"So what did Lowell Morgan do to deserve this? It was his grand-daddy you had an issue with, not Lowell."

"It was Lowell's testimony in court that got the jurors all emotional, and they sentenced my daddy to an asylum for the criminally insane for life. He refused to go, of course. Committed suicide in his cell. I'll never forget that, even though I was just seven years old at the time. It had been three years since old Doc Morgan died. Lowell was eleven when he took the stand, yet he bawled like a baby about what my daddy did to his grand-daddy that night. Lowell didn't remember me, but I never forgot him."

Without warning, Preston brought the cane down with a thud right next to my skull, but I managed to dart away just in time.

"Wait, wait. So what does this have to do with Dr. Morgan's ancestors?"

He lifted his hands in surrender, loosening his grip on the cane for just a moment. Then he lowered the cane and leaned his weight against it, grinning at me. "I thought you knew. His great-granddaddy was the doctor on Custer's expedition. Lowell's the last descendant of the man responsible for letting two men die of dysentery—a painful, humiliating death. Lowell found his granddaddy sprawled over the gravestone of the second soldier, who was buried there on the family's homestead. The second to die of dys-entery during Custer's expedition. The second soldier to die at the hands of Lowell's great-granddaddy."

"That's your story? You're killing people over diarrhea? Are you shit-ting me?"

He motioned as if he was going to strike me, then laughed. "You are an odd one, aren't you? Nice pun, by the way."

"I didn't mean it that way," I said, lowering the hand I'd raised in self-defense.

"All the properties I coerced these people to sell or donate to Nature's Way were significant historical sites along the 1874 journey taken by General Custer. The land deserved to be conserved, the owners honored for making the decision to preserve the land for eternity."

Stupefied, I voiced my thoughts, bracing myself for the inevitable blow that would follow. "But you took an oath to protect life, not to take it."

I didn't get the reaction I expected. Instead of striking me, he laughed once again.

"Why Tommy Jasper?" I asked, blurting out the first thing that came to mind just to stop him from laughing.

"Did you know there were several women who accompanied General Custer during his expedition? One particular photo shows Custer in front of his tent with a couple of them near Nemo. Based on my review of Illingworth's diaries, I would pinpoint that campsite to be located directly behind Jasper's house. I wanted that little honey hole."

"So why didn't you club him like you did the others?"

He coughed up that wicked laugh again. "Because I wanted that land for *me*. Not for Nature's Way."

"So you poisoned Tommy?" I asked.

He nodded his head. "Tom Jasper has a bad heart. High blood pressure, actually." Seeing my puzzled expression, he grinned. "Oh, what difference does it make if I give you the details. You'll never live to tell the story. His prescription is for Lisinopril. He has high blood pressure. Glyburide, a similar-looking pill, is used to treat type-2 diabetes, but is not recommended to be taken if the patient has high blood pressure. Heart attack. And Tom must have ingested the Glyburide that night after you two had dinner at Nemo Guest Ranch. It almost did the trick. You see, I added only one pill—the pill Tommy ingested—in his bottle of Lisinopril, knowing he would get to it eventually. I'm a patient man. And knowing his condition, one supercharged dose of the Glyburide would be the death of him, no one the wiser."

The pride he wore on his face was nauseating.

"And Glyburide causes a fruity smell, right? Because they know. The FBI. All of them smelled it." Rage mounted behind his eyes again, too late for me to correct my mistake, although I tried. Taking a step closer, he grumbled, "If you hadn't interfered, hadn't found him, the pill would have worked as intended."

"But it didn't. And now he's a witness."

"So before I kill you, let me thank you. Because now I have Tom Jasper as a witness to testify and confirm my story that Dr. Lowell Morgan tried to kill him. Killed them all."

And with that pronouncement, he whipped the cane above his head with both hands.

CHAPTER 45

"WAIT, PLEASE!" I YELLED.

He hesitated.

"Just tell me why? Why did you kill these people?"

This brought Preston up short, his expression now turning as quickly from rage to confusion as it had from boastful pride to rage a moment before. "I never *killed* anyone. I simply helped them along in their journeys."

"Their journeys? *Helped* them along? They were productive people. Ranching, working the land." I couldn't believe how casually this intelligent physician's assistant was discussing murder as though it was an everyday unobjectionable event.

"Most of them were lonely. Widowers with no one in their lives. They had lived their full lives and were either sick or dying. Don't you see? That's how I learned about their land and having no one to leave it to. *They* called *me*. They were sick men who had called Dr. Morgan to cure them. But it was me they called for a shoulder to cry on. So I comforted them."

"You didn't *comfort* them. You *killed* them." I saw the muscles in his arms twitch with fatigue. Time was on my side after all, it appeared.

"Whatever disease each of them had is what was killing them. I just put them out of their misery a little sooner."

"Tommy isn't sick," was all I could think to say.

His expression softened. "Creutzfeldt-Jakob disease. It's a rare brain disease that Tom was diagnosed with just two months ago. No one's ever lived more than a year after the onset. Tom will be dead before his next birthday. Didn't he tell you?"

My head was swimming with answers I needed to know.

"Tommy said he got confused, his vision blurred before he passed out. The doctors said he had a seizure. Was that from the disease or your death pill?"

"Could be either one. So you see? I was trying to spare Tom an agonizing death. CJD is cruel. The best Tom can hope for is to suffer a stroke and live out the remaining months in a vegetative state. He deserves better."

"What I don't understand is why you are Dr. Morgan's lover if you hate him so much. Why didn't you just kill him as your revenge?"

He smiled. "I thought about that early on. But that would have been too easy. For him. I needed to smear his reputation all over to hell and back like he did to my daddy's. Do you know how unmerciful kids can be about the criminally insane? I heard it all. I was a nutty buddy. The crazy's kid. Barking mad dog's puppy. Cracker's kid. A loony bin boy. Son of psych. Bonker's boy."

"Wasn't it enough that you were his assistant? You had to worm your way into his bed too?"

His crooked smile morphed into one that was simply brilliant and shining, like his eyes. Preston was absolutely giddy about this line of questioning. "Like I told you. I was his lover first. I hadn't planned on that, but Lowell fell in love with me. Head over heels. It made it so much easier to manipulate him as his lover than as his assistant, of course."

"Manipulate how?"

"I needed him to be willing to do anything. Like spend millions of dollars on land he didn't need. To donate to Nature's Way."

"But you had money. You said so yourself. Why didn't you buy the land?"

"I already told you. I needed him to have a reason for killing all these people. Besides, my money was earned the hard way, being orphaned like I was and then losing my wealthy grandparents who raised me. I wasn't about to spend one red cent on avenging myself for the Morgan family's crimes against mine. Why not spend *their* money?"

My face must have revealed how baffled I was, not knowing anything of Preston's background.

Noting my confusion, he continued. "Am I going too fast for you, Ms. Bergen? I was orphaned because of Lowell's grandfather's savagery and raised by my father's grandparents. Turns out, they were wealthier than my parents ever let on. Grandmama and Grandpapa died when I was sixteen, leaving me a trust fund. I'm worth millions, *millions*. But I learned early on that all the money in the world doesn't make the pain go away."

Stammering, I asked, "How will you convince the authorities Dr. Morgan did this and not you? It will be his word against yours."

"I have a note—a suicide note—in his handwriting. In it, he admits to all of these murders." He pulled a crumpled note from his pocket. "Of course, I've been crying over this note for hours, ever since he told me what he was going to do. I couldn't stop him from committing suicide. And I've been wandering all over town—in Rapid City—looking for him. Settled for hanging out at Storybook Island by the Crooked Man until the police come looking for me. Brilliant, don't you think? That's all the police need to know. And I will play the role of the grieving lover, the unsuspecting widow."

My stomach dropped and my throat went dry. He had killed Dr. Morgan. I hadn't noticed until now that he'd been using past tense every time he spoke of Dr. Morgan, but now it made sense. And I realized my own minutes of life were numbered.

"You are insane," I choked.

"Not insane. Committed."

A noise sounded behind him and he glanced quickly over his shoulder. I took that instant to look for my gun.

"What about Ernif?" I said, snaking my fingers under the overstuffed chair, groping for the Smith & Wesson.

Satisfied that what he'd heard was only a breeze blowing through the windows, Preston turned back to face me. "He had cancer. Testicular. Didn't want to scare Helma, so he didn't tell her about it." To my horror, the P.A.'s face twisted into sympathy as he asked, "Don't you see? They were each destined to die imminently. They were walking corpses already. Every one of them. So am I a murderer if I merely hastened their appointment with the Grim Reaper?"

"We're all destined to die, and yes, you are a murderer. Pure evil."

He clucked his tongue, scolding me. The expression on Steve Preston's face at that moment was almost wistful. "When Ernif and I went for our walk a week ago today, I could almost hear the sounds of the wagon train snaking along the creek, the men, the horses, arriving at camp in the distance below. I imagined General Custer, Colonel Ludlow, Private Noonan, and Bloody Knife kneeling at the very spot where Ernif and I stood that day. I was perturbed with Ernif since he was spoiling my perfect record, refusing to meet with me on the proper day—August seventh—which would have been Wednesday. It was the first time in twelve years that my calendar didn't match up precisely with the days and events of the expedition. I knew for a year in advance that the seventh would be a Wednesday, so I made sure my day off each week was Wednesday. But Ernif—stubborn Norwegian that he was—refused to reschedule Helma's weekly visit with Dr. Morgan late Wednesday afternoon. Wouldn't meet with him at any other time during that day."

"So you killed him? Just for that?"

"Oh no, dear. Are you not listening? I aided those ranchers along in their journeys for very specific reasons. With purpose. As Ernif lay on that rock for me, on his belly, I repeated these words perfectly from memory: 'He cocked himself on his hind legs, and showing his huge teeth, he grinned in defiance. But like all who fight Custer, he was compelled to surrender.' And do you know what? Ernif called me a strange little man."

"This is where Custer killed the grizzly. You posed Ernif like the bear. On the same rock."

"Good girl," he said, shuffling a step toward me. I scuttled away from him as he spoke, making it beyond the armchair, which gave me an opening to my left. "You know more about Custer's expedition than most people. And now everyone will know. This land of the Hansons will be bought by or donated to Nature's Way. And guess who's the leading expert on Custer's expedition locally? That's right. None other than Dr. Lowell Morgan. See how nicely that all fits together?"

From the resolve in his eyes, I knew he was about to make his move and so was I. "That's where you missed it."

His smile faltered, his swagger wavered. "Missed it?" he said, his voice carried a note of incredulity.

"All that planning you did. For nothing. This land has already been deeded by Ernif and Helma for another purpose."

"I know. Ernif spoke to me about their plans just before I asked to get a photo of him on that rock. The Saddleback Ranch for the wayward boys. How nice."

"No! I mean he and Helma already deeded the land to someone else."

"You're lying."

"I'm not."

He faltered, his mouth slackened, his eyes widened. "But, but . . ." he stammered. "But Ernif's dead."

"He signed the deed long before he died," I said. "I guess that means you lose."

I rolled in a sideways somersault just as he sliced his cane through the air, the brass ball narrowly missing my right shoulder blade.

"Beulah!" I screamed as I commando scrambled across the living room carpet, then rolled sideways and closer to the door.

Thwack!

CHAPTER 46

THE WIND SLICED BY my ear, the cane whipping to a thud on the coffee table, shattering it to pieces. Glass shards rained down around my head and arms so I curled up into a ball.

Beulah bayed and howled. I heard another thwack, thwack, my body slithering around on the floor to avoid the blows like a snake avoiding the beak of a starving, swooping hawk. I heard growling, gnashing teeth, screams. Thwack, thwack.

At some point—what seemed like hours into the battle but, later, I realized was probably a matter of seconds—my fingers landed on my pistol. I gripped it and flipped around into a seated position, facing where I thought I'd find Preston. His face loomed above mine, creating a monstrous image, the barrel of my gun inches from his nose. Behind him I saw Helma grabbing tightly to the narrow end of his cane. She swayed violently from side to side like a rag doll as Preston wrenched the cane in an attempt to free it so he could club me in the face with the lethal brass ball. In the milliseconds that followed a squeeze of my trigger finger, the shower of pink that exploded from where his nose and mouth had been branded my brain as indelibly as had the maniacal expression, eyes fixed on mine, he'd worn immediately before.

It was as if I were staring at a color version of an old Etch A Sketch, the lines of a smiley face instantly erased with one upside-down shake. Preston's face in front of me one minute, nothing but a blast of pink the next. I felt a hot spattering of something against my face and neck and I squeezed my eyes shut. But not before I saw Preston drop to the floor like a marionette whose strings had just been cut.

My ears were ringing, the explosion of sound all around me so deafening I thought my eardrums had burst. A rush of energy coursed through my veins that may very well have been the adrenaline I would have needed to leap to my feet and let fists, elbows, and knees fly until one landed squarely on Preston. Anywhere. To make sure he was dead. But my primal instincts told me to stay put, keep my grip on the pistol, and get a handle on my faculties before I sprang into any Jackie Chan action. Time stood still for eons as I tried to rearrange my senses, every one of them disoriented by whatever was happening in the tiny space of what I vaguely remembered as being Helma's living room.

Through the thick fog in my head, I recognized the pounding of footsteps and Beulah's incessant yelping, a mournful sound of renewed pain. I felt a hand touch my shoulder, and I pressed my face even tighter to my knees, afraid I'd imagined the whole scene and Preston's next blow from the cane would smash my nose and pop my eyeballs out of my head. The hand gently shook my shoulder.

"Liv. Liv. Liv, it's me."

I looked up to see Jack Linwood's face staring down at me.

"You?"

He smiled and wrinkled his nose, just like a grown-up Mowgli would do.

"Come on," he said, reaching out his hand to me.

I took it and unfolded my long legs and arms, eventually finding my way to my feet and steadying my dizzy head. I brushed the shards of glass from my hair and clothes, thankful I was wearing the boyfriend jacket and jeans, which protected me from death by a thousand cuts. I looked around Helma's living room, which had been completely destroyed, furniture smashed to bits, glass and blood everywhere.

"Did you shoot him? Or is that Beulah's blood?"

"Neither," Jack said, his grin fading.

"Steve Preston? Dead?"

He nodded.

"What happened?" I asked.

He looked away. I stared out the large picture window, the glass now missing, which explained some of the shards scattered all over the floor. Through the gaping open hole I saw Streeter and Jenna Tate interviewing Elizabeth. She was holding an ice pack to the side of her head, but other than that, she looked remarkably like herself.

"*She* shot him?" It took every ounce of willpower I had not to sprint out the door, grab Elizabeth's hand, and run off into the woods where no one could find us. Then we'd hug and laugh and cry and compare notes and thank God we were alive. I had to settle for a broad smile, a swelling pride in my chest that she was my sister.

"No, *you* shot him," Jack answered. "If Helma hadn't managed to regain her senses and grab his cane, you'd be dead. She saved your life. And Elizabeth's."

"Oh my word. How did she muster the strength?" I said. Then I remembered the tiny figure clinging to the cane behind Preston just before the commotion. Just before I shot him. "Behind Preston."

Just the thought of her witnessing all that violence in her condition made my stomach and legs grow weaker.

"Elizabeth said that Preston examined Helma and then pulled out a vial of something he said would relieve the pain. He was about to inject her with whatever was in the vial but Elizabeth began to protest. Preston flung your sister against the wall, where she hit her head and was knocked unconscious. She doesn't remember anything after that. Apparently, you must have come in around that time from what we can gather. Toxicology will have to determine if Preston ever managed to inject Helma or not. Either way, she managed to find the strength to get out of bed, jump into the mix, and hold tight to Preston's cane, giving you time to find your gun."

The disappearing face. The spray of pink.

"Holy crap," I said, my breath catching in my throat. Helma saved both our lives. Mine and Elizabeth's. My eyes trailed out the window and landed again on my petite sister.

Jack noticed. "Your sister out there keeps repeating, 'It's the widow's mite.' Wasn't that a nursery rhyme or something?"

"The widow's might—m-i-g-h-t—is what Elizabeth is talking about," I corrected him, briefly describing the story about how the widow gave everything she had, two tiny mites, as a sacrifice. And Helma had sacrificed herself for the two of us—Elizabeth and me.

The memory of that spray of pink came to me again. I wiped at my cheeks and forehead with the back of my hand, disgusted at the thought of Steve Preston's slippery mind anywhere near my skin. I'd never killed anyone, and I didn't take pleasure in knowing I had just killed a man, even though he was an evil one. But I'd be lying if I said I wasn't glad Preston was dead.

"Where is Helma, by the way? I want to thank her." His eyes dropped to the floor, then away from me. "Where is she, Jack?"

Jack wrapped his arm around my shoulder. "As I said, we'll have to wait on toxicology to tell us if it was something Preston injected into her or if she died from injuries sustained in her scuffle with Preston. Either way—"

I wept. Helma had succeeded. Elizabeth had lived and so had I.

When I regained what little composure I had left, I asked, "How's Elizabeth? Is she going to be okay?"

"She's going to be fine. She'll need to go to the hospital for a day or two for observation. She'll need to get a CT scan to make sure her concussion hasn't resulted in something more serious. She has a whopping headache, of course."

"And what about Beulah? Was she involved in what happened in here? This place looks like a war zone."

Jack sighed and studied the mess at their feet. "We found bite marks all over Preston's legs and arms, as if Beulah was protecting you. I imagine she latched onto Preston's arm with her teeth, clamping hard and holding on for dear life as he stabbed and beat her with the cane. Preston managed to destroy most of the furniture and shatter the picture window by swinging his cane. At some point, it appears, Helma had regained enough strength and awareness to get out of bed, to sneak down the hall, and to latch on to the cane. She fought valiantly from the looks of things. You fired off a shot just as Preston shook free of Beulah's grip. And of Helma's. That part we saw when we got here."

Beulah had contributed to saving my life too. And Helma saved us all. I smiled as my eyes went back to Elizabeth, standing with the agents outside. At that moment, Streeter turned toward me as if hearing my thoughts and offered me a smile, which I returned.

"Where's Beulah?" I asked Jack, still watching Streeter.

When he didn't answer, I turned to him. His smile had faded and he was looking down at the floor.

Again.

CHAPTER 47

MY BEULAH WAS IN bad shape. But before I could go to her, I needed to hug Elizabeth.

After clinging to each other in joy and thankfulness, we consoled each other over Helma's death. Elizabeth found solace in knowing her hero Helma was no longer suffering and, at the very least, would be thrilled that we figured out she was trying to warn us and had saved our lives.

As Elizabeth put it, Helma wouldn't have had it any other way.

Then we were instructed to switch places, each interviewed a second time by the opposite agents, Elizabeth by Jack, me by Jenna and Streeter. Divide and question. Streeter was full of remorse, saying he should have known that Steve Preston was targeting Helma and he should have been here for us earlier.

I told Streeter everything Steve Preston had said about Dr. Morgan, explaining as best I knew how the P.A.'s perverted altruistic reasoning for securing the properties and justification for accelerating all those men's deaths. And I warned him about Preston's primary motive of framing Dr. Morgan for everything that had happened. Streeter told me he had found Morgan alive by the headstone, and he had asked Streeter to go easy on Preston. I learned that Preston had tried to make Dr. Morgan's gut shot look like a suicide, and how Morgan had died on his way to the hospital.

I told Jenna and Streeter about what Preston said regarding Rowland Cowen killing Mrs. Aker's cat and Tommy being poisoned with the switched tablets, although I couldn't remember the fancy medicines he had named. Streeter told me about the two prescription bottles they had found in Dr. Morgan's home, and the names he recited sounded familiar to me. Jack explained that the lab confirmed the pills Dr. Morgan had tried to give Helma were indeed nothing more than sleeping pills.

When I asked to see Beulah, Streeter led me to where they had her immobilized. The EMTs had strapped her to a gurney and had sedated her. When I found out they had saved her life, I hugged each of them. And nuzzled Beulah's neck.

Streeter and Jack went back to work directing the incoming crime technicians and the activities of the EMTs.

Elizabeth and I found a place to sit on either side of Beulah, watching the agents comb through the crime scene and bag more evidence. Within the hour, Michael had arrived, and he appeared more dazed than I felt. Elizabeth and I tag-teamed telling him the story before the EMTs explained to Michael how his wife needed to be taken to the hospital for further observation.

The deaths of Helma and Steve Preston were confirmed. The medical technician who had checked on Beulah periodically reported that my bloodhound probably had a broken leg, three badly bruised ribs, and a concussion, but, thankfully, no internal bleeding. All of that assessment was preliminary, he cautioned, and he strongly recommended I get her to a veterinarian for X-rays as soon as possible.

Because I'd missed my flight and Michael had arrived, Elizabeth offered that I take her Jeep and follow the ambulance to Spearfish, the nearest animal hospital, and eventually use it to drive back to Fort Collins. I took her up on the offer and watched as the EMTs settled Beulah into the back of the ambulance for the ride to Spearfish. They even called ahead to the animal hospital, asking the staff to prepare a team to help when they arrived.

Beulah would live, but they weren't sure if she could continue her work as a trailing dog, which worried me.

I watched as Streeter, Jenna, and Jack were joined by the crime scene technicians, pouring over the mess in Helma's lovely home. I saw tiny Elizabeth tucked under Michael's arm, showing him the plans Helma and Ernif had for the land. For the lost boys. Michael was smiling, and I knew he would throw himself completely behind the design and construction of the bunkhouse and gathering hall before turning the keys over to Saddleback Ranch.

I said my good-byes to Jenna, Streeter, and Jack.

"I'll have to schedule that interview for a later date, Streeter," I said to him, wondering now if attending Quantico would even be an option, considering I had just shot and killed a man.

"There's no need," he said, placing his large hand on the small of my back.

I had my answer. I assumed that he meant he didn't think Beulah was ever going to mend enough to trail again, which meant they had no use for me. Before I could assess how I felt about the change of events, Jenna stepped beside us and spoke directly to me.

"You're in," she said.

"I'm in what? Trouble?"

"You passed. You made it into the academy."

I didn't understand what she was saying and looked to Streeter for the answer. "But I haven't even had my interview yet."

"This is the interview," Streeter explained. "The past few days have been, I mean. Special Agent Tate is actually the head of the training division agency for new recruits. Quantico."

I stared at him, then at her. Then at Streeter again.

"We were under a tight time frame and had to sidestep some of the processes to get you admitted. Tate volunteered to do some fieldwork on the Crooked Man case and assess your skills."

I looked back at Jenna, who confirmed. "Need to brush up on my fieldwork skills every once and awhile," she said.

"Besides," Jack said, holding up an evidence bag that held three sixpence, "we wouldn't know the significance of these coins that we found in Preston's pocket if it weren't for you."

"So this was your interview. You made it, Liv," Streeter said with affection.

Arms crossed, Jenna hitched a hip and said, "Yep, and you are now officially one of the new recruits for this fall's session. Three weeks at Quantico, thirteen weeks in D.C."

I stared at Streeter, still finding it difficult to comprehend what they were saying.

His eyes were pinned on mine. "Just remember," he said, "I told you to work on your honesty if you're going to work with me."

"Congratulations, Liv," Jack said. "Even though you didn't exactly go through the typical recruitment channels."

So, the dress, the high heels, the confidence—and most of all, the coziness and familiarity Jenna Tate shared with the agents. All of it made sense now. This had all been a sham to put me off guard, get me riled up, and see how I would handle myself. And apparently, I passed the test.

Jenna uncrossed her arms and gripped Streeter's arm. "Anything for you, Street."

Streeter never took his eyes off mine. "With or without Beulah. You made it."

I thanked them all, no longer resisting my urge to hug all three agents, excited to know I was headed to Virginia. I admittedly clung to Streeter longer than I probably should have, but what the heck.

Jack walked me to the Jeep and reminded me of our date next Sunday. I smiled, resisting the urge to see if Streeter was within earshot. I thanked him and patted his hand rather than encouraging a second kiss from him.

Just as I turned the key in the ignition, I heard Streeter ask if he could have a minute alone with me. Jack soon retreated into the throes of the crime scene.

Streeter was staring at me, his eyes once more locked on mine. "You scared me back there."

I smiled, even though for the first time since all this happened, I really felt like crying. "I scared *me* back there."

"You'll want to talk about this, Liv. Trust me. I know." He handed me his business card and I noticed he had scrawled his home, cell, and direct lines on the back.

"Thank you."

He brushed a loose strand of hair away from my face, allowing his fingertips to linger on my cheek. Then he was gone.

As I drove away, following the ambulance, I imagined Elizabeth and Michael spending the fall caring for the bees and preparing them for their winter's hibernation in the barn. They'd return in the spring to show the boys and the leaders of Camp Saddleback how to care for the bees and harvest the honey.

The lost boys would find a home here.

All because of the widow's might.

ACKNOWLEDGMENTS

I ATTRIBUTE THE INSPIRATION for this story to my love of the Black Hills and appreciation for the brilliantly written book *Exploring with Custer: The 1874 Black Hills Edition*, by Ernest Grafe and Paul Horsted. Mr. Grafe and Mr. Horsted made our ancestors—the courageous settlers of the west—come so vibrantly to life with their pictorial comparisons of then and now that I decided to create fictional feuding characters as descendants of those real-life cavalrymen. However, all of the characters in my book are truly fictional and have no relation to the men who participated in the scientific expedition led by General George Armstrong Custer. Any likenesses, misstatements, or mistakes about the actual locations where Custer's men camped during that expedition are all mine and were never intended to reflect badly on the hard work and reconnaissance done by Ernest and Paul. For the facts and a wonderful historical read, please refer to their book, not mine.

Linda O'Doughda and Jeanne Pinault patiently teach me the art of writing and I extend a huge thanks to these brilliant editors. I hope you enjoyed the book, thanks to them. A special thank-you to Jenny Simonson for her amazing help as my trusted reader before the manuscript was submitted, a friend who always knows exactly where to drag my finger when

I can't place it on my story's weaknesses. I want to thank my special book club beta readers for this book, the wonderful Mangelsen sisters, Ruthie and Sarah, and their friends Danielli, Jessica, and Jody. Without you, I could never have hijacked your book club and scared you all to death.

As always, the characters in the Liv Bergen Mystery Series are fictional. If you like the way I created them, feel free to imagine that I based a particular character on you. If you don't like the way I created them, and you insist I created one based on you, then let me know and I'll introduce you to Monsignor O'Connell for a much-needed confession.

Lucky me, you picked up this book.

READER'S GUIDE

1. The Crooked Man case was introduced in *Lot's Return to Sodom*, the second in the Liv Bergen Mystery Series, and became the focal point in this third book in the series. Did you find the technique of issues being carried over from book to book annoying or effective in heightening your anticipation?

2. Liv Bergen is blessed with numerous siblings and a strong family. How effectively does the author use the character's family members to further the story?

3. In *Widow's Might*, the author furthered the relationship between Liv Bergen and Streeter Pierce that began in *In the Belly of Jonah* and *Lot's Return to Sodom*. How effective is their caution toward each other in building their investment in a lasting relationship?

4. The author raised the ethical question about an individual's right to die. Although the Crooked Man clearly committed

murder, how much control should individuals diagnosed
with a fatal condition have with their own lives?

5. The concept of hospice, caring over curing, has been a god-
   send to many people. Although Helma Hanson appreciated
   the help, her decision was to feel the pain in her final days
   in order to have a clearer head. How would you choose?

6. Titles of books are often selected for marketing purposes.
   Sandra Brannan has created the entire Liv Bergen series
   around morphed biblical titles. How successful did the title
   tie to the story? Do you believe in the saying to never judge
   a book by its cover? How would you judge *Widow's Might*,
   both cover and content?

7. The author highlights how groups created to further a
   cause can sometimes lose sight of the purpose and instead
   justify the bad behaviors of individuals for a greater good.
   Describe some examples where you feel this has happened.

8. Although fast, the pacing and plot for *Widow's Might* differ
   from the first two books in the series in that the story was
   more of a traditional "whodunit" mystery. Which of Sandra
   Brannan's books is your favorite?

Sneak peek of Noah's Rainy Day, *the fourth in Sandra Brannan's Liv Bergen Mystery Thriller Series . . .*

CHAPTER 1

WALL TO WALL PEOPLE. Everyone was too busy to notice one another, let alone him.

PERFECT.

A tinny version of "Jingle Bells" scraped through the airport speaker system. Occasional pages punctuated the obnoxious and too frequent warnings that the moving walkway was about to end.

He hated the holidays. The loneliness. Everyone so disgustingly happy.

Tugging the blue vest over his expansive belly, he pushed the empty candy wrapper with his broom and watched the crowd scurrying about through the concourse. He kept a careful eye on the smallest of holiday travelers, particularly those whose parents made detours to the nearby restrooms.

Just one. He only needed one.

The frayed candy wrapper had tumbled across every inch of the concourse over the past three hours, backtracking over this particular section of tile at least a dozen times. The same wrapper. Companion to the sentinel line of dust gathered by the push broom. The wrapper that once contained his breakfast. A breakfast of champions. The wrapper that never quite made it from the floor to the garbage can, despite his diligence and effort to sweep it away.

No one noticed.

No one ever noticed the janitor. Not even the other DIA employees, who were supposedly his coworkers, but were far too important to befriend him. He was, after all, just a janitor. They had no idea how helpful they had been in their inattention of him or to his ineffectual efforts.

Didn't matter.

It's exactly what he wanted. He wanted to be invisible. If they realized his blue vest wasn't quite the same color as theirs or that his name badge wasn't quite the same size, the DIA employees may recognize him as an imposter.

That wouldn't do.

His cover as a janitor had been his most successful. Particularly in crowded public places. At the Rockies stadium. At Larimer Square. At Cherry Creek mall. His past experiences bolstered his confidence this morning. He would find at least one today.

But he hadn't expected it to take this long.

Holidays suck. Christmas was the worst. Too many people. Too many smiles. Too many packages being tenderly carried to their rightful places under countless trees. Didn't he deserve a little something under the tree this year?

Yes. Of course. That was why he was here. Patience. Patience and discretion.

The longer he remained huddled against the wall, the more likely someone would notice his ineffectual labors. But he was safe here. Under the overhang, away from the cameras' range. He escaped his cover being blown thirty minutes ago when he was down at the end of the other moving walkway. Only feet from where he stood, pushing his broom in the shadows, some old bat dropped her bag of popcorn in her awkward dismount from the moving walkway. Several travelers glared in his direction as they stepped over the puddled popcorn. They acted as if it were a minefield and as if he planted those mines. He pretended not to notice the commotion. He turned his back as he pushed the candy wrapper in the opposite direction. He wore his navy blue stocking cap, pulled down on his forehead. His thick black-rimmed glasses were bound with a strip of duct tape across the bridge. The pretense of limited peripheral vision was complete. Believable. The earpieces of his headphones were jammed deep within his protruding ears, which gave him the excuse to ignore their demands for his services. Just to be on the safe side, he meandered toward the bank of restrooms, hugging the wall under the overhang and pushing the tumbling candy wrapper.

But he was safe again. Invisible. Just a janitor. A janitor gripping his broom. A shiver dragged along his spine. Gripping a broom. A child's grip. In the closet. The closet filled with mops and brooms. Locked. Where his father kept him. Where he imagined growing up to be a janitor, pretending, just to keep his mind off the darkness. And loneliness. In a way, his father was to thank for this clever disguise, he supposed.

His stomach growled. It had been too long since he last ate and he simply hadn't eaten enough when he did. His large, doughy fingers uncurled from the broom handle and made their way between the ties of his blue vest into his olive drab jumpsuit pocket. Just as his fingertips reached the edge of the king-size package of peanut M&M's, he saw him.

Like a camouflaged hunter spotting a trophy elk in his scope, his movements were slow and deliberate. He eased the candy from his pocket without making a sound while he studied his prey.

A tall, lanky man wearing a BlueSky Airlines uniform was walking— more like prancing —toward the Buckskin bar and grill. The bar was across from his safe haven under the overhang by the restrooms. Just on the other side. Less than thirty yards away. The way this airline employee carried himself, it was no wonder to him where the term "light in the loafers" came from. "Skip" was making a beeline toward another man standing just beyond the row of barstools separating the restaurant from the concourse. The second man didn't look happy. His fists were planted on his hips. His foot was tapping. His eyes hard.

Perfect. A lovers' quarrel between "Skip" and "Thumper." No better distraction.

As the airline employee approached, he gave the irritated man a quick peck on the cheek and leapt into a long, animated explanation of whatever it was that had irritated the jilted, foot-tapping, ball-fisted lover awaiting him outside the bar. It was not important what the two men were so worked up about on this otherwise peaceful Christmas Day. What was important is that Santa had not forgotten *him* this year. His Christmas gift had just arrived. Delivered by "Skip," one of Santa's elves.

A boy. A beautiful, blond boy.

"Skip" had long since released the little boy's hand. The little boy was lingering beside the two quarreling men, circling around the area. Just beyond the bar, on the edge of the heavy pedestrian traffic ebbing and flowing through the concourse. Dressed in a beautiful, hunter green Christmas outfit, the boy danced and pounced about, oblivious to the tide of travelers. Oblivious to "Skip," his distracted escort. Oblivious to "Thumper's" fury. Oblivious to the invisible janitor across from the bar who fixated on his every movement.

Unaccompanied minor.

He spied the airline wings pinned to the little boy's vest lapel to confirm his assumption. It explained "Skip" and his inattention of the boy. The child was traveling alone, from one place to another and just passing through Denver International Airport.

What fortune!

He closed the distance between him and the boy, careful to stay close to the wall yet out of the quarreling men's peripheral vision. He stood between the boy and the small family bathroom, nestled between the expansive bathrooms dedicated to men and women only. The family bathroom, an oversized stall with locking door intended for mothers and fathers to help their young, offered him privacy.

Pushing the small line of gray dust and the well-traveled candy wrapper toward the door, he felt the weight of his concealed backpack against the small of his back, under his blue vest, and smiled. Opening the door, he set the broom just inside and turned back toward the child. He rattled the bag of M&M's. The child looked up. And stopped dancing.

The child saw the bright yellow bag and a dimpled grin spread across his smooth, white cheeks. After cutting a quick glance in his escort's direction, the boy tiptoed toward the man with the bag of candy.

"What Child Is This?" was playing overhead. He scanned the concourse before he ducked, unseen, into the bathroom with the bag of M&M's.

And the boy.

Fic   Brannan, Sandra
                Widow's might